Eli Amir was born in Baghdad in 1937 and, with most of the Iraqi-Jewish community, left for Israel in 1950. His earlier novel *The Dove Flyer* was published in English in 2010 and was shortlisted for the *Jewish Quarterly*/Wingate Prize 2011. *The Jewish Chronicle* wrote:

"Amir paints a throbbing, colourful picture of Baghdad with its soothsayers, rabbis, sheikhs, prostitutes, revolutionaries, Zionists and princes. But, ultimately like the wings of a dove, the dreams of all the main characters are broken as they go into exile. 'I write to show the pain, the sorrow, the insult, of losing a homeland,' says Amir."

A social activist, as well as a prize-winning author, Eli Amir said in Cairo on the Arabic publication of *Yasmine*: "How can there be peace without us knowing each other?"

yasmine

yasmine

Eli Amir

Translated by
Yael Lotan

HALBAN
LONDON

First Published in Great Britain by
Halban Publishers Ltd.
22 Golden Square
London W1F 9JW
2012

www.halbanpublishers.com

All rights reserved. No part of this publication may be reproduced,
stored in a retrieval system, or transmitted in any form,
or by any means, electronic, mechanical, photocopying, recording
or otherwise, without the prior permission of the Publishers.

A CIP catalogue record for this book is available from the
British Library.

ISBN 978 1 905559 23 7

Originally published in Hebrew under the title *Jasmine*
by Am Oved Publishers, Tel Aviv, 2005

Copyright © 2005 by Eli Amir

Translation copyright © 2012 the estate of Yael Lotan

Eli Amir has asserted his right under the Copyright,
Design and Patents Act, 1988 to be identified
as the author of this work.

Typeset by Spectra Titles, Norfolk
Printed in Great Britain by
MPG Books Ltd, Bodmin, Cornwall

To Lili

and to our children Yael, Harel and Hillel

and to

Yasmine, wherever you are

This English edition sponsored by

Dr Naim Dangoor CBE

The Publishers would like to thank
Sylvia Haim, Samir El-Youssef and Philip Simpson
for their help with the translation of this book

Contents

1	Seventh of June, 1967	1
2	Just Three Weeks Ago	23
3	Katamon and the One-Room Flat	39
4	The Minister in Charge	54
5	First Day in East Jerusalem	71
6	Kabi and Sandra	78
7	"*Vie krikhtmen arois?*"	84
8	Restoring Normality	101
9	Facing the Older Brother	109
10	Internal Disputes	119
11	From Paris to al-Quds – Yasmine	134
12	The First Meeting	152
13	An Off-the-Peg Suit	165
14	Kabi in Khorramshahr	171
15	Ghadir – Stream and Light	182
16	Yasmine, Nasser and Me	190
17	Two Orgasms	198
18	Soft Words	208
19	Morning with Yasmine	223
20	The Art of Haggling	229
21	Picnic with Michelle	235
22	Out of Prison	241
23	Two Authorities	254
24	The Voice of Israel	269
25	"What is there here for us?"	278

26	Thirty Lira and a Special People	288
27	Their Clocks and Ours	292
28	Father and Senator Antoine	299
29	Fathers and Sons in Hebron	308
30	Sealed Lips	319
31	"You're a minute and a half late"	323
32	"A kosher Christian"	332
33	"That Yasmina of yours"	337
34	Hizkel – Integration Blues	344
35	The High Windows	356
36	Ghadir	363
37	Kiddush Wine	368
38	An Ordinary Weekday	382
39	"Either I'm crazy, or they are"	387
40	A Dowry without the Bride	397
41	Ramleh and the Immigrant Camp	403
42	The Flight of the Gulls	409
43	"What could you have done?"	418
44	"There's no comparison! She's a woman!"	429
45	A Refugee, Son of Refugees	435
46	A Broken Branch	439

And the children struggled together within her and she said, If it be so, why am I thus? And she went to inquire of the Lord. And the Lord said unto her, Two nations are in thy womb, and two manner of people shall be separated from thy bowels.

(Genesis 25, 22-3)

1

Seventh of June, 1967

At daybreak on Wednesday, the seventh of June, 1967, As-Sayyed Antoine Salameh, senator of the Hashemite Kingdom of Jordan, peered out of the window and saw a group of soldiers approaching slowly, wearily, as if scarcely able to walk. Their clothes were torn and dusty and no wonder, thought the senator, they've been fighting all through the night. He had heard the shells whistling overhead and glass shattering. When the shelling began he hurried to turn off the lights in the entrance to the villa and in the living room, and paced nervously through the rooms, searching in vain for a place of safety. Never before had he imagined that a time would come when he would need shelter under his own roof. His wife, too, wandered about the house, trailing him in silence like a ghost. The two pills he had given her, the ones he took when he couldn't sleep, had not helped her. She was unable to relax and went on walking about in an old summer dressing-gown, her eyes wide open and her hair dishevelled. He could not help grimacing with distaste and pity at the sight of her.

He too, of course, had not closed his eyes all night. How could he sleep when the fate of al-Quds hung in the balance? He waited impatiently for the night to pass, and now the sun, as though it too was anxious for the welfare of the Holy City, rose early and shed its bright light at exactly four thirty-four. The senator took another look at the soldiers down the street and felt relieved. This must be the vanguard of the Iraqi forces who had volunteered to come to the aid of the Arab Legion, as he had been informed by the court minister from the royal palace. Iraq, our sister state, land of the two rivers, was always the first to come to the aid of Palestine. These soldiers and the Legion troops were risking their lives to preserve the integrity of his city. They would wipe out the disgrace of '48, they and the armies of Egypt's Nasser and of the other Arab states.

Clouds of dust hung over Sheikh Jarrah, the garden suburb north of the city. Taking advantage of a break in the firing, the senator urged his Sudanese maid to take bottles of cold water to the soldiers to revive them. Suddenly, strange black crows, with outstretched necks and huge wingspans, flew over his spacious house, heading towards al-Mudawara. Their flight startled him.

The senator opened the doors to the wide terrace that overlooked the high road and was struck by the acrid smell of gun-powder and smoke. He went to the balustrade and saw the soldiers resting their heavy rucksacks and weapons on the ground. Some of them leaned against the garden wall, others crouched down for a moment's rest. A few gazed at his well-tended garden, at the handsome villas in the vicinity and the luxurious Ambassador Hotel. As a representative of His Majesty King Hussein, he felt it his sacred duty to welcome the brave warriors and thank them on behalf of the entire Hashemite Kingdom. He raised both hands to greet them, and they turned to look at him with curiosity.

"*As-salaamu aleikum warahmatu'llah wabarakatuh* – peace upon you and the blessing and mercy of Allah, *ya guidan*, O brave warriors, *ya mujahdeen*, O jihad fighters, O kinsmen of our glorious Arab family, O bold spirits and dear hearts. I, Antoine Salameh, member of the Senate of the Hashemite Kingdom of Jordan, feel honoured to bring you the thanks and admiration of King Hussein bin Talal bin Abdullah bin Hussein al-Hashemi. Your glorious fight recalls the battle of Khalif Omar ibn al-Khatab, conqueror of al-Quds al-Sharif. With your sword you have repulsed the despicable Zionist enemy, the cruel, contemptible, miserable and cowardly infidel, and with Allah's help you will throw them into the sea."

The soldiers stared at him in amazement. Perhaps they did not fully understand his speech since he addressed them in the Palestinian dialect, and Iraqis had a dialect of their own that he himself scarcely understood. He should address them in literary Arabic, which all Arabs understood, but let them first refresh themselves with cold water. He wanted to go down and clasp them to his breast and listen to their stories about the brave battle they had fought that night. But, as he turned, one soldier, his shirt torn and his left arm bandaged, stood up respectfully, took off his helmet, raised his reddish head and said:

"*Ihna yahud, min hon* – we're Jews, from here, from Israel…"

"*Yahud? Min Israil?*" The senator was stunned. The blood drained from his face and for a moment his vision blurred and reeled. Abruptly he turned around and fled indoors, into his living room. For a long time he sat trembling on the edge of the sofa, like an unwelcome guest in his own house. What if the Jewish soldiers killed him, and his wife too? He should call someone. His knees trembled as he staggered to the telephone and for the fifth time since the shelling began phoned Abu George, his journalist friend and neighbour.

Abu George listened impatiently. Was the elderly senator

losing his mind? Had he not explained to him, repeatedly throughout the night, that there was nothing to worry about – on the contrary! Once more he described the interview that the sector commander had given the press the week before at the Legion camp in al-Mudawara.

"Our forces are well prepared. The Jews know what they can expect here. They wouldn't want to commit suicide, would they?" the commander of the fortified hilltop defending the north of the city had said. And it was precisely this restrained reply, spoken in his reserved British manner that had made the journalists smile. The commander also showed them the massive fortifications, the deep, concrete-lined trenches that twisted and wound around the whole of al-Mudawara, the forty bunkers with impenetrably thick walls, interspersed with observation posts, sniper nests, heavy mortars and cannons dominating every part of the hill. Underneath the bunkers was the vast command centre, carved out of the bedrock like an ancient cavern. The commander also showed them the stocks of ammunition. Who could possibly invade these hills? thought Abu George. The entire area was crisscrossed with landmines, and hundreds of trained Legion troops were only waiting to unleash a hail of fire on anyone who tried. "Who would dare to challenge us?" said the commander at the conclusion of the tour.

"*Yahud, min Israil*, believe me!" the senator insisted.

"*Shu Israil*, what are you talking about?" replied Abu George, pitying the delusional old man. He had been unable to sleep for several nights because of the war with the Zionists, and the past night had been the worst. The assault on al-Mudawara and the neighbourhood of Sheikh Jarrah had begun at midnight and continued uninterrupted. A barrage of fire, shells roaring, bullets whistling – the very ground shook. He realised it was not enough to utter reassuring words.

"Senator, please come to us, you and your wife. We'll be honoured to have you stay. You know my daughter Yasmine is in Paris, her suite is unoccupied – you can have the whole second floor to yourselves. I'm coming to fetch you."

"Thank you, Allah protect your Yasmine. I'm staying here, and if I'm fated to die, let it be in my own house," he replied in a broken voice.

After he replaced the receiver Abu George grabbed a pair of binoculars and climbed hurriedly to the roof of his house. He wanted to see for himself what was happening at the front, but a spreading *shajarat al-yahud*, a "Jews' tree" – a eucalyptus – blocked his view of the hill. He went up to the edge of the roof and held the binoculars to his eyes. Looking north he saw, outlined against the grey sky, burnt-out vehicles with black smoke rising from them.

Suddenly the noise stopped, but strangely it was the silence that made him choke. He threw away the burning cigarette and spat on the floor. Damned cigarettes, they were no use whatever. A fear awoke in him and forced into his mind sounds and sights he preferred to forget. Vividly the memory came back of the shots that had rained down on his house then, almost twenty years before, fired from Katamon towards his house in Talbieh. He recalled hurriedly packing some valuables and urging Um George and little Yasmine to grab whatever they could and flee.

The firing began again, seeming to come from all around. Was history about to repeat itself? Would he have to flee again? No. Not this time. Never again would he abandon his house, flee, escape, get out, absent himself, desert, go missing, wander away…*Sumood*, he said to himself, hold out, stay put, cling to the ground. He choked and coughed and kept repeating, *Sumood, sumood…*

What was wrong with him? Was he losing his mind too? And what was causing this strange cough? He took a deep breath, but instead of the crystal air of Sheikh Jarrah, his lungs filled with acrid smoke. Shaking himself out of a nightmare, he said to himself, Cheer up, they can't break into the fortress of al-Mudawara. It isn't the Jews who are firing but our people, the mortars and hand-grenades and machine-guns and rifles of the Hashemite forces. Maybe what the senator saw was some of their soldiers who had deserted out of fear, or a handful of them who had managed to sneak through the lines, or perhaps…But he didn't want to finish this thought. He went downstairs and ran to the telephone. This time he phoned the senator.

"Are the soldiers still there?" he asked anxiously.

"No, *al-hamdu lillah*, thank God, as soon as the firing began they vanished."

"Allah be blessed," sighed Abu George, his spirit restored. He sat down to listen to the radio. The Voice of Damascus broadcast yet again the song "*Idbah, idbah, idbah*" – "Slaughter, slaughter, slaughter", while Radio Amman described the valiant fight of the Legion and its conquests in the Kingdom's West Bank and in Jerusalem, including the UN headquarters occupying the old British High Commissioner's mansion on the Hill of Evil Counsel. "The bodies of the Zionist soldiers are scattered on the battlefield, preyed on by black crows," the announcer declared. Abu George wiped the sweat from his brow and, in spite of himself, could not resist turning the dial to the Arabic-language service of Israel Radio. The Zionist announcer calmly listed the positions the Israeli army had captured. The scene painted by his statements and the interviews from the front was utterly unlike the one broadcast from Amman. Doubts festered in Abu George's mind. They're all liars, he grunted. Psychological warfare, that's what it is – who can tell what's really happening?

He felt trapped in his house, cut off from events. Should he again call his partner Abu Nabil, at the Al-Wattan office, ask him for the umpteenth time what was happening, and listen to another recitation of Nasser's great victories over there and King Hussein's over here? Shame on him for doubting his friend and the mighty Arab nation. These calls made him look faithless and cowardly. He should have spent the night at the newspaper's office. He looked into the kitchen and saw his wife sitting there quietly, hunched, blowing her nose. Seeing him she tried to smile, and he knew that at this moment she was tormented by her longings for Yasmine. How could he leave her and go out? But he had to go into town.

Abu George sat beside his wife and she got up to bring him a pot of coffee and a jug of water with mint leaves. Then she stroked his head and pressed it to her bosom, as she always did in bad times, to subdue his inner demons. But now he shook free impatiently, quickly drank the coffee and the water and stood up. The coffee had scalded his throat.

"Why are you rushing off, my dear?"

"I've got to be at the office."

"*Ya Adhra*! O Virgin Maryam, can't you hear the shelling?" She stared at him in alarm.

"I've got to get to the teleprinter, I must find out what the news agencies are saying, Reuters, United Press. See the headlines in the newspapers."

"Isn't it enough that the radio is on all the time, and the phone keeps ringing? Bad news moves fast." She stopped, wondering how to detain him. The previous night he had come home after midnight, at the height of the firing and the explosions. Several times she had called the Al-Wattan office to urge him to come home, and when he set out she counted the minutes, wondering what was keeping him, then went and waited by the gate, listening with one ear for the engine of the Dodge coming up the narrow lane, and with the other for a possible phone call from Yasmine. The firing and the falling shells terrified her. She did not remember such a barrage even when they fled their house in Talbieh in '48.

"Don't go, *behiyatek*, on your life, I beg you," she pleaded.

"I must get some air," he snapped and went out into the garden. The volleys of gunfire and the reek of burning buffeted his head. The walls of the house trembled. The fish in the small pond flitted and hid under the rocks at the margins. He went back inside and stopped to look at Yasmine's portrait on the wall, his heart aching with longing. How was she, what was she doing now? He wished he could hug her, wished she were with them at this difficult time. The ringing of the telephone interrupted his thoughts.

"Abu George, I need you here urgently." Abu Nabil's voice was uncharacteristically hesitant. "It's to do with the Governor."

"I'm coming," he replied and replaced the receiver.

"But it's *harb wadarb*, battles and war, out there!" Um George protested.

"It is war, *ya ruhi*, my soul, and Abu Nabil doesn't get on with the Governor. He needs me. What should I say, that I'm afraid? Shame!"

"At least eat breakfast first."

"I couldn't swallow a thing." He kissed her on the cheek and turned to go. At the last moment he took his camera bag and added his binoculars.

"Phone me when you get there," she said behind him.

He turned around. "Close the gate and make sure I locked the roof door. Don't let anybody in!" he added and immediately regretted frightening her needlessly.

When he started the Dodge and emerged from the parking lot his heart was melting as he reflected on his good fortune at having the love and support of such a woman.

As he drove down Ragheb al-Nashashibi Lane, the sound of the firing grew louder, but Abu George couldn't tell from which direction it was coming. It sounded as if it was coming from all around – but where were the soldiers?

He saw the first sign of the night's devastation on the narrow road leading to the Sheikh Jarrah intersection, not more than a hundred yards from his house. A man dressed in a kumbaz and keffiyeh was lying dead on the road, one of his splayed legs blown off. Beside him lay a dead Legionnaire, and there were several more lifeless bodies nearby. For a moment he held his nose against the stench of blood and burnt flesh and felt a sharp pain in his chest. His throat began to burn again and he sneezed. He swung away from his usual route and turned towards the Ambassador Hotel. Suddenly a sheaf of fire spat out over the hotel roof. It's our people firing, he thought hopefully. But the luxury hotel looked abandoned, its windows were shattered and a body was lying over a windowsill. How strange, just two days ago the Ambassador had been swarming with guests. Why was it abandoned? When? And why wasn't he notified? After all, he headed the association of tourist and hotel enterprises.

Powerful explosions detonated behind him, any moment now shells would be falling on his head. Abu George turned around and drove away from the scene in the opposite direction, against the traffic. He was trembling all over. *Abuna el-Masih*, Jesus Father, have the Jews got this far? He shouldn't have left his house, and who's to say they aren't firing on civilians? If he'd thought rationally he'd have known that only a lunatic would venture outside at such a time and leave his wife alone. Oh shame, shame – what to do about the shame, and where does shame lead us? He confessed to himself that he'd been ashamed to stay at home and was now ashamed to return there. He stepped on the accelerator and drove at speed to Saladin Street, turned right and parked as he always did beside Al-Hurriyeh, the exclusive restaurant he owned. The gate was open and for a moment he thought of going in, but instead hurried to join Abu Nabil, who was waiting for him in the newspaper's office across the street.

"*Sabah el khair*, Abu George, good morning," his partner greeted him and then came straight to the point. "There are reports, still unconfirmed, that the Jews, damn them, have broken into al-Mudawara and are pressing ahead. I can't believe it's true, it's a fortified bastion, but…Maybe we should ask the Governor for information – what do you think?"

"Well, yes, we should publish a special interview with him. It's important to reassure the population."

"Right, that's why I called you. You know the Governor hasn't spoken to me since…"

Abu George nodded, remembering the Governor's fury about something Abu Nabil had written a few months earlier.

"So, could you go to him…?" Abu Nabil asked hesitantly.

"No, brother. First of all, your honour is as dear to me as my own. I couldn't possibly interview him without you. Secondly, it's an opportunity to bury that incident."

Quickly they crossed the street to the Governor's residence, passed the gate-keeper and almost ran up to the second floor.

"The Governor's in the conference room," his secretary said and led them into the familiar chamber. From the walls, portraits of the kings of the Hashemite dynasty stared down: al-Sharif Hussein, al-Emir Abdullah, Talal and Hussein. The Governor looked as though he hadn't slept and seeing Abu Nabil his face froze momentarily, but he recovered and rose to greet them and shake their hands.

"Pardon us, Governor," Abu George began, "for barging in like this. We needed to speak to you on such a day. We're going to print a special issue and wanted to interview you."

"You're welcome."

"Please be so kind as to bring us up to date on the news," Abu George went on, relieved to be where he was. Abu Nabil took a notebook and his favourite Parker-51 fountain pen from his jacket pocket.

The Governor, speaking in his graceful high-flown style, reported that at this very moment, over in the Sinai desert, the Egyptian airforce was pounding the Zionist army, setting its tanks and armour ablaze. Then he read them a letter he had received from His Majesty, and added that the King had received a telegram from President Nasser, assuring him of a complete Arab victory.

The telephone rang. The Governor picked up the receiver and seemed to move uneasily in his armchair as he listened. Then he rose, went up to the big map on the wall and marked something on it.

"And what is happening here, on our front? War?" Abu George asked.

The Governor compressed his lips. "Not war," he replied quietly. "I'd say, border skirmishes, nothing more. Though they are serious. During the night enemy soldiers managed to penetrate our lines here and there, and at this moment our soldiers are finishing them off. Our men are firing from every roof and every position, and they won't let the enemy raise its head," he concluded and leaned back in his armchair.

"On my way here I heard Israel Radio's Arabic service, claiming that they'd driven us out of the High Commissioner's residence. Is there any truth in that?" Abu George asked.

The Governor ignored the question. "You listen to the Zionists' radio?" he asked.

"I'm a journalist," Abu George replied, his eyes meeting the Governor's.

The phone rang again. "*Ahlan*, Mr Mayor go ahead." As he listened, the Governor fiddled with a pen on his desk. "You're right, my friend. We must reassure the public. These incidents are mainly on the border. Make sure the stores open as usual. There's plenty of everything, and the main roads to Amman are open." After he replaced the receiver he cast a worried glance at the wall map.

"Governor, many parts of the city are under fire," Abu Nabil intervened. These were the first words he had addressed to him since the article that had caused them to fall out.

"Naturally, they're firing at us and we at them," the Governor replied, restrained and authoritative. He wiped the sweat from his brow.

Abu George gazed at the two proud men, as full of themselves as their bulging bellies, and suppressed a grin. "On my way here

I didn't see a single policeman on the street. Where are our security forces?"

"Not to worry – they're where they are needed. Orders were given to step up their presence."

The phone rang again. "Good morning to you, reverend Sheikh. Go ahead, yes, I understand…" He covered the mouthpiece and said to the journalists, "Excuse me, please. It's the Sheikh of the Haram al-Sharif. Yes, reverend Sheikh, you can be absolutely sure that the army is defending the city as it would its own life and soul. We're distributing weapons to the inhabitants. The Jews won't dare approach the city walls."

When he turned back to them Abu Nabil asked if it was possible that the Soviet Union would intervene in the war.

"There is no need!" the Governor declared. "This morning His Majesty informed me that their Prime Minister, Eshkol, had sent him urgent messages begging him not to open fire."

Abu Nabil quickly made a note of this fresh news item.

"Eshkol didn't understand that he was giving himself away. You remember how a few days ago he addressed his people on the radio, and stammered with fright? *Miskeen*, poor thing! Ha ha…" The Governor laughed nervously. "Our King, who is as wise as his grandfather Abdullah, immediately spotted this and decided that now is the time to attack them, when they are weakest." He took a box of cigars from the drawer of his desk, chose one and trimmed it, then offered the box to the visitors.

"How long do you think this war will last?" asked Abu Nabil, greedily inhaling the cigar smoke.

"It depends. We have a manpower problem, though it's not too serious. We expected most of the enemy forces to be sent south to the Sinai, but apparently a few reserve units were left here, more than we thought. At this moment armoured divisions, tanks and infantry are advancing from Amman to al-Quds. Iraqi troops have also raced here through the night, and our Syrian brothers are ready to ignite the fire on the northern front. So everything is proceeding as planned," he concluded with satisfaction. "We have learned the lessons of *al-Nakba*, the catastrophe of 1948. Our new leaders, primarily Nasser and Hussein, God preserve them, are leading us to a splendid, speedy victory!"

Abu Nabil's eyes lit up at hearing the name of his hero Nasser. Abu George looked at him and at the Governor. Both were Muslim, born in East Jerusalem. He was the only one born in Talbieh, on the western side, the only one who became a refugee. In the 1948 war, too, the leaders had promised that a turning-point would soon be reached, that in a week or two they would return to their homes after throwing the Jews into the sea.

"Governor," he said, aware that he was spoiling their mood, "Your Honour, this morning Senator Antoine rang me to say that there were dozens of Israeli soldiers around his house. Do you know anything about it?"

"As I said before," the Governor replied sourly, "there have been minor incursions here and there. The sector commander told me this morning that at about four-thirty, at dawn, the Jews tried to climb up al-Mudawara hill, and were blinded by the rising sun. When they came too close our soldiers skewered and roasted them. The commander invited me to come and see the heap of bodies and dip my feet in their blood."

"*As-senator khatyar, ayyan wata'ban* – the senator is old, sick and weary," Abu Nabil said firmly. "Can you give us a quote from the King's letter?"

"I'm afraid not. I'd have to get His Majesty's permission. But you can certainly mention his reassuring, optimistic message." The Governor stood up. "Now, gentlemen, it remains for us to bless our brave, beloved King and, *inshallah*, victory will be ours."

Abu George raised his camera and took photos of the Governor standing beside the wall map, holding a long pointer.

Emerging on to the street, Abu Nabil put his arm through Abu George's. "The war has reconciled me and the Governor," he chuckled.

"With Allah's help everything will come right," Abu George sighed. He was feeling somewhat relieved, despite his lingering doubts. For all he knew Senator Antoine was imagining things, and, given his own history, perhaps he had caught the old man's panic.

Abu Nabil glanced at the colourful hoarding outside the al-Hamra cinema, displaying a scene from the old romantic film *Al Wardah al Baidha* – The White Rose – with Abdel Wahab.

"I'll book the four of us a box for next Sunday, *inshallah!*" he said expansively.

"*Ya reit*, that would be nice," replied Abu George.

On the way back they talked about the special edition, the headline with the King's message and the Governor's statement. Reaching the editorial office Abu George stopped.

"Abu Nabil, Um George is very worried. Our friend the senator phones every half hour and terrifies her. Perhaps I should return home, and you…"

Abu Nabil raised his hand and said, "*Ala ayni wala rasi*, upon my eye and my head, Abu George. Leave it to me!"

Abu George started his car but instead of turning right towards his house in Sheikh Jarrah, he turned left, driving down Saladin Street to the intersection with Suleiman Street. There he stopped and parked. He could hear gunfire coming from the direction of the Rockefeller Museum, and from Musrara on the boundary-line. Who's firing? he wondered, and walked faster to Bab el-Zahrah, Herod's Gate, where he entered the Old City.

There were few people in the alleys, perhaps only those who did not believe that war had broken out. For the past three weeks Nasser had been spitting in Israel's face, every day more copiously, and Israel didn't even wipe off the spittle. On the contrary, it seemed to be withdrawing into its shell, ashamed and scared. The Arab countries, Russia, France and half the world were against it – how could it hit back? Maybe the Governor is right and the Jews are being crushed under our soldiers' boots, and perhaps the people here know instinctively that nothing bad can happen to them and neither they nor their city are in any danger.

Someone recognised him and asked about the news. Two anxious elderly men stopped to listen.

"If I tell you, who will buy the special edition of my newspaper?" he joked, then told them what the Governor had said. They broke into cheers for Nasser and for the King. He smiled faintly at these simple people's naive enthusiasm.

Suddenly he noticed that his legs had carried him to the Haram al-Sharif, the place that the Jews called the Temple Mount and which they longed to seize. If they managed to break into the city they would no doubt go there. But what was the best observation post from which to see it? Of course, in the Church of the Redeemer, or rather on its roof! He began to hurry towards the Bab el-Amoud, the Damascus Gate.

Even this gateway to the Old City, which was usually lively

and crowded, was all but empty. The stone carvings, the loopholes and observation posts built by Suleiman the Magnificent, normally obscured by the tumult of everyday life, could be seen in all their glory.

Having descended the steps of the ancient Roman Cardo he stepped onto the Via Dolorosa. He stood for a moment on the worn paving-stones of the path followed by the Saviour, in the place where he stumbled under the weight of the cross. Are the Jews about to crush us under a new cross? he wondered. He felt the irritating cough starting again and hurried on. In a few moments he reached the church. Climbing its narrow, twisting stairs was increasingly difficult and he felt acutely short of breath. I'm no longer young, he said to himself, and mustered his remaining strength to reach the top. Once there, he clutched at the railing and tried to catch his breath.

"*Sabah al-khair*, good morning, Abu George!" said a familiar voice.

"Oh, good morning, Abu Shawkat!" he greeted the well-known photographer. "What are you doing here? You brought the child, too," he added, stroking the little boy's head.

The three stood side by side in the narrow gallery beneath the roof of the Church of the Redeemer and gazed at the expansive view. Before their eyes the Dome of the Rock glittered brilliantly in the sunshine, spreading a golden glow all around. To its right, the dome of the mosque of al-Aqsa looked dull and shabby by comparison. Why don't they polish it, Abu George wondered. Before him lay al-Balad, the city, to which they did not add "the Old", as did the Jews. Such a small place, yet it was the foundation stone, the bedrock and source of countless Arab traditions passed down from generation to generation for thirteen hundred years.

It was ten o'clock in the morning, and a light breeze dried the sweat on his face. The sight of the snipers' nests of the Legion and their civilian auxiliaries was reassuring. He set down the camera bag and took out a notebook. Both men looked towards the hilltop. They could hear gunfire, both near and distant, apparently aimed at the city and from it.

Then all at once the barrage intensified all around. They pressed their backs to the wall. Abu George thought a nearby minaret was being targeted, but before he could ask Abu Shawkat for its name, the little boy shrilled: "Daddy, look look, they're shooting at Bab al-Asbat!"

Abu George held the binoculars to his eyes.

"Look left, something's moving, a thin metal stick, probably a car antenna, with a small flag on it," said Abu Shawkat and he began clicking away with his camera.

"I think it's one of their armoured vehicles. But which way did it get in – through Bab al-Asbat? Impossible, it's too narrow…" Abu George said quietly and bit his lip. Had he really seen a military vehicle there, or was he imagining things?

The firing intensified and fell like hail on the swaying antenna. What could one armoured vehicle achieve in these alleys – it was sure to be destroyed with the men inside it. How could it advance as if on an open highway?

"There! There it is!" the little boy shrieked. The imagined armoured vehicle became real as it emerged from an alley and moved towards the Haram al-Sharif. The men looked at each other speechlessly. Abu Shawkat stopped snapping pictures.

"Baba, are these the Jews?" the child asked. "Baba, why don't you answer?"

"It seems so," said the father in a low voice.

"Where are our soldiers?"

"They're firing from all sides," the father said.

"Then why don't the Jews stop?"

The half-track turned left to the entrance gate of the Haram al-Sharif. A black motorcycle lay in its path. Maybe it's a booby-trap, *inshallah*, that will blow up in front of them and stop their advance, Abu George thought. But the vehicle did not stop, it rolled over the motorbike and moved on.

Now Abu George saw a Jewish officer, tall and broad-shouldered, rise from the armoured turret to look at the golden dome in front. "Allah, where are you?" Abu George cried silently, looking at the sky. He prayed that the snipers placed on every roof would destroy the intruder. Why don't they hit the arrogant officer standing so upright in the turret? But nothing deterred him or the vehicles which followed him up the path to the holy shrines.

"Baba, why don't our soldiers kill them?" the little boy asked. "What will happen now?"

Abu George looked at the child and thought he should have been spared the sight, just as he should have spared his daughter Yasmine, who was about the same age at the time, the flight from Talbieh. Thanks be to Allah that Yasmine could not see what was happening before his eyes at this moment. For the past five years he had urged her to return, but fortunately she had not. What would she see here now – the army of the Jews? What a horror!

"Allah will break their necks," Abu Shawkat whispered. "Is there no force that can stop them?"

"Stop, baba, stop! Let's go back!"

When the third of the Jews' vehicles drove past, one of its soldiers was shot dead by the King's snipers. "Die, dog! You and all your army!" the photographer shouted.

"*Yallah, yallah*! Go on! Bang bang bang!" the child shouted, clapping his hands. The shooting continued, bringing down more Jewish soldiers.

"*Yallah, idbah al-yahud*, slaughter the Jews! *Idbah, idbah!*" Abu Shawkat screamed, but the convoy went on.

Abu George lowered the binoculars. Who were these Jews? – dog's spawn, *owlad iblis*, sons of devils, *afareet*, demons! They know no pity and nothing can stop them. His father said once that the Jews were like stinging ants, no exterminator can stop them spreading. Donkeys' sons, how dare they enter Islam's holy of holies! What nerve! Don't they know the entire Muslim world will fight back? Monsters, there's no God in their hearts. That was how they raided our villages in '48, drove us out of Talbieh and brought the *Nakba*, the catastrophe, upon us, and how they joined the French and the English and attacked Egypt in '56. All our troubles come from them. How is it that they can bring the war into our homes, our lands, assaulting, invading, conquering. Hypocrites! Defence forces they call their army. They launch wars and call them defensive, may their homes be destroyed! What's their secret? Pathetic refugees whom nobody wanted, a humble minority, frightened, without dignity or shame, then all at once they're dominating and humiliating. Where did they get the strength? And we, descendants of the desert warriors, bold and mighty conquerors, builders of the greatest medieval empire, creators of a magnificent culture – how did the wheel turn?

"Abu George, what's going on here? Where is Allah, where is the Legion, where are Hussein and Nasser and the Arab states and Russia? Where?" Abu Shawkat wailed. "*Ya rab el-alamin*, Lord of the Universe, what will happen to us? Wasn't one *Nakba* enough? The land is gone and so is our honour!"

The leading vehicle stopped. The soldiers' helmets looked like miniature copies of the domes of the hallowed site. The shooting stopped. Abu George could not understand why the Legionnaires had stopped firing. Idiots, go on, keep on firing, he wins who has the longest breath.

The soldiers climbed out of their vehicles. Abu George thought he was going to faint. One group walked to the balustrade of the Haram al-Sharif, overlooking the Jews' Wall, also known as the Wailing Wall, where they used to pray and weep before the gates of the ancient city were closed to them in the terrible war of '48.

A soldier pulled a flag from his backpack, raised it and walked around the group of soldiers, then began to leap and dance ecstatically, till he stumbled. Then he walked to the top of the Jews' Wall and wedged the flag in it.

"Baba, they stuck their flag there! They beat us!" the child wept.

The two men stared at the hated blue-and-white flag flapping before their eyes. The soldiers stood to attention and sang their anthem. A heretical idea crept into Abu George's mind – perhaps the Ba'ath party, the Tahrir and the other nationalists were right when they insisted that the King wanted to get rid of the Palestinians...Had he really handed the West Bank over to the Jews?

Silence fell in the narrow alley adjoining the Mughrabi quarter. Only a single sound, subdued, as if from another world, a soft mournful sound arising from a dream, the sound of man face to face with himself, face to face with his Creator, pierced the stillness. Abu George had heard this before, once, many years ago, not in this place. He concentrated on the sound, trying to identify it. A ram's horn! That's what it was. Its notes seemed to be carved out of his own heart, a heart scorched and howling, weeping bitterly, moaning the cry of the defeated.

Abu George's body slumped, the bag slipped from his hand and he did not hear it hit the floor. He choked as his tears flowed freely, and he felt no shame.

2

Just Three Weeks Ago

I was tempted to start with *some time before the Flood*, or *before the earthquake*, but in fact it was only three weeks ago when on one warm spring evening in the middle of May 1967 I returned home late and found, pinned to the door of my one-room flat, a reservists' call-up order. It was headed Emergency Call-Up a scary phrase that tells you to drop everything you're doing because something else has begun. The order was to show up immediately at my unit HQ. What's going on? Has war broken out? With whom? My head started to spin. It was midnight – how could I get there? I unlocked the door, drank some water and took down my kitbag, uniform and boots from the top of the wardrobe. I packed shaving gear, underwear, a khaki hat, a couple of books, packets of halva and crackers, and went to bed.

But I couldn't fall asleep so turned on the radio. Cairo Radio was broadcasting a ballad sung by Um Kulthoum, which calmed my nerves somewhat – if there was an emergency over there, they'd be broadcasting nationalist marches or readings from the Quran.

When I did finally doze off my sleep was invaded by the red kestrels which had recently come here, migrants from cold lands faraway, who had built a hasty nest under the roof tiles of the house opposite. The day before I noticed that their eggs had hatched and one of the fledglings had fallen from the eaves and died...My sleep was shattered.

I got up and made myself a Basra lemon tea, and ate some halva to sweeten the vigil. As soon as daylight broke I left the house and took two buses – one to the main bus depot and the other to the mustering station.

Most of the passengers on the southward-heading bus were reservists. I sat in the front seat and looked at the changing scenery. It came to me that this morning I hadn't raised the window blind to look at my Orthodox neighbour. Every morning I watch her working in her kitchen or small balcony, surrounded by her young brood. I'd developed a sort of superstition that if I didn't see her first thing in the morning the day would go badly...What nonsense, I rebuked myself.

The radio sounded six a.m. and the driver turned up the volume. Total silence fell in the bus. In a deep voice, the announcer reported that Nasser had closed the Tiran Straits and barred our shipping to the Indian Ocean. Without stopping to draw breath he went on to state that Israel regarded this move as a *casus belli*. The scenery grew blurred. My brother Moshi must already have been called up. Fortunately Kabi was in London.

At the Bilu camp where we reported for duty, we were hastily equipped and divided into teams. We refreshed our memory of battle orders and of regulations if captured, and held practice exercises and instrument checks. We were going over the communications procedure – which I had almost forgotten – when we were summoned to the firing-range. All right, I told myself, this is serious.

My target-practice results were dismal. You're not ready, man.

Is this the way to go to war? Fortunately Trabulsi is on my team. "But where is he?" I asked the commander. "He's just had a son. He'll be here," he replied. I should have brought my transistor radio. Though what's the point, when the news is so worrying and the commentary even more frightening. In the evening, when we had set up our tents and got ready to go to sleep, I wrote an army postcard to my parents.

The next two days were spent in further training, and the third day Trabulsi arrived, having seen his son through the *Brit*, and brought us delicacies from the circumcision festivities – bagels, *melabas*, Moroccan biscuits. We all crowded around him.

"You can't imagine what's going on in Tel Aviv," he told us. "It's a ghost town, the streets are empty and apparently thousands of casualties are expected. The rabbinate has prepared land for a mass grave in Independence Park, and secondary-school kids are being enlisted to dig trenches. It's terrifying! People are running away, making macabre jokes: 'The last one out of the airport turn off the light!' that sort of thing…"

"Eshkol is scared shitless. He won't do anything. We should bring back Ben-Gurion," said Aflalo.

"Forget it!" said Trabulsi. "How long will that bunch of old-timers stay in power?"

"We're stuck here on our own. That's when you know you're in trouble," said Slutzky.

"Hey Nuri," Aflalo challenged me, "you work for the government. What kind of a leader is Eshkol?"

I didn't reply at once. I used to see the Prime Minister from time to time, going up the stairs to his office, humming little snatches of song, *ya-bam-bam*, like a kindly grandpa from an old shtetl. The Minister in charge of his office says he's a *Yiddishe kop* – a clever Jew, a good judge of people. And in fact once, when I accompanied him and his aides on a trip to Nazareth, I found him surprisingly astute and sensitive. But none of this shows from a distance or at a superficial glance.

"Just look at Nasser," Aflalo went on. "Young, handsome, tall, sturdy, charismatic, a brilliant speaker. And his opposite number? Eshkol! Old, bearish, balding, with a black beret flat on his head like a pitta, his belt under his armpits, and on top of all that, he's a lousy orator. Bugger it!"

Trabulsi laid a soothing hand on his shoulder and pulled some photos from his shirt pocket to show us the *Brit* celebration of his newborn son.

Evening fell, finding us in wistful mood. The talk turned to home, children, wives. I saw Yardena running ahead across the sands of Ashdod like a wild colt, with me in hopeless pursuit. Yardena is a ripe succulent fig, while I'm still green. In our first winter together she knitted me a fancy sweater with a zip, and I walked around the streets of Jerusalem looking like a storybook pre-State fighter. She taught me to eat goulash with potatoes, seasoned with spicy paprika, and for someone brought up on rice, like me, it was quite an achievement. But two weeks ago she ended our relationship. "You've been leading me on for three years. There's something screwed up about you," she flung at me on Emek Refaim Street, not far from her little flat, and stormed off, leaving me standing on the pavement, open-mouthed and sweating. I knew she wanted to get married, and once in a delirious moment I promised to do so but since then I'd been evasive about any commitment.

Now, in this parched desert, I remember her fragrance and

feel I'm dying of desire for her and going mad for a drink. Yardena detested the smell of slivowitz, to which I'm addicted, but as a special treat she would let me drink whisky. I'd massage her slender neck, her supple back, turn her over and pour the liquor into the hollow of her navel and suck it up noisily, while she giggled like an infant. Oh Yardena, Yardena, why did you discard me like an unripe fruit?

I borrowed Hermosa's transistor and moved to one side to listen to Sawt al-Arab radio from Cairo. I turned it on in the middle of a live interview with Ahmad Shukeiry, the chairman of the Palestine Liberation Organisation.

"Isra'il," he mocked, "your head is made of wax, so why are you walking in the sun?"

"Throw them in the sea! Throw the Jews into the sea!" screamed the interviewer, Ahmad Said, Nasser's loyal spokesman. But why is Egypt behaving like this? There's a whole desert between us. "Go on, Jews, pack your belongings and leave!" Said commanded in a different tone, a thick, warm and actually quite pleasant voice. I didn't know which was scarier, his screams or the quiet injunction.

I turned off the radio and on my way back a nagging thought occurred to me, again: why weren't we destined to live somewhere else, a safe, quiet place, far from this turbulent, crazy country? What did we need all this for?

Once, when I was a child, I heard an old man talking about reincarnation. He said that when the soul leaves the dead person's body it circulates around the family until it settles in a new baby. I was named after my uncle, my mother's brother, Nuri Elias Nasekh, who died before he was thirty. Perhaps my time has come, and the soul that I inherited from him will soon

27

leave me too. I'm not far from thirty. I said this to Trabulsi, only half in jest. He sensed the fear behind it and took me straight to Slutzky, our amateur palm reader, to read my fortune.

Slutzky rattled on at length about my character, my career, the women in my life, a great love that will appear and end with heartbreak, but said nothing about death. When I steeled myself to ask about it, he pointed to my life-line – long and clearly delineated. Then Trabulsi and Aflalo asked about their life-lines, and he told them they had nice firm ones too. Time would show that he was both right and wrong, but I mustn't anticipate.

A bad headache drove me to look for a quiet corner and try to calm down, so I slipped away from the racket in the tent area and sat in the shade of an old eucalyptus tree beyond the rows of tanks. I listened to the wind riffling through the leaves as if they were pages in a book of poetry, now stopping for a quiet read, now skimming fast, glancing and flitting on. The breeze made me feel better, though the headache persisted. Apparently, I was smoking too much.

I pulled off some leaves, crushed them in my hand and breathed their sharp, penetrating odour, the way Father used to. How was he feeling in the face of this imminent war, this innocent scholarly man who thought of Israel as a fragrant holy land, an earthly paradise? I remembered him sitting beside the radio, chain-smoking, listening to the BBC, to Israel Radio in Arabic and in Hebrew, to Sawt al-Arab radio stations from Baghdad, Damascus, Amman, Riyadh, reading all the newspapers and driving Mother crazy. "Why did we come here?" she would protest. "For war?"

My parents argued – about justice and about the Muslims'

Allah and the God of the Jews, about us and them and the lousy character of the Muslims, who don't know how to compromise and always leave something unresolved, and Mother repeated for the thousandth time the story about that folklore character Juha who sold his mansion but asked to keep just one nail on the wall in his possession. The buyer agreed and thereafter Juha made his life miserable by coming to inspect his nail before dawn and in the middle of the night, on holidays and festivals, on Fridays and workdays, and the buyer never knew when Juha would show up and disrupt his life, until in the end he quit the mansion just to get some peace…"That's the Arabs for you," Mother would conclude. "They always leave a nail in the wall and get worked up and fight. There's no ending with them!"

Because of the emergency call-up I hadn't gone to say goodbye to them and though I kept writing and sending postcards, I still had had no reply. Telephone? They'd been waiting for one for the past three years. There's a public phone near the grocery, but it's always out of order.

On the eighth or ninth day we had a visitor – the poet and World War II partisan Abba Kovner. We sat on the ground and listened while he talked of his fears for Jewish continuity, which was again in peril. "Once more its fate is in the balance," he declared, and though he managed not to mention the Holocaust, it hung over our heads: "What must we do when our existence is in danger? Should we confront the evil, or wait till it blows over? Once more we are alone."

His words depressed me. I felt I didn't have the strength to shoulder the anxieties of the Holocaust as well. Faced with Pharaoh, we didn't need Hitler too.

Another day of inactivity and waiting. We tried to kill time by playing backgammon, draughts and cards, and debated what more had to happen before Eshkol gave the order. At noon some of the family men were given a day's leave – so maybe there won't be a war after all? A group of us went to the canteen, and I asked the guy in charge to turn the radio to the Israeli Arabic-language station. "Again?" he protested, "What the hell do you want the Arabic station for? Screw them!" I explained and pleaded and finally he relented.

"President Gamal Abd el-Nasser, yesterday in Bir Gafgafa you said you would not retreat a single inch. Well, listen to these words from Israel: the Tiran Straits are an international waterway, open them up or they will be opened some other way, and an Israeli ship will pass through, flying the Israeli flag."

The statement did not mention war, but hinted at it. Nothing about force was said, but there was an implication that force would be used. "You do not threaten Arabs, you don't impugn their honour and you do not insult an Arab ruler!" That was the lesson I was taught by my older brother Kabi when he worked in the government information office for Arab interests, before he joined the Mossad.

"Son of a bitch!" Trabulsi burst out. "You heard Nasser? 'If Israel wants war – welcome, *ahlan wasahlan*!' Does he think war is a belly dance? Why don't we take the fight to them? They should be screwed to hell!"

I look at Trabulsi and I'm filled with envy. He's just got a new baby, a second child. As for me, I have nothing, no wife or kids, no house and no car. I haven't even bought that mustard-coloured jacket, like the one my late Uncle Nuri had, which I'd always dreamed of buying. I saw one the other day in the window of OBG, the most exclusive menswear shop in town, but it was too expensive. Now I wish I'd bought it anyway.

*

In the evening the order came to get ready to move. It didn't say where to. Aflalo's face turned pale, his mouth tightened as he packed his gear and he was ready before anybody else. We boarded the trucks and travelled in darkness. My mouth was dry and my mind blank. I don't remember how long we were on the road when we got the order to stop overnight in an abandoned orchard. "Sleep with your clothes on," the commander said. The rumour went round that we were on the outskirts of Gaza City.

We woke up to a beautiful morning, a bright sky and the air exceptionally clear. A pleasant breeze rustled through the abandoned orchard, which breathed a green freshness. If only we could stop right here, in the beauty, the light and the wind. But at midday the word came: "Tomorrow we go to war!"

I went to the adjutant and told him that I was an Arabist. "Wait here a minute," he said and left. The minute stretched to twenty, and I thought he'd forgotten me. Then he returned and took me to the Intelligence Officer, who took me to the Operations Officer, who took me to the Brigade Second-in-Command, and he took me to the Brigade Commander.

The Brigade Commander showed me a conference table covered with a green cloth, gave me a printed sheet headed "The Instrument of Surrender of the City of Gaza," and asked me to translate it into Arabic. I read the text and I didn't care for it. "Rewrite it as you see fit," he said. His calm manner and confidence in the city's surrender reassured me. But when I returned to the camp my anxiety reawakened.

"We need an Abu Gilda, a one-eyed pirate who will demolish Pharaoh," said Trabulsi.

"We need Moshe Dayan! The Arabs are afraid of him," said Aflalo.

"What can Dayan do now?" I asked, in the self-important tone of a government functionary.

I couldn't fall asleep that night. Fear haunted me. In the darkness I saw a man with his hands tied, being shot in the head. He fell and that was the end of him. One moment he existed, the next he didn't. A scene from a film. Was that going to be my fate? That night, on the outskirts of Gaza, I made a vow: if I survive this in one piece, I'll change my life.

In the morning I felt worn out, but was glad to get out of the sleeping bag, to drink the burnt coffee Trabulsi made and eat a slice of army-isssue bread with cubes of halva from the battle rations. The paper said Nasser was going to make an important speech at midday. I went to the Intelligence Officer and volunteered to translate it. He put me in a side room with a radio, paper and pencil.

What a voice he has, this Nasser! Soft and musical when he speaks about *Misr*, Egypt, bursting with vitality when he speaks about *al-karameh*, honour, furious when he attacks *al-istimar*, imperialism, lyrical when he speaks of *al-nasr*, victory. He has total command of his vocal cords and can hypnotise his audience. No question about it – Sawt al-Arab and Egyptian theatre have missed a great talent.

"I am your sacrifice, I am Egypt's sacrifice," he roared inspirationally, just as he did on 26 October 1954, when he addressed the crowd at Maidan al-Manshieh in Alexandria. I was a boy then, a student at the Da'at evening school in Mahaneh Yehudah in Jerusalem, and I heard the speech at Grandma's house before classes started. I remember the intense excitement that affected everyone, when suddenly in the middle of his speech seven shots were heard. And I've never forgotten what he said then, when the assassination attempt failed:

"Citizens, remain where you are...May my blood be your sacrifice, my life Egypt's sacrifice. O free people, I speak to you after an attempt on your lives. The life of Gamal Abd el-Nasser is yours, since he comes from among you...I am no coward, I have fought for your honour. If Gamal Abd el-Nasser dies you will all be Gamal Abd el-Nasser. I shall fight for you to my dying day...I shall be a martyr for your sake..."

Even then I understood what must be happening in the heart of a young Arab, because on hearing this speech I myself was seized with the urge to grab a gun and start shooting the British overlords, the American imperialists, the agents of the West, and whoever else he told me to shoot. I was a youngster, fresh from the kibbutz youth movement where I'd been taught all about Israel's founding fathers and the heroes of our war of independence. And here was their hero, a bold young leader who had seized power in Egypt, thrown out King Farouk, made General Naguib president of the new republic, and kicked out the British expats. In those days I dreamed of becoming a leader like him, and hoped he would make peace. Yet now the hero of my youth was giving the signal for his armed forces to pour into the Sinai desert and entrench themselves in its gullies and ravines in order to kill me. And for what? The Straits of Tiran were zipped open and then zipped shut. Was that a reason to kill and be killed?

Now, on the outskirts of Gaza, I am listening to Nasser's speech on the Intelligence Officer's radio, and hear him declaring that his goal is to restore the situation as it was before 1948. I try to concentrate on his words, not on his voice, but I can only retain the words when I listen to the tone and the music. It is thanks to the music that I remember his old speeches verbatim, like something learned in childhood – the emphatic repetitions, the rise and fall of the voice, the rage he let loose and the insults he flung, the stormy outbursts, the dramatic silences, the measured imprecations.

"I am your sacrifice, I am Egypt's sacrifice," Nasser yells again. How many cockerels will he slaughter to satisfy his whims? And supposing he wins…they say he has chemical weapons! That's enough, calm down, stop scaring yourself.

That evening the entertainer Shai Ophir was brought in. He caricatured Jews from here and there, in Arabic and in Yiddish, and we fell about laughing. For a few minutes I forgot the Sawt al-Arab broadcaster who had roared, in Hebrew this time, so we would all understand: "We'll exterminate you, we'll slaughter you, we'll grind you to dust!"

At night the choking sensations came back, as if a vampire had me in a stranglehold. Come on then, how much longer do we have to wait? Memories were flooding in threatening to engulf me. I was two when World War II broke out and we fled from the house where I'd been born in the Muslim al-Muadham quarter of Baghdad, but the rioters had caught up with us in the Jewish quarter, where they killed and raped and robbed. I was ten when Israel's war of independence began in Palestine. The Iraqis had arrested my Uncle Hizkel and we abandoned Baghdad like refugees fleeing for their lives. I was nineteen when the Suez War broke out, and my mother miscarried from anxiety. Now I'm approaching thirty and there is no end in sight!

The days pass at a snail's pace. Another day of nerve-racking anticipation, and another, and now it's Friday. It's hot. The air lies heavily like an ancient, immobile beast. People are silent, it's like a Trappist monastery. Only Trabulsi walks around energetically, singing nationalist songs off key, distributing little flags to the men who are sprawled in the shade of the tanks, half-tracks and armoured cars, and demanding that they put them up right away.

"How long can this go on? I can't live like this. Three weeks without Beitar Yerushalayim!" Hermosa grumbles, suffering withdrawal symptoms from his favourite football team.

"That really is too much," Trabulsi agrees.

"Who wants war?" I ask, and everybody, Trabulsi and Aflalo, Katzav and Slutzky and Antebi, stare at me as if I've gone mad.

"I'll tell you what I want, I want to eat cow's foot soup with a lot of pepper, wash it down with a shot of arrack, and screw my neighbour's daughter all night," says Antebi in a mock Yemenite accent, illustrating his intentions with an eloquent hand gesture. Everybody laughs, and my mind flies back to loving nights with Yardena, and the longing is eating away at my heart.

On Fridays especially my thoughts turn to home, to my everyday life. Three weeks away from everything, here in this desert, it's too much.

I want to sleep in my own bed, not in a sleeping bag, to wake up in underwear, not in uniform, in my little flat, not among tanks, to wash under running water without being inundated by sand storms, to crap in a toilet bowl and not in the field, to drink Noumi Basra tea rather than Trabulsi's burnt coffee. I want to rise early, walk for an hour, go into Leonid's Russian grocery for coffee with two fresh warm rolls, preferably scorched around the edges. I'm dreaming of the Mahaneh Yehudah market, where I'd buy fruit and vegetables from the

Iraqi stall-holder and demolish a portion of Suberi's falafel with fenugreek and pepper relish.

I even miss the crying of my Orthodox neighbour's latest newborn. Every year the woman produces a baby which wakes me at dawn with inconsolable wails, and she always takes her time before putting it to the breast.

I miss my routine, going to work in a leisurely way, arguing about trivialities with my fellow workers, chatting with Levanah, the delectable manager of the Minister's office, though she's always in a rush in case he needs her, even sitting in the canteen and gazing at the hairy legs of Flora, Brokelman's secretary, and wondering why she doesn't shave them.

I miss Fridays. Knock off work early, go home, wash the floor, take a shower, flop on the bed and listen to Classical by Request at five p.m., sit on my little balcony and watch my Orthodox neighbour lighting the sabbath candles, the glow on her face as she recites the blessing, her hands circling the flames to cherish the light. I like to pour myself a shot of slivowitz and at six-thirty listen to Um Kulthoum singing, then hurry over to Katamon to join my parents for the sabbath supper and eat cold *okra kubbeh*. God almighty, is this too much to ask?

Heat. Emptiness. Unease. Once again I drag myself to the silent shadow of the eucalyptus, lean against its trunk with my eyes shut, and try to calm myself by crushing leaves between my fingers.

"What the hell's the matter with you, Nuri? I've been searching all over for you. The Intelligence Officer needs you right now!" My peace was shattered by the Intelligence sergeant, who dragged me back.

I put on the headphones. "Your eyes take me back to the

bygone days, teach me regret for the past and its pains," sang Um Kulthoum. "What I saw before me, till my eyes fell on you, were my wasted days, how could they count as my existence?" God in heaven, Um Kulthoum used to sing me to sleep in my mother's arms...

"What's taking you so long?" the officer snapped.

"One moment, a little patience please," I allowed myself to answer him back, and gained time by muttering, "let me figure out what's going on here." For a few moments I plunged into a blissful *tarab*. What is *tarab*, you may ask? How to translate it? Well now, Mister Orientalist, didn't you spend four years studying Arabic language and literature? Call it a musical high, a thrill of excitement, sheer pleasure, intoxication by sound, a body's song, a spiritual uplift, a soul's orgasm, the oblivion of Allah and all His servants – all these add up to *tarab*.

For a moment I forgot the war. The queen was singing! Who can be compared to her, who can decipher the mysteries of her voice, the heart-thrilling quavers, the sweet ache she plants in the soul? Come on, don't get carried away. She deserves to die, this queen. Yes, right now, when her friend Nasser is declaring war on us and she is doing nothing to stop him.

"So, what's going on?" the officer prodded me.

"I think the wireless operators have silenced the network and are listening to Um Kulthoum. One of them has just told the other that communications will resume after the recital."

"Are you serious? Could it be a trick to fool us?" The officer stared at me as if I'd gone mad. "How long will it take?"

"Can't tell. Could be two or three hours. It depends..."

"I don't understand anything any more!" he exclaimed, grabbing his head with both hands, and walked out.

Then the announcer introduced Sheikh Abu al-Ayneen

Shaisha reading from the Surat al-Ma'ida: "The bitterest enemies of the believers in Islam are the Jews and the idol-worshippers." He went on to urge "Jihad is the duty of every devout Muslim, the only way to treat the enemy. It is a religious duty to kill them, and whoever does so has his place in heaven."

The Sheikh's voice is melodious and moving, an intoxicating *tarab*. I relish every syllable, drink in every word, and suddenly it strikes me. What an idiot I am! Hey, he's calling on Muslims to kill you!

3

Katamon and the One-Room Flat

There were still plumes of smoke in the desert sky and explosions could still be heard, when I was summoned to the divisional adjutant's tent. I rushed there with my heart in my mouth – my two brothers were in the Armoured Corps and I hadn't heard a word from or about them.

"The minister you work for has asked us to release you immediately. You're to be at his office tomorrow morning," the adjutant said and turned back to the papers on his field desk. What happened, why is he sending for me? I was agitated and it was a while before I took it in – I was free, discharged, going home, the war's over.

I had almost nothing to pack – most of my things had been scattered all over the place. I said goodbye to my mates and ran back to the adjutancy for my travel discharge. While I was there I enquired about my brothers. The girl who operated the field-phone took a long time to reach the right contact, and finally said, "Moshe Imari's OK, Yaacov has been slightly wounded."

"Yaacov?" It took me a moment to realise she was referring to my brother Kabi. "Where was he wounded?"

"They'll tell you at the Mayor's office," she said. And when I asked which hospital he was in, she couldn't say.

1 hitched a ride in a command-car that was taking soldiers

back from the Sinai. When we had taken refuge in the shade of the tanks, consumed by anxiety and waiting for the order to advance, I'd made all sorts of promises to myself if only I survived this war, even if slightly wounded, which would be a lucky outcome. Now, hearing that Kabi was wounded, I was desperately worried for him. What on earth had made him rush back from London?

I waited a while at the pick-up stop at Re'em junction, as one by one vehicles collected the waiting soldiers. When my turn came an ancient Susita with a bearded, burly driver of about forty drew up. "Excuse the jalopy," he apologised, adding that he had room for only one passenger. He straightened the kippah on his head, lit a cigarette and turned up the radio, which was broadcasting a report on the battle at Abu Agheila. His face was tight with tension and he muttered unintelligibly. I was totally exhausted, my mind in a fog of forgetfulness, my eyes sore and their lids heavy. Now and then I dozed off for a few seconds, feeling the sweet seduction of sleep, then shook myself awake, startled to hear what the bearded man was saying:

"According to the Midrash: When the Temple fell Abraham appeared before the Almighty, Blessed Be He, weeping and tearing out his beard and hair, rending his clothes and throwing ashes on his head. 'How am I different from all nations and tongues that I should thus be humiliated and dishonoured?' the driver quoted, his eyes glittering, while the cigarette dangled from his mouth and the ash fell on his clothes. "And here we are – Jerusalem the Holy is in our hands, the Sinai desert, Gaza, the Golan Heights and Jordan – all ours."

The car swerved off the road and when he swung back onto the broken asphalt, a huge truck appeared from nowhere in front of us. He steered sharply to the right, and again slid off the road. My heart was beating wildly.

"We turned their tanks into bonfires," came a voice from the radio, and in my mind I saw Trabulsi's tank bursting into immense yellow flames, while I was buried in the sand, in infernal heat, a thick smell of smoke and burnt flesh filling my nostrils. There seemed to be someone crying out behind the noise of explosions. Was it Trabulsi calling for help?

"You hear?" the driver shook me and turned off the radio. "Isaiah says: Behold, all they that were incensed against thee shall be ashamed and confounded, they shall be as nothing, and those that strive with thee shall perish. Thou shalt seek them and shalt not find them, even them that contended with thee shall be as nothing, and as a thing of nought. For I the Lord thy God will hold thy right hand, saying unto thee, fear not, I will help thee."

His voice seemed remote and indistinct, like a failing microphone. When I made no answer he turned the radio on again.

"But when I come today to sing your praises, to crown you with garlands, I'm but the least of your children, the last of the poets," Shuli Natan's silvery voice came over the radio. My companion happily joined in, nodding vigorously: "Jerusalem of gold, of copper and of light…" I had first heard those lyrics just a few weeks earlier when I was dozing in Yardena's arms in her roof apartment in the German Colony. The annual song festival was being broadcast, and when I woke up and asked which song had won, she said, "Something wonderful," stroking the back of my neck. Oh Yardena!

"Now they'll be crawling on their knees," my companion said with relish. "Nineteen years they didn't let us pray at the Wall, now the Almighty has settled their account. It is the day of joy in God," he sang again. "Why don't you sing? Want some coffee?" he stopped on the roadside and poured black coffee for me from an old thermos flask.

Now from the radio came the thick voice of Levi Eshkol, the Prime Minister: "This may be a time of destiny, from which a new order and new relations will spring in the region, so we may live in peace in our homes, on our lands, and continue the task of settlement, of the ingathering of the exiles, our spiritual, cultural and moral work. We have promised much to the world, to the Jewish people, and to ourselves."

On the steep ascent from Sha'ar HaGai where the skeletons of burnt-out armoured vehicles, mementoes of the '48 war, keep vigil on either side of the road, the jalopy began to sputter and cough. "That's it, no more wars," he said. "Now we can have some rest, huh?" I grunted and turned on my side, wishing he would leave me alone.

Up on the hilltop at Shoresh I sat up and opened the window. There they were, the mountains of Jerusalem. I love this air, the wind that blows here. I breathed deeply, excitement rising in my chest. For a moment I felt dizzy. Home. Who knows what news awaits me there, who came back safely and who did not, who was wounded and who remained whole. I felt tense, but also longed to sleep, not to see or hear or know anything, just hide till everything became clear. Anxieties overshadowed the joy of freedom. In a little while I'll inquire at the Mayor's office which hospital Kabi's in.

I took a deep breath and held it in my lungs, again, and again. Levanah, the priestess of health, head of the Minister's office, says it's an anxiety-relieving exercise.

"Can you drop me off at Teddy Kollek's office?" I asked.

"I can, it's on my way to the German Colony."
"The German Colony? That's better still…" I said, choking.

I used the public phone on the corner of Rahel Imenu and Emek Refaim to call Sandra, Kabi's girlfriend.

"He was wounded in the shoulder. They took him to the hospital in Ashkelon. I saw him there this morning. I'll go again tomorrow afternoon. Want to come?"

"Definitely."

"But don't tell your parents yet, all right?" she added, as if she'd been brought up in our family and trained like us to spare them anxiety and sorrow.

My dusty uniform, kitbag and bristly face indicated where I had been. A passerby nodded to me, saying, "Welcome back!" The notice board beside the municipal swimming pool – the "pool of abomination," as it was called by Orthodox Jews because of the mixed bathing – bore army bereavement notices in standard phrasing. I stood there a long time, reading the names. Then I went to a kiosk and asked for Escort cigarettes and the newspapers, but couldn't find my wallet. I must have lost it on the way. Never mind the money, call it a penance – but my documents!

"Here you are." The man handed me the papers and cigarettes.

"Sorry, I lost my wallet."

"Never mind. Pay me another time."

"No thanks." I walked away and immediately regretted it.

I walked slowly and stopped in front of the pharmacy. Here I used to buy lubricated condoms. Yardena wouldn't sleep with me without them. I'd slip into the pharmacy when it was empty and blush as I asked for "preservatives," as though calling condoms by name was too embarrassing and vulgar. I walked on, and finally made myself look up at Yardena's roof-top flat. Was she at home? Was she alone? If she hadn't ditched me before the war I'd be running up the stairs two at a time to fall into her arms in her spacious and colourful room, decorated with reproductions of Kandinsky, Gauguin, Manet. In the north corner of the room stood the bed – a huge bridal bed Yardena had found in the flea market in Jaffa, a real one-off. It had four wooden posts carved with pomegranates, and was scattered with lots of bright cushions that she had made herself. Right now I'd push some cushions under her to raise her rounded hips, and we'd plunge into frantic lovemaking.

   I gazed up at the flat. Go on up, I told myself – don't they say, "All is fair in love and war"? I took a step forward, but then stopped. What would I say to her? What if she's not alone? Keep your self-respect. Better walk away, she isn't yours any more.

My legs felt strangely weak, but I carried on walking up Yohanan Ben Zakkai Street and from there to the Katamon. The approach to the immigrant housing estate is pretty wretched, narrow dirt roads, the houses a clutter of little cubes of raw stone. Here too was a hoarding with death notices. Seventeen names! So many from one immigrant community. I read the names – one of them, Ovadiah Zakkai, hit me hard. I knew him as a boy in the neighbourhood, then we met again at the Hebrew University – he being the first Kurdish immigrant to make it there. He had hoped to get his doctorate in America. The notice told me he'd been a captain in the artillery. I remembered seeing him here, on Antigonus Street, after he received his M.A. in Chemistry – broad-shouldered and beaming, followed by the great Zakkai clan walking in procession, the women ululating with joy. My mouth became dry.

Yaacov Broshi was also on the board. Yaacov, the son of the synagogue caretaker, who became the owner of a wedding hall in another neighbourhood. He was a clever, sociable lad, who even in his teens had all kinds of money-making plans. Once his mother asked my mother, "Why don't your sons come to synagogue?" Mother blushed in confusion but they still became friends.

I saw her from afar, standing on the balcony. "Nuri!" she shouted, and immediately came out of the house, ran like a country girl down the hillside, and fell into my arms. She hugged and kissed me and stroked my stubbly face, tears running down her cheeks.

"*Ayni uwain al daghb*, my eyes are fixed to the road, waiting for my children to come, my heart felt you would come today," she said as we entered the house.

"Abu Kabi, get up, Nuri's here," she called to Father, while her hands probed my shoulders and arms like a mother examining her newborn.

Father was lying on the bed dressed, despite the heat, in thick cotton pyjamas. "*Al-hamdu lillah, ibni*, thank God, my son, welcome back!" His arms encircled my body and pressed me to him as they used to do when I was a child and his embrace was my absolute protection. He held me for a long time without loosening his grip. The warmth and scent of his body stilled my anxiety. "I thank God that you've come back to us safe and sound," he said with a sigh of relief.

"Sit down, son, let's look at you. Rest," said Mother, laying a hand on my shoulder. "Would you like to shower? There is hot water. Every day I turn on the boiler, hoping you will all come home. Blessed be He and blessed be His name, my Nuri has come back safely…" Her cheeks were wet with tears.

"That's enough, Um Kabi," my father said softly and turned to me. "Have you heard from Kabi and Moshi?"

"I spoke to Kabi yesterday," I lied. "Nothing to worry about. And Moshi should be discharged soon, being a farmer."

"Why did Kabi have to come back from London, aren't you and Moshi enough?" Mother protested, peering at me closely. "You've lost weight, my son. Stay here a few days, rest and eat properly."

She went to the kitchen and came back with a tray bearing a finjan of coffee with cardamom for me and tea with mint for Father. It was a pleasure to drink the excellent coffee, after so many days of sour dishwater. "Father, do you have a cigarette?"

"No, son. My throat was hurting so I didn't buy any."

My father without cigarettes? He's a chain-smoker and usually keeps several packets at home. He looked so weak and pale, lying in bed in the middle of the day, in the thick pyjamas.

"Have you consulted an ear, nose, and throat specialist?" I asked.

"What throat? Never mind his throat, he's had a heart attack!" said Mother, and I was struck dumb.

"Why are you worrying him, he's just come back from the war," Father hushed her. Deeply shaken, I drew my chair close to his bed, took his big hand and pressed it to my cheek. What had happened? Why a heart attack? Where did that come from? A deluge of pity flooded me, I wanted to hold his head and kiss it.

"Don't worry," Father said in a soothing voice. "I got over it all right."

Mother couldn't contain herself. "All right you call it? Don't ask what we've been through. I can't sleep a wink, I'm jumping at the slightest noise – footsteps on the stairs and I collapse. And your Father lights one cigarette with another, his ear glued to the radio all day and all night. *Matit Israil, jannat Israil!* – Israel is dead, Israel has gone mad! – they kept screaming, God damn them. Your Father couldn't rest, he fell asleep with the radio on, I turned it off and he turned it on again, and so on night after night. Then one morning – crash! He fell on the bed, couldn't breathe, was suffocating in my hands, his face all wet with cold sweat. God Almighty, what to do? How have I sinned? I ran out on the balcony and yelled and yelled. My soul almost flew away by the time the ambulance arrived. Don't ask what we've been through," she concluded with a heavy sigh.

I glanced round the room and saw just how abject it was: a small windowless space, low ceiling, a dangling lightbulb. On the wall hung a photograph of us before leaving Baghdad. Mother and Father in the middle, elegantly dressed, their faces bright with hope. Mother is pregnant, my brother Moshi is looking serious, Kabi is trying not to grin, I'm tilting my head to one side in a dreamy posture. I like this picture. Father cut it out of our travel document and gave it to a photographer who enlarged and framed it.

"Here, son, clean clothes. Go on, shower and leave everything behind you," Mother urged me and again clasped my neck. "Such days we've had, good God Almighty. The body's here and the soul over there…You heard about Broshi? What a fine boy! My eyes dried up from crying. And about Zakkai and Shkrachi and Skhaik? I don't know who to cry for first. You heard what Broshi did with the first money he earned from the hall? Bought his parents' flat from the government! Tell me, is there justice in this world? Why didn't all his good deeds protect him? His mother is a saint, an angel. She cleans and looks after the synagogue, and comes to prayers, and helps the poor. Nobody can be more righteous. We were together in synagogue when the shells fell on the neighbourhood. I said, 'Come down to the shelter,' and she said, 'Me, go down to the shelter when my son is at war? God forbid!' And look what happened to her."

"Enough crying, it's bad for your eyes," said Father.

"It's not the eyes, it's the heart. I remember his bar mitzvah as if it was yesterday. We were new in the neighbourhood, I didn't know a soul, and his mother brought me refreshments with her own hands, a big platter. 'Take it for the children.' Suddenly he's a soldier, and he's gone…Oh my oh my…"

"Um Kabi, why are you wailing now? Your son is back, thank God, he brought good news from the boys, and you're crying?" But his eyes were mournful too. So unlike his usual self, as if he'd lost all his vitality.

The carpet on the floor absorbed the feeble light. Mother had bought it in the market from an Iranian immigrant who was leaving the country. Two bus drivers refused to take her with the carpet, but the third one gave in when she shoved it in through the back door. Then she carried it a whole kilometre across the unpaved land between the last bus stop in Old Katamon and the housing estate. She came in, sweaty and proud, as if she'd recaptured the glory of the red Persian carpet in our home in Baghdad. Father had made a face.

I got into the shower, washed the dust off, shampooed my hair repeatedly to cleanse it from the sweat and dirt that stiffened it. The mirror showed me eyes that looked extinguished and a skinny face covered with black stubble. I threw my dirty underwear into the laundry basket, scraped the water into the drain and wiped the concrete with a cloth. I opened the window to let out the steam and the smell of mildew: this mouldy housing estate does not get much sunlight. Then I went back to sit beside Father.

"Tell me, son, where were you? What happened? Is it true the Egyptians ran away?"

"No, in some places they fought like the devil. We took heavy casualties too…"

"So what do you think, will Nasser make peace?"

"That lot make peace?" Mother put in, "God damn them. They don't know how to lose or how to compromise. Their honour! God save us from their famous honour."

"But if Nasser compromises they'll kill him," Father argued.

"What then? 'The old won't become new and an enemy won't become a friend.' That's the way it is," she replied. "It was Arabs in Baghdad and it's Arabs here. Where can we run away to now?"

"Um Kabi," Father said soothingly, "we've beaten them and their fathers and grandfathers to hell – why should we run away?" He turned to me. "What did Kabi say to you? Will he go back to London?"

I nodded.

"Of course he will," Mother said. "What can he do here? They ate his heart out, he was right to leave." She was chopping parsley at top speed. I watched her like a child watching a magician. She scattered a pinch of it on the meatballs and a lot on the salad and the hot green-pepper relish.

"Give us a little glass, we'll drink a toast," Father said.

"You see what he's like! You're forbidden to drink," she scolded him.

"You know anybody who was killed by a little shot of arrack?"

He went to the cupboard and took out the bottle. To please her, he said the prayer of thanks for having lived to the present and for God's will. "To you, son, to you and Kabi and Moshi and Efraim. To peace," he said and sipped the drink slowly, relishing the liquor. "The wars are finished, woman!" he said in a loud voice, then pronounced the blessing for bread, tore off a piece of pitta, wrapped it around some parsley, spring onion and pepper relish, just the way I liked it, and handed it to me. Only then did he lean back in his seat at the head of the table. The colour was returning to his face.

"Don't eat the meat," Mother commanded. "I cooked chicken breast for you." He looked at me and raised his hands, as if to say, "You see what she's doing to me?"

Mother ignored his silent protest. "You should recite the *HaGomel* for coming home safely, son. When Kabi and Moshi return we'll celebrate all of you coming home safely, and your Father's recovery, may God open the gate for us," she concluded in the words of the prayer.

When I got up to leave she hugged me again. "Sit down, Nuri. Where are you off to already? You just got here. Let me get a sniff of you!"

"Another time, Mother. I have to be at work tomorrow and I haven't any clothes here."

"Already back to work? What's so urgent?"

"*Al-wazir*, the Minister, has sent for me."

"Aha," Father said, impressed.

"Wait, wait! I'll do a *ghasas* for you," Mother said and right away set about preparing for the procedure – melting balls of lead over my head while rubbing my neck with water – a time-honoured protection against the evil eye. I sat in the kitchen on a low, cane-bottomed stool and waited patiently for the end of the ritual, which included various muttered incantations. She also stuffed into my pocket a pinch of salt wrapped in a bit of cloth and the remains of the melted lead. I never told her that I always carried them with me – I even took them to war. I preferred to pretend that I regarded the whole thing as meaningless superstition.

Before I left, Mother gave me a basket full of delicacies and pastries. "I found your favourite halva in the market, first-rate stuff, and got you some Noumi Basra tea," she said, following me to the stairs.

"Mother, tell me the truth. What did the doctors say?"

"He has to be careful, not get excited, not get worked up, not smoke, and he must diet, take pills and rest, that's all."

The moon lighting the night sky wore a pale halo. I was taking a shortcut across the stony field to Dostai Street when I remembered that I hadn't asked Father for money. My wallet was lost – how was I going to get to work tomorrow morning? I jumped down the three steps to the path that led to the housing estate on Elazar Street and a moment later stood in front of my bursting mailbox, stuffed mainly with bills. My heart was thumping as I searched for something, just a note even, from Yardena. In the past she liked to surprise me with letters, or notes under the door, "I'm with you wherever you go," that kind of thing. When we had a fight she'd send me colourful postcards with proverbs included, to signal that she wasn't angry any more and love was on the menu again. But this time there was nothing. Feeling disappointed and lonely, I climbed up to my little flat on the fourth floor.

Grushka, my neighbour's cat, came up to me on silent paws. How could I have forgotten her? A beautiful, thick-furred cat, white with a black band, she always waited for me, was never annoyed with me. I picked her up and rubbed my cheek against hers.

There was a thick, heavy smell in the flat, the smell of dust accumulated in closed, unused rooms. I turned on the light by the front door and stood in the doorway, hesitant, as if I wasn't really home. But Grushka leapt down and ran inside and drew me after her. She settled possessively on the worn green armchair that I'd sworn to throw out if I returned from the war. I put down my kitbag and Mother's provisions, and for some reason went around turning on all the lights – in the bedroom, the kitchen, the bathroom, the balcony.

The pretty potted plant on the balcony had withered and died. The fridge held rotting fruit and vegetables, mouldy cheese, stale bread, and a jar of pickled herring in congealed oil. The bathroom walls had shed bits of plaster. The water in the toilet bowl had gone down and left rust marks. When I turned on the kitchen tap it coughed horribly, spitting out rusty splashes. I left the water running till it cleared.

I wanted to run away, but where to? I took a hefty swallow of slivowitz straight from the bottle. Sharp as a razor, it scorched my throat, lit a fuse and rolled like a ball of fire down my gullet. Now for a cigarette. I usually had packets lying around the room. I searched everywhere, turned out all the drawers – nothing.

While sorting out clothes for the next morning, I discovered a ten-lira note in a pocket, which cheered me up no end, as if I'd found a hoard of treasure. I turned on the radio and closed my eyes. I'd dreamed about this moment, about stretching out on the sofa, having a quiet drink and listening to music. Why then the sadness and emptiness?

*

The sound of the alarm clock pierced my brain like a harpoon striking a fish. With my eyes shut I fumbled for the button and thumbed it down furiously. I sat up trying to recall the dream, to figure out what Trabulsi had yelled in the tank, but all that came was the image of the flames.

The last stars were fading, clearing the sky for a new day. It seemed a long time since I'd heard these early morning sounds, the dawn chorus. Daylight revealed the red kestrels on the tiled roof opposite, boosting my spirits a little.

The Orthodox woman came out on to her balcony, and this time she smiled and waved to me. Her latest baby began his early morning caterwauling, and I remembered that I'd missed his cries during those days of waiting. His mother calmly began to hang up washing, taking piece after piece from a big tub, until there was no room left on the line. Only then did she go inside to suckle the little screamer. In the meantime the water boiled in the kettle, and I poured in the remains of the Noumi Basra. It tasted stale. I ought to keep it in a ceramic jar, I told myself for the umpteenth time. The sound of piano playing came from the radio, then the voice of Michael Ben-Hanan: "Good morning everyone! And if you're in the mood for calisthenics, take your places, get ready…"

I cut myself shaving and bled. The face in the mirror looked weary, overhung by a thatch of hair in urgent need of the barber's scissors. Cheer up, union-man, you've come back safely. You have an appointment with the Minister, and Levanah is sure to be there. Then I managed a smile, at last.

4

The Minister in Charge

The door to the Minister's office was open, Levanah was not in the waiting room, and before I could greet Shula, the secretary, the Minister gestured to me to come in, swung his legs off the desk, stood up and squeezed my hand hard, his lion's mane shaking as he nodded vigorously.

The Minister in Charge was our cabinet minister, and this was our name for him because, though he didn't have a specific portfolio, he was involved with everything and his office practically adjoined that of the Prime Minister.

"Welcome back. How was it?" he asked, as if I had been away on some kind of excursion.

I grinned uncomfortably, not knowing what to say.

"So, we went to sleep as a state and woke up as an empire! Now all of the Land of Israel is ours." His eyes glittered under his bushy grey eyebrows. "This was the first war for your immigrant generation. I won't deny that we were worried, wondering how it would go, how the immigrant settlements on the border would cope, and what would happen if the people abandoned them." His frankness surprised me. "But I hear that you, the younger generation, proved yourselves in battle."

My stomach tightened and I pressed it with both hands. I

wanted to tell him about the seventeen boys from Katamon who fell in battle, but kept my mouth shut.

"Tell me, since you know them, did you think that the Egyptians would run away, barefoot?" he laughed and glanced at a big photograph of a group of pioneers that hung on his wall.

"I don't know…In my sector they fought honourably," I mumbled.

"You're tired. Well, it's to be expected." He told Shula to bring me a cup of coffee, but she didn't know I don't take it with milk. Levanah would have brought me coffee the way I like it. The Minister began to pace up and down. "It's a new historical era for us," he exclaimed, waving his arms. "Tremendous possibilities have opened up!"

"There is also the question of what the Arabs will do," I put in, and felt right away it was the wrong thing to say.

"What can they do? Even if the era of wars is not yet over, it's put off for many years, and we must take advantage of this time to build and develop. We'll turn Jerusalem into a metropolis, Israel's eternal capital," he declared, settling in his armchair.

The Minister had embraced this settlement vision since he was a boy and had met the pioneers from Eastern Europe, enthusiastic young people with rumpled hair and open shirts who captivated him. He used to see them at their meeting place not far from his parents' apartment, staying up till the small hours, and he adored them, brewing tea for them and washing their tin cups. He was filled with admiration for the way they ignored the conventions of appearance and property, content to live in tents and fortify their bodies and minds with the dream of an independent state. He wanted to be like them.

In his youth he worked in agriculture and construction and

developed a socialist world view. When he matured he dedicated himself to national objectives, acquired a style of leadership and became a popular speaker, aided by a powerful, far-reaching voice. His speeches, delivered in high-flown and even obscure Hebrew, were alive with Zionist fervour and as long as the road from Sinai to Jerusalem. Now he told me that he envisaged thousands of young people, successors of the pioneers he had known in his childhood, settling in the liberated territories and making the wilderness bloom.

"*Yungerman*," he said, borrowing a typical Yiddish word from his friend Eshkol, "let's get down to business." As he talked he took a big paperclip, straightened it and began to clean his fingernails. Then he tried without success to restore the wire to its former shape. "Listen here. I was really impressed by the position papers you prepared for me that time. And incidentally, you displayed considerable long-term understanding in the big debate with Professor Kishinevsky, I can see it quite clearly now. Altogether I think a fellow with your background should be in Intelligence, and now I find that you're in the Armoured Division," he said in passing. "Well, I've decided to take advantage of your capabilities and appoint you advisor on Arab affairs and put you in charge of our office in East Jerusalem." Seeing my surprise, he went on, "Sometimes we dive for pearls, and then discover them right under our noses. You combine two qualities – you're a child of the East who commands both Hebrew and Arabic, and you're also a product of our kibbutz movement, and had the privilege of serving the founding fathers." He sipped from his mug of coffee. "So set up an office in East Jerusalem, sniff around to see what's happening there, meet their effendis, and provide me with your evaluations."

I stared at him in astonishment, trying to take in the idea of such an important position.

"The Prime Minister has asked me to help him formulate policy regarding the Arab sector and the liberated territories, and you're the right person to help me carry out this mission," he concluded, throwing the spoiled paperclip into the wastepaper basket and picking up the phone: "Shula, can you come in and take dictation?" There and then he dictated my official appointment, told her to send it to all the relevant parties, and then put him in touch with the sector commander and the Mayor. "I want them to introduce you to the job without delay and…Shula," he added, "ask the Ministry spokesman to issue a communiqué to the press and radio today." He stood up – and my appointment was established, without my being consulted or even asked if I wanted it.

"We'll provide you with everything you need. Now, to work!" he urged me in a tone that reminded me of Shai Ophir's satirical skits when we were on the outskirts of Gaza. He came up and put his arm around my shoulders.

"I have a request to make, if I may," I said.

"I'm listening."

"I have an uncle, my father's brother, who was one of the leaders of the Zionist underground in Baghdad. He's been in prison there for twenty years, with the threat of being hanged at any moment. Maybe now we can save him? His name is Hizkel Imari. The Mossad are familiar with his case."

"Yes, yes, you told me about him. We tried at the time but without success. I promise you we'll do whatever we can to rescue him," he said and patted my shoulder. Suddenly his expression changed. "You heard about Levanah's brother?" he asked in a low voice.

"No."

"Fell in the battle for the Old City." I gasped. "Go, go and comfort her." Then, after a moment of gloomy silence, he said, "It is written in the Scrolls of Fire, 'In war people kill and are killed, and we need to cry for the living and the dead.'" He closed the door behind me. I knew that he had lost his paratrooper son in the Suez war in 1956.

I sat down in the waiting room and watched Shula as she coped with a stream of phone calls. After a while her image was replaced by that of Levanah, my usual link with the Minister in Charge. In fact, it was thanks to her that I had come to work for him. Two years before, when I had an administrative job in the Ministry, I used to see her in the cafeteria, and one day I told her that Arabic was my mother tongue and that I had a degree in Arabic Studies. A few days later she came furtively into my office, holding in her small hands a number of letters that needed translating. The Minister in Charge had received them from the heads of Arab local councils, following a controversial speech he'd made in the Knesset. I translated them on the spot and even suggested how to reply to them. That's how it started. Soon after, Levanah introduced me to the Minister in her typically gentle but businesslike manner: "This is the man who has been helping us with Arabic issues," she said, and in effect made me an unofficial advisor to the Minister and his office. I enjoyed the opportunity to make use of my training and knowledge, even on a voluntary basis and without an official position. Ever since then I had felt committed to my additional employment, and Levanah saw to it that I received up-to-date reviews from various sources, including classified material. I liked her company: there was something reserved about her,

her measured gestures, her quiet footsteps. Sometimes I kept her hanging around by telling her Arabic stories, since she knew no Arabic and very few Arabs. But I didn't want her to think that this was my entire world, so I made a point of talking to her about books, plays, concerts and exhibitions that I had enjoyed. She never stayed long, always apologising that she had to rush back to the Minister's office. Her loyalty to him was absolute, so much so that I sometimes wondered about their relationship. But then I'd say to myself, nonsense, think of the age gap, the different backgrounds and the risks involved. And anyway, why should she? The Minister was a kibbutz member and family man – what could he offer her?

I sat facing Shula, deep in thought and absentmindedly taking apart and re-assembling a ballpoint pen that was on her desk.

When she had finished making all the necessary calls she went to the security officer and came back with an official document stating my new position. "Now give me your home number…What, you don't have a phone? We'll take care of it immediately." She sat at the typewriter and wrote an official letter to the Director General of the Post Office, got the Minister to sign it and put it in the out tray.

I pondered the unexpected appointment, which had fallen like a fruit from a tree straight into my mouth. The Minister in Charge knew very little about me, we'd never had a general conversation that could have given him an idea what I was like. To his credit, he never asked if I was a party member or close to his political movement. Two years before, when I'd translated the letters from the heads of the Arab councils, he asked me to join him in a meeting with them, where I served as his intepreter, and a few months later Levanah asked me to prepare a memorandum for him on the teaching of Arabic in schools and universities, and invited me to take part in a meeting with a large group of people. The Minister presented the subject briefly and put a few questions to the participants. The first to speak was the scientific advisor, Professor Kishinevsky, who favoured strengthening Israel's Western orientation:

"You're wasting your time, Minister," he declared at the outset, and went on to argue that the Arabic language was petrified, inferior, lacking theoretical literature or any modern scientific and cultural terminology, that Arabic culture as a whole lacked the tools for abstract thought, and so on and so forth.

This was my first experience of attending a meeting of experts, whose knowledge seemed unchallengable, and I hadn't intended to speak at all. Nevertheless, I found myself proposing a different approach: "Our great lexicographer Eliezer Ben-Yehuda considered Arabic to be a language which was engaged in a process of revival, dealing successfully with the modern world. He even introduced Arabic words into Hebrew." The professor froze me with a glance.

I saw the Minister, himself an impressive and authoritative figure, rubbing his thick mane and listening uneasily. In the end he summed up by saying, "The issue is not ready for resolution." When faced with irreconcilable positions, he always found a neutral formula that the opponents could not object to. After the meeting he told me to wait. "You didn't stand up for your opinion as you should have," he said reproachfully.

"There is an Arabic saying, 'Who dares to tell the lion he has bad breath?'" I replied in my defence, and he laughed. "How can a person who doesn't know any Arabic and knows nothing about the Arab world make such statements about the language and the culture?" I added, saying what I hadn't dared to say to the professor and his colleagues. "We need Arabic speakers as much as speakers of English and French. We live in the Middle East and our future is here. We still have Iraqi and Egyptian immigrants who know the language, but if we don't take care there won't be any in the next generation."

"Don't be so pessimistic, young man," he said and stood up, and that was that.

A week later Levanah informed me that the Minister had decided to accept the scientific advisor's position. She invited me to have coffee, her way of sweetening the pill. But this was ages ago, before the war.

"Shula, could you get in touch with the hospital in Ashkelon, please?" I asked. "My brother is there."

She tried again and again but couldn't get through. Then, without warning, a bearded man in a black suit and black hat came into the office. Without bothering to introduce himself, he said, "I have to see the Minister immediately!" Shula asked him who he was and what he wanted, but in reply he launched into a passionate sermon calling for the restoration of the Temple, with verses flowing from his mouth like lava, and all the time swaying back and forth as if praying: "Since the destruction of the Temple there has not been a day that was not cursed…" He took out a glossy pamphlet with impressive illustrations of the Temples, the First, the Second, and even the Third Temple, "which will be built soon in our lifetime and will not wait for the coming of the Messiah. At long last we have triumphed and Jerusalem the Holy has been delivered from the hands of the Gentiles, God damn them!" he intoned.

Shula looked at me, at a loss, and I stared helplessly at the eccentric who, taking advantage of our confusion, barged into the Minister's office. She shot out of her seat to try to stop him and was stunned as the bearded one, smiling triumphantly, slammed the door in her face.

"What a nutter!" she exclaimed.

"The Minister told me about Levanah's brother," I said. "I'd like to visit her." So Shula summoned Chaim, the Minister's driver to take me there.

The entrance to Levanah's parents' house on Herzl Boulevard was white with pasted-up sympathy notices from friends and neighbours. I stood there a long time, uncertain about going in. How do you comfort the bereaved? Taking a deep breath, I pushed open the door. The living-room was packed. Levanah was surprised to see me and introduced me to her parents, her brother and two sisters. They were sitting on a low bed, not on the floor as we do. I mumbled something and sat down beside her. She passed me a photo album with pictures of a slim young man in his early twenties, smiling shyly.

"How did it happen?" I asked.

"After it was all over, someone fired a shot from the Old City wall, and…" She bit her lip. I didn't know what to say. I took out my cigarettes, but quickly put them back in my pocket. Levanah doesn't smoke and doesn't like it when people light up near her.

"It's all right, you can smoke," she said, nodding. "Did the Minister speak to you?" I said yes and thanked her, as I was pretty sure the appointment was her idea. I knew she had a lot of influence over him.

"You've lost weight," she said. "Take a few days off."

"I got the impression he wants me to start right away."

"What's so urgent? Will the Arabs run away?"

Two women came in and embraced her. Her face contorted as she tried not to burst into tears. When they let go I took her hand in both of mine and held it a long time.

I remembered I had no money and went to the bank, then took a taxi to Zion Square, which was packed with young soldiers and reservists standing around in groups. Some were silent, others were talking at the top of their voices, telling stories about the war. Instead of Ze'ev, the affable cashier I was used to dealing with, there was a young woman with a beehive hairdo who was busy inspecting her fingernails.

"Where is Ze'ev?"

"On the Golan Heights," she said without looking up. Finally she noticed the line stretching behind me and asked what I wanted. The army wages weren't in my account yet, while the mortgage payment was due. I withdrew the one hundred and seventy-three lira in the account and left.

The streets were livelier than ever. It seemed that overnight Jerusalem had acquired a whole new population. People walked around, stopped to talk to acquaintances, chatting or whispering, and the air held something new, something confused and unclear, a mixture of joy and sadness, hope and expectation, as well as the eternal Jewish question, "What's going to happen?"

I walked down Jaffa Road towards the centre of town. The roar of pneumatic drills made the ground tremble and deafened the ears. I walked on to see the concrete wall that separated the Old City, al-Quds as they call it, from our Jerusalem, but it wasn't there! Heavy equipment crawled on the hilltop, smoothing over no-man's-land. Clouds of dust settled thickly over everything, and all was noise and confusion, while hundreds of curious onlookers gathered to watch. I too stood there, hypnotised, realising that I had never imagined East Jerusalem would be opened to us.

I was eager to see it, but the way was still blocked. Someone said we should try the Mandelbaum Gate. There a crowd gathered where only the other day Jordanian soldiers and UN observers had manned the gate, now replaced by Israeli soldiers and policemen. The old sign, "Stop! Border Ahead!" lay on the barbed wire fence, which had collapsed.

I stood in line, gazing at the nearby Tourjeman post and chewing my lip, just like the last time when, nine years ago, I had crossed this border on the way to Mount Scopus. Good God, how the years had flown! I still remember the earnest expressions on the faces of my fellow squaddies.

"We're going abroad," Sergeant Major Efroni had said when he briefed us. To impress us with the importance of the occasion, he lit an American cigarette and launched into an emotional speech: "Going up to the Mount we'll be driving on the road where the convoy to Hadassah Hospital was ambushed in April 1948. This was just after Abd al-Kadr al-Husseini was killed on the Qastel, and four days after the capture of the village of Deir Yassin by the Irgun and the carnage that followed. Mount Scopus was cut off, and the British governor agreed that Jewish guards could accompany the medical convoy. In the afternoon the news came that everyone in that convoy, seventy-eight men and women, had been massacred in Sheikh Jarrah. The bodies of twenty-two of them were never found. That's the story in a nutshell," he concluded. "We kill them and they kill us, and the world looks on as if it's a madhouse."

When we reached Mount Scopus, the regular outpost commander, known as the king of the mountain, showed us around the hospital, the university buildings, the national library and the pine woods. I was part of a unit of soldiers who were specialists in all sorts of things and was personally responsible for wireless communications, but we were all ostensibly hospital workers. This was army life from a different world – a bit like a prison, since there was no going in or out, but we enjoyed a very comfortable existence during the month we were there. I still remember the smell of baking bread and the excellent meals, worthy of a high-class restaurant, cooked for us by an older reservist who in civilian life was the chef of the Dan Hotel in Tel Aviv. In fact, we were so isolated I was able to make friends with Ghadir, a shepherd girl from the other side of the border, but that's another story.

In our limited free time we were offered educational courses by the team of experts from the National Library and the hospital, academics who maintained the laboratories and facilities of the Hebrew University on the Mount. I especially enjoyed the lectures on the history of Jerusalem by Professor Meir Shadmi, the renowned scholar of Islam and an amiable elderly man with a Ben-Gurion-style mane, a boyish grin and prominent teeth. Being a child of the mass immigration of the 1950s, without any formal education, I was self-concious about knowing so little. By day I had worked for a living and at night I attended a school for working boys. It was thanks to the school and its dedicated teachers that I was able to matriculate, but my general knowledge was inevitably as full of holes as a Swiss cheese. Now Shadmi, this eloquent professor, a modest, friendly scholar, happily shared his vast knowledge with anyone who took an interest. Till then I had known next to nothing about Jerusalem. In Baghdad my mother had told us some stories, but they were naive and nostalgic tales that could not instil in me the sense of the city's holiness, the way it is felt by a religious Jew who prays to it three times a day, or by one who grows up in its alleyways.

That time on Mount Scopus – Jebel Sacobos in Arabic – Shadmi talked about Jerusalem as a poet speaks of his beloved. He told us that her stones are singing, that she is bathed in a soft, caressing golden light. He described the great Muslim shrines, the Dome of the Rock and al-Aqsa mosque, the foundation stone from which Mohammed rose to heaven on his steed al-Burak, and of course the Temple Mount's history, and our holy Western Wall, and the numerous synagogues and famous religious schools. But after lavishing praise on the ancient city through the ages, he concluded on a sober note: "Here were born the spiritual creations of the prophets and sages, kings and poets, who lived in Jerusalem and endowed it with extraordinary grace, and made it into a messianic city which, like a magnet, draws the madmen of this world and its would-be saviours, and everyone prays and their prayers are not answered, and they call on the Messiah and he does not come."

With the help of the field-glasses of the Intelligence unit on the roof of the hospital, he showed us the city within the walls. I saw houses crushed together, balcony touching balcony, roof adjoining roof, like an overturned sieve sheltering the city, pierced here and there by minarets and church steeples, interspersed by some green plumes – the few unruly trees and bushes that dared to reach for the sunlight while their roots pushed through the stony soil – and the whole crammed, in suffocating proximity, into less than one square mile.

I soon became used to the small sounds and rustles, the amazing rural calm, which was broken at dawn and four more times in the course of the day by the summons of the muezzin. I walked around and discovered the eastern flank of the mountain facing the mountains of Edom and the Dead Sea. When I woke up early I watched the peach-coloured glow of the rising sun over the mountains of Edom, and when the air was very clear the water of the Dead Sea was a brilliant turquoise, like a field of gems. I grew deeply attached to the landscape, the slopes and the gullies, the way I had discovered the beauty of the Jezreel Valley and Mount Tabor when I was a boy in the kibbutz.

Professor Shadmi was a fount of wisdom. More than once I had received a whole lecture in response to a routine comment, such as, "It's a pity the Old City is in Jordanian hands."

"But my dear Nuri, what matters is the essence, not the vessel. Even if we agree that the Temple Mount is the centre, the heart, that everyone wants, Muslims, Christians, and Jews, we still have to consider what is the essence, the core of the place. Do you know the story of Rabbi Yohanan Ben Zakkai? No? Well, he was the youngest disciple of Old Hillel, who regarded him when he was still a youth as the greatest of them all, and dubbed him 'a father of wisdom for the generations'. Before the downfall, during the siege of Jerusalem, Ben Zakkai was one of the leaders of the Sanhedrin, which occupied a hall in the Temple. While the Zealots wanted to fight to the last, come what may, Ben Zakkai realised that they could not possibly defeat the Romans, and he chose survival and the preservation of the spiritual centre. With the help of his disciples he slipped out of the besieged city to go to the Roman commander Vespasian, and said to him, 'Give me Yavneh and its Sages.'

According to tradition, Vespasian agreed because Rabbi Yohanan foretold that he would become emperor, and shortly after this a messenger arrived from Rome to inform him of it. You ask why Yavneh? Well, my friend, you should know that Yavneh was the seat of the Sages and Rabbi Yohanan Ben Zakkai, who wanted to ensure the survival of Judaism, installed the Sanhedrin there and made it the spiritual centre that preserved the future of the People of Israel. That is why I say, what matters is the essence. That is what preserved our people, not the stones, not the holy site; after all, no one knows when or even if it will ever be within our reach. Rabbi Yohanan Ben Zakkai believed that it did not matter who ruled over the stones and the Mount. If he had given in to the Zealots, we wouldn't be here today."

When at last I reached the officer responsible for the Mandelbaum Gate he asked to see my identity card, which I didn't have, but fortunately I had the new document I'd been given that morning by the security officer of the Ministry. "With a document like this you stood in line?" he asked, raising his eyebrows.

I boarded a taxi. The driver, a man about my age with a peaked cap on his head, waited for me to tell him where we were going.

"To the military government headquarters. But first I want to drive around the city. Slowly, I want to savour the views."

"Savour them, friend, savour and enjoy! We've got all the time in the world." His throaty Sephardic voice was music to my ears. Suddenly I envied him and felt annoyed with myself for having flattened my own pronunciation in order to sound like the kibbutz-born kids.

"You were born in the Old City?" I asked.

"Can't you hear it? Right there, within the walls."

"You remember much?"

"How could I forget? The Golden Gate, the Tower of David, Absalom's Tomb, the Via Dolorosa, the market…"

The street names were displayed on ceramic tiles in green, black and white, written in Arabic and English. I read them slowly, like a child. It occurred to me to check what the street name signs were like on our side. I'd never thought about it before.

"Everything's shut. Bastards. What's the matter, we aren't good enough for them?" asked the driver, lighting a cigarette.

"It's not them, it's us. The military governor imposed a curfew," I told him.

"Pity, I wanted to buy some electrical goods, before they learn from us and put up the prices." We continued driving through the empty alleys. Place names and concepts I'd learned from Professor Shadmi rose to the surface of my mind.

A dead city, bands of soldiers patrolling, and suddenly the voice of my Minister in Charge came from the car radio, full of his trademark pathos: "Jerusalem, the reunified city, the capital of Israel for all eternity…"

"It seems the bullshit's starting already," the driver grumbled and spat out of the window. "What eternity? One bark from Washington and we'll crawl back into the cage, like we did in '56."

"Where is Wadi Joz?" I asked.

"You should have said," he replied and drove towards the Rockefeller Museum and then turned left. We saw closed workshops, heaps of junk, broken vehicles and dead engines, rubbish-strewn plots, then suddenly – crash! A hail of stones fell on the car. I crouched low. The driver cursed. We looked around and saw no one.

"Sons of bitches, they aren't scared!" he said and stopped.

"Keep going, keep going," I urged him. "*Ibad an al-shar wughanilo* – avoid evil and sing for it!"

"But what's going on?" he protested. "We just finished smashing them in the war and already they're raising their heads!"

On the right were some wooden huts. Again, I thought of Ghadir, the pretty shepherd girl I had met on Mount Scopus nine years previosly. Perhaps she lived here?

Rubbish on the roadsides, bits of paper flying, shops and businesses shut, even the hotels were closed. Curious eyes peered at us from the windows, around the curtains. I smiled at them, then stopped. I didn't want them to interpret the smile either as triumphal or as a greeting.

"Everything's closed, damn their eyes. Let's go to Salah a-Din Street, where their so-called fashionable shops are."

"It's just a little shopping centre," I said when we arrived, disappointed, as if I'd expected to meet a beautiful cousin who turned out to be nothing special.

"Wait, wait, you haven't seen anything yet. This isn't the Old City."

"*Madinat as-salaam*, the city of peace," I intoned.

"What kind of *salaam* is this?" he muttered and slowed down again. "Siege, encirclement, breakthrough and liberation – again, and again, for ever and ever."

5
First Day in East Jerusalem

Hundreds of Jerusalem Arabs crowded in front of the iron gate of the military governor's HQ which had moved into the former Jordanian governor's house on Salah a-Din Street. A woman covered from head to foot was crying "*Ibni, ibni* – my son, my son!" – her eyes full of tears. I had seen the same tears in the eyes of the lovely Rashel, the wife of my Uncle Hizkel, and recalled how she had leaned, barely breathing, on my mother when they tore her husband from her arms and dragged him away to the dungeons of Iraq's secret service. I took a deep breath and pushed my way through the crowd, then went up to the second floor, to the office of the General's advisor.

"You're the General's advisor?" I was amazed. Aharon Amitai, a former classmate, was sitting behind the desk.

"*Ahlan wasahlan*, Nuri," he greeted me and stood up.

"*Ahlan wasahlan* to you," I replied. "This is a surprise." The room was richly furnished – massive leather armchairs, a conference corner, a huge dark desk, a bright carpet on the floor. On the wall hung an impressive photograph of the Old City as seen from the Mount of Olives.

"The General says to bring you up to speed," he at once began to brief me, in his typical businesslike way, on military and civilian matters, hierarchies, power relations and interests, and all in great detail. It was evident that in a matter of days he'd built up a whole network of acquaintances and sources and collaborators from among the locals. When he finished the survey he carefully collected together the papers on his desk, locked them in a safe and took me over to field security, to provide me with permits to enter the cities of the West Bank and various closed sectors, including military camps. When everything was done he said, "Come on, let's get something to eat and I'll introduce you to an interesting man."

Amitai was a few years older than me. At university he had been an outstanding student, and spoke fluent Arabic without a foreign accent. He used to take course notes on large cards and leave as soon as the lesson ended, never wasting time on idle chitchat. One girl in our class, Beanstalk we called her, was crazy about him and went out of her way to attract his attention, but never managed to get even a smile out of him. He and I became friendly only in the third year, when I organised a small group of students to help kids in the poor neighbourhood of Musrara to prepare for the State Aptitude Test. Beanstalk, who followed him everywhere, laid an ambush for him there too, worked with him, and eventually got him. Amitai continued his university studies and was the first of our year to obtain a doctorate. He joined the academic staff and was considered highly promising. Now he and I left the grounds of the military government HQ and went to a nearby restaurant. Al-Hurriyeh – Liberty – said the sign over the door.

"It's not a bad place. Belongs to Abu George, a Christian from a well-off family originally from Bethlehem. He's a journalist with political awareness. He's also the chairman of the tourist industry association."

A pair of colourful canaries chirped in a cage near the

entrance. A diminutive man was busy buffing the unoccupied tables and chairs and a pungent smell of polish hung in the air. We went through the empty restaurant into an attractive garden, where rose bushes bordered a lawn, and at the back stood a spreading pomegranate tree full of red buds that would ripen into sweet fruit by the end of the summer. A sprinkler freshened the hot air with flying showers of cool water.

A handsome, fair-skinned man in his fifties came to our table. It was Abu George. "*Ahlan, bil-colonel,*" he said to Amitai and shook his hand. Amitai introduced me by my grand new title, and Abu George gave me a feeble handshake. In his white jacket and black bow tie he reminded me of Humphrey Bogart in *Casablanca*. When he left us to order our lunch Amitai said, "This is where you and I must make each other look big and important."

"Why did he call you colonel?"

"They gave me that title the day I started here. They think I'm from the Intelligence Services."

In keeping with his new image as a secret service man, Amitai told me what he'd managed to find out about our host. Abu George, originally Ibrahim Hilmi, was born in the last days of the Ottoman empire. He had told my friend that when he was a child he saw General Allenby entering Jerusalem after the conquest, and described how the victorious General dismounted from his horse at the Jaffa Gate and entered the holy city on foot, humbly, to show respect. His maternal uncle had been killed in that war and the family did not know where he was buried. When he grew up he took this uncle's name, Abu George, and had been known by it ever since. He had only one child, a daughter named Yasmine.

A corpulent waiter, dressed in finery like the serving staff at the King David Hotel, brought us hummus and tehina, shishlik and a salad seasoned in olive oil, which immediately transported me to my childhood. The pitta bread was thicker than ours and its flour tastier, the hummus denser and more satisfying, not ground smooth as we tend to do it. But best of all was the tehina full of finely-chopped parsley and the right amount of salt and lemon.

"I apologise, we have no new fresh supplies. This is all that's left," said Abu George.

"Blessings on your hands," I said in a friendly tone. He nodded slightly and left.

"His employees follow him through thick and thin," Amitai went on. "He pays them well, contributes to their children's education, helps with medical costs. Like our old-time socialists…"

Abu George returned and sat down at the corner of our table. A pair of pigeons landed on the window sill, and their cooing blended with the silence that dominated the lovely garden.

"How are things?" Amitai asked.

"Hard. Hard…What more can I say?" replied Abu George glumly.

"All the same, tell us."

"What's to talk about? In '48 you drove me out of Talbieh. I escaped to al-Quds. Now you've invaded this place too. Where should I run to now?" His expression showed how severely recent events had devastated him, leaving him stunned and perplexed.

"And now what?" Amitai pressed him.

"Now? We wait."

"Wait for what?"

"*Ana maref*, what do I know? For the king, for Nasser, for

America, for Allah," he said despairingly, took a *masbahah*, a string of worry beads, from his pocket and began to run it through his fingers.

"But the issue is between you and us, brother," Amitai said impatiently. "Not with America or Russia."

Abu George took a deep breath, closed his eyes and considered. Then he said quietly, "You'll be out of here in two, three weeks, just like you quit the Sinai in '56."

Amitai dismissed the prediction with a shake of his head, lit his pipe and puffed on it, exhaling smoke-rings. The smartly-liveried waiter brought iced water and fragrant Arab coffee. My watch showed a quarter past one. I'd arranged to meet Sandra at three to go to Ashkelon to visit Kabi at the hospital.

"You're Iraqi, aren't you?" Abu George said to me and poured me a cup of coffee.

I nodded.

"Your Arabic is a mixture."

"Like life," I smiled.

"Thirty years ago, when I was a student at Beirut University, I knew an Iraqi Jew by the name of Somekh. He was planning to open a psychiatric hospital in Baghdad, something very advanced," he said and offered me a cigarette from his packet of Imperials.

"They're as good as American cigarettes," he assured me. The Virginia tobacco was aromatic and very strong. I coughed and my head spun, but I continued to smoke it out of politeness. For the next round I offered him one of my Ascot cigarettes. He inhaled a couple of times then said, "Too dry," and put it out. He became silent, withdrawn, not at all like a traditional Arab host.

"How much do we owe you, my friend?" I asked.

"*Mush mumken*, out of the question!" he said, startled out of his reverie. "You don't want to insult me."

"Narghile?" the waiter offered, Amitai nodded, and the two of us lounged beside the hubble-bubble like lords in their ancestral home. Unused to smoking a narghile, I inhaled too deeply, the water gurgled in the glass jar and I choked and spluttered. Abu George watched me and for the first time a little smile appeared on his face. In the empty restaurant the sound of bubbling water was like a distant melody, and I must have dozed off, because suddenly I was in a desert sandstorm, buffeted by a blinding wind while shells whistled around me. I woke up in alarm to see a big man standing before me, moustachioed and smiling.

"Meet Abu Nabil," Amitai said. "He's Abu George's partner in the *al-Wattan* newspaper, and the senior editor."

"You should add the former," said the newcomer when we shook hands.

"What happened, you split up?"

"God forbid, not at all! But, since you closed them all down, there isn't a paper any more. Why didn't you at least leave us the newspaper?" Abu Nabil protested. "Let me tell you frankly," he went on, "before the war when I wanted to feel good I listened to Sawt al-Arab, to hear about Nasser's glorious exploits. When I wanted to know the truth I listened to your Arabic service. And when I wanted to get away from both Nasser and you, I'd go to my desk in the newspaper's office. Now I've got nothing left."

"What are you afraid of?" Abu George asked us. "An egg doesn't break a stone, as we say."

"Allow us to let off steam, it's to your advantage, 'Colonel,' if only to get the orders of your military government published,"

Abu Nabil whispered like a confidential advisor, twirling the ends of his thick moustache. There was something attractively theatrical about his gestures.

"*Shwai-shwai*, not so fast, give us a chance to get organised," Amitai protested.

"You must be joking," Abu Nabil winked. "You are not Levantines like us. You are Westerners. With you everything is planned well in advance."

"The liberation of Jerusalem wasn't planned."

"*Mush ma'qul*, inconceivable. You conquered us at lightning speed," Abu George said and began to cough.

"That's what happens in war – there are always surprises," Amitai responded evasively. We stood up and said goodbye with the usual courtesies.

Having been assured of my future co-operation, Amitai accompanied me to the corner of Omar Street, where Sandra was waiting for me beside her car.

6
Kabi and Sandra

Sandra hugged and kissed me as if I were Kabi himself. "I've been so worried," she said as she started the big Peugeot.

Dear Sandra, a really sweet girl. She came from Georgetown University to Jerusalem to perfect her Hebrew, met this fellow at a dance in the newcomers' club and fell in love with him. But he went off to be a spy in Europe, and before she could work out what was happening the war broke out and her man came back unexpectedly, got in touch with her, rushed off to the battlefield and was wounded.

"Sandra, your story and Kabi's should be made into a Hollywood movie."

"Or an Italian melodrama," she laughed. "But we still don't know how it ends."

I told her about Father's heart attack.

"That's terrible! Kabi will take it very hard. Why didn't your mother tell me? I could have helped, if only as a chauffeur."

The hospital was bursting at the seams. Kabi wasn't in his room, and we had to search for some time before we found him in the cafeteria. There he was, with his upper left arm and shoulder heavily bandaged. We fell into a close embrace.

I took a good look at my handsome brother. He'd grown a

beard, which suited him. Kabi is taller than me. He's sturdy and broad-shouldered, and the wide arch of his rounded shoulders makes him look gentle. His eyes too are gentle, and warm, and his smile is boyish and attractive. I never flatter him, although I did say to him once, half in jest and half in earnest, "You're not only the first born, you also took the best from Father and Mother, and I got the leftovers." He blushed.

"What happened?" I asked now, pointing at the bandages.

"A piece of shrapnel tore a ligament and scraped the bone. It's nothing, I'll be discharged in a few days. I've got a slight fever and they're waiting for it to pass. Then I'll need physiotherapy, that's all," he brushed it aside. Then he asked, "Little brother, what do you think was the most important thing that happened in this war?"

"We screwed Pharaoh, but I don't suppose that's what you mean. I've no idea, tell me."

"It was our war."

"Really? Not England's, not France's?"

"You don't understand. Look around you, most of the wounded are from the mass immigration, as they call us. Jews from Iraq, Romania, Morocco, Tunisia, Libya, Turkey, Iran…"

"Seventeen from Katamon alone lost their lives," I told him.

"It's a revolution. From now on the State is as much ours as theirs."

"Kabi, I've got something to tell you. Don't be alarmed, but Father wasn't feeling well, something to do with his heart."

"What? When?" he asked in a low voice and pushed his plate aside.

"The night you were called up."

He frowned. "How is he? Tell me the truth."

I told him everything I knew.

"And how is he now?"

"He's all right. Mother's looking after him, and he's on a strict diet."

"Was that why you were sent back from the front?" he interrupted.

"No, not at all. The Minister in Charge sent for me. My job is translating petitions and announcements. He needs me to report to him on 'opinions in East Jerusalem', so he can show the Prime Minister that he has his own sources of information."

"Why is Father suddenly having heart problems?" he asked, his face darkening with worry. He lit a cigarette. Kabi and Father were deeply attached – he was the apple of Father's eye. Until his bar mitzvah Father would sit beside him at bedtime, as if he were a small child, and Kabi would hug him and hold his warm hand till he fell asleep. When Father went to a café to relax, or to hear his youthful passion Selima Pasha singing at Teatro el-Jawahiri, Kabi would stay awake until he came home. Father also shared with him, his eldest son, his secrets and his family business. Kabi alone had known about the weapons hidden in our house in Baghdad.

"How is he really? Tell me the truth," he repeated.

"He's better now, I promise. A bit thin and weak, but the worst is over. He's stopped smoking and Mother is a bit anxious, you know what she's like. Tomorrow or the day after I'll see his doctor and find out exactly what his medical condition is."

"Don't let them know about me."

"Of course not. I'm not crazy."

"Tell me, with your connections, can't you arrange for them to have a phone?"

"And you, working for the Mossad, can't you arrange it for

them? You know how many people are on the waiting list? I keep buttering up Elkayam at the post office till I feel sick. We'll see, maybe now the Minister in Charge will help me get one."

"You've got an important job."

"Well..." I dismissed the subject. I said nothing about the car, the phone and the promised office in East Jerusalem. With him I always played down my achievements, partly because I was living in the kibbutz while he was working in the transit camp, and partly because he was the eldest and his achievements had to be greater than mine. But he understood that I'd been given an important position.

"Little brother, listen to me, keep a diary while you're working there."

Then we talked about broadcasting to the Arab population, something Kabi had specialised in, which was now of the greatest importance. "I've got some ideas for them," he said.

"Why the hell should you help them after all they did to you?" Kabi had worked in the Arabic service of Israel Radio for five years, first as a news reader, then as a correspondent, editor and news analyst. His rich voice, his excellent Arabic, his general knowledge and sound analysis made him a natural choice for any role. Nevertheless, he was sidelined, in particular by the Iraqi-born department heads. "They can't get beyond their slave mentality," he used to say. For five long years he gave of his best, but was never offered a permanent job. Finally he quit in disgust. He tried the Ministry of Information, and there too they treated him shabbily. His skills were overlooked, he kept having to prove himself, convince the people in charge that he was good enough, and the only way to end this misery was to pull strings, which he refused to do. Either because of this, or because he was simply tired of the struggle, he finally accepted the overseas work that the Mossad offered him.

By the time Sandra brought me back to Elazar Street it was quite late. I emptied my mailbox and climbed the stairs, feeling worn out. The dirt and untidiness in the flat depressed me; I had to impose some order and turn over a new leaf.

"Miaow miaow," Grushka greeted me at the door. I let her in and gave her the cream Mother had given me (Mother knows I dislike cream, but keeps trying). Grushka lapped it up, whitening her whiskers. I understood that from now on she would despise the yogurt I used to give her before the war. I wrote on the shopping-list on the fridge: "Cream for the princess".

The radio was playing a Mendelssohn symphony which revived me, and despite my fatigue I plunged into housework and started cleaning. Mother had instilled these habits in me as a child, and I learned to be tidy during my time in the kibbutz. There I had a small section in a wardrobe shared with other kids, and had to keep all my clothes in it – underwear, shirts, socks, sabbath clothes and work clothes, even towels – and in time I got to be a dab hand at folding things neatly. Here in my flat I had a big old wardrobe all to myself, and it held everything – bed linen, clothes, tapes, files, notes, text-books and newspaper cuttings. In the course of the week it all got jumbled up, but periodically I put things back in order.

Soon the flat was sparkling and fresh-smelling. I took a shower and then sat down with a shot of slivowitz to read my letters. One was from Sonia, my group teacher in the kibbutz. After asking the usual polite questions, she wrote that our schoolmate, "Mister Universe", a.k.a. Amram Iwa, was killed on the first day of the war. Though he'd left long before, the notice was sent to the kibbutz because when he was conscripted he gave the kibbutz as his home address, hoping it would help him get into the paras. Sonia asked me to speak about him at the thirty-day memorial service at his family home in Netanya.

Tears were blinding me and I went and lay on the bed. I thought about our time in the transit camp on Mount Carmel, and in the youth group at the kibbutz. As sleep crept up on me scenes from the past flashed through my mind, one was especially memorable: Amram, tall, sturdy, surrounded by a crowd of boys and girls, breathlessly watching him bending iron bars with his hands. Cries of "Bravo!" from all sides, and Amram walking away, proud as a peacock, with a beautiful Romanian girl on his arm.

7

"*Vie krikhtmen arois?*"

I'm very fond of *The Book of Legends* by Bialik and Ravnitzky, which I received as a present from Professor Shadmi when I finished my national service. It's always on my desk and from time to time I dive into it for wisdom from our Sages.

These days I keep recalling the famous statement of Rabbi Yohanan: "The Son of David cannot come except in a generation that is wholly righteous or wholly iniquitous." I admit that I'm not waiting for the Messiah, and I don't believe that people will ever be all good or all bad, but with the liberation of Jerusalem there is something of the taste of Messianic times hanging in the air, and there is a sense that it's a great privilege but also a great anxiety that wrong actions could jeopardize it all.

Now that the Western Wall is in our hands, I could give Mother a real treat by taking her there. She was very excited. The night before, however, she dreamed about her father, who was a pious and humble rabbi, but she did not remember any details of the dream and it left her feeling vaguely uneasy. Since coming to Israel Mother had known many upheavals, but she never gave up her simple religiosity. She observed the Sabbath, kept a kosher kitchen and followed all the rules. Still, she became more tolerant with us, and didn't force her sons to be like her. It seems she accepted that it's possible to be a good Jew without sticking to all the laws.

When she saw the Wall her face shone with the same light and youthful vitality that glowed during the Kol Nidrei prayer on Yom Kippur. She stared at the huge stones with the patches of sprouting hyssop and scraps of paper wedged in the crevices, then looked at me. She said nothing and simply walked up to the Wall, touched it gently and then disappeared amid the throng of worshippers.

The dusty square was crowded that morning. There were religious and secular Jews, tourists, policemen and soldiers, but despite their differences they looked to me just like a crowd of pilgrims from the past. I watched from the side, trying to imagine the place in all its ancient glory. Mother was gone for a long time but at last I saw her walking towards me. Here, amid the mass of strangers, she looked so small and delicate. Her expression was relaxed – the dream about her father had come back to her, she said, and then added that he had always hoped to pray at the Wall.

The crowd swept us along. Thousands streamed through the shady passages and out to the sweaty alleys of the souk – the street of leather goods, the butchers' market where great hunks of meat hung on hooks, streets of clothes, of fruit and vegetables, foods and sweets – each alley with its own distinctive odours and colours, sweet or sour, fresh or mouldy, attractive, nasty and confusing to the nose. The smells reminded Mother of Baghdad and she was happy, holding herself visibly more erect.

We stopped and stared at the passers-by. Such a colourful

variety, such contrasts, different cultures side by side, although with no contact between them. There were veiled women showing only their eyes, dignified men wearing long robes, a wide sash, keffiyeh and agal, simply dressed peasants bearing baskets, and among them bare-headed women in revealing modern clothing. How did these men feel at the sight of the girls in tiny mini-skirts invading their alleys? What were the veiled women thinking?

Bustle and noise. Hundreds of people, most of them Jews, packed the speciality shops, buying baclava, pressed apricot, boza ice-cream, imported liquors, various cheeses, fish and smoked meats. They fell like locusts on the shops selling electrical appliances, household goods, furniture, antiques.

"Watch out for pickpockets," said Mother, alarmed by the crush.

"This is a city of saints," I replied, borrowing her stock phrase, and her eyes smiled back at me.

She wanted to surprise Father with the kind of dried white mulberries that he used to like, but finding herself at the entrance to a textile shop she could not resist going inside. The shopkeeper, his head wrapped in a keffiyeh despite the heat, showed her some fabrics, then turned to a customer who did not speak Arabic. Mother looked at the materials and now and then interpreted for the two of them.

"Learn Hebrew and you'll do good business," she said to the shopkeeper.

"What for? How long will you stay here? A month, two months?"

"*Khaliya ala allah*, leave it to God."

"Well, my son," she said when we left the shop, "this is just the honeymoon." She wouldn't rest until we found the *souk al-*

attarin, the heavenly spice market. There she discovered a shop that specialized in dried fruits and traditional eastern sweetmeats, and bought not only dried white mulberries, but also small dried fruits of the kind we hadn't tasted since Baghdad, dried apricots and plums, dates and pistachios, black watermelon seeds, and all sorts of other delights that caught her eye.

Loaded with all these aromatic goods from the Old City, we reached Jaffa Gate. I wanted to put her in a taxi, but she insisted on going home by bus.

I had some time to spare before a scheduled midday meeting with the Mayor and decided to visit my new office. It was only a few days since I had been taken to see it by Mr Solly Levy, but I already felt that it was my second home. Mr Levy, who represented the Israel Lands Authority, was a Sephardi Jerusalemite whose ancestors had come from Macedonia. He told me at our first meeting that his father had been the Town Engineer in the administration of Ragheb al-Nashashibi, the Palestinian Mayor who was married to a Jewish woman. After the June war, Solly Levy suddenly found himself responsible for all the public properties owned by the Jordanian government in Jerusalem. He showed me some spectacular buildings, then took me to a small house set in a beautiful garden in Sheikh Jarrah.

"This was the office of Ahmed Shukeiry, the founder of the Palestine Liberation Organisation," he told me. The name struck me forcibly. This was the man whose evil laugh spouted from all the radio sets during the run-up to the war: "Isra'il, your head is made of wax, so why are you walking in the sun?" Shukeiry himself was not a Palestinian but a Lebanese from

Tebnine, and was renowned as a sharp lawyer and brilliant speaker who hired out his pen and his voice to the highest bidder. He had served as Syria's ambassador to the UN, as deputy head of the Arab League, and even as Saudi Arabia's UN ambassador. Nasser appointed him chairman of the PLO – and here I was in his Jerusalem office.

The house had five rooms as well as the office, it had a handsomely furnished bedroom, a modern kitchen, and a living-room which contained a large sofa, a damascene inlaid table and two armchairs. All was comfortable and attractive, way beyond my expectations, but I was uneasy. Me in Ahmad Shukeiry's office? How could I work from the residence of such a bitter enemy?

Mr Levy broke into my thoughts. "Shukeiry ran away in the middle of the fighting, and these are the offices we've been given. Why are you hesitating? For myself I've chosen the Saudi consulate next door."

He's right, I thought. And this place suits my purpose. If I'm to make contact with their leading figures, it will be easier for them to come to this prosperous secluded neighbourhood, to an office set among trees and diplomats' villas, far from malicious eyes. Perhaps here I'll be able to establish relations of mutual respect and openness. So instead of avoiding the dark shadow of the previous occupier, I chose to use the elegant house as my starting point. I felt there was a good spirit in the air, a new hope – perhaps a new order will prevail, perhaps the country will know peace at last.

Later I tried to pinpoint the moment when the seeds of future enmity were sown. When did the open hearts close, when did the smiling faces begin to frown?

Was it when the bulldozers demolished the houses of the

Mughrabi Quarter to make room for the Western Wall plaza, a huge open space that made it easier to reach the Wall, but dwarfed it and deprived it of its hidden, mournful glory? Or the moment when the inexperienced military governor insulted the Mayor of East Jerusalem, Ruhi al-Khatib? Or when another stanza was added to the song *Jerusalem of Gold*: "We have come back to the water-cisterns, the market and the square", as if they hadn't been inhabited since time immemorial?

Who can tell, who can define the moment after which nothing was the same any more? Perhaps there was no such moment, no time of acceptance and reconciliation, only an interval after the shock of defeat. Perhaps while we were celebrating our revival, their old hostility, burning jealousy and intolerance continued to simmer, as well as their natural rage about the plunder of their land, and all these festered secretly like malignant tumours that devour the body and leave nothing but raw bones.

As in previous meetings in the office of the Mayor, Teddy Kollek, I tried to figure out his personality – a good-looking man, impressive and distinguished, full of charm and very influential, who seemed to be able to open all hearts and doors. Businesslike, impatient and self-confident, he was in a hurry to join together the two cities that lived side by side with a chasm between them.

"In Vienna," he declared, "there were Czechs, Hungarians, Slovenes and other minorities, and they all saw themselves as Viennese."

"But this is the Middle East, not Europe, and we're dealing with Arabs, not Czechs, Hungarians and Slovenes," said Haramati of the Ministry of the Interior.

The Mayor gave him a hard look and proceeded to discuss measures to relieve the plight of the Arab population that had just been added to his jurisdiction. He was obviously torn between two impulses. On the one hand, he wanted to be an enlightened victor, a liberal governor, while on the other he did not want to give anything for nothing.

"In discussing these measures," somebody pointed out, "you're overlooking something essential: the Arabs don't feel they are being granted something when they're given back part of what used to be theirs."

"My dear friend, you cannot turn the clock back."

From the Mayor's office I went to Rehavia, to visit my old teacher Professor Shadmi. He led me into his spacious flat, where a pleasant smell of baking hung in the air. The flat was divided into two – one part was where he lived, the other contained his immense library and study. Whenever I visited him I felt as if I was entering a shrine. Thousands of books in many languages filled the shelves that rose from the floor to the ceiling. Vast regiments of volumes, ancient and new, thick and thin, stood crammed together. I felt that the shelves were groaning under the weight of wisdom, not because having a lot of books necessarily means wisdom, but because their owner was a real sage.

The professor gave me a friendly hug and congratulated me on my new appointment. He even insisted on toasting the occasion, although it was the middle of the day.

"I telephoned your office as soon as the war ended, and they assured me that you'd come back safely. Then I read about your new appointment in the newspaper, and I was pleased that I had a share in persuading you to take up Middle East studies."

"A new world calls for new roles, doesn't it?" I said, trying to sound sophisticated. "But what's going to happen now?" This time-honoured Jewish question was sure to elicit an illuminating answer from him.

"What I have to say has already been said in part, so my reply will be something of a paraphrase. Sir Arthur Wauchope, the first British High Commissioner in Palestine in the 1930s, compared his role to that of a man who rides two horses – one is dynamic, efficient and has a vision, the other is slow, confused and indecisive. In that sense things haven't changed much. Today the horses are still not starting from the same line. Nevertheless, I do have a feeling that there is a positive current running between the two halves of the city, 'reunified Jerusalem'. Perhaps at last we'll realise our dream of a life of productive co-operation and partnership. One side will provide modernity, scientific objectivity, rationality and the desire for peace, and the other will contribute its glorious history and its religious-ideological origins. I'd like to believe that we've been granted a moment of grace, a chance that Jerusalem will flourish with a plurality of cultures and languages and faiths, and will be a source of hope and light. We must not miss this opportunity."

"You believe that we will achieve peace?"

"Well, that's difficult. At this moment I'll be happy if the killing stops, if we achieve even partial co-operation, but right now peace doesn't seem realistic. The Arabs are a proud people. After such a rout they won't make peace," he concluded.

I phoned the department to check something, and Levanah, unusually for her, interrupted me and asked me to come in at once. "Something urgent has come up. Not for the telephone." I raced back to the office of the Minister in Charge.

*

"I'm glad you phoned," Levanah greeted me. "I didn't know where to look for you. The Prime Minister is going to visit the Old City and the Minister wants you to come along. Go down and wait in his car."

The interior of the car was very hot, just as it was two years before when I had accompanied Eshkol on a visit to Nazareth. Then, too, Levanah recruited me to help with the first visit by an Israeli Prime Minister to the country's biggest Arab city.

The director of the Prime Minister's office, then as now, was a short smiling bespectacled man, who always made lists of the day's schedule in tiny handwriting, as if to cram Israel's whole agenda on to little bits of paper. Being short-sighted, he would push his glasses up to his forehead and peer closely at his notes. He asked me to prepare data about the problems of the Arab sector in general and Nazareth in particular, write down the main points for the Prime Minister's speech, and also co-ordinate the visit with all the relevant bodies. I worked day and night, enjoying the sensation that I was acting on behalf of the powers-that-be, and everyone complied willingly with all my requests. I even went to Nazareth ahead of the Prime Minister's visit in order to be there to receive him. On the day of his arrival I waited tensely at the entrance to the city together with the local Mayor and dignitaries. Nazareth was decorated and looked festive, school-children lined the streets and cheered, and the heads of the different churches lavished praise on the important visitor. "Too much flattery," I heard the Minister in Charge whispering to Levanah. "And the Jews don't flatter you?" she responded in her quiet way.

The festive lunch was followed by official ceremonies. The leader of the opposition in the city, a Communist, well-known for his caustic attacks on the government, stood up to speak. Eshkol rested his head on his hand and fell asleep. This could be a disaster, I thought, disappointed and embarrassed.

"The Prime Minister is asleep," I said urgently to the director of his office. "It will offend the Arabs, and he won't know what to say in response to their speeches. All our efforts will be wasted!"

"What do you want me to do?"

"Go and wake him up. Give him a glass of water, a note, anything…"

"Take it easy, young man. Relax."

But I couldn't relax. The faces of the Arab guests clearly showed their dismay. But when the speeches ended Eshkol opened his eyes, looked around at the people seated beside him on the podium, looked at the audience in the hall, and began to answer all the points raised one by one. His statements were thorough and persuasive, based on solid facts. He did not fail to respond to any of the complaints, admitted that one or two of them were justified, promised to set things right, and won the audience's hearts.

The director shoved his elbow into my ribs, beaming. "You see? Old Labourites, when they want to concentrate they close their eyes."

Now, once again, I had the privilege of joining the entourage of the Prime Minister, this time on his first visit to East Jerusalem. Levanah and the Ministry spokesman came too, and we waited in the Minister's car until he and the PM came out.

Inside the Old City we were met by the Minister of Defence, the Chief of Staff, the Mayor of Jerusalem and other VIPs. At first, as we walked through the winding alleys towards the

Western Wall, Eshkol was smiling and relaxed. But gradually his expression changed, and he seemed perplexed, even sad, though mainly thoughtful. Countless eyes watched him as he passed, defeated eyes, eyes filled with silent fury. When we approached the Wall, Eshkol was greeted with applause from a group of Jewish worshippers. He raised his left hand, with the damaged finger, and made a V sign.

"Is that V for victory?" his office director asked.

The Prime Minister's face was grim. "No, it's V for *Vie krikhtmen arois?* How do we get out of this?"

I couldn't shake off the impact of Eshkol's remark and his extraordinary reaction on visiting the Western Wall. Such sobriety in the midst of the euphoria that engulfed all the rest of us. Such humanity amid the roars of triumph. Again and again I have asked myself what he meant. Was he thinking, as people said then, of the difficulties and complex problems ahead of us, which he foresaw from the start, or did he mean literally how to get out, how to separate ourselves again from the Arab population?

As we were leaving the Wall, Eshkol stopped, saying earnestly: "Normality must be restored without delay!"

An hour later all the personnel involved met in the conference room of the Regional Commander to discuss how to implement the Prime Minister's order. There wasn't enough room for everybody around the long table and an extra row of seats was added, creating a kind of class system – those at the table and those further from it. After a tense meeting in which all sorts of assignments were given out, I undertook to speak to one of the Palestinian dignitaries to whom Amitai had introduced me – Abu George.

In the evening I phoned Al-Hurriyeh, Abu George's restaurant, but no one answered. I was about to try his home number but, worried that he might refuse to meet me, instead decided to act in the Middle Eastern manner and simply go to his house on Ragheb al-Nashashibi Lane in Sheikh Jarrah.

Abu George's house, like others in the neighbourhood, was surrounded by a fence of iron posts with sharp spikes. I rang the electric bell beside the heavy gate and waited some time. At last the gate swung open slowly, not much more than a crack, and Abu George stood before me, his eyes dark and his mouth shut tight.

"*As-salam aleikum*," I greeted him, though it was for him to greet me first.

"*Wa-aleikum*," he replied drily, without adding the usual "and the mercy and blessings of Allah". Feeling awkward, I smiled at him, wondering if he'd forgotten me and our recent chat in his restaurant.

"Could I have a few words with you?" I asked. He nodded silently, and after looking up and down the silent street to make sure there were no witnesses he opened the gate wider, though he did not say the customary "*Tfadal*".

We crossed the garden and entered the house without saying a word. The walls of the wide hallway were hung with an impressive collection of ancient pistols, swords and scimitars. The living-room didn't look like a traditional Arab *madafeh*, with low divans and hard cushions, such as I usually saw in Israeli Arab houses, but had modern furniture – leather sofas and armchairs, vases filled with flowers, decorative statuettes. On one of the walls hung photographs, presumably of family members, and in the centre was a studio portrait of a very beautiful young woman, with blue or grey eyes. Another large photo that caught my attention was of Hajj Amin al-Husseini, the mufti of Jerusalem, in splendid traditional robes. I turned away from the Palestinian leader, a man who collaborated with Hitler and hoped to exterminate the Jewish people. Abu George invited me with a gesture to take a seat but remained standing in front of me, not even trying to hide his displeasure at my uninvited visit.

"I'm sorry for disturbing you in the evening," I said.

"What will you drink?" he asked coldly.

"If I were in my father's house, I'd ask for a chilled beer, but…"

This approach must have appealed to him, because his forehead cleared and the tension in his face eased. He left the room.

The house was very quiet. I remembered something I'd heard from the Minister in Charge: "When you go into a Jewish house and it's quiet, you know someone is ill. When you go into a non-Jewish house and it's quiet, you know everything's all right."

Abu George returned with bottles of Dutch beer and filled glasses for both of us. Then he sat down opposite me, took a big *masbahah* from his pocket and began to roll the beads rapidly through his fingers. The clicking was loud in the silent room.

"Handsome jars," I said, pointing to a collection of antiques in a display cabinet.

"Inherited from my grandfather," he said impatiently.

"The pictures on the walls must have historical value too."

Instead of responding with polite phrases in the customary Arab manner, he leaned forwards, and stuck out his chin, as if to say, "Get on with it!"

So I did. "I'm here on behalf of the government. We're asking for your help in restoring normal life."

He frowned, closed his hand on the string of beads and sniffed at them. "Why should I help you?"

"People need to go on, to make a living, to work. We want life to proceed normally. I'm told that you have dozens of employees who are out of work."

"If you go away and leave us, everything will soon be back to normal."

"History follows its own course and it can't be turned back. Nor are we here for the short term." Then I added: "Try to see us as partners who want to help you and be helped by you."

"You have wounded our honour, shamed us before our children and the entire world, driven thousands of our people from the country, taken over our holy places. Then you come to me after dark and ask for my help? You want to turn life back to normal? What life are you talking about?" He began to cough till his eyes turned red.

"Frankly, I don't know how I would act in your place. But please, Abu George, who can solve the problems between us if not us, if we don't communicate?"

"This land speaks Arabic!"

"This land also speaks Hebrew – and Latin and all the languages of worship," I said quietly but firmly. "And it's on this land that you and we must live."

"Why not leave things as they are, without work, without supplies, without services, without anything. Let it all blow up and burn!"

"Doing nothing is also an act. Sometimes it's the most destructive act of all, as a wise writer once said."

Abu George made a dismissive gesture. "You won't be allowed

97

to stay on in al-Quds al-Sharif. You'll quit this place just as you quit Sinai and Gaza in '56. The business people here are not willing to commit themselves to more than a week or two. They're waiting for you to leave."

"Abu George, it's true that politics are volatile and anything is possible, but in the meantime you still need to live," I insisted.

"Conquerors have rolled in and out of this place like footballs – Crusaders, Ottomans, the English. They all left, and the same will happen to you. No conqueror ever lasted here." He wiped the sweat from his forehead.

"You haven't been here since the days of Adam and Eve either. In fact, we were here before you. But let's not go into that. Even if, as you say, we're going to quit this place in a couple of weeks, why hurt commerce, why not take care to keep life on an even keel?"

He stared ahead of him with a stony expression and continued to roll the beads with nervous fingers.

"If you, the public figures, don't help out, things will develop by themselves without you." Suddenly I remembered our first meeting, together with Abu Nabil, and I went on, "Abu George, now you can restart your newspaper, just as you always wanted."

"Has it occurred to you that I might be accused of collaboration," he replied, "that people might say you bought me? And what would my answer be – that you asked for my help and consent?" He slammed the beads on the table.

"The situation is painful and embarrassing, but life must go on," I repeated.

His face was grey. I felt deeply sorry for him and for his world which had collapsed. Unlike many others, I did not believe that this was a case of an advanced Western civilisation beating a backward oriental one. The oriental culture was part of my world, I'd grown up in it and I cherished it. If we were not standing on opposite sides of a barricade, and if they had not tried to destroy us, I'd have felt not only compassion but also pain for a rich culture gone bankrupt. How to help them overcome the humiliation? How to save them, and us, from frustration and vengeance? I didn't know what to say and I didn't know him well enough to share my thoughts with him. He might think I was condescending so I said nothing.

Again there was an awkward silence, and he picked up his beads and began to roll them slowly, his gaze wandering over the room.

"You know I'm a refugee from '48?" he said at last.

"I know."

"Everything is dead," he sighed. "I can't promise anything."

"Why not? Don't you want to start publishing your newspaper again, reopen the hotels, bring back the tourists, provide employment for your workers?"

"These things are not up to me alone. I'll have to summon a meeting of the board to decide. I'll do this only if I get a written order from you," he concluded and put a visiting-card on the table.

"Tomorrow morning you'll get an official letter," I said and stood up.

"Why didn't the 'Colonel' come?"

"It's a civil matter."

"You're mistaken. It would be easier to obey an order from the military governor."

He won my respect precisely because he promised nothing and made no effort to please me. I was familiar with the rich ceremonial customs of greetings and courtesies, pleasantries, good wishes and gestures, embraces and kisses, a complex system of manners cultivated by the Arabs over the centuries, and it made them the world's finest hosts. But this excessive courtesy can mislead. Experts in camouflaging their feelings, masters of prevarication, they are not always wedded to the truth, and they can be brazen liars.

But I was not the kind of naive Westerner who falls for Arab charm. Nor was Abu George a typical Arab, using courtesy and bonhomie to disguise his true feelings. His lips and his heart spoke the same language. He expressed what he felt, and was obviously choked with grief. He couldn't understand our history, couldn't see into our hearts or recognise our wounds. To him we were oppressive conquerors treating his city as if it belonged to us. I had to treat him like a man who has fallen into a chasm and broken his bones, and every little movement causes him pain.

8

Restoring Normality

As soon as the Israeli official left, Abu George went to the telephone. Then he hesitated. What could he say to Abu Nabil, and anyway, what was the urgency? Was his ship sinking? Haste comes from the devil, in the words of the proverb. They want to restore the normality of life? Let them try!

To take his mind off the problem he went down to the basement to fetch a bottle of Dutch beer but couldn't find any. God damn them, he thought, now I won't be able to import the stuff without seeking a permit from them. He poured himself a glass of vodka instead. Since the events that led up to this devilish war he had been drinking more and more. At first in elation, hoping that the coming war would wipe out the humiliation of the *Nakba*, and restore the people's rights and properties. Then after the *Nakseh*, the error that led to the new calamity, he began to drink out of grief, loss, failed dreams – and there was more to come.

What's he going to say to his colleagues tomorrow? The nerve of the man! The Minister's counsellor presents himself at my house and demands in the name of his government the restoration of normal life. Why hadn't the "Colonel", the one who calls him "brother" in a familiar way, given him the slightest hint? Yet they're all fingers of one hand. Who else did they approach? The Jews are shrewd, they're using British tactics, divide and rule. In a little while, when Senator Antoine comes over as he has every evening since the war, we'll find out if they have approached him too. And where is Um George? Why is she out this evening? He picked up the receiver to phone around for her, but changed his mind. Let her enjoy' herself, poor thing, take her mind off Yasmine who isn't here with us. A long and insistent ring at the gate announced the arrival of the senator. That's the kind of man he is, more like an impatient child. It might be better not to involve him in these deliberations. His views are clear and razor-sharp: "There must be no co-operation with the Jews. No helping Israel! And the worse things get, the better."

In the morning Abu George went to the restaurant earlier than usual. He watered the geraniums in the window-boxes, plucked the withered leaves, gazed wistfully at the lemon tree and decided to send for the gardener to mow the lawn and trim the hedge. Then he sat at his table and sipped the hot water with mint that the head waiter had prepared for him. He looked at his watch and wound it up. Abu Nabil was due at eight-thirty. For the past ten years, since they acquired *Al-Wattan*, the two had breakfasted together every day at Al-Hurriyeh, spent an hour or two talking, discussing their joint enterprises, and decided on the subject of the day's leading article. Only rarely did they break this habit.

Abu Nabil was a fluent and stylish writer. Once he familiarised himself with an issue, he would dash off sheet after sheet with his Parker-51 filled with green ink. His career in journalism had begun in Egypt, when he became a reporter on the famous daily *Al-Ahram*, and he was trained by the best men in the field. From the start of their partnership they had divided the work in the most natural way – Abu Nabil wrote mainly about political issues, while Abu George preferred social subjects and the arts. Perhaps it was because he was a Christian, a shrinking island in the sea of Islam, that he hesitated to express his own unorthodox views publicly, choosing rather to influence the Muslim Abu Nabil from behind the scenes. Um George tried to persuade him to avoid political involvement, and in fact doubted the wisdom of owning a newspaper, but once bitten by the bug of public commitment he could not give up journalism.

Abu George dearly loved the printing press, especially the machine which spat out thousands of identical copies, a truly magical process. He would come in at night and, dressed in a suit and tie, would stand beside the printers in their grimy overalls and wait for the first sheets to emerge – like a father waiting for his child to be born.

He edited the weekly arts and letters supplement, played down the gossip about stage and film stars that characterised other newspapers and gave generous space to poetry, short stories and serious writing. The editorial role led him back to poetry, an early love of his. In the '40s, when Yasmine was born and his joy was unbounded, he published a collection of poems which was regarded by the literati as a gem. As the newspaper became established, he began to publish his old stories and poems that had languished in a drawer, but under imaginary borrowed names – Antara ibn Shaddad, an Arab hero from pre-Muslim times, Tarik bin Ziad, the Arab conqueror of Spain, Saladin, the Kurdish warrior who defeated the Crusaders. He could not explain why he chose military heroes, but the well-known names intrigued and thrilled the readers. Even Abu

Nabil did not know he was the author. The poems that bore his name dealt with everyday concerns – such as the *Nakba* of 1948, or wandering, searching for a home.

Then came exciting times. Gamal Abd el-Nasser rose like a bright star in the world of Arab leadership and swept everyone away, even him, not to mention his adolescent daughter who worshipped the Egyptian president like a god. Inspired by him, Abu George published a new book of poems under the pseudonym Saif al-Arab – Sword of the Arabs – dedicated to "Gamal, the banner of Arabism". Nasser wrote to him to acknowledge the dedication, and revealed that in his youth he too used to write and wanted to be "an author like Tawfik al-Hakim". Abu George was thrilled – Tawfik al-Hakim was an enlightened writer who aspired to social justice and humane democracy, detested fascism and the Nazis and mocked the antics of Mussolini and Hitler. Perhaps Tawfik al-Hakim would serve as Nasser's mentor and encourage him to devote his energies to the war on poverty, to education and the redistribution of national resources. But the more he listened to Nasser's speeches, which veered between grand phraseology and self-pity, the more he suspected that the promising new leader was another man who sought, in the words of Kwame Nkrumah of Ghana, "monarchy in politics".

At this stage he tried to cool the enthusiasm of his daughter Yasmine. "No human being can achieve so much," he told her. And indeed, the dreams of a new, free and democratic society that would break out of isolation and backwardness and take its place in global culture, dissolved in the heat of extremism and Nasser's lust for power.

When Abu George realised that he and his contemporaries could not reform Arab society, he decided to take care of his own. He went into the tourist business and opened a restaurant and hotel in partnership with Abu Nabil. As a Christian who was not identified with any of the major rival clans in al-Quds, and thanks also to his good nature, he made friends and acquired status and soon found himself involved in public affairs. But now, after the debacle, his business was stuck like a car in the sand.

Once more he began to contemplate leaving the country and joining his brother Younes who had settled in America. In 1950 he had stayed with him for three weeks in the New York borough of Queens, where Younes had opened a shop specialising in condiments and sweets from Beirut and Damascus. It was a thriving business. The two brothers used to walk up and down Atlantic Avenue, discussing their lives.

"Come on, Abu George. Come over here and settle in America. We'll go into business together. We'll lease an old apartment building, renovate it and rent it out, and in a few years we'll recover the investment and start making a profit."

"And leave home?"

"Home? What home? It's a crazy region, never at peace," said Younes. "Who knows how long the Arabs and the Jews will go on killing each other. Leave that place behind, bring up Yasmine in a free and safe country."

Abu George wandered about Queens and Manhattan and tried to imagine his life there. He saw himself getting lost in the huge department stores, smothered by the clamour and frenetic pace. Life in New York struck him as neurotic, a constant chase after riches, and their slogan "Time is money" seemed oppressive – like a saddle on a wild horse.

"Forgive me, brother," he said to Younes, "this life is synthetic." He believed that a man should sleep in a bed that fitted the shape of his body, move around in a stable where the horses spoke his language. Surprised by his own conservatism, he confessed to himself that even the transition from his house in Talbieh to Sheikh Jarrah had broken his heart.

Abu Nabil arrived on time, punctual as a Prussian officer, as usual. They greeted each other the way they always did, asking after each other's health, their wives and children and the rest of their families. In the meantime the head waiter brought them breakfast with milky English tea for Abu George, his custom since Mandatory times, and Arabic coffee for Abu Nabil.

"*Akhbarak*, what is your news, Abu George?"

"Last night the advisor to the Minister in Charge came to my house – you remember him, the skinny young man the 'Colonel' introduced to us here a few days ago," said Abu George and described the conversation.

"Let them drink sea water! Restoring normality to life would serve their interests, not ours. On the contrary, we must disrupt their life, start a *muqawamah*, a resistance movement," Abu Nabil said, narrowing and widening his big eyes in the manner of Yusuf Wahbi, the famous Egyptian actor and director. "Our energy must be directed towards one single aim – to get rid of them."

Abu George looked at him dully but said nothing. His partner dug a spoon into a dish of plum jam and ate it with obvious relish. "I tell you, now that the borders have been broken down and the damned Zionists have themselves destroyed their precious 'green line', we must make sure that our Palestinian brothers gradually infiltrate Israel, work there and marry our brothers and sisters there, and eventually become the majority. This way, our Arab brothers together with the anti-Zionist

Orthodox Jews will slowly but surely strangle Israel with a pincer movement." He burst out laughing and went on lapping up the jam until he finished it.

Abu George ignored his friend's febrile daydreams and tried to tackle the question that was troubling him. "Leave aside for the moment what will happen in the distant future. The question is, what do we do now? Right now we depend on the bastards – our freedom of movement is in their hands, taxes and customs duty, commerce and construction, even the permit to import Dutch beer…"

"We don't have to do anything, we're inside their guts now, we've got them by the balls. Look at the map – they are squeezed from the east, pushed from the south, harassed in the north. Wherever they turn they find us. They have only one outlet – the sea! Why are you worried?" He laughed aloud and Abu George envied his optimism. "We can make their life hell," he concluded, rubbing his hands together.

"How?"

"Like I said – from now on we're inside their guts. We can poison them, we can shaft them from the front and the back."

"For that we need a tool we can count on," Abu George said heavily. "All right, we Arabs have Mig fighter-jets, tanks and radar and television, but our mentality is that of cameldrivers."

"Abu George, no offence, but you're a Christian, you don't appreciate the power of Islam. This must be made into a religious war, and that will soon bring it to an end. Let me remind you of Hassan al-Bana, how his call to love death more dearly than life captivated Egypt? We sell this message to some of our hotheads, and the fire will blaze all by itself."

"So what do you say, should we restart the newspaper?"

"Did you ask the man how come they're letting us publish it all of a sudden? *Dir balak*, look out, be wary of him."

Abu George went into another fit of coughing.

"You deserve compensation for war damages," chuckled Abu Nabil. "Five-star treatment at Hadassah Hospital." He drained the last drop of coffee in the pot, looked around and leaned closer to his friend. "Two days ago Abu Ammar, alias Yasser Arafat, called my Nabil and inducted him into Fatah. I said to him, '*Ibni*, son, why are you doing this? You've just got married, your wife is pregnant.' You know what he said? 'It's how you brought me up, Father.'"

"I'm worried too, desperately afraid that my Yasmine will be stupid enough to join Abu Ammar's people in Paris," Abu George sighed.

"What can I tell you, brother? We honoured our parents like God himself. Who dared disobey them, who dared look them in the eye? Today the children do what they please and nobody can tell them anything." Abu Nabil rose, shook the pitta crumbs from his jacket and said, "I'm going to the newspaper office."

"What newspaper? Everything is at a standstill."

"You know what they say, man's nature is broken only when he's buried."

9

Facing the Older Brother

Kabi looked back at the hospital as if to say goodbye and good riddance. "That's it, come on! I can't wait to see the old people, to get the smell of home in my nostrils."

"And then we'll go to the Galilee?" Sandra suggested hesitantly.

"Good idea. We'll swim in the Sea of Galilee and wash away the memory of the yellow dust and those white beds."

I wondered if Sandra was pressuring Kabi to get married the way Yardena pressured me. Sandra fitted Kabi like a ring on a finger, but she had none of the sabra-style assertiveness that pushes a man into a corner. On the contrary, her good manners and gentleness strengthened the relationship. Mother liked her, and urged Kabi to buy her presents, to bring her home, to take her to Eilat, and on the few occasions she came to the house she pampered her like a daughter.

In the car she turned on the radio, which was again broadcasting the song "Jerusalem of Gold." Kabi grew serious and listened attentively. "What a song!" he said, visibly moved.

"Nationalist kitsch, more suited to our Arab cousins," I teased him.

"Little brother, this is our song, the longing for Zion, the anthem of the mass immigration which has bought a right to this place with blood."

"Big brother, the song was composed by a privileged sabra, born in Kibbutz Kinneret – what's she got in common with the mass immigration?"

"The Jewish soul," Sandra interjected.

"Bravo," said Kabi and stroked her arm, in a rare demonstration of affection. "Did you know that Sandra has translated Agnon's *The Doctor's Divorce* into English?"

"Really?"

"The story is in Kabi's kitbag. You're welcome to read it," she said, embarrassed but pleased.

Sandra always surprises me. She's only been in Israel six years and already she can translate Agnon. Kabi, on the other hand, has had an awkward relationship with Hebrew. He wasted years in the Arabic section of the Israeli Broadcasting Service, a stifling, overcrowded colony of journalists and entertainers totally absorbed in the Arab world and isolated from Israeli life. If he'd mixed with native Israelis he would have breathed different air. When I spoke about it he would tease me, "Yes, my little sabra," or, "All right, my little kibbutznik." I wasn't sure that he had found his place in the Mossad, on the dark side.

A bizarre thought occurred to me. Could it be that my new appointment has shaken him? In Baghdad he was seen as destined for great things, and I lived in his shadow. When Father bought us new shoes Kabi would put them on at once, delighted, and show off. And as for me, I would put them aside and wait for a special occasion, enjoying the mere fact of having new shoes. I admired him, but didn't want to be like him or to compete with him. I wanted to follow my own path. Only here in Israel, starting from the kibbutz, did I discover a new world, and it kept growing bigger. Who'd have thought it?

We reached the suburbs of Jerusalem and drove straight to Katamon, to 422 Antigonus Street, Apartment 1.

"Wouldn't you like to rest in my place for a few days?" Sandra offered, looking at his bandaged shoulder.

"Thanks, but I want to be with Mother and Father. In two days we'll take a trip together and see the Golan Heights."

She stood by the car, waiting for him to invite her in, but he didn't. "All right then, I guess it's a family occasion..." she said softly and drove away.

"Why didn't you invite her in?" I asked.

"Forget it, it's not the right time. Mother with her tears and father ill."

Yardena would have chucked me if I'd treated her this way. But the truth is, I had also been looking for excuses to avoid commitment.

Father jumped out of bed, hugged and kissed Kabi for a long time, but seeing his bandaged shoulder he shook his head at me reproachfully.

"What's happened to you, God save you?" Mother asked and fell into his arms, her sobs expressing both anguish and relief.

"A piece of shrapnel scratched me, that's all." But Mother didn't let up till he told her exactly where and how it had happened and if it hurt and who looked after him and what the doctors said and how soon he would be well. He replied briefly, as if anxious to move on to a more important question.

"And you, Father – what's all this about your heart?"

"Thank God, they must love me in heaven. They sent a warning." He laid a hand on Kabi's arm. "The main thing is that you've all come back safely. And you, Nuri, you shouldn't have worried him with my problem."

I smiled to myself, because at that moment, like a contradictory echo, Mother scolded me, "Why didn't you tell us he was wounded? The kibbutz spoiled you."

I had become used to these reproaches, especially since the fiasco of that Yom Kippur when I brought them an obviously non-kosher, headlesss cockerel from the kibbutz and insisted it had been slaughtered according to religious law. Since that time Mother had taken to calling me "Abu Fairytale".

Once again, she brought out the lead pellets, melted them into a bowl of water that she held over Kabi's head, and rubbed him with the water. Later she wrapped the piece of melted lead with a little salt and stuffed it into his pocket, a talisman against the evil eye.

We sat in the kitchen where delicious smells wafted from the saucepans on the stove. Kabi got up, took a meatball from a pot, blew on it and swallowed it quickly so as not to scald his tongue. Mother whispered to Father, "If he's sticking his head into the pots it means we don't need to worry about him," and she smiled for the first time since we came in.

"Mother," said Kabi, noticing her smile. "Tomorrow, how about making your pilau bejij?" This dish of rice with chicken and chickpeas, seasoned with fried onion, almonds and raisins, was his favourite.

"Why didn't you bring Sandra?" she asked, and when he did not reply she said, "That's not nice" and wiped her hands on her apron.

Father had something on his mind but he waited until after Kabi had taken a shower, Mother's cure-all, before asking, "Will you go back to Europe?" Kabi nodded, and Father looked down as though he'd been rejected.

"Father, I'm new in this business and must make my mark. I'll come to see you as often as I can," Kabi tried to reassure him. "You're fretting already, Abu Kabi?" said Mother. "Enjoy your son, he isn't going anywhere yet. The wound has to heal first." With the authoritative manner of the eldest son, Kabi changed the subject. "Well, what do you think? Your son Nuri has been made advisor to the Minister and the head of his office in East Jerusalem. He'll have an official car and already has a telephone at government expense."

In Arabic it sounded much grander than in Hebrew, and Mother ululated as if it was my wedding day. "May you both become viziers!" she said.

"Nuri, let me remind you again," Kabi continued in his masterful tone, "to keep a journal. These are historic times, you hear!"

"You'll have coffee?" said Father, an earnest expression on his face. Kabi and I exchanged smiles. An invitation to coffee meant a serious talk. Father brewed coffee even the Bedouins admired. In his hands it was an art form. He could take dull grocery coffee and make it superbly fragrant and tasty – two or three sips would bring you back to life. We sat together in the narrow kitchen around the bulky standard-issue table, on wooden stools that Father had made and Mother fitted with homemade cushions. The coffee boiled and Father used a small spoon to skim the foam, divided it equally between the cups and poured the coffee on top.

"So, son," he turned to me. "What will you do in this job?"

"I don't know yet. I'll try to be a mediator between the two worlds."

"Son, do you remember," Father asked Kabi, "what I said to you when we sat day and night in front of the jail in Baghdad, worrying about your uncle Hizkel?"

"How could I forget? You said if we were fortunate and made it to Israel, we were to treat the Arabs here the way we wanted the Arabs in Iraq to treat us," Kabi replied fluently, as though it had happened the day before.

"You hear, Nuri? You were small and we spared you the pain we suffered when your uncle disappeared into the clutches of the Department of Investigations."

"Don't worry, I told him everything," said Kabi. "I wanted to impress him." We both laughed.

"Fortunately we won," Father went on. "Nuri, now that you're the *wali*, the ruler, treat them with respect. Give them what is due to them with an open hand, so they won't feel you're doing them a favour. And don't let it go to your head. Remember that power and domination are passing things, like the smell of this coffee."

"And talk to them gently, damn their eyes. You know the proverb, a soft tongue breaks the bone," said Mother, who was ironing.

Kabi clenched and unclenched his hand to regain the muscle tone in his injured arm. "It's not a simple matter, Father. And I also want to remind you of something. You remember I worked as a mechanic in the police force, before my national service?"

"Of course I remember. Your mother and I were so pleased you got into the police."

"But it was hard. There were some Arab workers there too, from those villages in the north which make up the Triangle. There was a lot of tension. They suspected me and I didn't feel safe with them."

"I remember," said Mother from behind the ironing board. "They thought you were from the *mukhabarat*."

"That's right. I often heard them talking among themselves.

Father, their main theme was that their Arab brothers would defeat us and take back the land that we stole from them, and an Arab takes revenge even after forty years, and another forty years. And all those slogans: – '*Lu blad bladnah, wil yahud klabnah*', – The land is ours and the Jews are our dogs."

"You hear, Abu Kabi," Mother intervened. "It's what I always said, there's no trusting them."

"There was one, Asad, a real clown, who kept on saying, '*Kalam fadi*, nonsense! All you need is patience and an active prick, and we'll win.' He used to laugh and say, 'Whenever I screw my wife I get twice the pleasure – once for screwing her, and once for screwing the Jews by making another Arab child.'"

"You're right, son. I'm not denying it. We're in for a difficult time, a testing time. The victory itself could become an obstacle…Why don't you come back here," he went on. "There will be a lot of opportunities for someone like you."

"I know. Some Information Department types came to the hospital and tried to recruit me for some kind of project – 'selling' democracy, freedom of expression, the status of women to the people in the territories," Kabi scoffed.

"They think they can reconstruct the heads of the Arabs, eh? Make them into Englishmen?" Father chuckled and took out his beads.

"They'll never understand the Arabs. I admit that I don't always understand them myself," my brother went on. "Who'd have thought that when Nasser resigned, after leading them to such a defeat, they would pour into the streets, wailing as if the Prophet Mohammed had just died?"

"*Yallah*, enough of politics. Tomorrow morning you have to go to the synagogue and say *HaGomel*," Mother told him. She emptied Kabi's kitbag, and dumped his clothes in the laundry basket. "Kabi, Friday evening I want you to bring Sandra here for dinner. How much longer are you going to keep her dangling – till the rope breaks? Come on, my son, you and Nuri are weighing heavy on my heart. Don't I deserve a little happiness?"

"What's this, woman? You're starting again? It's bad for your eyes."

"It's not the eyes," she said, wiping away her tears. "It's the heart."

I felt it was time to leave. I didn't want to get involved in another marriage discussion while there was nothing I could say in my own defence. But I thought about it on the way to my little flat. Mother dreamed of having us marry wealthy high-class Iraqi girls, but did not insist. Today she gave her approval for Kabi to marry Sandra. She didn't judge Yardena by her origins either, only saying, "She isn't for you, son. She's too hard." Perhaps she was right. How suddenly Yardena had walked out of my life. All at once a door had slammed! Not even a single phone call after the war.

I turned on my bedside lamp and stood in the dimly lit room looking out at the flat opposite. My Orthodox neighbour was walking about without her kerchief. Her shaved head excited me. It was the first time I'd seen her like this and I watched her entranced, my mouth dry. I got into bed and stared into the dark, my body burning. It had been weeks since I'd been with a woman.

In the morning I opened the wardrobe and wondered what I should wear. How could I call on Arab dignitaries dressed in my ordinary clothes?

I went to a clothes shop on Ben Yehuda Street where the salesman, a thickset Iranian, made me try on a number of suits till we both gave up. At the door he stopped me. "Tell me, young man, do you have a wife?"

"No. Why?"

"It shows. If you can't choose a suit, how will you choose a wife?"

Then I went to OBG in the Generalli Building, under the statue of the lion. I'd often wanted to venture inside but never before had the nerve. The salesman saw that I was unsure of myself and asked what I did for a living and what the suit was for. When I told him that it was my first suit and that I needed it to represent the government in East Jerusalem, he recommended merino wool. "It's good for the demi-saison, and for summer and winter. How about ties?"

"One will do."

"All right, first try on the suit."

In the fitting-room he held his head to one side and told me to turn around. "The jacket fits you very well. We'll just shorten the trousers a bit," and went off to consult an elderly man who was sitting behind a desk at the far end of the shop. Returning with a number of ties over his arm, he said "You had better take two. It will enrich your appearance."

"And impoverish me," I said.

"Don't worry, I've arranged for a discount of twenty per cent in two payments, and one tie is on the house," he said. "I told the owner it was your first suit."

Before I left, the owner stopped me. "As you're going to work with our cousins, let me tell you a story. My nephew commanded a battalion in the War of Independence. When they took Ramlah the Arab dignitaries came to him, trembling all over. The oldest one said, 'Commander sir, we want to know what you intend to do to us?' My nephew looked at him and said, 'We'll do to you exactly what you would have done to us.' They were terrified and burst into tears. You understand what sort of people they are?" he finished with a sigh.

"What can we do?" put in the salesman, and added a bit of advice: "There's no trusting a goy, even after forty years in the tomb."

I arrived late for the meeting at the military government headquarters. This time it was chaired by Amitai, not the Regional Commander. Speaking in his dry, pedantic manner, he surveyed the new political groupings and foresaw changes in the Palestinian leadership.

"They'll kick out Ahmad Shukeiry," he said.

Shamluk, representing the security service, reported on a new leader who was rising to prominence – Mohammed Yasser Abd al-Rahman Abd al-Rauf Arafat al-Qidwah al-Husseini, known as Abu Ammar; an unmarried engineer, educated in Egypt, a follower of Hassan al-Bana, the leader of the extremist revolutionary movement, the Muslim Brotherhood.

"They influenced his political outlook," said Shamluk, adding that the man had again managed to escape from our security service.

"That slippery eel, he could swim on land," muttered Harish, representative of the Ministry of Religious Affairs.

10

Internal Disputes

Abu George woke early. Having bathed and shaved he went into the kitchen and made himself early morning tea. He then filled his pipe, stuck it in his mouth unlit, and sat like this, in his dressing-gown, for some time, periodically removing the pipe to take little sips of tea. He was trying to understand the new reality, to follow the changes taking place before his eyes. The Israelis were euphoric, dancing on top of the world, their generals bragging that they could reach the steppes of the Urals, the whole world admired them, spoke of them as a major power, while his own people were still in mourning, unable to comprehend their downfall.

The human landscape itself had changed. The Jews Abu George used to know before '48, Valero, Havilio, Mazursky, had good breeding and courteous manners, respect for people like himself, even an innocence and a genuine desire to live together in harmony. In the twenty years that had passed it seemed that strange Jews had displaced the older ones, or else a different spirit ruled them. Seeing the greedy eyes in the market, the rummaging hands, the eagerness, as if they were newly-freed prisoners frantic to make up for lost time, was more than enough. It could take a generation or two, perhaps more, he thought, before they calmed down and we get our feet back on the ground, and all of us become mature enough to live as neighbours. Our people are keeping their eyes shut tight, he thought, they are clinging to denial. Even he, Abu George, went to bed every night hoping to wake up in the morning and find the occupier gone, disappeared. The occupation was driving him out of his mind, as if a stranger had invaded his bed and was making free with his wife.

He kept waiting and waiting, God only knew for what. Likewise with the newspaper. The skinny young man, the Minister's advisor, had said they could start publishing again, but still he did nothing. He meant to do it, but recoiled at the last moment, again and again. What he needed before anything else was a break from the tension in this place. He thought he would send Um Zaki, the housekeeper, to his winter residence in Jericho, to get the place ready, but he kept forgetting to do so. Even for a rest you need peace of mind.

If only his health were better. If only this crazy cough would go away. It had been plaguing him since the night the Mudawara was shelled. The doctors at the Augusta Victoria Hospital thought it was asthma, then an allergy, they did all kinds of tests and found nothing. Told him to stop smoking – but how? They suggested he should consult specialists in Israel, and he refused. Um George said he was sabotaging his own health. "Why not go to the Jews? We used to go to Hadassah Hospital before the *Nakba*, didn't we?"

He tries to maintain a measure of routine in this world that has turned upside-down. He has breakfast with Abu Nabil, but when his partner goes to sit in the editorial office, though the newspaper is shut down, he himself goes into the restaurant office, casts an eye over the accounts, checks the stores, chats vaguely with the employees, but feels empty inside. He wanders restlessly about the streets, saunters into the shops, sits in their doorways drinking coffee, gazing at the passersby, exchanging meaningless remarks with the owners, and walks on.

Every morning he waits for the evening, and then for the twilight before he goes home. As soon as he enters the house he takes off his jacket and tie, puts on a dressing-gown, takes vodka from the freezer, pours himself a glass and goes out to the garden. There the sight of the water plants in the illuminated fountain, where the colourful fish glide about calmly, dissolves the lump in his throat. But then the memories he wants to discard come crowding back – the *Nakba* of '48, the flight from the house in Talbieh, the temporary stay with relatives in Bethlehem, exploring the possibility of emigrating to America like his brother, and the *Nakseh*, the failure. The failures and catastrophes don't let up. He sits in the garden on the edge of the fountain, waiting for Um George to return from her work in the restaurant, and prepares a mint and verveine tea for her. When she comes in she will kiss his forehead and he will embrace her and press his head into her bosom as if he were still a youngster.

The night before she told him about a dream she had dreamed several times: Yasmine, wearing white slacks and a white shirt with a red kerchief around her neck, disembarks from a white ship and runs into her arms.

Five years earlier, when Yasmine left for Paris, Um George had said, "Maybe it's for the best. Maybe it will be a change of air for her, where she can pick up the pieces after Azme's death, study, meet young people from all over the world, get over her mourning, and leave behind the pitying looks she gets here in al-Quds." But when Yasmine did not return and the years passed, Um George sang a different song: "Our girl is bold and resourceful. She left behind a safe and cosy nest and started a career of her own, a journey of her own, an independent life. Patience! Soon, *inshallah*, our daughter will come back to us freed from all her fears and sadness. She needs her own time." But time did not heal, and Yasmine was too afraid to come back. "Everything in al-Quds reminds me of Azme and the collapse of my world," she wrote.

Life is a mystery. Who can tell how things will turn out? If he hadn't fled from Talbieh in '48 perhaps Yasmine wouldn't have met Azme and they would have been spared all this suffering. But what is the point of such speculations, he thought, and what does this say about my state of mind?

After the wedding the young couple lived with them for a while, in the upper floor that was entirely at their disposal, until they decided to move to a flat of their own. "What do they lack in this house?" Um George lamented, and he agreed with her. But they came round when they saw how eager the young couple were to start living in their own home. They waited impatiently for the first grandchild, but instead there was tragedy – Azme died in the fullness of his youth, and the world turned dark.

Again he recalled the parting scene that he was unable to get over – Yasmine walking towards the departure lounge in Amman airport, her back to him. He wanted to say something but his vocal cords would not obey him, until at last a weak cry burst from his throat: "Look after yourself!" Um George hugged him: "Calm down, my dear. She's not going to a refugee camp. She's going to Paris, the world's capital." But he could not calm down. You bring up an only daughter and she abandons you. How could that be, oh Lord Almighty?

Five years have passed and the pain still stabs at him. If she was here he'd have someone to consult. Perhaps through her he would understand the mind of her generation, perhaps she could have interpreted the new reality to him. After all, she could speak Hebrew as well as the young Jewish women, like Edna Mazursky. If Edna had been with her she wouldn't have let Yasmine go abroad, she wouldn't have abandoned her in her mourning. Her father, too, was a true friend. Why did he not listen to his urging not to leave Talbieh?

He breakfasted as usual with Abu Nabil. This time, he made up his mind, he would speak to him firmly about restarting the newspaper, but to avoid being overheard they held the meeting in the office. Abu Nabil leaned back in his armchair, holding a silk handkerchief in his hand, which was adorned with a signet ring set with a brown stone – like the Sultan's seal – and sucked on the mouthpiece of the narghile.

"At long last, we'll be getting back to work!" This was the first time he had responded favourably to the suggestion to restart publication.

"I would also like to change the contents," Abu George went on. "I'd like to publish a series of articles of re-evaluation, open the paper to young talent, involve women, turn the defeat into a springboard for an examination of ideas and social concepts."

"Why do we need to re-examine our ideas?" Abu Nabil asked dismissively. "It's obvious enough, it was a Soviet plot against us." Seeing his friend's astonished expression he added, "Wasn't Karl Marx, the father of the Russian Revolution, a Jew, and wasn't his revolution a way of solving the Jewish problem?"

"You may be right," Abu George said to avoid a pointless argument. "But we still need to re-examine our positions."

"What are you talking about? Outside elements sabotaged us.

Otherwise, is it conceivable that little Israel could defeat us like this, like a stroll in the park? We were unlucky, that's what it was! And after the Israelis' sneak attack there was no other option. Abdul Hakim Amar, the Egyptian commander, had to retreat to the Suez Canal to save the army, just like in '56, when the British, the French and the Zionists attacked together…"

"Come on, Abu Nabil, we're always blaming others for our problems – the Ottomans, the British, the colonialists, the communists, and now the Jews. When are we going to accept responsibility for our own mistakes?" He leaned closer and continued in a low voice. "Look at Nasser. He promised social change, land redistribution – instead he ruined his army, involved the King and Syria in the mess, lost his lands and ours, and he still blames everyone but himself. We're stuck in the past, brother, and we won't move forward until we stop blaming everybody else. Look at how the Israelis have succeeded in combining the old with the new, modernism and religion. Look at their enthusiasm when they reached that Wall of theirs."

"Bravo, Abu George! That's exactly the point. Soon their madmen will start talking about their Temple, and our loonies will declare a jihad, and that will be it…Just what we need! *Al-jihad*, brother, is the Muslims' finest invention." Abu Nabil slammed the table as he used to do in the days when he played ping-pong in the students' union. "Nasser understands this. Look at the cable he sent the King: 'We believe in Allah. It is not possible that Allah will abandon us. In the future Allah will bring us victory. He will help us, and we must be guided by His will.'"

"And this is the man you're counting on? A revolutionary who appeals to Allah when he's beaten?" asked Abu George.

"Abu George, you're a proud Arab, but you're *nasrani*, a Christian, you don't understand Islam." This was a delicate subject. "You don't understand that it is necessary to speak of Allah, that it's the key to unity, to victory. Re-examination? What for? You want us to become a cheap imitation of America? The backside of the West?" he protested, stressing every word. "We must cling to Islam. We're the offspring of one of the greatest, most glorious civilisations in history. For more than a thousand years we were at the forefront of all human endeavours – science, economics, the arts, medicine, philosophy, politics. We laid the foundations of astronomy, algebra...It was from us that Europe learned the decimal system, Ibn Khaldun was the father of sociology, Ibn Sinna was the greatest physician and philosopher who ever lived..."

"And now what?" Abu George broke in gently, though he was growing impatient. "You're lecturing me as if I were a total ignoramus. How long can the bankrupt cling to his past glory?"

"Only until the war. The third round," said Abu Nabil, blowing smoke rings.

"How many wars must we fight?"

"As many as it takes. We carry on until we win."

"I suggest we translate and publish the leading articles of the main Israeli newspapers," Abu George returned to his theme. "That way we'll understand them better."

Abu Nabil leaned back in his armchair and laughed aloud. "I neither want his sheep nor wish to see him," he quoted the familiar saying.

Abu George felt weary. It was so discouraging to find that behind the facade of the intellectual and sophisticated editor was a Muslim in full regalia who showed no inclination to free himself from the primitive reins of his heritage.

I can't change Abu Nabil and I don't want to hurt his feelings, he thought. In the absence of a river, settle for a stream. But he decided to drop his second bombshell: "Tomorrow afternoon I'm going to call a meeting of the tourist board to discuss the Israelis' request to restart the tourist business."

"I can't stop you from doing what you think best, my friend, but be careful, I expect you'll encounter tremendous anger."

Abu Nabil was uncharacteristically late for the board meeting in the spacious conference room in the Al-Wattani hotel so Abu George had to start without him. He read out the letter he had received from the Minister's advisor, Nuri Imari, asking the participants to help with the restoration of normal life and when he finished, there was a storm of protest.

"Restore normality? That's treachery!" declared Abu Masoud, the cinema owner. "They want us to accept their domination and their laws. To put it bluntly, it's nothing less than a call to collaborate with the Zionist enemy!"

Abu George breathed more easily when he saw his friend enter the hall, mount the podium slowly and importantly, to take his seat among the leading members.

"*Mukawamah* – resistance, blood, sweat and tears, as Churchill said. You cannot defeat a vicious and treacherous enemy by sitting still," stated Abu Izzat, the owner of a large textile plant.

The argument raged. Abu George had hoped that Abu Nabil, who was popular with the extremists because he had supported the rebel Izz al-Din Al Kassam against both the British and the Zionists, would intervene and try to cool things down, but he remained silent, smoking and twirling his moustache. Abu George threw him pleading looks, and at last he spoke.

"If we co-operate with the occupier, we shall be releasing our people and the Arab states from their duty to wage war. We must pull out the thorns stuck in our flesh with our own hands, die like lions rather than live like sheep," he concluded, held his head up like a peacock and twirled his moustache.

Bourguiba was right, thought Abu George. The Tunisian president had said that rhetoric was the Arabs' best possession, as well as their misfortune. The discussion went on late into the night. He realised that he was on his own and he had no choice but to adopt an unequivocal position.

"Gentlemen," he began. "Let's be honest. If the businesses remain closed, then we, who are sitting in this room, will not be without resources. Furthermore, Amman will continue to pay the wages of the officials and senior functionaries. But please tell me this: who will feed the children of our employees? I am well aware that the Zionists are pulling a dirty trick – they seem to be asking us nicely. But so what? You know the saying, if you crave everything you will lose everything. The facts are hard and admitting them is even harder, but brothers, we lost the war! We lost, and now we can extend our legs only as long as the blanket that covers us. Why not play their game, perhaps on one or two conditions? Is that not better than military orders that will take away all our initiative and offend our honour? Will taking care of our workers make us criminals? Did not other nations in history do the same in similar situations?"

Abu George had spoken passionately and when he finished he felt dizzy. He needed to breathe fresh air and prayed that he wouldn't have a coughing fit. Abu Nabil opened the windows, but a cloud of smoke still hung in the room. It was midnight and they were all exhausted. Abu George wanted to wind up the session and called for a secret ballot, so they would feel free to follow their conscience. The decision to re-open the businesses passed by a single vote. There was uproar and someone demanded a second ballot. Abu George wiped his brow, stood up and said:

"*Ya jamaat al-khair*, good people, we have debated and decided. Let us respect the position we have adopted. Let us enter into negotiations with them, and whoever disagrees should face his own destiny." It was plain to see that while disaster had unified them so far, from now on there would be divisions among them, and he would have to confront friends who turned into enemies. As the saying goes, "The stone that hits you is thrown by he who stands closest."

"You're afraid of the Zionists. You're leading us to defeat," Abu Nabil chided him after the meeting. "Your efforts are in vain. I promise you deliverance will come soon. My father always said that there is no problem without a solution."

That night Abu George could not sleep. He walked around the house, warmed up some milk for himself, but remained awake. His stomach was upset and he was fearful about the future. Finally he wrote a note to Um George asking her not to wake him in the morning, because he meant to stay at home. He left it on the chest of drawers.

The next morning he felt an invisible wall rearing up between himself and the rest of the board. It was in their eyes, their sudden silence when he entered the club, their whispered exchanges, as though he was no longer their leader and flesh of their flesh.

"What the hell are they thinking – that I've been bought? That I've become a collaborator? What would they have done in my place?" he protested bitterly to Um George after a day of wandering through the streets.

"Don't you know, my dear, that people are ungrateful?"

He complained of aches and pains and she massaged his back with a thick, pungent oil that softened and sucked out the pain.

"Bless your hands," he groaned. "They are charged with electricity!" Her smile soothed and reassured him. This house is my solid foundation, he thought, and said: "I'll resign my position, I swear by Yasmine's life. Let them choose a new chairman to do the work."

"You can't. It would be like justifying the muck they're throwing at you."

"If only Abu Nabil would back me up."

"Maybe he's being pressurised. Don't forget his son is in Fatah," she whispered, as if she might be overheard in her own house.

Abu George recouped some of his prestige when he led a delegation of journalists, writers and academics to the Hebrew University. The formal invitation came from Professor Meir Shadmi, after he had lunched at Al-Hurriyeh with Nuri Imari, his former student and the Minister's new advisor. Abu George could hardly turn down the eminent scholar's invitation, and so agreed to go and see his life's great enterprise, the *Concordance of Ancient Arabic Poetry*. He was accompanied by Abu Nabil, of course, as well as three journalists, two young poets, three lecturers from Bir Zeit University, and the owner of a well-known Nablus bookshop.

Imari and Professor Shadmi met them at the gates of the campus and led them to the National Library, an unimpressive rectangular block with a dimly-lit interior. The erudite academic lectured them at length about rare texts, speaking a high literary form of Arabic with a strange accent. He beamed like a young lover as he read them ancient elegiacs set in the *qasida* style.

Abu Nabil, who had been watching the elderly professor with narrowed eyes, interrupted him. "*Ustad* Shadmi, do you have children?"

The professor raised an eyebrow, "I have a son, Menahem."

"You know so many outstanding Arab poets, and yet you named your son Menahem?" Abu Nabil said provocatively.

Abu George cringed, embarrassed, but the professor did not seem offended. He gave his bad-mannered visitor a look that Abu George thought held a trace of mockery.

"In fact, my son's name is Mehammed," he said with a wink.

"How is that?" Abu Nabil grinned.

"Mohammed's name was Mehammed or Ahmad, Paraklete in Greek, and in Syriac – which is Christian Aramaic and was once Jewish Aramaic – Mohammed is Menahma, or in the short form, Menahem!"

Abu Nabil was speechless.

"Did you know this?" the professor asked with a raised finger, his tone changed to that of a pedantic teacher.

Abu Nabil shook his head, then challenged him: "What about Menahem Begin, is he also Mehammed?" Everybody laughed.

The bookshop owner, a self-taught man who had learned the *Hadith*, the oral tradition of the Prophet, from a great scholar who had been deported from Syria for his extremist views, said "Ustad Shadmi, my teacher heard about you and read your scientific articles, and he says that you're a secret Muslim."

"Oh, yes, I've heard all about *El-shakhs yiktum dinu*, 'the man who hides his religion'. Tradition has it that when such a man dies and is buried in a Jewish grave, angels come by night and carry his body to a Muslim burial ground," said the professor.

"So are you a Muslim or not?" the bookshop owner insisted.

"I tell you what. When I'm dead, open my grave and see if the angels have taken me away. Then you'll know for sure," he concluded with a smile.

Abu Nabil spoke up again. "Let me ask you a Jewish question, that is, a question about Jews."

"That is not my speciality, but a guest is a guest. Ask your question."

"You Jews are a wandering people. When do you think you'll grow tired of this place and wander off somewhere else?"

Abu George flushed and put a hand to his mouth to suppress a cough. What was the matter with Abu Nabil, why was he behaving like a tiresome adolescent?

"If you want a proper answer, I must introduce you to Jewish issues. So, please, make yourselves comfortable, help yourselves to soft drinks and biscuits."

Abu George took a honey biscuit and grapefruit juice, but Abu Nabil leaned back, clasped his hands behind his head and waited.

"Time was," said the professor, "when living in exile was the existential condition of the Jewish people. Survival was paramount. Our forefathers seemed to say, 'We have no present, so we must interpret the past and ponder the future.' But then the Zionist revolution returned to the Land of Israel, the place of action, and it said, 'Now we are the interpreters of the Jewish condition, we are the ones making new precepts, because we have to act. We will bring the Jews to the present by means of the tree that we plant, the war that we fight.' Herzl was a kind of prophet who said that building a home for the Jewish people and immigrating to it was the paramount precept for our time. In other words, Abu Nabil, *ya azizi*, my friend, we are not going anywhere else and will not return to the exile. At long last, we're home."

"And the Arabs who are here, what about them?"

"Modern history is not my field," the professor replied evasively.

Working on the newspaper in its new form was good for Abu George, making him feel young again. The first night he and Abu Nabil stayed up till three o'clock in the morning, and jumped like young billy goats when the first sheets emerged from the old printing press. He returned home close to daybreak, and was met at the door by Um George looking excited and pleased, trailed by Senator Antoine.

"What's all the fuss about?" he teased them with a smile. "And why are you up so early? It's not the first newspaper we've printed!"

"Dear heart, my love, don't flatter yourself and your papers. It's about Yasmine – she's coming home soon!"

"What? When did she phone? What did she say?"

"What does it matter what she said," the senator linked his arm with Abu George's. "The main thing is, she's coming. What a girl! And how much she's suffered."

"*Inshallah*, she'll stay with us now," said Abu George, hoping he could keep her with them. She had only to submit the results of her research and put in some course-work, and she would have her doctorate. He began to think he might persuade her to do her training in al-Quds in some recognised institute, or in Ramallah. If he couldn't find a suitable place, he would look in West Jerusalem. There and then he resolved to consult Nuri

Imari, his mediator with Israel. He knew that just as in Arab society, in which you always need a go-between to shorten your path and save your dignity, the Israelis had a similar custom which they called "protektzia".

11

From Paris to al-Quds – Yasmine

The heat struck Yasmine like a physical blow when the plane door opened on landing at Amman Airport, and she hurried to put on her dark glasses to protect her eyes from the searing sunlight. Her father and mother hugged her tight for a long time. How she had missed their love and the reassurance of being close to them. Now she saw that they were looking a little bowed, somewhat sadder. "Yasmine, Yasmine," her father mumbled, and her mother cried and laughed and patted her cheeks.

After passing through customs they got into Abu George's black Dodge. The scant traffic moved slowly, so very different from the fast-flowing river of vehicles in the City of Lights. Yasmine stared at the sights, looking for graffiti such as decorate the walls of Paris like make-up on a woman's face, but the walls here were mostly bare. Here and there she saw war slogans which brought a bitter smile to her lips: *Al-nasr qarib!* Victory is coming! and *Ta'ish al-wahda al-arabiyya*. Long live Arab unity!

Approaching the Jordan River near the Allenby Bridge, the traffic came to a halt, and they joined a long line of cars that stood bumper to bumper, flanked by families waiting to cross on foot. She didn't remember such scenes in the past. Then she noticed soldiers checking documents, examining baggage and vehicles. They were older than national servicemen, bareheaded, their uniforms untidy. This was her first sight of Israeli soldiers, and she didn't know they were reservists.

"What's this?" she asked her father.

"The occupation," he replied.

She closed her eyes. Would they search her baggage? In one of her cases were three secret letters given to her by Fayez, the head of Fatah in Paris. When he instructed her how to conceal them and who to give them to, she felt she was fulfilling an important patriotic mission. Turning round she saw a long queue of cars forming behind them and sighed – she couldn't warn her parents, and there was no turning back; there was a tailback behind her and the occupation troops in front. She tugged her skirt down over her knees and squeezed into the corner of the car, regretting her courier mission. Resting her head on her mother's shoulder, like a tired child, she tried to look apathetic.

After half an hour their turn came. "*Binti*," said Abu George, "present your French passport and leave your Jordanian identity card in your bag."

"Documents, please," the soldier who approached their car said in strangely-accented Arabic, which reminded her of North African Arabs she had met in France. Abu George handed them over and the soldier examined them closely.

"I see you're a journalist, sir?"

"A reporter, also the owner and editor of the *Al-Wattan* newspaper."

"And what were you doing in Amman, interviewing His Majesty?' the soldier jested.

"No," replied Abu George. "I brought back my princess."

The soldier peered into the car and bowed slightly. "Where is the princess coming from?"

"From Paris."

"Ah, Paris…" The soldier hummed one of Yves Montand's songs as he continued to examine the documents. "What was the princess doing in Paris?"

"She's studying at the Sorbonne. Getting a doctorate."

"Does your father always speak for you, mademoiselle?" he surprised her by asking in French.

"Madame. Not mademoiselle," she corrected him drily.

"Why did you enter with a foreign passport? Don't you have Jordanian citizenship?"

"Of course I do," she replied.

"A friend from your government recommended that she enter with her French passport," Abu George explained.

"I see."

A tall sergeant approached them. "Why are you messing around? Get on with it! Can't you see the queue?"

Yasmine pricked up her ears at the sound of Hebrew. But what did "messing around" mean? She didn't remember the expression from her childhood. Could it be a coded expression?

"There's a problem. A Jordanian citizen came in with a French passport," the soldier said, showing it to the sergeant.

"So what? They wanted to avoid the family reunification process," the sergeant replied, examining the passport. "All right, take her to the Ministry of the Interior and search her. But get a move on!"

Yasmine felt herself going pale. The soldier instructed Abu George to park on the side and asked her to accompany him. "Madame la princesse," he said, "please wait until you are called by passport control. When you are finished there, wait for me here by the tent."

Another thirty-five minutes of waiting outside the Ministry

tent, oppressed by the heat and the crowd, the palpable tension of the others who were waiting like her, the distress of those who came out of the tent with the order to go back to Jordan, Yasmine thought about the freedom of life in Paris, the political ferment at the university, and told herself she was watching the Theatre of the Absurd. The sun beat down mercilessly. Her mother waved to her with a scarf she had taken off, urging her to come and take it to protect her head, but she remained where she was, stubborn, as if punishing herself.

When her turn came, she was interviewed by a fair-haired older woman who was smoking a cheap cigarette. The smell of tobacco prompted Yasmine to take out her own thin filter cigarettes. She lit one and put the pack on the desk. With a gesture, the woman asked for her documents, examined her French passport and Jordanian ID, and looked at Yasmine closely to compare her appearance with the photographs.

"How long have you lived in France?" she asked in English.

"Five years."

"What do you do there?"

"I live."

"Okay, but what is your occupation?"

"I'm studying for a doctorate at the Sorbonne."

"In what subject?"

"Special needs education."

"What is the purpose of your visit?"

"Do I need a purpose to visit my homeland?"

"All the same."

"I've come to see my parents and my friends."

"Okay. How long will you stay?"

"Two, three weeks. Not more than a month."

"Who are your friends in Paris."

Yasmine's eyebrows rose, then she shrugged. "The books in the university library."

"May I see your airline ticket?"

Yasmine handed it to her.

"Are you planning to stay?"

"I just told you I've come for a short visit."

"Sorry to have troubled you, madam. Enjoy your stay."

When she reached the door she heard the woman call out, "Mrs Hilmi!" and froze. "Your cigarettes!"

The French-speaking soldier was waiting for her outside. He went with her to the car and helped her take out her three suitcases and carried them to another tent. Inside there were a table, two chairs and a bare lightbulb dangling from the roof. She thought there might be a hidden camera somewhere, such as she had seen in films, and reminded herself not to appear uneasy and to behave naturally. Now that they were alone the soldier looked her over with a cheeky smile on his face.

"Please open your cases."

Yasmine opened her handbag, took out her set of keys and placed it on the table. "I'm not opening anything. You want to check, go ahead," she said, holding her head up.

The soldier seemed amused, again asked her to open the cases and she shook her head. "I see you're not just a princess," he said laughing. "You're a queen."

The first case was full of neatly packed clothes – elegant dresses, blouses, scarves. The soldier took out one garment after another and laid them carefully on the table. When he reached the silk knickers and bras in the bottom of the suitcase his movements slowed down and his touch became decidedly suggestive. Yasmine felt as if he was groping her breasts, her stomach, her intimate parts. Her skin crawled. The sight of his fingers handling her underwear made her sick. She wanted to claw at him, to push him away from her personal clothing.

In the second suitcase he found a couple of cardboard boxes and held one of them as if it were explosive.

"What is this, *madame la princesse*?"

"Open it and see."

He tore open the wrapping of one of the packets. Small white tubes fell out of it and scattered.

"What are these?"

"Cotton tampons. Women use them for their periods. They're more hygienic and convenient than cotton pads."

The soldier stared at her in disbelief, crushed one of the tampons and grinned in embarrassment. "You can pack your cases. You're free to leave."

"I'm not packing anything. You opened, you can pack."

The soldier grumbled but began to pack, stuffing the clothes quickly into the suitcases. She stood like a pillar of salt, staring at the ground. A pair of pink satin knickers fell on the floor. The soldier picked them up delicately, blew on them as if to remove the dust, finally closed the case, locked it and gave the keys back to Yasmine. Then he pointed to the door. This time he did not help her carry the cases.

Her parents had waited in the car, their nerves fraying. Seeing her come out, her father rushed to carry her cases and they drove off. Yasmine's gaze was frozen and her mouth tight-lipped. The car crossed the bridge and turned on to the road leading to al-Quds. When they had put some distance between them and the bridge she suddenly remembered something she had repressed during the search – the third suitcase, the one which held the books and the secret letters, had not been examined at all.

"Is there another checkpoint on the way?" Um George asked.

"I don't think so. The worst part is behind us. I was afraid they wouldn't let her enter and we'd have to apply for family reunification, and that's no end of trouble," he replied. Yasmine didn't know what he was talking about but hadn't the strength to ask.

As soon as they entered al-Quds she felt more alive. She wanted to see and sense the pulse of the city she had left five years before. She was also curious to see it in its new situation – what did an occupied city look like? But before she could ask her father to take any detours, he turned towards Wadi Joz, and a few moments later they reached the little square near their house, and the car climbed up narrow Nashashibi Lane.

Strangely, she did not feel festive or even as excited as she had expected to be. For a moment she recalled the other house, the one in Talbieh, not as a distant memory, but as vivid and attractive. Why think about it now? Would she care to see it now?

The car stopped under the awning. Yasmine hurried back to the iron gate, pushed it shut with her shoulder as she used to do, and stopped to take a deep breath. There – the smell that followed her everywhere, the scent of a hot summer tempered by the fragrance of the water-sprinkler and the fish-pond. The pond was smaller than she remembered, but the trees fringing the garden had grown taller and the roses seemed more vibrantly red. The three wrought-iron seats in the middle of the garden were still in place, but their feet had rusted. A great weariness fell on her. She sank down on to one of the seats, as though her body had been waiting for this moment when she would rest in her garden, surrounded by the stone wall and the trees. She wanted to drowse, to sleep. But her father and mother came up to her, smiling and eager for more embraces, beaming with joy, as if she'd arrived at just this moment. Here, in their fortress, she was safe at last.

They went inside. Her face looked back at her from a large photograph Azme had taken soon after their wedding. The portrait was radiant with happiness. Why didn't Azme let her take his picture on that occasion? In the kitchen she slipped off her shoes and felt the pleasant coolness of the marble floor. Her father went to telephone the senator and Abu Nabil, to tell them that she had arrived safely. Her mother said to him, "Get it through to them that she's tired, that they shouldn't come today."

"How can I do that?"

"Simple, invite them for tomorrow evening."

Yasmine climbed the stairs to her own suite. How spacious it all seemed compared with the poky rooms in Paris. When she opened the suitcase the soldier had rummaged through she wanted to dump everything in the wash, as though he had defiled her clothes, but on second thoughts she threw into the laundry basket only the pink knickers that had fallen on the ground. She took out a negligée and a wash bag and left the suitcase open on the floor. She did not feel up to unpacking her clothes, hanging them up and folding them, and the other two cases remained untouched. After her shower she lay on the bed and tried to sleep.

After dinner the senator arrived with his wife. "Sorry, I couldn't wait," he said, grinning like a mischievous schoolboy, and hugged her. "Thank God, you look wonderful!" he said and gave her a present – a rare book on Arab architecture in Andalusia. The old man is trying to console himself and us with memories of our glorious past, she thought compassionately.

Before long Abu Nabil and his wife also arrived. "I waited five years and couldn't wait another day," he declared and enfolded her in his huge arms. He had always loved her and had even dreamt of marrying her to his son Nabil, and had never stopped loving her even though in the end she had chosen Azme.

After the kisses and emotional exchanges and descriptions of the scenes at the bridge, the three women retired to the kitchen, and Yasmine wondered if she should not join them there. But she was anxious to hear the men and get firsthand information about the situation. Abu George sensed her hesitation and gestured to her to remain.

"Sit with us, daughter, feel like a guest today."

The conversation quickly turned to politics and the new state of affairs. The senator described a difficult exchange he'd had with the minister of the royal Jordanian court; Abu Nabil spoke in detail about an argument with the editor of the Cairo daily *Al Ahram*, who told him what Nasser was planning in the aftermath of the defeat.

Yasmine would have liked them to be more explicit, and in particular to criticise the King, who was responsible for the defeat of his Kingdom, but she kept her mouth shut. How could she intervene in this male discussion, which the senator dominated by virtue of his age and status, and in which the two newspaper editors took part thanks to their gender and their profession. She, as a young woman, was supposed to do nothing but serve them. She must not misinterpret the privilege of listening to their talk. Smiling sadly to herself she thought about the students who were capturing more positions of influence in France. Here everything was petrified, immobile. She would have to accustom herself again to the old way of life.

Senator Antoine was looking old and was visibly tired by the conversation. He was the first to announce his departure, and moved by compassion she accompanied him and his wife to the gate. The many fragrances of the garden flowers, borne by the warm evening breeze, enveloped her like silk veils. In Paris, she thought, the flowers are lovely to look at, but not the same kind of treat for the nostrils.

Later that night Yasmine turned on the television and watched a Lebanese musical show. What are they celebrating, she thought angrily, switched off and turned to the wall. She slept badly, waking up several times. Towards morning she dreamed that Azme was sitting in her father's seat in the garden and that she had moved towards him to give him a hug, but when she came close he disappeared together with the chair. She woke up in alarm and went to the window. The three seats were in their place. Still agitated, she lit a cigarette and went downstairs.

"Where's Father?" she asked, worried.

"He's gone to the office."

"Why so early?"

"Since the war he's been too restless to stay at home."

"Mother, the garden seats are rusting."

"Who's had the leisure to think about them?"

After coffee and a light breakfast she went back upstairs and prepared to go out. She took out the three letters that Fayez had asked her to deliver as soon as she arrived, but stuffed them back among the books. They can wait till tomorrow, she thought. Today is Azme's birthday. She would go to his grave now, early in the morning, even before his parents.

She picked flowers from the garden and went up to the cemetery, which was quite deserted. She had been right to go there early. Now she could sit beside Azme's grave and be alone with him, undisturbed by anyone. For a long time she talked to him silently, telling him of all that had befallen her, her longing for him, her desolate nights, the loneliness that had undermined the whole of her life, and finally, after many days of numbness, she began to weep. "*Inta umri*," you are my life, she muttered, recalling a favourite song that they used to sing together.

She stood facing the marble tombstone and caressed the carved letters of his name. The heat was intensifying and her head began to ache. There was no escaping this light. She had forgotten how the sun and the blinding light shaped existence itself in this place.

On her way into town Yasmine entered their beloved restaurant, which was still empty. Abu Rashid, the stalwart head waiter, and the rest of the staff welcomed her with cries of joy. She loved the look of the place – sparkling clean, the tables brightly polished, the garden flourishing, and there was her favourite pomegranate tree, taller and now covered with blossom. She sat down, patted its branches, its budding fruits, and suddenly started: where was Father? She went across the street to his office at the newspaper, but he wasn't there either.

When she returned Abu Rashid brought her a bunch of flowers, a pot of coffee and a glass of chilled water. "*Ahlan wasahlan, binti*, you've lit up the place," he said, beaming.

She relished the familiar aroma of the coffee and picked up the newspapers offered by the restaurant. Reading them closely she wondered at herself. In Paris she merely glanced through the weekend edition of *Le Monde*, interested only in the column of Eric Rouleau, the Middle East commentator. Now she pored over all the papers, Jordanian, Egyptian and Syrian. She even read the ads, anxious to pick up every scrap of information, to restock her empty store. The reports distressed and infuriated her, but she couldn't stop reading and drank glass after glass of water, as if to flush away the contamination. When only the Israeli papers were left, the Arabic-language *Al Yom* and the English-language *Jerusalem Post*, she pushed them aside and went out to Saladin Street.

Milling before the gate of the governor's residence was a cluster of enemy soldiers, talking at the tops of their voices in a vulgar, grating accent Yasmine thought. Car horns blared and the traffic was slow. The pavements and the road were choked with people, and for a moment she hoped that these were manifestations of *mukawamah*, resistance, but soon enough she realised that these were Jews crowding the shops of East Jerusalem, buying up everything in sight. This too was painful and offensive. Were these the people who defeated the great Arab nation?

She needed to go to Bir Zeit, speak to the students and lecturers and find out what they were thinking. It occurred to her to meet Nabil, Father's partner's son, who had always been a nationalist revolutionary. She could phone him. Then she stopped. How could she ask for a meeting with a man, much less a married one? The thought annoyed her. A day after her arrival and already she was succumbing to the old customs, as though she hadn't lived for the past five years in the liberal heart of a modern, tolerant world.

Yasmine went into *Dar al-Kutub*, her favourite book and stationery shop, but Um Yassin, the saleswoman who had always welcomed her with a motherly smile wasn't there. She browsed through the new books and translated novels imported from Egypt, leafed through a few, then went to the poetry section and was pleased to see two of her father's pseudonymous collections, as well as a new collection by Fadwa Toukan, the poet from Nablus. Yasmine felt at home among the shelves of Arabic poetry and history and decided she would come again soon and buy a book or two.

On her way out she asked the new, young shop assistant about Um Yassin.

"*Rahat*, passed away," came the reply.

Saddened, she left and walked out on to Suleiman Street. Here too there were swarms of shoppers. Yasmine remembered a small, quiet city whose inhabitants ambled along, and everyone knew everyone else, not this maelstrom of tourists flooding the streets and overpowering them with their foreign speech.

The previous evening she had heard that Bab al-Khalil, the Jaffa Gate, had been reopened and walked over there and on an impulse carried on to the Church of the Holy Sepulchre. There everything was the same, the ancient smell of the walls, the massive furniture and the incense. She went upstairs to the office of the Mutran, the bishop, where a handsome young priest stood in the doorway. Yasmine introduced herself and asked, "Is the Father in?"

"Mutran Krachi is busy. He has visitors. Sit down in the meantime."

When after a while she rose and said she would come another time, he asked her to wait a moment longer and rang the inside office. The Mutran came out immediately and hugged her tight for a long moment. Too long, she thought.

"Abu George didn't tell me you're back already."

"I only arrived here yesterday. Father didn't have time."

His eyes moved to her handbag. "Has Fayez sent anything?"

"Yes, of course," she replied, thinking about the packet hidden among her books.

"We have to meet. There are many things we should discuss."

"Certainly, Father," she replied and again he hugged her tight. She flushed as she went down the stairs. She would never forget the strength the Mutran gave her in her bereavement, when all she wanted was to join Azme in his grave, but his embraces and fond looks embarrassed her.

Descending the wide steps to the market, Yasmine caught the lines of an Abdel Wahab song she hadn't heard for years – "You travel alone and abandon me, go far from me and rule my heart." She stopped to listen in the doorway of a traditional dress shop.

"*Shoof hash-shafeh, ya Salam!* Look at that bit of stuff!" she heard the youngest salesman saying to another, devouring her with his eyes.

"Careful, brother. Shame," said the other.

"You want to bet she's English?"

"Why?"

"Her clothes, her sunglasses, her smell," he enthused.

Addressing her in broken English, bowing, he invited her to enter the shop. She suppressed a smile and on a whim decided to play the part of an English tourist. Maybe she'd tell them she'd come all the way from London to show solidarity with their plight and express support for them in these tragic days.

She kept her dark glasses on inside the shadowy interior. The young salesman hastened to bring her coffee, firing questions at her – where had she come from and for how long – while spreading embroidered kaftans and blouses before her, and further items he produced from the drawers. She felt flattered, courted, valued – unlike her experience in Paris, where she often waited at the counter for someone to come and say, coldly polite: "Vous desirez, madame?"

Indeed, the common people here possessed a distinct charm and were warmly hospitable. No doubt this was the image of the Orient in the minds of European visitors. In her role as a curious tourist she asked the salesmen how they felt under the occupation.

"Good, very good money!" said the young one, rubbing two fingers against his thumb. He drew closer but she stepped back, gently but firmly placing a distance between herself and him.

Three Jewish women entered the shop and began to feel the fabrics and examine the embroidered dresses, consulting each other loudly, as if they were in their own backyard. Now and then they addressed the salesmen in a ridiculous mishmash of Hebrew and broken Arabic, and seemed quite unconcerned about their clumsy speech and the fact that they were among Palestinian Arabs. For that matter, the owners didn't mind and fussed around them in a friendly way. The scene was of shopkeepers wanting to sell and buyers wanting to buy, nothing else. No enemies, simply people who wanted to make a profit, or get new clothes or cushions. Where were the flags? What would Fayez say if he saw this? She abandoned her subversive intention of telling the shop staff that she had come from England to show solidarity with their plight.

One of the Jewish women was wearing a Star of David pendant, like the one worn by Yasmine's childhood friend Edna Mazursky. Sweet Edna gave her a gold one just like hers, and she wore it for a few days until she realised that the people around her did not appreciate it, and put it away. She still had it – had not forgotten it even when they fled from their home. She wished she could find Edna again.

Before leaving the shop she pointed to a colourful kaftan and made no attempt to try and reduce the price the salesman quoted, either in reaction to those noisy Jewish women who haggled over every penny, or from loyalty to her image as a foreign tourist, or simply to please the young man who danced attendance on her.

Yasmine continued to wander about the souk and was enticed by the familiar odours of a sweet shop – *rahat lokum* and baklava, as well as *knafeh*, with its rich smell of salty cheese and melted sugar. Giving in to temptation, she entered the big shop, ordered a large plate of *knafeh* and was momentarily transported back to her sweet-toothed childhood. Never mind, she told herself, tomorrow she would be grown-up again. Her mood improved and she decided to buy gifts for her friends in Paris. For Fayez, who headed the Fatah group over there, she bought Damascus pistachios and watermelon seeds, and for Suha, her friend at the university, she bought her favourite, candied, bittersweet orange segments. Finally, she purchased five silver chains with crucifixes for occasional presents.

She also found the stationers' shop where she was supposed to deliver one of the secret envelopes. Fayez had given her a photograph of the owner, and when she went in she asked him a pre-arranged question and received the expected answer; she promised to return the next day. The third and last destination, a mailbox in the centre of town, could wait for the time being.

After a painful visit to Azme's parents, who had moved to Ramallah, Yasmine returned home in the evening. Her mother suggested throwing a little party in her honour, but her father said nothing, only wrung his hands. She looked at his face and at her mother's and observed how they had changed since she went to France. She had to reconstruct her relations with them, determine the limits of acceptable conversation, and the ground-rules of mutual involvement in one another's lives.

"You're afraid your friends won't come?" her mother asked him.

"I don't know. This is no time for a party."

Something had happened between him and his friends, Yasmine realized, but she didn't ask about it. They would tell her if they wanted to. Though it was late she decided to phone Nehad, her friend since they moved to East Jerusalem, and was greeted with cries of joy: "You arrived yesterday? I must see you!"

"Let's meet tomorrow in Café Ambassador."

"How? The Israeli army have turned the hotel into their headquarters."

Yasmine's blood rose to her head, but she contained herself. "All right, so let's meet at Al-Hurriyeh."

Their meeting was very pleasant. She had always liked Nehad. A simple soul who took no interest in politics, she remained the same as she had been as a girl, warm-hearted, affectionate, earthy, full of laughter. I wish I had her simplicity and love of life, thought Yasmine, admiring the snapshots of her friend's three small children.

"Little angels, and their chatter is my music," Nehad gushed, and described each of them in detail. Yasmine's attention wandered, she tried to keep smiling but the tears threatened to fall. She didn't want to sink into past sorrows, but couldn't help thinking that if she had not miscarried during the mourning for Azme, she would now be a mother to a five-year-old child.

Nehad brought her up to date on all the social news – who had married whom, who now had a son or a daughter, who had built a house and who remained single. Yasmine became conscious of the gulf that had opened between them and asked herself what kind of woman and wife she would have been if Azme had lived and they'd had children.

After Nehad rushed off to take care of her children, Yasmine checked the telephone directory for West Jerusalem. She pored over the lists of names but did not find Edna Mazursky.

12

The First Meeting

Abu George phoned me to ask for an urgent meeting. He came to my office in Sheikh Jarrah but after a relatively short exchange of the usual courtesies seemed to get stuck and couldn't say why he wanted to meet. I already knew him well enough to understand that he found it difficult to ask for anything, and in fact so far he'd never asked anything for himself.

"*Tfadal! Talab! Khidmah?*" I prodded him. "Is there any request or service I can help with?"

He moved uncomfortably in the armchair and finally grasping the end of the rope I had thrown him, he said formally, without the familiarity which was developing between us, "I need some advice."

"A dear man has asked for a trivial thing," I replied with the well-known saying.

"My daughter Yasmine has come home. She studied special needs education for a PhD, and all she needs now is a period of practical work. I'm afraid she won't find a suitable institution among us. Not that she's planning to stay, but…" He took out a silver cigarette box, lit a cigarette, inhaled loudly then squashed it in the ashtray. He tried to smile. "*Yaani*, I mean, I just wondered if you have such an institution." He wiped his forehead. I poured him a glass of water and he thanked me with a nod but didn't drink.

"We, my wife and I, we so much want her to stay. She's our whole life…Maybe you…" He fell silent and looked down.

"I'll do my best," I said and touched his shoulder lightly as a gesture of friendship. I walked with him to the door and he left in a hurry.

I phoned Levanah, who knows everything there is to know about the government ministries, and she advised me to ask at the Ministry of Social Welfare: she even gave me the name of the man in charge of the relevant department. I contacted him immediately and he recommended me to the director of the special education youth village in Kiryat Menahem in Jerusalem with whom I made an appointment for Yasmine.

But on the day she didn't show up. I apologised to him and made another appointment, but just when she was expected at the youth village Abu George came to my office again, deeply embarrassed and apologetic.

"I want to ask the director's pardon, and…I'd like to make a donation to the youth village," he said.

"It's not necessary."

"What can I say to you, brother? I…" I nodded and urged him to go on. "You see, Yasmine feels that to do her research at your institute means recognising the occupation. The young are suspicious; they don't think, they see every move as collaboration with the enemy. I don't know what to do," he sighed.

"Abu George, why don't you remind her what happened when Mustafa Kamel refused to hold any negotiations with the British before they left Egypt. His rival, Sa'ad Zaghloul, was just as much a true patriot as Mustafa Kamel, but he was a practical man and thought he should try to get as much as possible out of the British. He went to London and in the end scored some major achievements on behalf of his country. Tell her she can make use of our services with an easy conscience. It will not commit her to anything."

"Everyone is urging her to try, even Senator Antoine. Have you heard of him? Even this senator, who does not recognise you and refuses to accept the fact that you're here, even he tells her that she should complete her training in one of your educational institutes. He loves her and wants her to stay with us," Abu George explained frankly. In the silence he frowned then smiled slightly. "Actually, in spite of his total rejection and resistance to you, Senator Antoine is sure that training at an educational institute in your country will be first-rate professionally."

A few days later he came to see me again. "*Al hamdu lillah*, she agreed," he announced, and I quickly made a third appointment with the director of the youth village. Abu George said hesitantly, "Could you perhaps come with us, if it's not a problem for you? And perhaps we could even drive around a little in West Jerusalem?"

"At your service. Shall we leave from here?"

"No, no. Not from your office," he replied in alarm. "Could we meet at the American Colony?"

"Certainly. By all means."

At the appointed time I waited for them, dressed in my new suit, in the hotel café. Unlike modern luxury hotels with their ostentatious settings, here the café was a spacious patio, breathing freshness. A small fountain played in the middle, surrounded by beds of bright pansies, trees and shrubs, with tables and chairs scattered around invitingly.

Abu George arrived with his daughter on his arm. He looked like a different man. With his daughter at his side his face shone openly with tenderness, pride and devotion. The light summer suit he wore on this occasion seemed to reflect the light of his love. He looked around and when he spotted me he came over with her, solemn and dignified, and introduced us. We shook hands, though her hand barely touched mine. She was wearing a very fine perfume. What is more, she was as beautiful as she had appeared in the photograph I noticed the first time I entered their living room, though there was now a touch of sadness in her eyes.

"So you are the saviour?" she said mockingly in French.

"My French is poor. We can speak Arabic or...Hebrew?"

"My Hebrew is not up to date and my accent is poor," she surprised me by saying in fluent, sabra Hebrew. "We'll speak English!"

The waiter moved the chair closer for her and she sat down, supple and graceful, but held her back very straight and her shoulders stiff and high like a pair of bodyguards on full alert. She took out a packet of foreign cigarettes and laid it on the table, and her turquoise-blue eyes, the colour of a dreamy lagoon, looked straight at me.

The waiter quickly brought a jug of water and glasses and poured for her first instead of for her father, then remained to receive the order, staring at her in amazement. I must admit I didn't know what to do with myself. I began to sip the water, wondering about her air of sadness which made me want to stroke her gently, to make her smile. I forgot the purpose of our meeting and instead of talking like a man about the subject at hand I fell silent like an awkward boy. Abu George drank some water, cleared his throat, took out his beads and began to roll them between his fingers.

The uncomfortable silence was interrupted by the waiter, returning with our order: lemonade for her, and for us *sadeh* coffee in little white china cups edged with gold. The aromatic coffee was as black as her hair. I breathed in the aroma and looked at Yasmine. Her gaze forced me to keep alert. Abu George sipped his coffee slowly, and when I remained silent he overturned his cup on the little saucer, waited a moment and handed it to me. I reversed the cup and examined it solemnly.

"You can tell the future?" Yasmine asked, still mocking.

"*Ya rait*, I wish," I replied.

She looked around, her full lips tight, took out a slim cigarette but did not offer me one. Before she could light it the waiter appeared and lit it for her with a flourish. Didn't he have any other customers to serve? Yasmine spotted the headline in the daily *Al Quds*, announcing that a curfew had been imposed on Jenin.

"So once again you're imposing a curfew on innocent people," she snapped at me.

I stroked my thick sideburns, fashionable at the time, but didn't know how to reply.

"*Binti*," said Abu George breaking into a nervous cough, "it's not him, it's the army."

"It's not the same government?"

I said nothing but looked at her – her somewhat elongated face, her fair complexion, her expression in which contempt and embarrassment were mingled. She straightened her blouse and looked at the full glass ashtray in the centre of the table. Right on cue the waiter materialised and replaced it with a clean one. His hovering must have annoyed her, because she put her dark glasses back on and turned her head away. Her right foot was swinging restlessly.

I decided to get straight to the point. "The youth village we're going to is one of the best in the country. People come from other countries to specialise there, and some are also doing research."

Abu George nodded. "Yasmine hasn't made up her mind yet. She just wants to see the place."

Well, thank you very much, I thought to myself, beginning to resent the visiting princess. Her father glanced at his watch, took a deep breath and gestured to the waiter.

"I'm paying," I said.

"That's not our custom," he smiled and put a bank-note down on the table.

Abu George settled comfortably in the driver's seat of his Dodge and turned on the radio. The voice of Fairuz filled the car, sultry and yearning. *Aatini al-nai waghani.* Give me the flute and start singing! Yasmine relaxed a little and nodded her head in response to the beat.

"Do you know Fairuz?" Abu George asked me.

"I prefer Um Kulthoum."

"I like Fairuz more," said Yasmine.

"Fairuz is splendid, but she's too controlled. Um Kulthoum is warm and speaks straight to the heart," I said.

"They're both good," said the father.

Reaching the road where until recently the concrete wall separating the two parts of the city had stood, Abu George became tense and slowed down. He began to point out the sites he had known since childhood: "Mamilla. It's changed so much...Under the Mandate it was a commercial centre, fine shops, not dirty garages…Look, there's the Palace Hotel. It's where the Mufti of Jerusalem stayed, did you know?" he asked, seeking my eyes in the rearview mirror. "And here's Terra Sancta. Yasmine, you remember?" She gave it a glance and her face twitched.

"This is a new hotel, Kings Hotel," I told them. "But when King Hussein comes we'll put him up at the King David, of course." My attempt at a joke failed. Why are you playing the tourist guide, I asked myself. These people are visiting their own city.

We drove down Gaza Street. I watched Yasmine from the back seat. Her eyes seemed fixed between the road and the sky. Was she remembering? She was eight or nine when they had fled from their house, and should remember quite a bit. I was twelve when we came to Israel and Baghdad remains engraved in my memory.

At the end of Herzog Boulevard I said, "There on the left is an immigrant neighbourhood. My parents live there."

"It's al-Katamon," said Abu George.

"And there, ahead, is Kiryat Yovel, also immigrant housing."

"*Yaani, Bait Mazmil*…Looks like toy bricks."

"And over there is Manhat."

"Al Malhah!" he said. In his mouth the old names had a different flavour. He slowed down and looked around. "You've been building and building. Nothing is the same."

The gatekeeper at the youth village bowed as we entered, an unusual gesture for an Israeli. "The director is waiting for them," he told me in Hungarian-accented Hebrew, pointing to the office.

A well-dressed young woman came hurrying to meet us. "You

must be Yasmine," she said with an attractive smile. "Welcome! My name is Michelle and I'm the village psychologist. I also studied at the Sorbonne."

"Good morning, Michelle, I'm Nuri," I broke in, extending my hand. "Please meet Mr Hilmi, Yasmine's father."

"'Oh forgive me! I was so curious to meet the new trainee," she chuckled and shook hands with everybody, just as Mr Lishinsky, the director of the youth village, arrived to greet us and invite us to follow him into his office. His secretary brought refreshments while Lishinsky, thin and bespectacled, fired questions at Yasmine – where had she studied and for what degree, had she finished her course obligations and what were her grades? Yasmine remained silent. Abu George hung his head, took out his beads but changed his mind and put them back in his pocket. We all looked at Yasmine, who still said nothing. Finally she removed her scarf, exposing a garnet necklace on her long neck, slowly opened her handbag, took out a packet of documents, and put it on the director's desk.

Michelle took the documents and looked through them. "She graduated with exceptional grades, better than mine... We studied with the same professors. This is splendid, extraordinary!" There was something very attractive about this Michelle – her easy attitude towards Yasmine, the way she touched her, as if they were old friends, and above all her big warm smile. Yasmine's eyes wandered over the room, but the tension in her forehead showed that she was listening to every word. I was afraid that the director and Michelle would speak carelessly in Hebrew, as I hadn't told them Yasmine would understand every word. Then Lishinsky launched into a tiresome speech about the contribution of the youth village to the rehabilitation of children with special needs – you'd think he was addressing potential donors – and I lost interest and watched Yasmine and Michelle, two beautiful, educated women.

Michelle smiled at Yasmine, looked at the director, who was still speaking, wrote something on a piece of paper but crushed it and threw it into a wastebasket. "Excuse me, Mr Lishinsky," she interrupted him in full flow. "I think it's best if we go and see some of the classes now. The children will be going to lunch soon."

I thanked her with a nod. Her charm and liveliness were very attractive. As we walked towards the classrooms I approached Lishinsky and told him in a low voice that the director-general of the Ministry of Social Welfare was very enthusiastic about the idea that a Palestinian woman would do her research here. "He said that this would be the start of co-operation between them and us."

"Why didn't he speak to me then?" he replied. "Listen, your mademoiselle looks like a film star, not a psychologist for children with disabilities."

Michelle stayed close to Yasmine, though the visitor remained distant and reserved. Michelle took her arm and chatted to her in rapid French. "Here we can try to apply what we learned at the Sorbonne!"

Yasmine only looked at her in silence.

In the classrooms the children greeted Michelle enthusiastically, and she responded with kind words, hugs and caresses. Yasmine's shoulders began to relax; she bent down to the children and, to our surprise, spoke to them in Hebrew, and also hugged them impulsively. For the first time that day I saw a different Yasmine; it was as if she had dropped the heavy burden that weighed on her mind. She sat with the children, enjoyed their chatter, looked at their paintings and asked Michelle who had sent them to the village. Abu George watched his daughter livening up and nodded to me, as if to say, *Inshallah*, it will be all right.

Michelle led us along the village paths. She walked like a panther, supple and strong. Through her thin skirt her buttocks were clearly visible, round and firm, and being a lifelong admirer of women's behinds I couldn't take my eyes off hers. When the hawk-eyed Yasmine caught me staring at Michelle's rear, I blushed and grinned like an idiot.

When we entered the dining hall Michelle took me aside and whispered, "If we hadn't gone into the classrooms, I'd have thought she was an iceberg. She's very intelligent as well as beautiful. And what eyes!"

"Where are you from?" I inquired.

"From Paris," she smiled, examining my features. Losing my usual shyness, I smiled right back into her eyes.

"Would you like to join the children for lunch?" the director asked, looking at Yasmine. She thanked him but refused.

"Miss Hilmi, you're welcome to come here any time. You won't need me, Doctor Michelle will be available." With this he left us and went back to his office.

Michelle walked with us to the car, shook Abu George's hand, then gave Yasmine a hug and parted from her in a friendly way. I stood back a little and waited for her.

"Well, what do you think?" I asked, feeling my face growing hot.

"We have to see what she wants," she said seriously.

"We should talk," I stated, hoping to see her again.

"I'm off to Paris this week. My mother is ill. I'll be back in a couple of weeks and then we'll see." And she walked away.

*

"*Shukran*, thanks, Nuri. It was an interesting visit, and the children are very appealing," said Abu George when I got into the car. Yasmine was silent.

"What's your impression?" I asked.

"They're professional," she replied, and withdrew back into herself.

Abu George wanted to drive into Kiryat Yovel, to look at the housing that appeared from a distance like a bunch of toy bricks, and he was impressed by the construction work in progress and the public buildings in the lively neighbourhood.

"Take me home, please, Father," Yasmine said.

"Why don't we go through Talbieh?" he suggested. Yasmine froze. "Just for a quick glimpse," he added. She looked at him, with an air of cold indifference. "We'll just take a look," he almost pleaded.

A few minutes later we were in Talbieh. Abu George stopped by the Sherover villa and stepped out of the car, leaving the engine running. Next door was their house, looking proud and handsome, as if time had stopped for it. Good Jerusalem stone, tubzeh-cut, always retains its freshness. The only sound was the rustling of the palm fronds in the wind, the young palm tree had grown tall and slim, like a boy turning into a man.

Abu George approached the house slowly. I watched him examining the carved doorway, the joint of the wall and the lintel, where there was a bit of cracked plaster. "Here we had a ceramic tile with the inscription 'Hilmi House', in Arabic and English. Where has it gone?" He patted the door. "My father carved this door and the windows with his own hands, it was the last work he did himself. He put in so much love."

Hilmi House stood on the corner, a two-storey residence set

in a large garden, unfenced, as if inviting visitors. At first glance there was nothing very special about it, just a handsome, pleasant house, made for people to live in, not to impress others. My eyes were drawn to the polished front door and to the round terrace with a balustrade of stone pillars on the upper floor.

Yasmine didn't approach and didn't say anything. She stood some distance away, immobile, her eyes on the house of her birth.

Abu George turned around, his face flushed, and got into the car. I looked at the nearby Sherover villa, its facade decorated with colourful mosaics and with a thick screen of trees around it, their tops rising above the high stone wall. A splendid villa indeed, but not a liveable house like its plain neighbour.

"You have built a lot, an awful lot. When did you have the time?" asked Abu George as we moved on. "My father, *Allah yirhamo*, may he rest in peace, was a timber merchant. He made as a toy for Yasmine a model of our house in wooden blocks. He enjoyed seeing her taking it apart and building it all over again, from the ground up." He glanced tenderly at his daughter, who was sitting beside him chilly and distant, spurning the encounter with her childhood home.

"This is where Yasmine was born," he went on. "A Jewish woman delivered her, Mrs Breilovsky, the best midwife in Jerusalem."

"Me and Kabi, my older brother, were nursed by our Muslim neighbour, Hairiyya, and my mother nursed her son Ismail," I said.

"Those were the days," he said.

"They aren't taking good care of the house," Yasmine said.

"Do you think they'll let us go in?" Abu George asked.

"First let's find out who it belongs to…"

"What do you mean, who it belongs to?" Yasmine interrupted me.

"In our *madafeh* we had a Persian carpet," her father recalled, "every strand a distinct colour, and together – a symphony. I've searched everywhere and haven't found a carpet like it. In '48 we left in a hurry, left everything behind, thinking we'd be back in a few days."

"Take me home, father," Yasmine said.

13

An Off-the-Peg Suit

Yasmine was deep in thought and didn't want to talk. Abu George, sensing her mood, pretended to concentrate on the road. She looked at him and smiled sadly. A gentle man, her father. Perhaps too gentle. What had happened to him lately? He was not the self-confident man she used to know. During the war his voice on the phone sounded hoarse and broken, as if some savage beast had him by the throat. Was this the reason he behaved as if he'd lost his faith in the justice of the Palestinian cause and his people's abilities? Was this the reason he was beginning to adjust to the new reality instead of resisting it? Her stomach was upset. Perhaps she, too, was falling ill, her body revolting against the reality that was being forced upon her. Why had she given in and agreed to go to the youth village? So what if they all pressured her? She felt she was losing control of her life, and thought she should try to figure out the strange world she had fallen into since leaving Paris.

The first thing that occurred to her, for some reason, was the Jewish official. Who was that Nuri? A young man in an off-the-peg suit that was too new and already wrinkled, a cheap tie knotted carelessly, untidy hair and thick, supposedly fashionable sideburns. Her father called him *al-wastah*, the man of contacts, the mediator. She thought he was a pimp peddling collaboration. Was he really the Minister's influential advisor? And who was the Minister? And why was Nuri trying so hard for Father?

This was the first time she had associated with Israelis. Since her arrival she had seen them only from a distance, swarming like tireless ants over her city, gnawing at the soil that held its stones together. They struck her as low-grade, undignified conquerors – the soldier who rummaged in her underwear with clumsy fingers, the gatekeeper at the youth village who spoke broken Hebrew with a weird accent, the desiccated, tedious director, and Doctor Michelle, a ready-made Frenchwoman recently imported. Were these the new landlords? Were these the dispossessors who had overturned her life and destroyed her father's health?

What did that Doctor Michelle mean, calling her "our new trainee", when she herself was still wondering what she was doing there. And the director, who had the nerve to fire questions at her as though she had come to ask for a favour. She was ready to get up and leave, but her father began to cough in that nervous way and she didn't want to upset him. It was painful to see him looking so desperately at the Jewish official. Oh, the shame of it!

The eyes of the others, watching her while the director was firing his questions, reminded her of the mocking looks of the children at the YMCA. It was in one of her first Hebrew lessons, when she was getting her letters mixed up, confusing *b* with *p*...A trivial episode, but it's always unpleasant when people look down their noses at you.

Michelle must have sensed how she felt, because she was anxious to flatter her. An odd type, this Michelle, and funny that they should meet here. What was a French psychologist from the same university doing in this little youth village in Jerusalem?

Stranger still was Father's friendship with the Jewish official. He went to see him, took trips with him, even led him to Hilmi House and let him see his terrible pain over losing their home. Oh Mother of God, how her heart raced when they reached the place, how awful to see her home appearing before her like a ghost. Her father moaned, his face flushed then turned grey, as if he had been struck by a fatal illness. They shouldn't have gone there. What demon had compelled her father to lead them to what had once been their home and had now turned into their cemetery?

She remembered scenes from the past, most vividly the whistling of bullets over the palm tree, which was shorter then and spread over her and Edna Mazursky like a big umbrella. She remembered that they had stopped playing and watched wide-eyed as bullets whizzed overhead, only half understanding that something momentous was happening. She remembered Ramzi Khir, their Protestant neighbour, running into their courtyard, his face contorted with fright, and her father's hoarse voice calling the girls to come inside at once, then saying they had to pack a few essentials and leave.

And Edna, oh her dear sweet Edna, said nothing but ran home and a few moments later returned with her father, Mr Mazursky who, sweating and out of breath, pleaded with her father, again and again, not to leave. "Come to us, there's plenty of room. Stay, Abu George, better a good neighbour than a distant brother!"

"I love you all too, but we're at war, and it's stronger than we are," her father replied. Why hadn't he listened?

Edna, dear wise Edna, still a child, had sensed disaster. She wept and hugged her and refused to part, as if they would never meet again. Father patted her little head, saying, "Don't worry, we'll be back in a week or two, when it's all over." And so in one moment they lost their home and peaceful beautiful Talbieh, with its spacious houses and its neighbourly relations with the Jews. Neither they nor the Mazurskys imagined that this catastrophe would hit like an avalanche, burying a world that would never return.

And now another world was collapsing before her eyes – the al-Quds of her youth. On their way home they got stuck in a traffic jam. Local labourers were working on the road and blocking the traffic. They were operating pneumatic drills, their faces like shadows. Everywhere drills and bulldozers were demolishing her city. They had even invaded Al-Hurriyeh. So many soldiers and officers and secret service men came to eat there, their very presence intimidating, their eyes stripping her, and she had to hide behind her dark glasses.

Overnight the dream of liberating their homeland vanished. How the bubble of pre-war euphoria had burst in a moment! She had anticipated returning to Hilmi House in triumph, dreamed of meeting the Jewish girls who had mocked her at the YMCA; they called her Turquisa on account of her eyes, till she pleaded with Father to buy her a pair of sunglasses, "like Soraya, the queen of Iran". Only yesterday Nasser was calling the shots, dominating the headlines, Nasser whom she had admired since she was thirteen, collecting every photo of him she could find and every speech he gave. Why had she come back? To see the Jews celebrating? She took out her cigarettes and lit two, one for herself and one for Father, who remained silent.

You had to hand it to that official, who rejoiced in the Arab name Nuri, as if to mislead – there was no arrogance about him. He treated Father and her with respect. She watched him when they were about to leave the youth village, when she waited in the car and the Frenchwoman was flirting with him. She saw a slender, boyish young man, listening with his head inclined. For a moment he reminded her of Azme, and a shudder went through her…Oh Lord, no, what nonsense! She passed her hand over her forehead to dispel the lunatic idea.

Her father stopped outside Al-Hurriyeh and went in to check on things. He returned with a tall, Israeli officer.

"Yasmine, meet our friend the 'Colonel.'"

"I'm not a colonel, I'm Doctor Amitai," he said and extended his hand.

She shook his hand but was unable to force even the shadow of a smile. "What is your speciality?" she asked, just to say something.

His answer surprised her: "Arabic language and literature."

But she reckoned this was all part of his supposedly friendly façade. Increasingly angry, she feared that some mysterious force was driving her father, as though he was living his life in another world.

The "Colonel" turned to go to the governor's house, and her father came back to the car.

"Father, why do you associate with them?"

"*Ya binti*, this man holds a lot of power in his hands." Then, after a brief silence, he added, "I haven't found anything wrong with him, at least not so far."

"And why are you sending me to do my training among the enemy?"

"What's wrong with doing your specialised training with Jewish children? Will it affect the quality of your research, does it require that you love the Jews?"

"They'll soon be driven out of here."

"I wish."

"Father, are you helping them?"

"Shame on you, *binti*!"

"Then how is it that a senior official and the director of the youth village set aside their work and devote time to you and your daughter, and even arrange for her to be escorted by a person who just happens to speak French, and happens to have studied at the Sorbonne, and happens to have a doctorate in psychology, and just by coincidence happens to work in the place where I may do my training…Why are they doing all this? Just to honour us?"

"*Binti*, this is a big world, it doesn't exist just to persecute us. And Nuri is like an *ibn arab*, a son of Arabia…"

"How? He's an enemy!" she broke in.

"Yasmine, there are human beings among them too. When this war began we thought there would be another Deir Yassin, but it didn't happen."

"If we had won, would you have helped the enemy?"

"For now they're here, and we must make the best of the situation."

"What we must do is make their life a misery and drive them out."

"Who's going to drive them out? President Nasser? King Hussein? President Nur al-Din al-Atassi of Syria? Or perhaps Shukeiry of the PLO? They're all big-mouths, and they are the ones who inflicted this catastrophe upon us."

"We will drive them out, we the Palestinians."

"Is that why you want to return to Paris?"

"I can't stay here."

14

Kabi in Khorramshahr

Before returning to London, Kabi met Siomka, his chief, for a regular briefing. But even before the coffee was brought in, Siomka told him, "We've decided to change your field of activity."

Kabi was astonished. He pulled his chair closer to the chief's desk and, looking straight into his eyes said, "May I ask why?"

"After the war, the head of the Mossad decided it was time to update our priorities. We've concluded that we need to invest a major effort in Iraq and the Persian Gulf, and who better for this mission than you. You're to go to Khorramshahr. The area is swarming with Iraqi Shi'ite smugglers, an ideal site for agent recruitment."

He offered Kabi a cigarette, and watched him staring blankly at the ashtray.

"Khorramshahr?" Kabi said at last, stunned.

Siomka took off his glasses and said in a softer tone, "I know it sounds like being exiled to the ends of the earth, but it isn't. The region is beautiful and exciting, and I'm sure you won't be sorry. Incidentally, London will wait for you, and one day we'll send you back there. You're leaving in two weeks, and in the meantime learn a little basic Persian, so you can get around. Anyway, you will hardly need it in Khorramshahr – they mostly speak Iraqi Arabic there. Our head of station in Iran, Amram Teshuvah, is expecting you. You coordinate your cover with him." With this he ended the interview and stood up.

Kabi left the chief's office with the mission file in his hand. Inside he found the name of a Persian teacher who lived in Tel Aviv and decided to look him up straight away. Why Khorramshahr? He had become familiar with London, and even liked the place. There he had found Miss Sylvia, the legendary English teacher from his school in Baghdad; he had renewed contact with George Imari, his childhood friend and relative, and had also managed to recruit a few agents. Iran had never interested him. Now and then he read something about the Shah, and noticed the beautiful Soraya, sister of King Farouk of Egypt, who had become Queen of Iran, and who aroused his pity when the Shah cast her off because she was infertile.

In Tel Aviv he went into Braun's bookshop on Allenby Street and searched for titles in English about the geography and history of Iran. He found what he was looking for and a saleswoman took his order and promised to send the books to his address.

Kabi then found a public telephone to call the Persian teacher, who immediately invited him to his house on Aliyah Street.

The elderly and infirm man set him times for their lessons, but added, "Always make sure that I'm home before you come from our holy city. Unfortunately, I spend much of my time in the emergency ward."

From the very first lesson Kabi realised that he had a first-rate teacher, and his own familiarity with Arabic characters which were fortunately also used in Persian, made study all the easier. The lilt of the language as spoken by the old man also pleased him, and he made a point of imitating it. In the following days the teacher also taught him the vocalisation of the muezzin in Iranian mosques, and lent him tapes of prayers and Quranic readings in the Iranian manner.

Two weeks later, close to midnight, Kabi landed in Tehran and took a room in the Kiyan Hotel. The next morning he met Amram Teshuvah in the hotel lobby; Amram was a stocky, moustachioed type who invariably had a cheap local cigarette dangling from the corner of his mouth. He briefed Kabi, set him targets and tasks and handed him a file of information including maps and phone numbers to learn by heart. It was decided that he would present himself as Amir Abbas Mahmoud, an Iraqi from Baghdad who had emigrated to London when the Ba'ath Party came to power.

Before he left, Amram said, "I suggest that you tour the city."

Amir Abbas Mahmoud, alias Kabi, sat in the hotel lobby, drinking coffee and watching the guests. He was especially intrigued by the sheikhs in their traditional robes, presumably visiting from the Gulf principalities and Saudi Arabia. His time in Europe had taught him that the first hours in a strange city were most instructive in absorbing its atmosphere and sensing its pulse, and he looked forward to touring the place on his own. Outside he found himself swallowed up by the crowd – Kurds in their colourful garments, slant-eyed people from Khorasan, Turkomen who looked like the pictures of Genghis Khan's horsemen, Tehran's ragged poor, wandering aimlessly, and peasants in rubber sandals from different regions. He listened to their voices and tried in vain to identify their dialects. Was this the famous Persian diversity he had read about?

Wherever he went he saw the eyes of the Shi'ites' revered Imam Ali, which reminded him of the Shi'ite town of Kifl that he and his family used to enter when they made a pilgrimage to the tomb of the Prophet Ezekiel. Once, when was a child, and they were passing through the market he had innocently touched an apple. The stall-holder was furious, screaming "Unclean Jew!" a cry that still reverberated in his soul. To placate the man, his father had bought the whole box of apples and later threw them all on a rubbish heap...

As he walked he attracted pedlars like leeches, and began to fear that he was being followed. To shake them off, he went into a small mosque and prayed like a regular Shi'ite.

In the south of the city, on the bank of a canal, he saw women washing clothes and sellers of food washing big tin bowls. The bowls were for serving *Kale pache*, a greasy soup made from the heads and feet of sheep which, once cooked, were proudly displayed on wooden benches beside the cauldrons of soup.

Walking north he noted that the canals, which carried the melted snow from the Alborz mountains, were running cleaner. The streets also looked different, lined with tall chestnut trees. In the Shemiran district there were grand houses, fine villas, and Niavaran Palace, the home of the Shah. Here the women were wearing European dresses and the men fashionable suits and ties.

That night, in the hotel room in alien Tehran, where he had never expected to be, Kabi lay awake for a long time. When at last he fell asleep he dreamed of his beloved Uncle Hizkel, whom they had left behind, imprisoned in Baghdad. He woke up in alarm, drank some water and tried to calm down.

*

In the morning Amram Teshuvah took him to Tehran's bazaar. Kabi was astounded – it was many times bigger than the souk in Jerusalem, or even Baghdad's Souk el-Sharja. There were countless shops selling superb carpets, scores selling gold jewellery, and crowds of women in traditional robes that enfolded them from head to foot.

Amram stopped at an unimposing shop where a money-changer sat on a bench in the doorway, stacking handfuls of coins in a mechanical way. They both went inside the long narrow shop and, behind a coarse cotton screen at the end, they entered a side chamber furnished with a Persian rug, a Damascene table and cane armchairs in the middle. There they waited a while until they were joined by a grey-haired man with big ears and a furtive manner.

Teshuvah introduced him: this was their contact man, an agent and spy handler who was famous in the Mossad. Kabi was curious. The man looked like any one of the money-changers in the market, not in the least like a living legend. Settling in an armchair the contact man took out a string of beads and rolled them deftly, chatting easily with Amram Teshuvah about everything and nothing. Not once did they mention their work.

The next day Kabi flew to Abadan with the contact man, who talked at length about Shi'ite mourning customs. Kabi noted that he was still discussing extraneous matters, as though they were not in the midst of an important mission. Preparing to land, the plane passed through Iraqi air-space, between Basra, the city of palms, and Kuwait. The landscape that revealed itself was enchanting – the Shatt al-Arab waterway flowed through the great yellow desert, flanked as far as the eye could see by tall date palms.

"Khorramshahr," said the contact man, pointing to the city

they were approaching. "It has the Shatt al-Arab to the west and the Karoun to the northwest."

"So much water...we should be so lucky."

A wave of moist heat smelling of rotten cabbage hit them when they emerged from the plane. The smell clung to nose, face, hair, clothes – everything. Kabi feared he'd never get rid of it. It was the petroleum stink of the huge oil refineries in Abadan which, prevented from evaporating by the humidity, turned the air into soup. The contact man seemed unperturbed by the stench and Kabi didn't know what to make of this strange and mysterious man. He wanted to be alone, to bemoan his fate for landing him in this hole. How the hell would he live with this smell, the humidity and the infernal heat? The contact man launched into another leisurely lecture, this time about the climate. Kabi wanted to tell him to shut up but didn't dare. They boarded a taxi and drove straight to a used-car lot, where they bought a second-hand jeep.

All the way to Khorramshahr the contact man sang sad Iranian songs and the heat grew worse and worse. Kabi remembered that someone had told him before he left for Tehran, "Some days in that region the temperature reaches 115 degrees. The tar melts on the roads and you feel the end of the world is coming."

The landscape actually looked familiar – an abundance of palm trees lined up in endless avenues, fellahin watering their fields, standing in channels with their gowns hitched up to their sashes, digging in the muddy loess soil.

"These are the Mediyyah, Iraqi Arabs who speak a dialect of their own and inhabit the marshes in the border area. These people are your clay, with them you will make your bricks," said the contact man. He put his hand on Kabi's shoulder and looked at him as if seeing him for the first time. "You look like them. You'll easily blend into the local landscape, and everything will be all right." These last words he said in Hebrew.

They stopped beside a big single-storey house. A man wearing a keffiyeh tied around his head opened the door and greeted the contact man with a kiss as if he were a brother. They exchanged greetings in the Iraqi-Muslim Arabic that Kabi knew so well.

In the living room, a boy brought them chai with sugar cubes. "Amir Abbas Mahmoud is my new associate here in Khorramshahr," said the contact man. "Please regard him as a member of the family."

"*Ala ayni wa'ala rasi*, upon my eyes and upon my head," promised the host. "You're Shi'ite?" he asked Kabi, who nodded.

"*Ya Ali!*" said the host, naming the revered imam. He led them to an adjoining apartment consisting of two furnished rooms. He showed them the rooms and made Amir Abbas Mahmoud swear that if he needed anything at all he would not hesitate to ask for it.

Kabi fondled the moustache he'd begun to grow from the moment he was told he was going to the Iran/Iraq border, and carried his two cases into the apartment, his mind already on his mission to acquire agents and find smugglers who had connections in the military, the CIA and the Iraqi government. At first glance they all looked the same, humble Muslims dressed in robes and keffiyehs. The heat and humidity exhausted him.

"Let's go out for chai," said the contact man. He led Kabi to a *chaikhaneh*, a shadowy tea-house with stools and tables made of unpolished wood, as in the common tea-houses in Iraq. Kabi looked at the big copper samovars, the heaps of charcoal and small pots of concentrated tea, and was elated by the old familiar sight. They put sugar cubes in their mouths, drank strong fragrant tea from small glasses, smoked a narghile and played *mahbous*, a variety of backgammon that called for skill, ingenuity and patience. The contact man's game was surprising, full of unexpected moves, but, none-the-less, he lost two games in a row. Although Kabi thought it was impolite to beat his host, he didn't want to lose intentionally as the man was shrewd enough to notice.

"How do we operate here?" he asked.

"Money and women. Sometimes also men, mainly adolescent boys and children. But don't make the mistake that Amram and the Europeans make. Your best prospect is not a man who lives with another man, but a man who likes to screw both men and women, preferably a pretty young arse…"

"And ideology and other motivations?"

"No ideology or anything else, just what I told you." The contact man signalled to the waiter to bring another narghile, and leaned closer to Kabi: "This waiter is an encyclopedia. He knows all there is to know about the leading families in Iraq, and who has influence where. Grease his palm now and then, but don't be too generous or he'll take it for granted."

After a short silence the contact man said, "You played *mahbous* with much patience. That's what's needed in our work. Remember that. And don't stay too long in that house. Get the most out of it, then find yourself a small place of your own." He stood up and asked Kabi to drive him to the airport.

In the evening there was a knock on his door. It was his landlord. "Mister Abbas Mahmoud, it's your first evening in our town, please do us the honour of dining with us."

Entering the main house with his host, he saw that the table was already laid. There was a jingle of bracelets, followed by the covered arms of the lady of the house passing dish after dish through a small hatch, her ten-year-old son carrying them to the table.

Kabi was especially delighted with the roasted fish, which reminded him of *samak masgouf,* a Baghdadi delicacy popular on summer nights on Jazeera, the island in the Tigris. He would have exclaimed in excitement, but had to maintain an air of respectability.

At the end of the meal his host offered him a glass of arrack, and Kabi feared a trap. If he did not drink he might offend his host, but drinking it would damage his cover as a Muslim. He refused, and remained adamant even when his host misquoted the scripture, saying, "The Quran forbids us to drink wine, not arrack..."

His first night in Khorramshahr seemed endless, filled with weird dreams, sudden awakenings and longing for home and for Sandra. What a fool I am, he thought, I should have proposed to her, put my life in order. I might even have brought her here. How will I survive in this isolation? He felt comfortable with Sandra and thought he might marry her in the end. Why did he always hold back? What was it about love that made him recoil from plunging into it? Only once had he felt its full intensity – with Amira, the daughter of a dove flyer in Baghdad. She had lit a fire in him, caressed him, drew him into herself. He would never forget their first kiss, flavoured with quince preserve and her special scent – sheer bliss. Then the profound calm when they lay side by side on the bank of the Tigris, under a silvery canopy of moonlight. The next day she had left Baghdad unannounced and emigrated to Israel; he did not know why and was shocked to the core. Since then he had feared such tigresses. But Sandra was right for him, everybody said so, he thought, and fell asleep.

He made a habit of visiting the *chaikhaneh* every day. Before long he succeeded in befriending the waiter, and after bribing him with a few coins he asked him to introduce him to merchants, border crossers and members of prominent Iraqi families who happened to be in Khorramshahr. He found partners for games of backgammon, dominoes or cards, and discovered which of them were compulsive gamblers in chronic need of cash. He would tell them stories about himself and his business here and in Tehran, and soon they responded with stories of their own, so he learned who could be tempted with what bait, and for whom he should wait until he got into trouble. In this way he acquired a couple of agents, if only for minor missions, but it was a start.

Among those introduced to him by the waiter was a Shi'ite of Iraqi origin, a native of Khorramshahr, a well-groomed, well-dressed man of about forty, who claimed to have connections in Basra, as well as relations and friends in Baghdad. The man, named Shahin Pur, crossed the border surreptitiously from time to time and was involved in smuggling – tea and jewellery from here, carpets and other goods from there. Kabi discovered that he was a gambler who dreamed of travelling to Las Vegas to play backgammon with the biggest gamblers there. "Here in Khorramshahr," he would say, "I've no worthy opponents." Kabi pretended to be a mediocre player, although he had been familiar with the intricacies of the game since childhood.

His relationship with Shahin Pur grew closer, and thanks to him he was able to expand his activities and set up a network of smugglers from Baghdad to the Shatt al-Arab, and from time to time Shahin Pur brought him a suitcase full of dates and other delicacies.

One day Shahin Pur told Kabi about a casual meeting he'd had with a relative who had been promoted to the post of governor of the prison at Nograt Salman. Kabi could hardly believe his ears – this was the prison where Uncle Hizkel was held! He took a deep breath and hoped Shahin Pur had not noticed his excitement.

In flagrant violation of the rules of the profession, but not without the caution that had become his second nature, Kabi determined to try and find out what had happened to his uncle.

15

Ghadir – Stream and Light

Almost every morning on the way to my office in Sheikh Jarrah, my eyes would automatically turn eastwards, to Mount Scopus, following the sun rising over the ridge that fronts the desert, and the face of a sweet girl would come to mind – Ghadir. What had happened to her? Was she still there? Did she remember me, the boy doing his national service nine years earlier?

I had met her on the mountain my first morning there, when I woke up at dawn to see the sunlight polishing the mountains of Jerusalem. Suddenly, beyond the barbed wire fence that surrounded our enclave in East Jerusalem, a shepherd girl appeared with her flock. Her walk was supple and springy, like a wild colt's, and her long dress flapped in the morning breeze. She seemed mysterious and secretive, and she charmed me from a distance. When I approached the fence she stopped where she was.

A young girl, her complexion the colour of ripe wheat with a beauty spot on her cheek, she stood facing me, staring at me curiously but uncertainly from the other side of the barbed wire fence. We looked at each other in silence. The flock stopped nearby, some twenty sheep and goats – one goat was sneezing repeatedly in a pitiful attempt to say something I didn't understand.

The next day, at the same time, when I was standing guard in the watch post near the entrance to the enclave, I saw the girl approaching with a big basket on her head.

"For you all," she said, laughing, pointing to the heaped spring onions, mint, parsley and other vegetables in the basket.

On the third morning she appeared wearing a straw hat on top of the kerchief on her head.

"*Sabah el-khair*, good morning," I greeted her.

"*Sabah el-nur*, morning of light...How come you speak Arabic?"

"*Ana ibn arab, Baghdadi.* I'm of Arab descent, from Baghdad!"

"Then what are you doing here with the Jews? *Inta jasous*, a spy?" she picked up her staff as if ready to leave.

I told her I was a Jew, born in Baghdad, and my name was Nuri.

"An Arabic name! Nuri, it means light, fire. Are you their spy or ours?" she inquired with a cheeky smile. I laughed and asked her her name.

"Ghadir."

"Ghadir – stream. A beautiful name, musical, like water running through gullies."

"Stream and fire, water and sun, *ya salaam*, it's beautiful!" she smiled, showing brilliant teeth.

Twice a day, morning and evening, she appeared – once from the east, wearing a white straw hat like an English lady, and once from the west, in a kerchief that matched her special beauty, and always with her flock. The lambs and young goats danced around her, bleating in chorus, obedient to her staff as a choir to the conductor's baton. Now and then she brought a basket full of vegetables, and once a week I paid her.

"Maybe you'd all like goat's milk too, or fresh eggs?" she suggested one day.

"I'll ask and let you know."

She picked up a stone and tossed it in my direction provocatively, her brilliant green eyes flashing. Her proud upright form, the long dress that hid her whole body, the intense life in her, everything about her captivated me. I sensed a mysteriousness that was much more intriguing than the provocative behaviour of women in our society. Suddenly she looked serious and turned to go.

"Stay a little longer," I pleaded.

"It's almost night."

"The darkness is good for talking," I persisted.

"I must go." She shook her head and walked away.

In the morning a vapour rose from the Dead Sea and spread below the rising dawn, finally surrendering to the white rays beating on the mountainside. A spring day. The birds were beside themselves with glee, the mountain was still a rich green sprinkled with vivid wild flowers, and you could hear your own heartbeat. But she wasn't there. I waited beside the barbed wire fence, and at last the flock arrived and behind it Ghadir appeared from the scrub, graceful and full of mischief.

"I hear the song of the desert, warm as the sound of the flute," she sang, weaving and gyrating like a dancing snake.

"*Ya majnuna*, crazy girl, where's the music?"

"Listen carefully and you'll hear it too," she said. "Yesterday I went with my mother to the Dead Sea. Down there, you see it?" she asked, still whirling, pointing to the blue abyss gleaming in the dawn light. "Jewish soldier, tell me, is Jaffa beautiful?"

"Very!"

"And the sea there?"

"Beautiful!"

"My mother doesn't want to bathe in the Dead Sea, only in the sea of Jaffa."

"When there is peace I'll take you and your mother to the sea of Jaffa," I promised.

"Liar. You're like all the soldiers, you come here for two weeks and then you vanish," she smiled and swayed like a flower in the wind.

In the afternoon she returned, bringing wafer-thin pittas. While I bit into the brittle dough she pressed her shepherd's staff to her belly and began to sing the stanza:

"What arouses love,
The eyes or the heart?"

"The eyes," I said, but she shook her head. "The heart." No again. "Both!" I tried once more, sounding like a petulant child. But she shook her head for the third time and smiled with her smouldering eyes.

"It's the smell! Smell is like love, fleeting and blooming!" She picked up one of the young goats and stroked it. "Tell me about your life," she said.

So I told her.

"Water and light, stream and sun," she said, her eyes full of tears.

"Pretty gazelle, why are you crying?"

"What does any person cry for?"

"*Ana aref*, how should I know?"

"For himself."

"And what does a person laugh at?" I asked.

"At himself if he's clever and at others if he's stupid. That's what my mother says," she replied, smiling again. "Oh what

185

rotten luck!" she exclaimed, suddenly alarmed. "Night is falling, what am I doing here? They'll kill me." She turned, picked up a stone and threw it far down the slope, then another and another, and raced after them.

That night the "king of the mountain", as our commander was nicknamed, told us that the scheduled exchange of convoys would not be taking place, so we would have to stay here another week. I was pleased. I loved the place, the tranquillity, the ideas opened up to me by Professor Shadmi, and of course, Ghadir, the wild colt on the other side of the fence.

The next morning I woke up late. I've missed her, I thought, and hurried to the western side of the mountain.

"You're late this morning."

"I had a nice dream."

"And I had a horrible one. They want to marry me to a cousin in Amman. He has pimples on his face and I don't like him."

"Don't agree to it then."

"I'm an Arab girl, not a bee that can drink from any flower she chooses. My mother understands, she says it's better when a girl marries the man she wants, but when my father hears any such talk, there's uproar. Who can say anything to him?" She picked a flower, sniffed it and threw it over the fence. Then she told me about her family – they were refugees who had fled from Jaffa to the slopes of Mount Scopus and set up a tent there. It was the first time I had met a refugee like her from '48.

On my last day there I told her I was finishing my tour of duty, and gave her my colourful silk scarf. "A present to remember me by." She held it in both hands, sniffed it, rubbed it against her cheek, and then flung it back. "You want them to kill me?"

"God forbid!"

"Kind soldier, may Allah protect you and give you His blessing," she said in parting and ran down the mountainside.

I waved to her and threw the silk scarf over the fence. Perhaps one day she would find it. I looked down but she was already out of sight. I stood there a long time, moved and confused by what had and had not happened between us.

I knew that Mount Scopus had been besieged during the most recent war and heavily shelled too, but in my dreamy way I kept on hoping that I would still find Ghadir on the slopes, herding her flock as before, wearing her kerchief or white straw hat, or even the silk scarf I'd left her. I wondered what she was doing now, nine years later, and what she looked like.

One day in the summer I went to look for her. I walked past the Ambassador Hotel, where the military government had its headquarters, turned near the Mount Scopus Hotel, which had been standing empty since the war, passed Nashashibi Lane, the home of Abu George and Yasmine, and started climbing the mountain not far from there. My path was blocked by legions of yellow thorns with high stalks, cheeky hands, sharp fingers and faces ugly as the faces of spiders. A dry wind rose from the desert and whipped my face, while pulsating waves of hot air clutched at my throat.

I stood and stared for a while at the wall of thorns. Perhaps I'd taken a wrong turn? I left the open field, found the old access road and reached the mountaintop exhausted and sweaty. The old approach to our camp had been erased, just like the wall separating the two parts of the city. Bulldozers and tractors were working there and raising clouds of dust. I climbed up on a big rock and looked eastwards, trying to retrace the shepherd's path used by Ghadir. Perhaps she had married the spotty man she disliked and had moved to Amman, I told myself, and turned back.

Then one evening I met her by chance. I was walking, deep in thought, not far from the villa of Senator Antoine, trying to figure out what had gone wrong with my last memo to the minister – had my Hebrew let me down, or were the facts too complex to summarise – when suddenly a woman covered from head to foot stopped in front of me.

"Nuri?" she said, doubtfully.

"Ghadir!" I couldn't believe it.

"*Allah yinawer alaik*, may God shine his light upon you! Light and water, stream and fire," she smiled. "I worried about you."

The evening sun lit her tawny face, and her wolfish smile delighted me. She was even more beautiful, taller, more mature. The beauty spot on her cheek was more prominent.

"What are you doing here?" she asked. I told her.

"I'll pray to Allah that you succeed in opening hearts, yours and ours. We poor Palestinians have no *wali*, no protector, this one kicks us here, another kicks us there…Is your office in our city?"

"Here, in this alley," I pointed.

She bent down, picked a blue thistle and gave it to me. "I waited for peace. Maybe my fate would turn around. I didn't want to marry, didn't want children, didn't want a house. They thought I was crazy. In the end they married me to my cousin."

"The one in Amman?"

"Yes, the spotty one I told you about. Since the war he's been stuck over there, in Amman."

"I thought about you," I said.

"Naughty!" she laughed. "How many children do you have?"

"I'm not married."

"Impossible."

She looked at me, blushed and lowered her eyes. Evening fell, a pungent smell of heat and dry dust hung in the air. We looked at the horizon, at the sun sinking like a burst pomegranate behind the mountains, slowly draining away.

"Nuri, Allah sent you to me from heaven. Maybe you can help me. I won't tell you what my problem is now, I've got to go home, but I'll come to your office."

16

Yasmine, Nasser and Me

The pretty pair of canaries at the entrance to Al-Hurriyeh were singing happily, unaffected by the heavy midday heat. I stood on the threshold, enjoying the sweet chirping, seeking out Yasmine in the packed restaurant. I found her sitting near the cashier's desk, deep in conversation with a young woman, probably her friend Nehad whom Abu George had mentioned, and wondered if it would be all right to disturb them.

"Hello Yasmine," I said finally with a nod.

She gazed at me absently as if she didn't recognise me. Perhaps it was my new haircut, I thought. The day before I had dozed off in the barber's chair and when I opened my eyes I had a shock – the man had got carried away and chopped my hair and sideburns short, setting me back several fashion years.

"Ah, the advisor," she recollected. "This is my friend Nehad."

I bowed slightly to Nehad, who returned a brief smile.

"Please," Yasmine said in a low voice, but it was unclear if she really meant me to join them.

"Thanks, I don't want to disturb you," I said. "Maybe later." Flustered, like a shy schoolboy, I passed a hand through my hair and looked for a waiter to show me to a seat. Yasmine fixed me with a stare that I countered with a forced grin, trying to avoid her gimlet eyes, but she wasn't letting up. I lowered my eyes but she still kept staring. Why was she looking at me like that?

I usually avoided eating at Al-Hurriyeh, because Abu George refused to charge me but on this occasion I decided to order something and wait for Yasmine to be free, so she wouldn't suspect that I'd been sent by her despairing father. Once I had sat down at a corner table near the pomegranate tree she became absorbed in her conversation with Nehad and never gave me a glance. With her friend she was lively and free, totally unlike the frozen woman I'd met at the American Colony. Her black hair was shiny, and now and then she pushed it aside gracefully, laughing. I had with me the latest issue of *The New East* devoted to Egypt and tried to read it.

Eventually Nehad got up to leave, shaking her head like a puppy coming out of the water. Yasmine walked with her to the door, then turned and looked around at the customers till our eyes met. She came to my table, like a gracious hostess, but her walk betrayed her tension. I laid down my knife and fork to show I'd finished eating, leaned back and invited her to join me with a gesture.

"You don't like our food?" she asked, looking at my plate.

I quoted the old Chinese saying: "In the morning eat like a king, at midday like a prince, and in the evening like a pauper. Which means that I should now be eating like a prince, and the food here really is fit for royalty, but I'm simply not hungry. Where is Abu George? How is he? I'm worried about him."

"My father is well," she said brusquely.

"When we came to Israel, my father suffered from a similar cough."

Her look became colder, spurning the opening of intimacy I was offering.

"Will you join me if I order watermelon?"

She shook her head stiffly, her expression deadly serious.

"It was good to see you looking so cheerful with Nehad."

"I like sitting with my friends," she said, looking away. Her eyes fell on the magazine with the picture of Gamal Abd el-Nasser on the cover. Her curiosity aroused, she picked up the magazine with both hands. "What's this?"

"There's an article here about Nasser's resignation," I said. "It says once he resigned he shouldn't have changed his mind so quickly about being re-instated, that the downfall needed time to sink in…"

Her response struck me like a whiplash. "Don't you speak to me about downfall." She glanced again at the cover photo. "Jesus, it's the picture that appeared in *Le Monde* the day he resigned. He looked so sad and so tired…I'll never forget that night. Every proud Arab who loves freedom can tell you where he was that night."

"As for me, I was at home, listening to his speech with my father."

"And I was about to go to a Beatles concert. When Father phoned me in Paris and said Nasser was about to make a speech, I rang my friend and cancelled. I usually looked forward with excitement to hearing Nasser speak, but that evening I was anxious and restless. It was his first speech after the war…"

"And what a speech!" I broke in and, lifting my hand, began quoting whole passages from it. "O my brothers! We have been together in times of triumph and distress, in the fine hours and the bitter ones, we are accustomed to sitting together, to speaking to each other with open hearts…O my brother citizens, I have decided to retire finally and completely from every position, official or political. I shall return to the ranks of the masses…Imperialism fancies that Gamal Abd el-Nasser is its enemy, and I want to make it clear that the entire Arab nation is opposed to it, not Gamal Abd el-Nasser alone…The hope of Arab unity began before Gamal Abd el-Nasser and will persist after Gamal Abd el-Nasser…"

Yasmine stared at me in disbelief, tears in her eyes, and I fell silent. She swallowed. "No outsider can understand this," she said. "My whole world collapsed that evening. I cried and cried…"

"My father and I were shocked too," I said, surprised to see her softening.

"What went wrong?" she said bitterly. "Nasser himself announced the defeat. The father of Arab unity, the leader who gave us back our pride, stood up and admitted defeat! What went wrong? Who made the mistakes? Who was the traitor? I saw the pictures – people tearing at their clothes, pulling out their hair, weeping and whipping themselves bloody, like the Shi'ites on Ashura. Everything collapsed like a sandcastle." Words failed her for a moment. "Everything was wiped out – the hope, the honour. I couldn't bear to stay inside. I walked and walked through the streets, feeling I was thousands of miles from my people, blind in a foreign city…" I poured her a glass of water. She passed her fingers over the photo of Nasser, sipped and fell silent.

I sat hunched, leaning towards her.

"Yasmine, can you explain this to me? How is it that when Nasser announced his resignation millions poured out into the streets and pleaded with him to take it back. A Western leader wouldn't have survived such a defeat. Even Churchill, the great victor of the Second World War, wasn't re-elected after it. The

British wanted another leader in peace time. Even our Ben-Gurion, the founder of the state, was deposed by his colleagues when they thought he was making too many mistakes. How could Nasser survive, promising such great things but then inflicting disaster on his people and the entire Arab nation?"

She thought a moment, then said, "He restored our honour, made us stand tall, he was our great father. We don't throw father figures on the rubbish heap as they do in the West!"

"You remember the ending of that speech?" I asked, and the words came to me by themselves: "My heart is entirely with you...I would like all your hearts to be with me...May Allah be with us, sow hope in our heart and give us light and guidance..."

"Light and guidance..." Yasmine echoed and sank into a world that I was not a part of. Her hair was strewn around her smooth neck, and her lovely elongated face was blank and immobile. Suddenly she shook herself. "Jesus, you know the whole speech by heart! And your accent, when you declaimed it, pure Egyptian! Tell me, did you learn that at spy school?"

"That speech was a masterpiece," I explained.

Her turquoise eyes looked at me searchingly, and for a moment they softened and a smile lit up her face. In the brief moment that flashed past, the world was full of possibilities, and countless hopes blossomed.

She leaned forward, as if to speak in confidence. "Masterpiece, you say? I say, it's a statement of life. The scholars in the West, including your people, understand nothing about the Arab soul. You dissect us as if we are a corpse on the mortuary slab, not a living soul," she sighed.

"You're right. My older brother Kabi says the same. He argues that all those university scholars who look so important wouldn't even be able to order a glass of tea in real Arabic. They're products of the West and Western culture, they don't know the life of the Arabs and can't understand their minds."

"None of you will ever understand our frustration, the damaged honour, the humiliation, the need for achievements and recognition, as well as the need for revenge," she said and motioned to the waiter to bring a jug of water.

"Why do you need revenge? We're educated people, we're supposed to enjoy life, love, raise children, dance, sing. Not die or avenge."

We looked at each other and she blushed. I looked down at the watermelon the waiter had brought, which was still untouched. I offered her a share, but when she ignored me I took a big chunk and bit on it. *Ya salaam*, I wanted to say, but instead said in English that it was excellent. She picked up a piece and chewed it slowly. I looked at her mouth and wondered who she reminded me of? Ah, Jeanne Moreau! Princess of my youth, in a childish hairstyle with a centre parting, a girl of twenty, her big eyes peering through round glasses, her arched lips pouting like a baby's.

"I dreamed of such a watermelon in Paris. With salty cheese and a fresh pitta in the evening on the terrace," she said in a low voice in which I thought I sensed an opening to be exploited. I brought my chair closer, but she sat up straight and her eyes became veiled.

"Mister Advisor, do you know how much harm you caused my father when you persuaded him to open up his businesses?" she asked.

"Your father is a patriot and a practical man. He knows people need to raise their children and bring bread home," I said, hoping to lead on to the subject for which I'd come.

"It's bread kneaded with poison."

"You have greetings from Michelle. She's expecting you."

"Michelle? Ah, the Frenchwoman you planted in the youth village to recruit me into your *mukhabarat*!"

"That's an interesting idea. I hadn't thought of it," I smiled.

"I can hardly remember anything about that visit, except the children. Everything seemed very suspicious to me – Michelle, and the director, and you. Why should you want to help me?"

"You're very distrustful, like an amateur spy. It's really quite simple. I saw that your father is anxious to keep you here, as you're his only child…"

"Oh really? And your sympathy as a father made you decide to help him…"

"I'm unmarried," I said, and suddenly felt annoyed. "I like your father. Can't you understand that?"

A faint smile appeared at the corners of her mouth.

I picked up her cigarettes. "May I?"

"Help yourself. Mister Advisor, can you tell me how many Jews there are in Israel?"

She was trying to crack a watermelon seed but couldn't.

"About two and a half million."

"Impossible. The restaurant is packed, the markets are bursting at the seams, the goods are flying from the shops, the West Bank is flooded with Jews."

"We lived in a cage for twenty years, now everyone wants to go outside."

She didn't try to crack the next seed, just turned it over and over in her mouth, her lips opening and closing, pouting and pursing.

"There must be at least ten million of you," she said and swallowed the seed. "I wanted to ask you something else. Could you help me locate an old friend of mine, Edna Mazursky? I knew her when I was a child, in Talbieh. Her name doesn't appear in the telephone directory," she added apologetically.

"I'll try. By the way, did you count the names in the directory and reach ten million?"

She grinned and crossed her arms on her chest, uncrossed them and toyed with the match box. Her lips continued to communicate a mysterious message. She spat out another watermelon seed and put it into the ashtray. Then she looked at her watch. "We've been talking for more than an hour. Don't you have to work to do?"

You're my work, Yasmine, I wanted to say, but stopped myself and instead made a promise in a solemn tone that surprised both of us: "I'll do everything I can to find Edna Mazursky!"

Yasmine stood up and took out her car keys. "I'm going home. Can I give you a ride?"

"No thanks. I like to walk after lunch."

Outside, a dry desert wind competed with the crazy pitiless sun. My nostrils dried up, I walked in a daze. I tried to reconstruct what she'd said to take it in, and above all to purge myself, to shake off the burdens of hatred and anger, spite and incitement, humiliation and defeat which were piled on our forefathers and on us, in distant times and in our time, and which had built up the jagged partition between Yasmine and me.

An Arab woman sitting on the sweltering pavement was selling fresh, juicy figs. I bought a few and on my way to the office couldn't resist eating them unwashed. As I sucked the soft ripe fig I wondered if Eve could have tempted Adam with an apple – surely it was a fig?

197

17

Two Orgasms

"You have to build up a relationship with her. Maybe you should phone her," I urged Michelle.

"I don't think I should suck up to her," she replied. She was clearly disappointed and annoyed that Yasmine had neither been in touch nor returned to the youth village. In the end I invited her to have dinner with me at the Rimmon restaurant, but she said she was too busy. Nevertheless I phoned her again two days later to invite her to a concert in Tel Aviv.

"Thanks, it sounds wonderful, and I haven't been to the Culture Hall yet," she said and asked me to phone her again on the day of the concert. Clearly this wasn't going anywhere, as tickets had to be bought in advance, but I rang her in any case.

"I don't really feel like going tonight," she said. "Come to my place and I'll cook you dinner."

Now that was something. Who'd have thought that the pretty French brunette would cook for me? What should I give her in return? At the last moment I bought one of the fancy victory albums, with photos of all the generals and stories of heroism, designed to stir the imagination of the new immigrant. At least with Michelle I didn't need to apologise for not losing.

I drove to her house in Beit Hakerem. Her flat was tastefully furnished in a light modern style, the pieces probably imported from Paris, and frighteningly spotless. Kabi's girlfriend Sandra had told us that new immigrant privileges had recently doubled, and Kabi said, "It's obvious why – they want to encourage immigration from the West, because they're afraid of us orientals. First they thought we might run away from the battlefield, and now that we've shown them we can fight, they're even more afraid of us."

Unfamiliar cooking smells were coming from the kitchen. The slightly hoarse voice of Juliette Greco filled the living room: "If you think love's season lasts for ever, you are mistaken..." I sank into an armchair and surrendered to the music.

"Wine?" Michelle asked.

"Only for the Sabbath eve blessing."

"Another provincial, like all Israelis," she complained in her charming French accent. "I've yet to meet a single Israeli man with European culture."

"I suppose I also fail that test. Incidentally, I'm not a sabra – can't you tell from my funny oriental accent?"

She poured us red wine and raised her glass. "*L'Chaim!* And here's to the Israel Defence Forces!"

These new immigrants really take Zionism seriously, I thought.

"To victory!" she raised her glass again.

I took a small sip and made a face. "It's sour."

"When will you Israelis become worldly?"

"We are Levantines, *ma chérie*. Zahlawi arrack is our drink."

"Now let's drink to the task you've given me."

"*L'Chaim*," I tried the dry wine again and decided this was a taste I just wasn't going to acquire.

"I've cooked you a shoulder of beef with *champignons*, prunes and a little Dijon mustard."

"Oh no, beef with prunes and mustard?"

"What did you expect, hummus?"

"What's a *champignon*?"

Michelle laughed. "At least you're not ashamed to ask. I went out once with a sabra who pretended to know everything. There was no second date."

"Heaven, take pity on me!"

"Now tell me about this Yasmine of yours."

"It's an interesting story, but I'll tell you another time."

"Why are you being so mysterious?" She spread a white cloth on the table and set it with stylish china and cutlery, as if we were at a fancy restaurant.

"Your Hebrew is very good."

"My father, God rest his soul, was a Zionist, a Hebrew teacher in Lyon. He spoke Hebrew to us, but unfortunately the French accent has stuck."

"That's what makes it so attractive."

"Flatterer." She lit the candles on the table, then turned off the record player.

"Why turn off the music?"

"Two orgasms don't work together. Food is food and music is music."

She served the beef with steamed vegetables, salad and French mustard, a mélange of colours and smells.

"Bon appétit," she said and sliced the steaming meat. She tasted it, chewed slowly, and her nostrils widened, "Hmm…good. Why aren't you eating?"

"Do you have any bread?"

"Isn't there enough food on the table?"

"An old habit," I replied. "Comes of growing up poor." She handed me a little basket containing rye bread.

The smell of the meat was delicious. I tasted a little – it was rich, interesting, unlike anything I'd ever tasted.

"I don't cook dinner for everyone, certainly not on the first date."

"Why am I privileged?"

"I don't know. I really don't. Before you visited us I had been expecting a boring seedy bureaucrat with a pot-belly. But from the start your voice on the phone sounded so gentle, like a bird with a broken wing..." She stopped chewing and her eyes scrutinised me closely. "Excuse me for asking, but who cuts your hair? I can send you to a first-rate French barber."

I put down my knife and fork, beginning to resent the barrage of comments and tests. I'd expected a relaxing evening, but her temperament kept me on edge. After dinner she brought in a tray of pale wood loaded with a variety of cheeses. Her eyes shone when she examined them, sniffed them and gestured to me to taste them. Her hands were big and strong – I hadn't seen such hands outside the kibbutz.

"What's wrong now? Why don't you have some?"

"I never eat cheese."

"*Merde!* This is crazy! Real French cheeses that I brought from Paris...Ah, such flavour, sure you don't what to try?"

Later she made coffee in a percolator and brought in Gitanes and Cointreau. "It's very sweet, just for you!" But when she saw me gulping it down she told me off: "Take it slowly, I don't want you to fall asleep."

"No danger of that."

"So tell me, was this Yasmina a spy of ours?"

"Certainly not!"

"Then why are you all taking so much trouble?"

"For humanitarian reasons."

201

"I see. Is that why you wanted to meet me too? Is that also part of your job?"

"I wish it was my job, having dinner with beautiful women."

"*Oo la la*, at last an Israeli who knows how to pay compliments."

I got up to help her clear the table, but she ordered me to sit down. I settled back in an armchair, relaxed and contented, enjoying the dry aroma of the cigarettes.

"So why doesn't your Yasmina come to the youth village? I've been waiting and waiting, but mademoiselle doesn't show up."

"It's madame. She's a widow. Her husband died in unknown circumstances."

"Maybe he was a spy."

"Maybe. Or a fighter, one of the fedayeen…"

"I don't understand anything any more," she said, pouring me more of the good strong coffee. "Another Israeli conundrum."

"If you're so critical of us, why did you come to Israel?"

"That's the whole point. I'm curious, from an anthropological point of view, to see if Jews can live together in a state of their own. I get the feeling I'm researching a madhouse. Everybody is against everybody else," she said, carried away by her own eloquence.

"Very impressive. All the same, why? Why really?"

"To tell you the truth, I like it here. From the moment I arrived I've felt part of a big family. I've met so many people in such a short time, more than I knew in my whole life."

"You're exaggerating."

"Not at all. You sabras have no idea what it's like to live in a cold, uncaring city. Like on the Metro, for example. People don't even look at you. On campus you're not allowed to walk on the grass. Here the students not only walk on the grass, they lie on it, getting tanned and enjoying life. This appeals to me."

We moved to the sofa and I flopped into it, emitting heat like an oven. My eyes began to close and my head was drooping. It was time to leave.

Michelle's hands dropped in disappointment.

"*Merde*, these Israelis. They either jump on you, or they walk away like strangers. Don't I at least get a little kiss?"

On our second date I brought her a book of Omar Khayyam's poetry, mostly wine poems, as well as hummus, which is believed to be as good for you as red wine. She opened the door in a white bathrobe, brushing her hair with her free hand. "Come in, make yourself comfortable. I just washed my hair and it's still wet."

"I like wet hair, it's sexy." I wasn't sure she heard me, because at that moment she switched on her hairdryer which roared like a pneumatic drill. When she finished she emerged in a very short miniskirt and a very big white blouse which accentuated the mounds of her breasts.

"I've got news for you. But first, what will you drink?"

"Do you have arrack?" I asked doubtfully.

"I bought some for you, I already know you're hopelessly conservative," she laughed unwrapping the book. "Oh, that's wonderful. Thanks! To tell you the truth, I wasn't crazy about the victory album you gave me. Those pompous generals...not exactly chic. A little modesty wouldn't hurt them."

She went to the kitchen cupboard and took out the arrack, but immediately put it back. "I'm not going to let you drink this cleaning fluid. It's so bad for you," she declared and turned to the fridge instead. She took out a bottle of white wine, plus a bottle of vodka from the freezer compartment. "This is excellent wine from the vineyard of my friend Jean-Claude. He wants to come here, marry me and start a vineyard here. Maybe in Judea or Samaria. Any suggestions?"

I shook my head. She turned on the record player and the voice of Edith Piaf, warm and strong, filled the air and made the angels dance in heaven. I leaned back in the armchair and took deep gulps of the sublime vodka.

"Your Lady Yasmina telephoned. We had a strange conversation. She asked about my working hours, and if it wouldn't be too much trouble for me if she came again, but she didn't mention a time."

"Be nice to her, please."

"Why is she so important to you? Every time I mention her your eyes light up."

"Really? I...well, strictly between ourselves, some anti-Israeli elements in your city, in Paris, have been trying to win her over...We're hoping to separate her from them. I can't say any more," I said in a tone full of importance.

"More mysteries!" she protested in her delightful accent. "Here's to the IDF!" she added, and drank her white wine. "Today I made you a special meal, French cheeses, salad and a quiche, everything seasoned with garlic. I must get you accustomed to eating cheeses!"

"*Merde*," I said, imitating her accent. "Isn't my mother enough? And I brought you the best hummus in town."

"Really? I've never tried hummus."

Again she spread a white tablecloth, lit candles, and before we sat down she turned off the music. I recalled her saying she couldn't cope with two orgasms at the same time. I tried to spread the hummus on the platter the way they do in restaurants, poured olive oil on it and showed her how to wipe it off with a pitta. She tasted it and made a face. "What is this? Sand with oil? How can you eat it?"

"It's original hummus from Abu Shukri in the Old City."

"I'm afraid of them. I don't trust their hygiene," she pushed her plate away. I took it and finished it with pleasure.

"Taste the cheeses. I prepared everything for you. Try the camembert – such a smell, and the garlic one, such a delicacy…oh…" she moaned with pleasure. I licked the olive oil from my fingers, added hot pepper relish and moaned like her. We also drank a lot, during the meal and afterwards – she guzzled her Jean-Claude's white wine, I kept on tippling the vodka. After the meal she brought in cognac. My head was swimming and my eyelids grew heavy.

"You're falling asleep on me again?" she protested and turned the record player back on.

Edith Piaf woke me up. I'd seen her once in an old film, a little birdlike woman with a mighty, heartrending voice; she was sad and not good-looking, but when she sang she was beautiful.

Michelle sat down beside me, snuggled against me, unfastened some of my shirt buttons and slipped her hand in. "You have a hairy chest, that's why I pamper you," she laughed. I was fascinated by her uninhibited spirit. "Why are you so thin? You're like a boy." I undid the rest of the buttons and let her do what she wanted. "Why aren't you sighing? In love you have to let yourself go."

The vodka and cognac were making me dizzy. I needed fresh air and asked her to open the window. When she returned she took me by the hand and led me to her bedroom. I took my drink with me, although I knew that alcohol suppresses the libido. She turned off the music again. "Leave it, leave it. I like music with loving," I said. Never mind her two orgasms – who's to say we'll even have one? I had difficulty unbuttoning my trousers, then got the laces of my left shoe tangled up and had to pull it off by force, almost falling off the bed. I was left in my underpants.

"Take them off, take them off," she urged, slapping my arse. "Ah what a sound!"

She was naked. She took her time stroking me and whispering French incantations in my ears. I got up and put the record back on – sing to me, Edith Piaf, sweep me away as you swept Jean Cocteau away. He loved you so much. You died on the same day, first you, then him just a few hours later. Sing to me, Edith! I said to her. Her anguished voice blended with that of Michelle, who was writhing and twisting, and my whole body sang with joy, the relief of being with a woman after three months of forced inactivity.

I went to the bathroom and stood for a long time under the shower, torn between the Jerusalemite's habit of saving water and the wonderful freshness of the cool current. While drying myself my eyes were drawn to an attractive display of creams and perfumes. An unusual impulse made me open them and sniff the wonderful, foreign scents. Finding a light jasmin-scented spray I squirted some on myself and came out.

Michelle was asleep. I settled in an armchair in the living room and leafed through the poems of Omar Khayyam.

> How long, how long, in infinite pursuit
> Of this and that endeavour and dispute?
> Better be merry with the fruitful grape
> Than sadden after none, or bitter, fruit.

*

After Michelle woke up she came into the living room in a light silk negligee, which she'd left hanging open, displaying most of her brown, suntanned body. She sat on my knee and asked, "Did you come?"

"There's a curse hanging over me."

"You've got to be kidding!" she protested. "What about children?" she added, sounding worried.

"There's a certain rabbi in Safed who said he could fix it for me, but only after a proper wedding ceremony."

18

Soft Words

At 4.30, earlier than usual, the latest baby began his morning concert. Why didn't she pick him up and give him a nipple to suck? Maybe the little thing is screaming because he has a tummy ache and the poor mother can't calm him down. After all, she must want to sleep too. My annoyance turned to sympathy. Looking out of my big window I saw her, my Orthodox neighbour, wearing a new light scarf. She's younger than me and already a mother of six. Her figure has thickened with all this childbearing, but she radiates a sweet, mature and modest femininity. Perhaps it's the effect of the scarf framing her face, her quick smile, or the full, soft body covered from head to foot. I wondered how she and her husband "commune", as they call it. How does modesty affect the passion, the physical contact?

I like to see my Orthodox neighbour at least once a day, preferably in the morning, otherwise my routine is upset. When I return her shy little smile, she looks away as if she's committed a sin. Sometimes I wish I could have a casual chat with her in the way of neighbours, make her laugh at a joke or a spicy story. Does she ever think about me as I think about her?

At this hour, when we both open our windows, she looks at me in silence. Maybe she's curious to know who spent the night with me. Once, out of consideration for her, I didn't raise the blind in the morning. Someone had spent the night with me and we coupled joylessly – a man and a woman joining together for a night of love when there is no love between them – and I didn't want my neighbour to see our gloomy faces after the miserable and frustrating sex we had shared. Things were different when Yardena slept at my place and we enjoyed our carnal pleasures; the blind was raised at dawn to greet the new day, and it seemed to me then that my Orthodox lady was glad to see Yardena. When I marry I'll invite her to the wedding; it will be nice to have her accompany me on that day.

Two floors below her lives another Orthodox family, also well endowed with offspring. They multiply like the Palestinians – a birth-rate which is three times the norm among us.

The Minister didn't want to know about the natural increase among the Palestinians, any more than he fretted about his bulging belly. I continued to show him the statistics and bombard him with forecasts. "These will become reality in our time," I told him, but he stopped me irritably. I persisted: "Your grandchildren and my children will have to contend with this situation. My father brought me here to live in a Jewish state but at this rate it will just go on shrinking." His bushy, greying eyebrows rose angrily and he began to pull hairs out of them. You had to see this to believe it – a senior government minister sitting in his office pulling out his eyebrows like a specialist in the removal of unwanted pubic hair. He paced up and down his office, prophesying the arrival of millions of Jews from the USSR: "They will melt the Iron Curtain and come to their historical homeland en masse, with their grandparents and babies…" His arms outstretched, he was all set to hug them.

How will they get out of there, I wondered to myself, although as it turned out, my scepticism would prove to be unfounded. The Minister dreamt of a new settlement movement in the occupied territories, like the one undertaken in the days of the British Mandate. "Our cousins," meaning the Arabs, "will work in our enterprises, will earn good wages and will gradually come to see our presence in the territories as a blessing, and will get used to it just as they got used to the fact that Jaffa and Ramleh and Ashkelon and Acre are ours."

I tried to cool his enthusiasm. "They have different dreams."

"You believe they'll lay down their lives for an ideology, as we do?"

"They've been doing it for more than seventy-five years."

But he'd stopped listening to me. My boss drove me crazy. He asked for my advice but didn't take it.

I went for my early morning walk. It was cool outside, with pleasant scents of autumn. A pale yellow light showed in a nearby house. A car drove drunkenly past, its headlights making the shadows dance. I stuck to the pavement, my eyes down and my arms swinging briskly. When I returned home *Ha'aretz* was not yet in my mailbox. The paperboys didn't work as hard as I had, an immigrant youth of the previous generation. When I quit the kibbutz and came to Jerusalem on my own, I delivered newspapers. It was difficult to get the job and not easy to keep it. My predecessor missed one morning and was fired.

Out of breath and sweaty from my brisk walk, I climbed the stairs, waited at my door and rang the bell. Sometimes I dreamt that a woman would be waiting for me inside, would open the door with a warm smile, hug me and thaw all the fears and anguish in my soul. Why didn't I get married? Of my class only Sultan and I were still unmarried. He was working on his doctorate, but what was my excuse?

I went to the office early to sort through my heaped in-tray. There were classified letters, invitations to various events, analyses by self-styled experts, appeals for help. I read the letters marked Classified first, placed some of them in the safe and left the rest, which were so designated merely from the sender's sense of self-importance, to be filed. Invitations I chucked in the waste-paper basket. Since starting this job I received invitations to every ceremony, opening night and exhibition. At first I felt flattered and went along, until I discovered that people turned up just to see and be seen, and in reality, to share the communal experience of boredom.

The other letters I spread on the desk like goods on a market stall. I glanced at the headings and set aside the "scholarly surveys", written by frustrated historians and the various would-be experts who infest the government service. If I didn't know that my Minister loved these things, I'd never have written any. For myself, I'm satisfied with basic facts, numbers and other data of essential significance. You soon find out that even the best-founded evaluations end up on the rubbish heap.

Finally I got down to the correspondence that really interested me – personal letters, requests and complaints from ordinary members of the Arab community. Their handwriting was sometimes hard to read; some wrote illiterate Arabic, others wrote in the elaborate high language of Arabic tradition, and a few opened with unctuous flattery. I could tell they were following the adage, "Kiss the hand you dare not bite, and pray that it break!" Many of the complaints were about the prevention of family reunification, difficulty in obtaining various permits, expropriation of lands and structures. Unfortunately I was no expert on civil rights, land and immigration laws, or the status of absentees. It was necessary to bone up on these subjects as soon as possible.

One letter written in tiny handwriting caught my eye. It was from a widow who was searching for her son, missing since the end of the fighting. I put her letter aside with others whose writers I meant to invite to come and see me. I wanted to find ways to make a real difference, and I also wanted to show them that we were human beings. In the past we had been the victims of the Gentiles, but now unless we were careful we could become our own victims. One of the last letters I looked at was a friendly note from Abu George asking me to get in touch.

My secretary Aliza wouldn't be in before eight, so I propped my feet up on the desk, detached myself from the matters at hand, and let my thoughts drift. My job meant that I had to submit to the dictates of my Minister's politics, and in fact there is something comfortable about obeying someone who knows what must be done. The trouble was that occasionally I thought he was wrong, and I myself was still groping and searching for the right way and wasn't immune from errors. I disliked his patronising attitude towards the Arab population, and felt uneasy when he indulged in his grand, pathos-filled visions while refusing to face reality. I wasn't willing to view the Arabs as "our cousins who will work for us", as inferior people without ideology and dreams. I wanted to help this post–occupation population as if they were regular immigrants, destined to be our neighbours for the rest of our lives. East Jerusalem was a new experience even for people who were born there, like Haramati of the Ministry of the Interior and Harish from the

Ministry of Religious Affairs, and how much more so for me, the youngest of the group, so it meant I had to be doubly careful. For now I was able to carry out my duties in my own way, but what if a time came when I was unable to do so?

Instead of imposing my ideas, I looked for relationships based on trust, on seeking out the local leadership and co-operating with it. I devoted a lot of time and energy getting to know the prominent families – Khalidi, Husseini, Asali, Budeiry, Ansari, Afifi, Nusseibeh, Barakat and others – and studied their histories in the records of the Sharia courts. When we met they were pleased to find that I knew something about them and their families and by degrees they opened up to me. Then I studied the Christian families – Salameh, Atallah, Jamal, Faraj and others – and learned which of them had always lived in Jerusalem and which settled recently, who were ancient Jerusalemites and who had originally come from Hebron. Some had Jewish friends from the time of the British Mandate who helped steer them through our bureaucratic maze. But I also spared no efforts to help the ordinary people, to act as a mediator, to represent and listen to them, to understand and feel their frustrations, and hoped that we would be able to live together. Building up trust is like weaving a complex tapestry which demands knowledge and subtlety, and there was still a long way to go.

Aliza arrived at eight on the dot, and after we had discussed her assignments for the day I thought I'd see Abu George at Al-Hurriyeh instead of phoning him. Perhaps Yasmine would be there too. I found him giving instructions to his staff, but when he saw me he hurried over and hugged me so tight that I almost blushed.

"*Mabruk, ya akhi!*" he congratulated me. "You succeeded in persuading Yasmine. She starts working at the youth village next week – *inshallah*, now she'll stay with us. Um George is weeping for joy. We want to invite you to dinner at the Intercontinental or the Al-Wattani hotel. Which do you prefer?"

"Many thanks, but neither one nor the other."

"Why?"

"Invitations have to be returned, don't they? And I'm an official with a modest salary, I can't afford such hospitality."

He looked at me as if he didn't understand. "*Yaani*, you mean this is *bartil*, a bribe, unless you repay me? These are our courtesies, as you very well know."

I shook my head firmly.

"All right, so come to dinner at our house."

"An invitation must be returned," I repeated the unwritten law. "And I'm a bachelor living in a one-room flat and can't invite you back."

He gave up and fell silent.

"What about you, how is your health?" I asked.

"Fortunately, having Yasmine here is giving me strength to cope with all our troubles. The Israeli flag is flying over my head, our Fatah think I'm a collaborator, your *mukhabarat* suspect me of being a Fatah agent, the army doesn't listen to anybody and has just expropriated buildings of mine in Ramallah and Nablus. Now, on top of everything, my friend Nuri, who helped me with Yasmine, the apple of my eye, is too conscientious to dine at my house. What's wrong with my invitation?" He broke into one of his frenetic coughing fits. "Maybe I'll go to Paris, there's a well-known Armenian doctor there."

"What is the matter with you, my friend? We moved mountains to persuade Yasmine to stay here and now you want to go there?" I protested, taking the liberty of interfering in his private affairs. "You refuse to let a Jewish doctor treat you? That's more Abu Nabil's style."

"You're more right than you know. Now Abu Nabil is refusing to accept advertising from Jews. I tell him it's business, not politics, but he won't budge."

"Have you talked to the 'Colonel' about the houses in Nablus and Ramallah?"

"He's busy. Since he started working with the Minister of Defence there's no getting hold of him. And he doesn't come to the restaurant the way he used to."

I asked him if he would agree to meet my Minister, which would give my boss a chance to hear about the problems and difficulties in the Arab community. "Would that hurt your standing, or be interpreted as collaboration, God forbid? Tell me honestly, we're like brothers."

"They say, 'One who is wet is not afraid of the rain.' Since I'm accused of all kinds of things anyway…"

I set off on one of my periodic tours of the government offices in East Jerusalem. The long lines stretching outside the local offices of the Ministry of the Interior, the Department of Social Security and even the Post Office were distressing to see. But people waited patiently, didn't grumble, probably didn't dare to protest aloud. Additional staff at these offices would make their life easier, so why wasn't it done? I should raise this matter, I thought, though carefully so as not to offend my colleagues.

The desert wind blew at my back and when I returned, hot and sweaty, to my office I found Aliza waiting for me impatiently. "The list of calls and the post are on your desk!" she announced and left. Aliza was like the flowers planted by the Labour Federation – opening at eight and closing at three. Sometimes I wished I had a more flexible secretary.

I phoned Amitai's unlisted number. "Abu George is upset – he has a problem. Could you talk to him?"

"I know, Nuri, but unfortunately nothing can be done about it. I checked. His buildings are in a vital strategic location which the army needs. He'll get reasonable compensation."

"He doesn't want any compensation, he just wants to keep his property."

"Nuri, we're in an ongoing struggle for survival, and it's hard on everybody."

I put down the receiver with a heavy heart and started reading an analysis by Harish from the Ministry of Religious Affairs, in preparation for a meeting with Mutran Krachi. Halfway through I phoned my Minister and suggested that he might invite Abu George to his office, or even meet him at his restaurant. I knew that he didn't like meeting people from East Jerusalem and had no interest in getting to know them, let alone in learning their language or touring the Arab towns and villages. Nevertheless I kept trying to involve him in their lives and to introduce him to those who held key positions in the Arab community, thus giving them the feeling that their issues were being addressed by the Israeli leadership.

"Such meals come at a price," said the Minister, rejecting the suggestion.

A week later I went to Al-Hurriyeh and was delighted to see Yasmine at the till. After some polite exchanges she challenged me, "You always say you're *ibn Arab*, don't you? So why did you turn down Father's invitation to dinner at our house?"

"Now I can't refuse," I said, and she looked pleased.

In honour of the occasion I had my hair cut at Michelle's French barber, shaved meticulously and wore my one good suit with a starched white shirt, a new tie and a matching handkerchief. I felt as if I was going to a *maayana* ceremony, when the matchmaker introduces the groom to the intended bride and her family. At the last moment I took the handkerchief out of the front pocket, in case I was seen by one of my neighbours, meaning to replace it when I reached Abu George's house. I took the present I'd prepared, a reproduction of *The Virgin's Spring*, by the amiable Jerusalem painter Ludwig Blum, and drove over to pick up Professor Shadmi and his wife Pe'era. I was reassured to see that he had a handkerchief in the front pocket of his grey suit jacket. Pe'era was wearing an evening dress and looked elegant and excited.

Abu George's front gate was wide open. Pe'era admired the garden and especially the ancient olive tree which, Abu George said, was at its best this autumn. He received the Shadmis with open arms. "We can start," he said, "now all the guests have arrived, except the senator. What can I do, his head is turning to stone."

Seated at the table were Abu Nabil and others from the tourist office, as well as Abu Shalbayyeh, an East Jerusalem teacher and journalist. "Colonel" Amitai, Dr Dovrat, a Foreign Ministry diplomat and expert on the history of religions, and Solly Levy who'd persuaded me to move into Ahmad Shukeiry's abandoned office – were chatting in a corner of the room. Two well-known restaurant owners from West Jerusalem were arguing volubly by the window. Abu George placed me, as the guest of honour, at the head of the table and he sat at the opposite end. I hoped he would seat Yasmine beside me.

She entered last, wearing a floating lilac blouse that resembled a delicate wisteria blossom in the wind, and sat down next to Professor Shadmi and his wife. Well, if not beside me, at least next to my associates. Our eyes met for a moment. Abu George welcomed the guests, thanked Um George and Yasmine, and concluded with *Tfadalu* to signal the start of the meal.

First came the hors-d'oeuvres and salads – *tebouleh, baba ghanouj,* aubergines baked in *tehina,* hummus with whole chickpeas, *tehina* seasoned with lemon and chopped parsley, a salad tossed in thinned *tehina,* broad beans, *kubbeh niyyeh,* raw ground meat mixed with *burghul, warak dawali,* vine leaves stuffed with rice, Nablus *kubbeh,* stuffed vegetables, tiny pittas with ground meat, and of course a variety of pickled vegetables including cucumbers, aubergines, luubieh and okra, spicy black and green olives – altogether an aromatic and colourful spread.

The conversation was lively and flowed easily. Professor Shadmi and Dr Dovrat talked at length about ancient times, the growth of the myths around Moses, Jesus and Mohammed, as well as what united and separated the three religions.

Then the talk switched to discussion of the British Mandate, an era of which many echoes remained – and I was surprised by the change in attitudes. In its time the British Mandate was seen as rule by an alien colonial power that took over the country and held on to it, until driven out by force. Now, in retrospect they viewed the Mandate as an orderly, even enlightened, regime which had laid down social norms, implemented regulatory laws and even promoted cultural and aesthetic values – for example, the statute that all Jerusalem buildings be faced with stone. I wondered if the Arabs would ever change their perception of us – would we be remembered as an enlightened regime that promoted progress, rather than an alien occupier?

Abu Nabil and Abu Shalbayyeh tried to divert the conversation to the present. Abu Shalbayyeh referred everyone to a series of articles he'd written, in which he called for a Palestinian state in the occupied territories.

Those of us who represented the authorities naturally avoided discussing the current situation. Abu George did the same, choosing to speak about Professor Shadmi's great concordance project at the Givat Ram campus, and the ancient manuscripts which were kept at the National Library. I worried that Abu Nabil would again make sly digs at the professor, but this time the crude mockery was replaced by a friendly spirit and obvious respect. He mentioned the recent discovery of centuries-old Hebrew Bibles, and of course offered to use his connections to enable "our Abu Mehammed", aka Professor Shadmi, to examine them himself.

The next course consisted of a steaming roast lamb, served up on an enormous tray. A waiter carved the meat skilfully with a large knife, then removed the lamb's tongue and laid it on a bed of chopped parsley on a plate in front of the host. Abu George rose, came up to me with the plate, sliced off a piece of the tongue and said, "Nuri, my brother, it is our custom that the host feeds the guest of honour the tongue of the lamb," and he fed me the slice with his own hands.

I was unfamiliar with the custom and for a moment felt that the piece of tongue was going to stick in my throat, but seeing the joy on my host's face I suppressed all my reservations. Just take it easy, I said to myself, you're a guest and this is an honour.

Yasmine's eyes were on me, twinkling mischievously, and I swallowed the meat as if passing a test, and felt a hot blush rising to my face.

Abu George went back to his seat and the waiters served everyone slices of roast lamb, Pe'era trying in vain to make the professor keep to his diet. The final course was fruit, including figs and watermelon, followed by sweet pastries and black coffee.

At midnight, when we got up to leave, Professor Shadmi said to our host, "My dear Abu George, I'm supposed to visit Bir Zeit University soon, and I don't want to go there empty-handed. Would you be so kind as to help me choose an appropriate gift for my hosts there? Perhaps an ancient pottery jar?"

"But of course! What wouldn't we do for Abu Mehammed?"

Yasmine's mischievous grin at the dinner party was succeeded a few days later by a fit of rage. The next time we met at Al-Hurriyeh my attempts at a pleasant chat failed, and our exchange grew so heated it became a quarrel. She called me "the occupier with the fine soul", and Moshe Dayan "the Casanova of wars", even arguing that Um Kulthoum was "an Israeli agent whose songs are designed to dope the masses". I was offended by such words as "enemy", "occupier", "dispossession", then annoyed at myself for giving so much weight to her anger, for making efforts to soften her rancour, and for being naive enough to quote to her Hamutal Bar-Yosef's poem, "Palestine":

> In this narrow bed
> Beside an earthen wall pocked
> With burrows for spiders and geckos,

> If I turn over I shall fall in the sea.
> In this hard and narrow bed
> Do you come to know me, *ya habibi,*
> Or to smash my head
> And my infant's head
> Against the Wall?

"Whose narrow bed is it?" Yasmine raged at me. "If the title were Israel I'd understand, but to call such a poem Palestine!"

"Now I don't understand anything, neither you nor the poem."

"Let me tell you a parable, then maybe you'll understand. A man set out on his donkey. On the road he saw a weary straggler. He took pity on him and offered to take him on his donkey. They rode together a while, then the straggler said, 'What a fine donkey – it carries both of us so well.' 'Thank you,' said the man. 'I try to take good care of it.' They rode a while longer, and the straggler said, 'Oh this really is a splendid donkey!' 'Thanks!' said the man. 'I make sure to feed it well and let it rest sufficiently, and it serves me accordingly.' They rode a bit longer, and the straggler said, 'Our donkey deserves all praise.' The donkey's owner stopped and said, 'That's enough, sir. Please get off the donkey.' 'But why?' asked the straggler. 'Because you have started calling it our donkey, and I'd rather you leave now, before you start calling it your donkey.'"

"A fine parable indeed, very apt…Now, instead of exchanging fables and labels, let's change the subject, all right? Michelle told me you're starting to work with her tomorrow."

"You and Michelle," she said with a sneer. "Like a pair of pincers trying to close on me."

"Sometimes I get the impression that you think I'm a devil who's out to harm you."

"Are you offended?" she asked, suddenly calmer. My eyes met hers and caressed her face. Yasmine took the jug of cold water that stood on the table and slowly filled our glasses. She looked at me clear-eyed and said, "Would you come with me tomorrow morning to that youth village of yours? It turns my stomach to think I'm going to do my final training among you people."

19

Morning with Yasmine

The morning I was to meet up with Yasmine – and what a morning that was! – I arrived early at Al-Hurriyeh and found Abu George already there. "Today we're going with Professor Shadmi to the antiques dealer, aren't we?" I said.

"Of course. How could I forget our Abu Mehammed?"

"When do you want to meet?"

"We'll leave here at eleven-thirty."

Yasmine arrived on time, looking glamorous in an aubergine-coloured shirt and black jeans, but her face was tense.

"We have time for coffee?" she asked.

"We'd better get a move on. Michelle is punctual. Do you want to follow me?"

"I'll go with you and take a taxi back."

"I meant to stay there for a while but I've got a busy day today, and I also have to prepare for a meeting with your Bishop Krachi," I said when we were in the car. "Do you know him?"

"Mutran Krachi? He helped me in the bad days after the death of my husband Azme." She took a deep breath and her breasts rose under the purple blouse. "When you see death before you, black becomes blacker still." She lowered her eyes and my hand, reaching out for the ignition, stopped in mid-air.

"The Mutran came to our house every day, and when he saw that I was in a state of shock and couldn't even cry, he sat beside me and told me a story that helped me more than all the comforting and consoling phrases I got from everyone else. It's about Abdel Wahab. Once when he was in his early twenties he was invited to sing at a celebration in Aley in Lebanon, where he was accompanied by the prince of poets, Ahmed Shawqi. While he was there he received the news that his father, whom he adored, had just died. He broke down and cried, 'Father, Father, Father!' Shawqi tried to calm him down, 'I'm your father and your friend who loves you,' but it made no difference. The Egyptian writer Taha Hussein, who was also there, tried to comfort him, but he couldn't stop crying and wanted to call off his evening performance. Then Taha Hussein said to him, 'Is all music joyous, is it all happiness? Is there no pain and sorrow in it? Sing to us, *ibni,* my son,' he begged. 'Your singing will move our hearts and we shall grieve with you,' and thus he persuaded him. In the evening Abdel Wahab stood before his admiring audience and sang and wept and the entire audience cried with him. That's what the Mutran told me, and I went up to my room, locked the door, listened to a record of Fairuz, and the dam holding back my tears broke."

I felt my whole body turning to her, and wished I could embrace her.

We reached the intersection near Mount Scopus and saw pneumatic drills breaking up rocks, bulldozers shaving the stony hilltop, chewing up the rubble and laying the groundwork for a new housing development. The air smelled of dry dust.

"You people are destroying the beauty and the character of the city," she said.

She's right, I thought. Jerusalem was changing visibly, day by day, and I was beginning to feel nostalgic for the quiet city I'd come to as a boy when I left the kibbutz. I loved the dappled hills, the variegated neighbourhoods, the tranquillity. I'd liked to see the modest girls walking in the streets in their long skirts. Before coming here I had pictured Jerusalem as a big city, an international metropolis with a style appropriate to the sanctity of the place, and was surprised to find a small and thinly populated town. With the addition of East Jerusalem, as well as areas to the south, north and west, roads were being built, machinery was burrowing into the underbelly to install telephone lines and sewage pipes, and the city seemed to be turning away from me – as embarrassed and perplexed as a barren woman who has overnight conceived septuplets, all of them impatient to leave her womb and go their separate ways.

"There is a man in Paris," Yasmine went on, grinning, "who hates the Eiffel Tower, yet he climbs it every day. Whenever people ask him why he does so if he hates it, he says, 'Because it's the only place from which you can't see the Eiffel Tower.' And apropos this anecdote, I think you people don't know what you're doing to yourselves, and how can you? The only place from which you can't see Israel is Israel itself."

I listened attentively to every word she said. I always loved this style of delivering ideas through anecdotes and parables, and she did it with the ease of an old peasant grandmother.

We passed a group of Orthodox Jewish men in black coats walking along the verge of the road. "These people we could get on with," she said. "They have no territorial ambitions."

"Drop the politics!"

"What can I do? Politics is in the blood, like a chronic illness. Once you catch it you can't get it out of your system."

"Tell me a little about the Mutran. I know nothing about him."

"He's a handsome man, impressive, intelligent, sharp, fancies himself and talks a lot. He's not a narrow-minded cleric. I may ask for his help in starting a certain enterprise," she said but did not elaborate. "Now let me ask you something. Can you explain to me how your Zionist mind works? Explain it to me as if I were an *olah hadashah*."

"I'm the new immigrant," I pointed out. "You're a Jerusalem-born sabra."

"Let me tell you," she went on. "I studied Hebrew as hard as I could so as not to be different. I finished the course at the YMCA with top marks in Hebrew composition. I even got a gift – a beautiful volume of Bialik's poetry."

"You see the difference between us? I learned Hebrew on the street, and you learned it from our national poet."

"You still haven't explained to me how your Zionist mind works."

"I want to live in peace with you and you're forcing me to quarrel," I said, and asked her to light me a cigarette.

She focused on my eyes with the concentration of an archer taking aim. "There's something scary about Zionists. They've developed their arguments to a fine art, like that fib about historical rights. They have a gift for selling sand as if it were gold, with a kind of devilish blend of pathos and power." She put the burning cigarette between my lips.

"We're a small state surrounded by tens of millions who want to destroy us. Has it ever occurred to you that we might be afraid?"

"Since when does the conqueror fear the conquered, or a strong man fear a weak one?"

"All our victories have been punches into a soft cushion. One victory on your side and we'll be in the sea. Please, give your chauffeur a break. Enough politics!"

"It's the strong who do politics, the weak can only talk about it," she protested.

I stopped at a kiosk in Kiryat Moshe and bought fine quality chocolate and two bottles of juice. "Here you are."

"Chocolate? Only Sylvana, our national chocolate! Did you know that at our weddings people sing to the bride, 'Oh little Sylvana'?"

"What a fool I am! How could I fail to connect chocolate with the national problem? May I give you a bit of advice? Don't talk politics with Michelle."

"What else do you expect me to do?" she replied, childishly mischievous.

"*Bonjour* Nuri, *bonjour* Yasmine!" Michelle greeted us. "How beautiful you look! This dark purple suits you well." She immediately drew Yasmine into a discussion about fashion and clothing in a hot country, and somehow moved on from there to Simone de Beauvoir's latest book, declaring that she couldn't understand what a woman with such a spiritual face saw "in that ugly mug Sartre".

Gossip about the famous couple didn't seem to interest Yasmine very much, and she began to speak about another thinker, Franz Fanon, the black psychiatrist, who had become a guru among Third World activists as well as the Black Panther movement in the United States. I gathered from what she said that he was born in the Caribbean, studied medicine and psychiatry in France, and wrote a great deal about the impact of racism and colonialism. Yasmine was especially enthusiastic about his work, *Black Skin, White Masks*, which dealt with his experiences as a black intellectual in a "whitened" world.

Michelle made a face, as if to say, What's it got to do with us? I watched and listened, ignored by two opinionated women who were trying to outdo each other in awareness of the contemporary intellectual scene in Europe.

Then Michelle remembered my presence. "Coffee?"

"No thanks, I've got to go."

"Shall I see you this evening?"

"Sorry, I have an appointment with Mutran Krachi," I said, annoyed that Michelle chose to mention our date in front of Yasmine, who pretended she had heard nothing.

20

The Art of Haggling

On the way back from the youth village I got stuck in a traffic jam – another sign of the times – and arrived a little late to meet Professor Shadmi at the American Colony. He smelled of pipe tobacco and I thought I might get myself a pipe too – it gives a man a touch of importance. We walked over to the nearby Al-Hurriyeh.

Abu George was waiting at the entrance, and it was only a few minutes' walk to a fine gallery of antiquities. The owner, Abu Sharif, welcomed us warmly, sat us down in the hospitality corner and exchanged polite chitchat with Abu George. Professor Shadmi carefully examined the artefacts and chose a splendid antique pottery jar and, as agreed, he left the bargaining to Abu George.

"This is our finest piece," said the owner, looking at it lovingly. Abu George turned his hand in a gesture that asked, How much? Abu Sharif went to his desk, put on his reading glasses and declared, "Two thousand lira."

"And for me?"

"Whatever you say."

"Meaning what?"

"One thousand nine-hundred and fifty."

"Is that a price for a friend?" Abu George took out his *masbaha* and began to roll the beads.

"For Yasmine, one thousand and eight-hundred."

Abu George's hand made a small movement indicating displeasure, as if to say, You're shaming me. Abu Sharif lowered the price by another fifty lira.

"*Mush maakul*, unbelievable, that you're doing this to me in front of my honourable guests…Do you know who they are?"

For a moment I feared that he would use our identities by way of pressure, and we would appear to be abusing our position for personal gain. But throughout Abu George had spoken to us in French, as if we were visitors from France, and the price went down by another fifty lira.

An Israeli officer came in with his wife and after a few minutes selected some ancient coins. The owner looked into the catalogue and named his price.

The officer asked in English, "Excuse me, but is this the final price?"

Abu Sharif took off his reading glasses, laid his hand on his breast and with a severe expression and in a slightly offended tone replied, "Of course, sir. We do not bargain."

The officer paid up and they left.

Abu George hummed under his breath and suppressed a smile. "Can you imagine a Jordanian officer paying you like this and leaving?"

"Don't even remind me. That lot! They drank my coffee, took whatever they fancied, and at best threw me a few coins."

"*Wallah*, what can I say? You're throwing us out," Abu George said bitterly in a low voice, as if to say, Maybe I should have taken them to the rival shop.

Abu Sharif, knowing the next move, went over to his desk,

picked up the latest issue of *Falastin al-Thawra*, and said, "Abu George, have you read the interview with Musa al-Alami?" And without waiting for the reply he began to read aloud: "The Arab armies came in '48 to defend the Palestinians from the Zionist tyranny, but abandoned them, forced them to emigrate and leave their homeland, put them in political and ideological quarantine, and threw them into ghettoes...I ask you, is this how a leader of ours should be speaking?"

In the meantime tea was brought in, and the two continued to discuss the political situation and the Arab countries, and for a while it looked as if they'd forgotten all about the purchase and turned the gallery into a debating club. The bargaining process became a battle of attrition between the two sides. At one point Abu George became annoyed and stood up as if to go. The gallery owner put on a grim expression.

"*Tayeb*, all right," he said. "Final price: one thousand and fifty lira."

"We've known each other for twenty years, haven't we, Abu Sharif? You're like a cousin to me, and if after all this...And for a few measly lira...I don't know what to think," said Abu George, clearing his throat as if words failed him.

It was obvious that Abu Sharif was uncomfortable, and to gain time he offered Abu George a pinch of snuff. He was about to offer some to us, but Abu George stopped him with a glance that said, Can't you see they are French? What would they do with your snuff?

"There used to be honour among us, a sense of shame, Arab generosity. Where has it all gone?" muttered Abu George as if talking to himself, staring vaguely into space. After a few hearty sneezes he stood up. "*Esma*, listen brother. Wrap up that jar and with it the little pitcher beside it and this plate, and take what's owing to you." He took out a bundle of notes and began to count them, with Abu Sharif's sharp eyes watching his fingers. Abu George put nine hundred lira on the table.

"The pitcher and the plate alone cost three-hundred and fifty lira, I swear by my children," Abu Sharif said mournfully.

"*Yallah*, brother, pack it up and let us go," Abu George pronounced the final verdict.

Outside Professor Shadmi shook Abu George's hand, thanked him warmly and invited him and Um George, Yasmine and me to his house for a drink.

"What wouldn't I do for you," said Abu George, looking pleased.

"Bargaining is a confusing experience. You always come out feeling you've been had," I said.

"Bargaining is an art form with its own laws," opined Professor Shadmi. "It's a subtle and oblique power play expressing the natural interests of the two sides, until they reach equilibrium. It also calls for considerable dramatic talent and knowing how far you can pull the rope without breaking it. In short, it's a whole subject that needs studying, and not everyone has the inborn ability for it, like tightrope walking."

"Bless your brilliant tongue, Abu Mehammed," said Abu George. "It's part of the ancient civilisation of the East that the modern West doesn't fully understand and despises as untrustworthy and silly pretence. 'You can't take them at their word,' they say, with superficial condescension. Only a few see it as you do...And now, gentlemen, let me invite you to lunch."

"Many thanks, but Mrs Shadmi will kill me if I break my diet," the professor winked, hailed a taxi and went off.

Aliza came into my office and put a jug of cold water and a bundle of letters on my desk. A pretty blue envelope addressed in

English caught my eye. Inside was a poem with a note that said, "Dear Nuri, when we met at Al-Hurriyeh after the dinner at my house you read me a poem. Here is another one. Yasmine."

The Face of the Homeland by Tadeusz Różewicz:

> Homeland is childhood's land
> the place of birth,
> the small and nearest land.
>
> A city, town or village,
> street, house, yard,
> a first love,
> a distant wood,
> graves.
>
> In childhood you learn
> the flowers, herbs, wheat,
> animals,
> pastures,
> words, cows.
>
> The homeland laughs
>
> At first homeland
> is near
> accessible
>
> Only later does it grow
> bleed
> hurt.

I folded the note and the poem, tucked them back into the pretty envelope and put it in a drawer. The naughty girl, when we met this morning she said nothing about sending me a letter.

21

Picnic with Michelle

Michelle phoned and asked me to join her on a family picnic by the sea on Saturday. I tried to put her off, saying I had a lot of work to do, but couldn't resist her urging. "Please come, I need you. Helene and Robert, my sister and brother-in-law, who happens to be my future husband's business partner, are here, and they've joined my sick mother in pressuring me to get married. They won't give me a moment's peace unless you're there."

We left early in her Peugeot 404, which she had bought tax-free as a privileged new immigrant. After a smooth ride, and sooner than I expected, we arrived at an attractive site between Herzliya and Kibbutz Gaash. Settling under a big beach umbrella facing the calm sea, we enjoyed the salty breeze. Helene and Michelle set a lavish picnic table from which rose tantalising smells of smoked fish, choice salamis and, naturally, strong French mustard.

Robert produced wine from the vineyard he owned with Jean-Claude. He poured a glass for each of us and breathing deeply he said in a solemn tone, "Just sniff! Sniff!"

I did, and smelled an aroma that caressed my nasal passages. We raised our glasses and I was pleasantly surprised by the smooth, lively taste, delicate and not rough on the throat.

Michelle was affectionate, obviously in control of things, and I admit I co-operated with her. I knew I was helping to show her family that her life did not depend on Jean-Claude.

After a number of glasses Robert declared that he was hoping to settle on the West Bank and start a big winery. "Can you help me with this, Nuri?" he asked, and suddenly I wasn't enjoying the wine quite as much.

"I know nothing about it. What do you need to start a winery?"

"Grapes!" he laughed.

"Why now?"

"The wars are finished, my friend! It is time for wine, for restaurants. You deserve to live like human beings, like the French and the Scandinavians, to occupy your minds with the really big issues, like where to go on holiday, where to have fun."

"The Messianic age, no less!"

"A normal life, *mon cher*, that's all. You people don't know how to live, and if you'll forgive me, you could learn something from us," he said, stroking Helene's arm.

"It's useless talking to him about leisure," said Michelle. "It was hard enough getting him to come out with us today. And he's never been abroad in his life."

"Why on the West Bank in particular?" I asked.

"Because there it's possible to grow high-quality grapes. We found Bordeaux-quality grapes in Bethlehem and Hebron."

"And if we give the territories back?"

"Why should you? Because of some Leftist Israeli intellectuals who suffer from a double guilt complex – as if we crucified both Jesus and the Palestinians? If I'd known that you read French I'd have brought you some of their articles in *Le Monde*. Why should we give up the land that was conquered with our blood?" He lit a cigar and flung the match on to the sand.

"Take it easy, Robert. Those intellectuals are not the left, they are advocates for the Palestinians," said Michelle. She took Helene's hand and they went for a swim.

A young couple were playing with a bat and ball nearby. The regular thump of the ball against the wooden bats was the backdrop to Robert's grandiose speeches about "the land of our forefathers". I felt like telling him he should come over here first, serve in the army and pay taxes, before setting up his winery in Samaria. He talked as if he was one of the old pioneers, eager to take his place, and from his residence in Paris compose another verse for the pioneer song "We shall be the first".

The woman playing beside us was young and tall, with shapely thighs. She moved lightly over the sand, but her strokes were powerful. God had given this woman so much beauty, grace and charm. Who could say what was best about her – her hair, face, shoulders, breasts, waist, hips, thighs? She was fantastic.

"You see what I see, huh?" Robert winked at me. He was dipping sausages in mustard and chewing happily. "Eat some of these sausages, they are kosher," he urged me. He poured more wine, following the same ritual as before – sniffing it first and sighing with delight. "Wine has a delicate soul," he explained. "It needs a loving home, the right temperature and darkness. Light and heat can make it lose its flavour."

I joined Michelle and Helene in the sea and lay without moving in the salt water, floating like a tarred fishing boat on the Tigris. A rare calm enveloped me. I must bring Yasmine here, I thought.

*

In the late afternoon, as the Sabbath ended, we returned to Jerusalem. Back in her apartment and after a shower, Michelle embraced me. An invigorating scent like that of a fresh melon wafted around her while in the background was the passionate voice of the French-Armenian singer Charles Aznavour.

Michelle kissed me. "*Ooh la la!* You're still drunk."

I was thinking about Aznavour, feeling that I'd just grasped the distinct quality of his singing. It was a blend of overflowing heart with the melancholy of a refugee clinging to a slender branch.

"Yesterday I had a weird day with your Yasmina," Michelle's voice came through. "She curdled my brain talking about that Negro, that Franz Fanon of hers…"

"Franz Fanon?…Ah yes, the intellectual guru she talked about when I brought her to the youth village."

"She says, quoting him, that 'racism creates psychological structures which prevent the black man from perceiving to what extent he is enslaved by the pseudo-universal white norm, and that the racist culture destroys the mental health of the black person,' and so on and so forth…"

"What's it got to do with us?" I asked.

"Don't you see the analogy? Clearly she is drawing a parallel between the Negroes and the Palestinians. In her eyes we are white racist colonialists. I told you your Yasmina is a tough case…"

"That's enough, you're doing my head in."

Michelle's face froze.

I stopped myself. Why was I taking it out on her? "I'm sorry…I had a really awful argument with my boss and I've no strength left for any more aggro."

"Something is eating at you the whole time," she said.

"Ideas, doubts."

"A revolution needs decisive people, not the Prince of Denmark. Maybe this job isn't right for you."

I said nothing.

"Why didn't you take me to the dinner party at Abu George's?"

I was stumped for an answer. "Well...I thought it would be a boring formal dinner..."

"You don't even know how to live," she declared.

I stood up and spread my arms wide. Michelle apparently interpreted this as an invitation to dance and she came into my embrace. I took hold of her waist and we moved slowly. Her body felt soft and her eyes were dreamy, but I felt dizzy. "I must sit down," I said.

"You never forget yourself, do you. Your mind is always in control, always working. You want coffee?"

"Water – and coffee," I said to please her.

"Your Yasmina has a Palestinian friend in Paris, did you know?" she asked, looking at my face. "Fayez is his name. He's also an admirer of Fanon. She says Fayez has concluded that our occupation has created the Palestinian nation, and that only their peasants and the refugees will liberate the Palestinians from the colonial yoke of Israel. Do you understand?"

"Interesting, with me she's never discussed these ideas."

"She's cleverer than you think," Michelle declared and sat on my lap. "You haven't given me one kiss today, and you haven't even noticed that I have a new hairdo," she whispered.

"I was waiting for the right moment," I said, my hand on her back.

"Yes, yes, *mon amour*, stroke my back, it makes me feel so

good, go on..." She unbuttoned my shirt and led me to the bed.

My head felt heavy. I shouldn't have drunk so much wine. I wanted to sleep, to curl up in my own shell. How will I drive home? Perhaps I should stay. Michelle silenced the music.

"The light," I pleaded. "Turn it off."

"I like it in the light," she insisted, muttering words of love in French. I echoed them in her ears, until my head sank into the pillow and I slept soundly.

When I woke up I dragged myself to the shower, her cave of fragrances. After a while she joined me, a glass of white wine in one hand and a Gitane in the other. I could only envy her free spirit. I dressed quickly, bashful about standing there naked.

"You're not staying?"

"Sorry, I don't have a toothbrush or a razor..."

"I got them for you," she opened a drawer and showed me.

"I need a change of clothes."

She looked at me sharply. "Why are you leaving me alone?"

I avoided her eyes and went out into the cool autumn night. I started the car and suddenly felt a cry rising inside me: Yasmine! Yasmine! Damn you! Why are you an Arab, a Christian, a Palestinian? Why? Come to me. I want to love you in Arabic and in Hebrew and in all the languages of the world. I want to make babies with you. Yasmine, Yasmine, Yasmine, where are you? I hit the steering wheel repeatedly.

I stopped the car. Take it easy, I told myself.. Don't gamble with your life. That's one sure way to lose Yasmine. And tonight, after all that drinking, what you really need is a bucket beside the bed.

22

Out of Prison

"I'm happy to inform you that your uncle, Hizkel Imari, has been released from prison in Iraq and will be arriving at Lod tomorrow," Mr Katz, of Special Operations in the Ministry of Defence, informed me by phone.

"I don't believe it. Are you sure?"

"I talked to him last night. He's feeling well and will land here tomorrow afternoon. We shall expect your family in the VIP lounge at the airport at 3.30."

My heart was racing as I reached for the phone. I wanted so much to share the great news, but who with? My parents still didn't have a phone. Kabi was out of the country, and I had no idea where he was. Should I phone Yasmine? No, that would seem odd. I couldn't stay in my office a moment longer and hurried to my parents' home. On the way I bought drinks, nuts and a huge bunch of flowers.

"You're bringing good news, son. Are you getting married?" Mother gave me a wink at the sight of the flowers. Father got up and laid down the Egyptian weekly he was reading.

"You won't believe it! Hizkel has been freed and will be here tomorrow!"

Father stood still, his mouth open and his hands trembling.

Mother ordered him to sit down and not get excited, and began to ululate with joy.

"Stop your *halahel*," Father warned her. "Don't tempt fate!"

"Blessed be He who made miracles for our forefathers and for us." Mother kissed me and continued ululating, undeterred.

We sat in the kitchen. The weather was cool. Father lit a cigarette, despite his doctor's orders. His eyes were red and he covered them with his hand. I knew he was thinking back twenty years, to the night when the police raided our house in Baghdad, searching for weapons and Hebrew books. Father pretended to be ill and stayed in bed, and Kabi, who was sixteen, followed the police in their exhaustive search through our spacious house, the seven rooms on two floors, plus the attic. I can still remember the thumps, and the screams and cries of Hizkel's wife Rashel and my mother, and how they dragged my uncle off to their dungeons. Only after months of nerve-racking anxiety and lack of information did Father locate his brother in Baghdad's Central Prison, but despite all his efforts to get him released he remained there. Since coming to Israel Father had not ceased punishing himself for leaving his brother in prison in Iraq, under the hangman's noose.

"Why isn't Kabi here?" Father asked.

"Nuri's here," Mother said, offended on my behalf.

"Sorry, son, I didn't mean to hurt you," Father apologised, laying his hand on my shoulder.

I knew I could never take my elder brother's place in Father's heart. Kabi would speak for Father when he went to the Labour Exchange, to the Sick Fund clinic, to Hadassah. They used to sit together in the café, smoke a narghile, drink arrack and discuss the state of the world. Father had no other friend, and since Kabi had gone to Europe he felt lonely, despite my best efforts.

"Here's to Hizkel," said Mother, and as a special treat offered Father a glass of arrack with a plate of almonds.

"Woman, I won't believe it till I see him with my own two eyes," Father said, rejecting the drink, afraid of celebrating too soon.

"Did they say anything about Rashel?" Mother asked and I shook my head. "What? She's staying with the Muslim?" she fumed. Later, when she calmed down, she asked me to take her to the market in the city centre to shop for the occasion.

Back in my office I called the emergency number in Europe that Kabi had given me, but there was no answer so I asked his contact man in Tel Aviv to pass on the good news, and turned on the radio. The announcer said there had been an explosion on Jaffa Road, in the city centre.

I jumped in the car and drove like a madman. I didn't know where to start looking for Mother. Part of King George Street was closed to traffic, so I ran to Ben Yehuda Street and Jaffa Road, to the Number 4 bus stop and the Mahaneh Yehuda market, but couldn't see her. If I'd only known what she meant to buy and where! If only they had a phone at home! What kind of a state was it that boasted its army could reach the steppes of the USSR, but couldn't provide telephone lines to its citizens? I should have stayed with Mother to help with the shopping and take her home. Maybe she'd already gone home? I jumped back in the car and drove at high speed in the opposite direction, to Katamon. Covered with sweat I rushed up the shadowy path leading to the housing estate. It was then that I saw her, standing on the kitchen balcony, smoking. I stood where I was for a few moments, catching my breath, and drove home.

I was due to meet Yasmine in an hour, to return an article she had written and wanted my opinion on. As I didn't trust my own judgment, I gave it to someone in the Ministry of Social Welfare to read: he praised it highly and drew attention to the writer's keen acumen.

To my surprise, the first words Yasmine spoke when we met were, "You heard what happened on Jaffa Road? Are you and your family all right?"

She's human after all, I thought to myself, relieved. "Thank heavens, yes, you can't imagine how worried I was – I had left my mother there as she wanted to do some shopping." I couldn't resist telling her about Uncle Hizkel.

"I suppose it's part of an exchange of prisoners of war."

"I haven't the slightest idea!"

She wanted to know about him. I commended his literary and journalistic talents, his efforts to start a school for working boys, his political foresight in urging the Jewish community of Baghdad to pack up and leave…I was like a mule claiming that its uncle was a thoroughbred racehorse. We chatted for some time. I asked her what she thought about the terrorist attacks by infiltrators, like the one in the centre of town today. She viewed them as a revolt against the defeat, a message to Nasser that he was sour milk and to the King that he was a withered tree. My body was intensely awake, my hands burned to touch her, to communicate to her the wonderful tenderness I felt for her, but outwardly I remained frozen, immobile.

The next day, on our way to the airport, Father was distracted. "Well, son, what do you think?" he asked repeatedly and didn't wait for an answer. He kept an unlit cigarette in his mouth, eventually lit it and took short puffs from it, to make it last.

A stewardess met us, took us to the VIP lounge and brought us some soft drinks, but we didn't touch them. Then the door opened and two men came in – Mr Katz from the Ministry of Defence and Hizkel, whom I hardly recognised. His shoulders were slumped, he looked tired, very thin and dull-eyed. His hair was sparse and greying, his cheekbones stood out, his nose looked bigger than I remembered, with deep grooves on either side of it. His old Clark Gable moustache was also grey. He and Father stood and gazed at each other for a long moment. Then Hizkel dropped his bag, Father stepped towards him and they fell into each other's arms and cried as men do, in suppressed sobs. Then Father turned his head towards me, and Hizkel said hesitantly, "Nuri, is that you?" He hugged and kissed me, his eyes wet. When he let go he turned back to Father. "Where is Kabi?"

"We haven't had a chance to tell him," Father replied.

Mr Katz watched us, his face stiff, as if the emotional encounter disturbed him. He gestured to us to vacate the lounge for a group of VIPs who had just arrived and before leaving he asked Hizkel to meet him the following afternoon at the Ministry of Defence in Tel Aviv.

On the way to the car park Hizkel blinked in the sunlight and tried to disguise the stiffness of his right leg. He and Father sat together in the back. "Blessed be He who has kept us alive to this time!" said Father. "We turned everywhere and to everyone, and we never stopped expecting you. Last night Nuri told us that at long last you were coming. I couldn't sleep all night. You know how many times they said they were getting you out? Broke our hearts. But Um Kabi always said you were a righteous man and God would not abandon you. How do you feel, brother, how is your health?"

"*Al-hamdu lillah*, all right, thank God."

Father produced a packet of cigarettes and they smoked in silence.

"Are the boys married?" Hizkel asked.

I said quickly, "In Israel people marry later," and Father added, "Kabi has a girlfriend from America. I think they're ready."

"Where is he?" my uncle asked again.

"In Europe, in *al-mukhabarat*," Father said in a solemn whisper. "Our son Moshi is married and has two children. He's a farmer in a co-operative village, and our sabra Efraim is in a kibbutz."

Hizkel was silent for most of the journey, his eyes on the road. When we reached Bab al-Wad, where the road begins to climb up the mountainside, Father opened the window and took a deep breath, filling his lungs: "The air of Jerusalem!"

"It's good air, very good," said Hizkel, as if knowing what was expected of him, and again he fell silent. "There was nothing I could do," he said at last, as if in reply to an unspoken question. "She stayed there. She has two children by him."

Father lowered his eyes. "That's life," he sighed, then added, "*Inshallah*, a new door will open for you here."

As we entered Jerusalem, Father became animated, naming the neighbourhoods we drove through and talking about the city with a new touch of pride. "In Jerusalem all construction is in stone, no bricks. It's a law from the time of the British Mandate," he said, and Hizkel nodded. "The Old City is a bit like Baghdad. Actually, no…Nuri will show it to you. He has an office in East Jerusalem, he's the advisor to the Minister, to *al-wali* of al-Quds."

Hizkel did not react. He was in shock, I thought.

"Well," Father went on apologetically when we reached Katamon, "we actually live in immigrant housing. It's nothing much, four walls, *al-hamdu lillah*."

Hizkel's limp was even more noticeable when we walked up the path to our house. I wanted to take the bag he had hanging from his shoulder, but he refused the offer. Mother was waiting for us, dressed in her finest, and when she saw us she waved, whooped and threw sweets and flower petals at Hizkel, as if he were a bar mitzvah boy. He smiled for the first time.

"The day we have longed for has come, blessed be His name!" Mother said, wiping away her tears, and she hugged Hizkel the way you hug a brother who has been lost for many years – she always held a special affection for her brother-in-law. She went to the kitchen and came back with tea and freshly baked pastries. As he sipped the hot tea Hizkel's face relaxed, like a thirsty wanderer finding an oasis in the desert.

"Home!" he said, underlining the word with a gesture that embraced the whole room.

"Take a shower," Mother advised, "to wash off the prison." She gave him a towel and new clothes, as well as a shaving kit she had prepared for him.

"I've got my things," he said, pointing to his bag.

"Throw everything out, take new ones."

When we heard him showering she whispered, "*Wawaili*, there's nothing left of him! And what about Rashel?" Father made a dismissive gesture. "Went with the Muslim, huh? Poor thing!"

"Don't raise the subject," Father warned, knowing how it upset Mother to talk about Rashel. It was she who had introduced her to Hizkel, and she always thought of her as her younger sister.

"I smell the smells of home," said Hizkel when he came out of the bathroom.

Father took a big bottle of arrack from the cupboard. "First we'll have a drink and say the blessing. This is arrack from Ramallah that I bought after the liberation of Jerusalem and I vowed we'd open it when you came. I was not sure if I'd live to do this…"

Mother filled a plate with various delicacies and gave it to Hizkel. He ate slowly.

"A blessing on your hands," he said. "Do you remember you used to send Kabi to bring me Sabbath *hamin* in prison? The smell of it kept me alive inside."

"Where did they hold you?" Father asked.

"In Nograt Salman, a hell hole, no roads lead to it, seven hours' drive through the desert from the Samawa railway station. In winter it's cut off for four months, only an experienced navigator on camelback can reach it. It's a horror. Burning by day, freezing by night. Revolting food, filthy water. And you can't run away. Anyone who tries ends up dead. If the guards don't kill you, the desert will."

"How did you get out in the end?" Mother asked.

"*Wallah*, I don't know. A prison officer came and told me someone important in Baghdad was going to smuggle me out. I was sure it was a trap, but he swore by the Prophet and by his children. Then the commander of the Central Prison in Baghdad came to inspect the place. They say he would sell his mother for money, that he used to be a general in the army but after Abd al-Karim Kassem was killed he was transferred to the prison service, a humiliation which he swore to avenge. One night I was taken to him, and he said that important people in London wanted to free me and would pay a lot of money…"

"London?" Mother interrupted. "Kabi is there."

"What are you thinking of, woman?" Father laughed.

"I didn't sleep for many nights. I didn't believe it. But I thought, why trick me now, they had twenty years in which to hang me."

"We moved heaven and earth to get you out," Father repeated.

"After a couple of weeks I thought they had forgotten about it. Then one night, after roll call, the officer took me out of the fortress, drove for hours in a military vehicle, handed me over to three Bedouins and said, 'These are your guides. Goodbye.'

"The Bedouins made me put on a woman's abaya, headscarf and a veil, and forbade me to talk. We drove and drove, I don't know where. Now and then they warned me about checkpoints. At night we got out of the vehicle and started walking. We walked for hours in the darkness, then they handed me over to three other Bedouins, who had two more 'mute women' with them. It was hot as hell, so I knew we were in the south. By the evening I smelled water and there was a nice breeze, so I guessed we were near a river. Then we reached a big marsh, and they put me and the two other 'women' on a boat and in the night we crossed the border into Iran."

"Iran?" Mother said excitedly. "A Thousand and One Nights!"

"In Iran too they passed me from hand to hand like a parcel. Finally they took me into a cheap inn and told me to open the door only if I heard two knocks, then nothing, then two more knocks. What can I say? A regular spy story. Near midnight I heard the knocks and someone said, 'Shalom' in Hebrew, then in our Jewish-Iraqi Arabic, 'Don't be afraid, you're in good hands.' The contact gave me men's clothes and we went to the airport, I don't know where it was, and we flew to Tehran. There he gave me a case of documents and said, 'You're flying to Israel – safe journey!' And here I am."

"*Ya Allah*, blessed be His name!" said Mother. "Abu Kabi, tomorrow morning take your brother to the synagogue to say the *HaGomel*."

After the meal Hizkel took off his shoes and sat cross-legged on the bed with the glass of arrack in his hand.

"How is our communist cousin, Selim Effendi?" he asked.

"Charcoal on his face, he and his communism," replied Father. "Have you heard about Khruschev's speech? The millions killed by Stalin?"

Hizkel nodded.

"All kinds of things happened to him. I don't know what he's doing nowadays."

"He's opened an import-export agency dealing with the West Bank and the Gaza Strip," I said.

"Exchanged the Communist Manifesto for dinars," Father chuckled.

"But Abu Saleh el-Hibaz, who saved his life, was hanged!" said Hizkel bitterly.

"That's how it is," sighed Father.

"What about your dream of growing rice in Israel?"

Father remained silent and rolled the beads of his *masbahah*.

"We'll see what they've got for me in the Ministry of Defence," said Hizkel.

At midnight I left and drove home, tired and dispirited.

The next day, though he was still visibly tired, Hizkel was excited about his forthcoming visit to the Ministry of Defence. His eyes were red, and Mother put her prescription drops in his eyes.

Father wanted to come along – "Let's have no more

separation!" – but as soon as we left Jerusalem he fell asleep and started to snore. Hizkel looked at the landscape and said nothing, then he also fell asleep.

I escorted him to Mr Katz's office in the government complex and after their meeting, which did not take long, I took Father and Hizkel, who used to be a well-known journalist, to the café of the Press Association in Tel Aviv. I thought he'd want to tell us about his meeting with Katz, but he remained silent, frowning, and we didn't press him.

From there we drove to Aliyah Street to buy clothes at the shop of Father's old friend Abu Yusef, an Iraqi Jew who spoke Hebrew in the classical, prayer-book manner. Abu Yusef clothed the three of us from head to foot, gave us a large discount and blessed Hizkel.

"You've spent a lot of money on me, brother," said Hizkel on the way to the car.

"I've got it all written down, and when you start working you'll repay it with compound interest," Father joked. Then he turned serious and finally asked, "What happened to your leg?"

"They crushed my knee, the Iraqi Bureau of Investigations."

"We'll take you to Hadassah, maybe something can be done," I suggested.

"It's irreparable."

We had lunch in the Hatikvah Market in south Tel Aviv. I phoned Aliza to find out what was happening in East Jerusalem, and called Levanah to hear about the western city. I asked to speak to the Minister and thanked him for his effort. "Blessed be He who unshackles the captives," said my socialist Minister. "Look after your unshackled captive. The Arabs of East Jerusalem will not run away, and if you need anything don't hesitate to ask." It made me feel better.

"What did they offer you in the Ministry of Defence?" Father asked Hizkel over steaming chai after a light meal.

"Nothing."

"So why did they ask you to come in?"

"No idea. They asked about the Ba'ath party, not that there was much I could tell them, and they asked what the political prisoners are saying and the communists, and if there are revolutionary cells. A waste of time. I thought they would ask about the movement, about those who sacrificed their lives, about Abu Saleh, may he rest in peace. They didn't."

"The past is dead," Father concluded gloomily.

On the way back Father said, as if getting a painful weight off his chest, "It still tears my heart that I had to abandon you and Rashel."

Hizkel compressed his lips, shifted in his seat and stared out of the window. "Could you have saved me, or her?"

We went on in silence but when we entered the house the mood changed. Mother had come back from the Old City with a hamsa and other amulets for good luck and against the evil eye, gave some to each of us and kept some for Kabi, Efraim, Moshi and the grandchildren. She had also bought fresh roasted coffee, which filled the house with its aroma, dried figs, dates and white raspberries. We opened our packages and showed her the clothes we bought at Abu Yusef's. "Wonderful!" she congratulated us. "Why didn't you buy more?" Then she turned beaming to Hizkel and asked what housing and what sort of work they had offered him.

"You mean they offered you nothing?" she said, astonished by his vague replies.

"They told me to go to the Jewish Agency, the Ministry of

Absorption. I didn't understand it all...They wrote it down for me." He showed us a piece of paper.

"Charcoal on their faces! Is that the way to treat a 'prisoner of Zion'? Next time I'll go with you!"

"You take care of your uncle, son. You lived in a kibbutz, you understand the way they think," Father said, handing Hizkel over to me. He had said the same when he decided to move from the immigrant camp in Pardes Hanna to Jerusalem.

"Soon," Mother added, "we'll all celebrate together, please God. Phone Kabi, Moshi and Efraim, and don't forget Sandra!"

23

Two Authorities

About a week after I met Ghadir in the street she came to my office. Hesitant, her eyes lowered, she stood in the doorway. She was dressed in a grey gown that reached her ankles, with a white scarf on her head, and holding a large wicker basket.

"Sit down, *ya* Ghadir, welcome!"

She perched on the edge of the chair, glancing at me and around the office – a place so far removed from the fields of Jebel Sacobos, Mount Scopus, where we had met nine years before. I was delighted to see this now mature young woman, who was as lovely as she had been then, if not more so, and was curious to find out what had brought her to me.

"*Mabruk*, may you succeed!" she greeted me and took from her basket a bunch of Bedouin pittas wrapped in a white cloth, and laid them on the table with some salt beside them, the way they are offered to guests at the gate of a city. To this dish she added a bottle of olive oil and some za'atar in a twist of paper.

Her humble offering touched me. "Blessing on your hands," I said, and to please her I fetched a plate from the kitchen, took one of the fresh pittas, dribbled olive oil on it, sprinkled it with salt and za'atar, and chewed it with loud lip-smacking noises. She smiled at me with her gleaming teeth:

"You eat like a born son of Arabia!"

"What will you have, coffee, tea, cola?"

"You serve me? Impossible! I'll get it."

"You're my guest. It would be shameful if you made the coffee in my office."

"You don't have someone to make you coffee, like they do in the Ministry of the Interior?"

"I do, but she's left already. Why did you mention the Ministry of the Interior? Does it have to do with the problem you haven't told me about yet?" Guessing that she felt uncomfortable bringing me her troubles, I raised the subject first.

"I have problems, and don't know what to do anymore," she said, looking at me. "I told you that in the end they married me to a cousin from Amman, Issam. He's all salt through and through, not a grain of sugar. But what can I do? I can't leave him, that's how it is among us. Now things are difficult. A few days before the war he went to Amman to see his family, and now he can't come back and insists that I must go to him. What will I do in Amman with just him and his family? We don't even have children, Allah didn't want us to. Here at least I'm in my own home with my mother, but there I'll be like a dead woman. He should come back here – it's how we planned it, that he would go, see his family and come back. We didn't know there would be a war and al-Quds would be separated from Amman."

"Have you applied for family reunification at the Ministry of the Interior?"

"Every day they say come tomorrow. You know Mr Haramati?"

"Yes, I'll talk to him. First give me all the details."

"I thought you'd want them so I brought our documents," she said and produced a bundle of creased papers from the pocket of her gown.

When I'd copied all the necessary information she said, "I'm afraid. I'm terribly afraid of him. He's a strange man, capable of anything. It's not a simple matter. Issam is religious, a Sufi, like my father, and they have some strange customs. One night I followed them in secret, I wanted to see what they did in their ceremonies. And what did I see? Issam and my father and all the men there standing in a circle, holding on to each other, their eyes shut, singing and dancing, jumping up and down like the billy goats in my flock." She smiled faintly. "Suddenly they went crazy, started shaking themselves like maniacs, tossing their heads from side to side and shouting 'Allah, Allah, Allah!' and foaming at the mouth…"

"*Allahu akbar, allahu akbar!*" the muezzin calling the evening prayer broke into the quiet office, startling Ghadir. For a moment I too felt that the muezzin's call was an angry admonition from another world, like a deluge of stones falling from the sky on unruly mortals.

"Don't worry," I said, walking her to the door. "I'll talk to Haramati."

The very next day I went to Haramati's office on Nablus Street. I knew him from joint meetings where he gave the impression of being a bundle of nerves. He chain-smoked, holding the cigarette between his yellowed third and fourth fingers, sucking on it till the embers scorched the skin. He had worked for years in the census bureau, and got his present job because he was a native of the Old City and spoke Arabic. Overnight he turned from an insignificant clerk into a powerful man able to decide people's fates.

The open space in front of his office, which I had passed many times before on my tours of East Jerusalem was, as usual, packed with people. Long lines had been waiting for hours, preoccupied and tense like people awaiting surgery. How would they come out of the encounter with the man who dominated this office? With or without a future life? Would he relieve their distress, or break them?

The daily presence of so many people had turned the open space into a market, the background music provided by the cries of various vendors, individually or in chorus. They sold pretzels with sesame and za'atar, a tamarind drink chilled with ice cubes, fresh pittas and sweet pastries, the usual fare of Arab streets. One curly-headed boy peddled Israeli ice-lollies, calling tirelessly in a sweet high voice, "*Kartiv, Kartiv…*" I pushed through the crowd to reach the door.

"No more numbers," said the usher at the door.

"I'm here to see Mr Haramati," I replied in Arabic and gave my name and title.

To my surprise, Haramati received me affably, like an old friend. He talked volubly and was keen to stress how deeply he was touched by the woes of the local population.

"We're honoured, Mr Imari! Welcome, welcome! You've seen what is going on outside – terrible! The crowding and the pressure, people waiting. So many of them need help, I swear my heart aches for them! We're doing our best for them, that's what we're here for, aren't we, Mr Imari? But how much can we do, and and with all these problems, my head is bursting," he declared and lit another cigarette.

"I'm aware you're in a very difficult and demanding position, Mr Haramati, so I came along to learn from your experience," I said to flatter him, and felt we were duelling with compliments in the time-honoured local tradition.

"Will you have coffee?"

"Many thanks…I came about a particular case, to ask you to see if anything can be done to help." I put Ghadir's and Issam's details on his desk.

"Certainly, certainly, anything I can do. If you came in person it must be important," he said and buzzed for his secretary, who came in. He glanced at the paper I had put before him. "Make a note of these details, look up the case file and let me know how matters stand. This is Mr Imari's particular case, you understand?"

When I gave him my hand in parting he said, "Won't you come with me to the Jewish Quarter? I'm going to the Hurvah Synagogue. The Sephardi Community Board has asked me to see if and how it can be restored."

"Why not?" I replied. "Let me just tell my secretary that I'll be late."

When we came out of the building people rushed at him with questions, appeals and entreaties, and he responded with a smile and sweet talk, much the way he received me. But when we got into the taxi he grumbled, "They jump on me and make my life a misery, who can stand them?" The words and tone contradicted his extravagant show of kindness, but I said nothing.

The taxi entered the Old City through the Jaffa Gate, into the Omar Ibn el-Khatab square, on to the Armenian Quarter and stopped at his request near Zion Gate where we got out and walked to the Jewish Quarter. Construction work was in progress, clouds of blinding dust swirled in the air, and I regretted coming along. We headed for the Hurvah Synagogue which was also known as "The Ruin Synagogue" of Rabbi Yehuda Ha-Hassid, and on the way he told me its history, from the fifteenth century to the arrival of Rabbi Yehuda Ha-Hassid in 1699, to the present time.

"You're amazingly knowledgeable," I said.

"Don't forget I was born and raised in the Jewish Quarter," Haramati said. "During the War of Independence the Jordanian Legion blew up the Hurvah Synagogue. Typical. Doesn't the Book of Genesis say of Ishmael, 'He will be a wild man, his hand will be against every man and every man's hand will be against him.'? You think they've changed?"

His question hung in the air, unanswered.

"Remember what Haramati tells you, a seventh generation child of the Old City: our cousins the Ishmaelites murdered, exiled and kidnapped our brothers, they erased the settlements they seized, not even sparing synagogues and cemeteries and ritual baths, and did not allow a single Jew to remain. Their hour will come."

He looked around him and his face became grim. "This is where they murdered my father. Every time I come here my heart breaks all over again. God Almighty, they even turned the Stambouli Synagogue into a stable. And after all they have done, our Minister of Defence – before my very eyes – hands over the keys of the Temple Mount to the Mufti! What for? So they can go on inciting hatred against us and stop us from entering? What a monstrous scene! The day that Moshe Dayan met the Mufti I couldn't work, I couldn't continue to serve the malefactors, our sworn enemies. What was Dayan afraid of? Did we not capture the site with the blood of our sons? Ever since that damnable day I have lain awake at night. My heart tells me that this is the end, that we lost even though we won." Then he walked up to a cold-drinks kiosk, gulped down a bottle of soda water, and lit a cigarette.

*

I could understand Haramati's emotional outburst. I too had been astounded that day when the Minister of Defence made his historic tour of the Temple Mount, shortly after the liberation of the Western Wall.

"Colonel" Amitai and I were in an army jeep following the car that was taking Dayan to meet the Mufti of Jerusalem. Everything happened very fast. Dayan stepped out of the car and was immediately mobbed by officers, aides, reporters and photographers, as if he were a divine being. He tried but failed to extricate himself from the close ring of his entourage and the cameras in order to speak to the local people. I was also disappointed that on my very first visit to the Temple Mount I was unable to see anything.

Suddenly Amitai and I found ourselves sitting within the inner circle. To our amazement the Minister sat down cross-legged and the Mufti of Jerusalem sat beside him. We did the same. The Minister opened with some Arabic pleasantries, then continued in Hebrew, and Amitai acted as an interpreter for the two men.

I was extremely uneasy. Just a few yards away, on the nearby steps of the mosque, King Abdullah, grandfather of King Hussein, had been assassinated fifteen years before. What if someone tried to assassinate the Minister? They said he was a totally fearless man who sometimes risked his life for no good reason. It was utterly insane to sit cross-legged on the floor near the Moslem shrines, surrounded by Arabs whose world had just collapsed on them, with the smell of their dead still hanging in the air. It seemed as if nobody was thinking of the danger, least of all the Minister himself.

I examined the face that was recognised all over the world – fine features, a reddish-brown complexion, a big bald head, a careless grin on his face, and the famous black eye patch. Was that the secret of his charm? So many stories were told about him. It was said that hidden under the patch was a black hole and constant, searing pain. They said he was impatient and short-tempered, but here there was no sign of it. He was charming, grinning like a boy, attracting all eyes.

Anxiety upset my concentration. Relax, calm down, I told myself. Are you taking the security of Israel upon yourself? You think the army and the Shin Bet and the police are asleep? Don't worry, take it easy the way he does and listen.

The Mufti of Jerusalem spoke calmly, raised issues, Amitai interpreted and the Minister dealt with them on the spot, like Haroun al-Rashid who walked about the marketplace and judged the people there and then. Dayan stated that he wanted the Arabs of Israel to come and worship on Fridays at the Temple Mount shrines from which they had been cut off for two decades, beginning the very next Friday. The regional commander glanced quizzically at the chief of operations.

"And the Arabs of the West Bank?" the Mufti asked.

"They will be welcome too."

"And who will be in charge of the mosques?" the Mufti asked, encouraged by the gesture.

"Your people," Dayan replied impassively.

The Mufti raised his head, looked left and right, and passed his hand over his face as if to hide his expression of smug satisfaction.

Mr Harish of the Ministry of Religious Affairs appeared to have turned to stone.

The excitement was overwhelming: I thought I could hear the wings of history beating overhead, could see its heroes, hear their breathing. Generations to come would remember this event, I thought, and here I was in the middle of it all, hearing every sound, capable of writing the chronicle of this time.

Dayan stood up and everyone followed. "From now on, stay close to me," he said to Amitai, and I envied him.

I left the Temple Mount feeling both elated and uncertain. Had the Minister been too hasty in his historic decision? The rumour had spread through the Old City and Muslims began to dance and shout for joy, blocking the narrow alleys. I felt lonely in the midst of the happy commotion, as if I'd been defeated in battle.

I hurried to report to my boss on the scene I had just witnessed. The Minister was shocked, but before he could launch into one of his analyses, Levanah came in and said I had been summoned to the Mayor's office for an urgent meeting.

More than twenty people crowded into Teddy Kollek's office to discuss the imminent opening of the Temple Mount for prayers. I had long before learned that such meetings were simply a managerial ploy, intended to foster the illusion that the management mattered. The really important decisions were taken privately by individuals: Ben-Gurion consulted and listened to various views, but in the end decided on his own, sometimes collapsing under the burden; Eshkol also took difficult decisions and developed his best ideas when alone, mainly by consulting himself while shaving; now the Minister of Defence had taken a unilateral decision to turn the Temple Mount over to the Mufti.

Since joining my Minister's consultative team I had learned it was not what was said that counted, but who said it. A triviality spoken by a person in power could sound like an important statement, and this made most meetings useless. If the person in power knew his own mind the meeting was at best a ritual. Nevertheless, if you were not invited you were as good as dead in the eyes of your colleagues and superiors. Years later the participants would tell everyone that they were present at that meeting, and I would tell my grandchildren that I was there when the one-eyed Minister of Defence entrusted the Temple Mount to the Mufti of Jerusalem.

I looked at the people present and wondered who would dare to speak up in such a forum. The Mayor, charming, impatient, sharp-tongued, was liable to interrupt you and leave you feeling you had wet your trousers. You never knew when this hyper-energetic man might explode; in a flash the enchanting smile would disappear from his face to be replaced by a severe and menacing expression. It was said that on occasion he smashed telephone receivers if he was not answered immediately. Everyone knew he was in a hurry to develop Jerusalem and establish new and solid facts on the ground.

Teddy Kollek leaned back in his seat and puffed on a thick cigar – one of his weaknesses. Haramati had the floor and he launched into a fierce tirade against the permission granted to the Arabs of Israel and the territories to pray at the Temple Mount. He made no mention of the handing over of the site to the Mufti, which he considered a catastrophe. Perhaps he was afraid to overdo the criticism of his superiors.

"Nuri, how many do you think will come to Friday prayers?" the Mayor asked me.

"Masses," I replied. "They will rush to the mosques as we rushed to the Western Wall. It will be necessary to manage the stream of visitors, to make sure the media bring the news to the world and the Arab states, and to involve the heads of the Arab communities in Israel so they'll feel part of the endeavour."

"Why take chances so soon?" said the chief of Jerusalem police. "The no-man's land between the two parts of the city is peppered with mines, a serious danger."

"Security problems will still be with us a month from now," I argued. Young as I was, I always preferred to take the decisive and unequivocal line.

The Mayor telephoned the Minister of Defence and urged him to postpone implementation, at least until after the mines had been cleared. His expression and the way he slammed down the receiver left no room for doubt: "He won't budge," he said.

Now Haramati and I walked back through the maze of alleys which confused me but not him. He made his way confidently, as if by smell.

The subject of Ghadir came up again the following Thursday, in the weekly team meeting. As we entered the conference room Haramati said, "I haven't forgotten your problem. Ghadir al-Sadek! Such a nice name, rare and unforgettable. Give me a little time. I'm waiting for some material. She came to my office and my secretary brought her in to speak to me. A real beautiy," he winked at me and sat down beside me.

We were joined by Shamluk from the secret service, the Shin Bet. He was wearing one of his colourful checked shirts which always seemed too short, perhaps because of his awkward long arms that he didn't know what to do with. Nevertheless his posture showed that he fancied himself an attractive male dressed in a bohemian style. At our meetings he would report in a clipped authoritative voice about current security and Hostile Terror Activity – as opposed to non-hostile terror activity? He constantly urged us to gather information about everything and everyone: properties, family connections, relations between the leaders and the various ethnic and religious communities, and seek out personal weaknesses, information about intimate relations, tendencies and hobbies. He thought of himself as an Arabist, an orientalist who understood the Arab psyche, and liked to season his speech with appropriate expressions and clichés.

"*Sakhtin wa-hana*, here's to your health and pleasure," he greeted me with a sly grin. "I saw you chatting with Yasmine Hilmi, what a beauty! Can she be recruited?"

I was taken aback. "Leave her alone," I said firmly.

"You'd better watch out! She's connected with Arafat's people, probably her father is too. Did you know that the son of Abu Nabil has joined Fatah? Keep your eyes peeled, sniff around, and if you find out anything give us a buzz."

"Who is this Arafat fellow that you haven't been able to catch?"

"A slippery customer who keeps falling on his feet," he snapped. "Don't worry, we'll smash them for him!"

After the meeting I went to Al-Hurriyeh. Yasmine was behind the till and she gave me a nice smile. I turned around and fled to my office. Then I felt ashamed – what was I scared of, Shamluk's gossip? And anyway, what business is it of his whom I see in my private life?

The phone rang. "Did you run away because of me? Don't stay hungry. Come and eat. I'll even let you pay." Yasmine's voice was warm and humorous. It was the first time she had rung me.

Ghadir showed up in the evening, looking agitated. "Am I disturbing you?"

"*Ahlan wa-sahlan*, welcome, come in," I said, rising.

"I thought I should tell you," she said apologetically. "I went to the Ministry of the Interior and Mr Haramati was furious with me. He asked why I went to you, how come I know you and since when, but I didn't tell him anything."

"I'm glad you came, and don't worry." I tried to reassure her, and waited a few days before phoning Haramati.

"Oh, hello, Mr Imari, good to hear from you!" the man gushed. "How are you? Ah yes, about Ghadir. What a lovely name and such a beautiful woman, I swear! She came to see us, did I tell you? We received her very cordially, out of respect for you, of course. We do have a little problem. You surely know that she has a lot of relatives in Jordan, and her husband too is Jordanian. Perhaps it would be best if he stayed among his own family and clan in his own country, and if she also sought her happiness there. I'm only thinking of her welfare, that's my only consideration, I assure you. Perhaps you could tell her this. I'm sure you have influence over her. Sometimes people don't realise what's good for them, and we must open their eyes. Especially our cousins – their history is full of missed opportunities because of their blindness to what happens before their very eyes. As the saying goes, 'Pissing beside the bowl instead of into it', if you'll pardon the expression…What? She doesn't want to move to Amman? But it isn't a deportation! She has already been to the place with her husband, spent a week there, and it would be natural for them to stay there. You surely know that Arabs living in a Jewish state feel ill at ease…"

"Mr Haramati, this is a genuine family issue. Her husband went to visit his father in Amman, and he has the right to return to his wife, to the city where he lived and worked before the war. Otherwise, what's family reunification for? In this particular case it's especially important to let the husband return for her own security."

"Oh, you're suggesting that there's some risk to her life, as it were? You surely don't think her husband will hurt her? Who will cook and wash for him and make his bed and…?" His crude laugh rang down the receiver. "My dear Mr Imari, you wouldn't believe the tricks our cousins use to get what they want, believe me! And there's another point. We have no precise information about her family in this country. It's not clear if they really lived in Jaffa, as she claims, or in Ayn Mahel. What did you say? Ah yes, right, I see in her file that they have relatives in Ghayna, in Galilee. But the record is incomplete. If she could provide us with additional information about her relatives, how long they have lived in this country, and so forth, and if it checks out, we'll reconsider the case – out of regard for you."

"I'll go there and look into it," I said.

"Really? You'll go all the way to Ghayna on her behalf?"

"I have to go to Karmiel soon on business, and Ghayna is not far."

"I understand…My dear Mr Imari, I'm always delighted to talk to you, and please don't hesitate to come to me with any request or problem. After all, what are we here for if not to help?"

My hands were shaking. Why did every exchange with him irritate me so intensely?

Several days passed and Ghadir did not show up. Finally I went to the little pasture alongside the Shimon Hatzadik neighbourhood. Ghadir was sitting on a boulder facing west. Two goats stood near her feet like sentinels. Seeing me she jumped off the rock.

"*Ahlan wasahlan, ya* Nuri!" she called out. "I thought you were angry with me. I pray to Allah every day to take care of you." She hung her head.

"Ghadir, we have to go to Ayn Mahel and to Ghayna."

"*Ya salaam*! I swear I dreamed just this – that I'm going in your car and you're going to meet my family and see that I'm not lying, as Mr Haramati thinks. Allah bless you!"

"Your mother should come with us too."

"Why do you need my mother?"

"You don't know your relatives, you were just three when you left Jaffa. And anyway, how can you travel alone with me? Too big a risk for both of us."

24

The Voice of Israel

A grey wind, laden with leaves and dust, cooled the city. Abu George and Abu Nabil were having their usual joint breakfast while listening to the Arabic language service of Israel Radio. The news reader promised a rerun of a special programme devoted to the "reunification of Jerusalem".

"Dogs!" Abu Nabil roared and silenced the radio. "Say annexation, robbery, plunder, theft, pillage! But reunification? What reunification?"

"Why are you getting so excited? At the most they'll mix their sewage with our sewage," said Abu George, pouring him a glass of lemonade with fresh mint.

"All the sanctity is on our side – the mosques, the churches, the history, even their precious Wall is on our side...Thieves, bandits..."

"Sanctity or sewage, what's the difference? Life is stronger than we are. The Jews came and settled in Jaffa, Haifa, Akko, and changed everything. The smell is not the same smell, the flavour is not the same flavour."

Abu Nabil stared at him and twirled his moustache. In their youth they had both been supporters of the armed struggle, admirers of Izz al-Din Al-Qassam, the Palestinian rebel leader executed by the British. At one point they had even rejected the old Mufti al-Husseini – he wasn't extreme enough for them…What has happened to Abu George, Abu Nabil wondered? It seemed all his vigour was draining away. Was it his age, the troubles, or the last war which had broken his spirit?

He glanced at his watch, and left in a hurry for an appointment with Abu Ammar, the leader of one of their factions. The venue and the time had been changed three times, and they told him to stay at home and wait for instructions. He waited all that day and the following day – nothing. Finally a couple of men he didn't know showed up. They made no mention of the forthcoming meeting with Abu Ammar, only asked in his name for a hardening of the newspaper's political stance, to prepare the ground for the *muqawameh*, the resistance movement, in al-Quds, the West Bank and Gaza. Finally they gave him a message from his son Nabil, who had been training in an unnamed Arab country for the previous three weeks.

Sitting in their office, Abu Nabil wondered whether he should tell his colleague about the previous day's encounter with the two mystery men, even though they had warned him not to do so. But he and Abu George had never had secrets from each other. Despite differences, they had been like brothers ever since they began working together.

"I feel that our revolution is about to start," he said eventually.

"Of course it is," said Abu George.

Abu Nabil did not notice the irony, so Abu George went on, "We're so desperate that we clutch at every glimmer of hope." He stared at the stone wall which had been repaired before the war and was again showing a crack. He wanted to warn Abu

Nabil against nurturing another illusion, this one regarding the new star Abu Ammar.

"I'm telling you, the masses will rebel," argued Abu Nabil.

"Why should they? Israel provides them with work, with a decent income."

"That's the Zionists' dirty trick. They always try to buy us with money. I promise you that this time the Palestinians will fight, it's only a matter of time."

Abu George looked at him as if he were a foolish child. He wanted to say that the conflict was between states, that because Nasser and the King were now weak they were allowing the Palestinians to misbehave for the time being, but once they regained their strength they would quickly clip their wings, if not chop off their hands. He wanted to predict that it would not be long before the Saudis muffled the mouths of the Palestinians with black gold. But he said nothing. He didn't want to have to listen to another speech about the Muslim holy war, which "as a Christian he wouldn't understand". Inwardly he admitted that these days his partnership with a Muslim was an insurance policy he needed more than ever. He got up to tune the radio to The Voice of Palestine and they heard the news that a band of insurgents had penetrated West Jerusalem and blown up the Israeli Arabic-language radio station.

"*Yaeesh, yaeesh*! Bravo! What did I tell you!" Abu Nabil rejoiced.

"...The Palestinian heroes, who were ready to lay down their lives, proved that Israel is not an impenetrable fortress. The heroic band of warriors broke into the heart of the Israeli establishment, the fortress of its evil propaganda, razed it to the ground and spread fear and anxiety in the hearts of the residents of West Jerusalem. The Arab people in the occupied

271

territories, who are groaning under the yoke of the ruthless Israeli army, have erupted in joyous demonstrations in the street," the broadcast claimed.

Abu Nabil jumped up and danced around the room. "Liberation is at the gate, victory is near!" He embraced Abu George and turned the tuner to the radio stations of Cairo and Damascus, Amman, Baghdad, Saudi Arabia, Tunisia and Libya. "Let's do a spread about the fighters," he said, thinking about his two visitors. Perhaps their appearance foretold the start of Abu Ammar's revolt. Certainly such a report would gratify the new leader, and guarantee the safety of his son Nabil. "Let's go and check it out."

"Why not ask Nuri, the advisor, to take us to the broadcasting station?" suggested Abu George.

"Are you mad?"

"Come on, brother, he will save us a lot of hassle and take us straight to the right place in a dignified way."

Abu Nabil extinguished his cigarette, adjusted his tie in the mirror on the wall and said, "They have press freedom, don't they? So why worry? Who will harm us? They like to appear enlightened, liberal. We don't need anybody, just take a camera and go to the field of action."

"Why not send a reporter?" said Abu George, rubbing his glasses with a handkerchief.

"I want to see it with my own eyes, to rejoice. I'm also curious to see how the operation will be reported in Israel. If you don't come I'll go by myself," said Abu Nabil.

Silence fell. It was not every day Abu George heard a threatening note in his friend's voice.

"It's the start of the revolt. We have to contribute something to it," said Abu Nabil. He checked the address of the Israeli broadcasting house, then phoned Hamdi Nubani, who was fluent in Hebrew which he spoke with the accent of an Old City rabbi, and asked him to translate every item in the Israeli press about the explosion. Nubani muttered that if the broadcasting house had been blown up he'd have heard it, since he lived not far from it, and though he was old he wasn't deaf. Abu Nabil hung up on him.

He took a camera and the two set out via Musrara, up Heleni HaMalka Street, and moments later stopped in front of the broadcasting house. It was all there, a handsome house built by the Abyssinian Empress Taytu next to what used to be the Evelina de Rothschild School for Jewish Girls. They looked at the fine stone building through the surrounding fence, examined the wall and looked closely at the asphalt pavement under their feet, like a woman searching for a lost diamond earring. There was no sign of destruction.

"Are you sure this is the place?" Abu Nabil asked, his face darkening. Abu George began to cough.

"Where is the collapsed building? Have these devils repaired it already?" Abu Nabil grumbled, then went to the concierge.

"We are looking for the site of the explosions," he said, showing his press card.

The concierge, who realised who they were and what they had come for, replied in Arabic, "No need for documents. Here," he pointed to a couple of stones in the surrounding wall which showed some minor damage.

They stood still, exchanged glances and alternately looked at the stones and at the concierge.

"*Behyatek*, on your life, are you mocking us?"

"No, no, brother, this is the wall, see for yourself," and he showed them the entire length. Abu Nabil glanced into the inner courtyard, and the concierge offered to give them a guided tour. He showed them the spacious courtyard with its flagstones and flowerbeds, palm trees, a cypress and an oak in the middle. Abu Nabil glared at a thick-furred black cat that was peeping at him impudently from behind the cypress tree. The concierge invited them to have coffee in the cafeteria, and offered to introduce them to the radio station's political commentator, but they declined politely and hurried away.

They said nothing on the way back and remained silent after arriving at Al-Hurriyeh, where they took a side table under the pomegranate tree.

"And we keep kidding ourselves that we'll throw them into the sea."

"Ever since the war," said Abu Nabil, "you've been eating your heart out, and breaking mine."

"I hate having to acknowledge that Israel is strong," Abu George said, slamming the table with his fist.

"When you say Israel is strong it means we are weak. Who is the Arab who will accept this?"

"I tell you we're living a lie. The power and the money and the blood are going to war, instead of to rehabilitating our society."

"So what would you have us do? The Jews have ruined our lives, undermined our world," Abu Nabil lamented. "There was a time when everyone knew his place, there were ranks – fellahin at the bottom and upper-class townspeople above, there were rich and poor. It used to be said if you had a piastre you were worth a piastre. Suddenly every peasant who carries a rifle is a resistance leader, and the bald woman is equal to the one with hair. Since when did the sons of people like us become soldiers? This business with Nabil is driving me crazy. I can't sleep at night…"

"The world is turning upside down before our eyes. We've lost our authority over our children. Perhaps it's because we don't offer them any direction, any road except war. Whatever the resistance organisations haven't demolished, the occupation will. The markets are open, the economy is unrestricted, Arabs work for Jews and make money. People won't be satisfied with little – they will be liberated, greedy, competitive," Abu George concluded and asked for a narghile.

"Stop smoking, brother. You're coughing too much, don't pour oil on the fire."

"The great writer Taha Hussein wanted us to become part of the West. The Khedive Ismail built an opera house and theatres, wanted to turn Cairo into Paris on the Nile. You can't stop the course of history. The whole world is following the West, and we're stuck in the camel's arsehole."

"You're a Christian, brother. You don't understand Islam…"

Abu George, in desperation, began to laugh. He took a handful of cloves from his pocket and scattered them on the embers of the narghile. A sharp fragrance spread through the air.

"Our modern history is full of mistakes. We rejected the Peel Commission, the Mufti chose to ally himself with Hitler, we rejected the 1947 Partition plan and lost the 1948 war. Now we've chosen the Soviets, and they have thumbed their noses at us."

"We chose our enemy's enemy – what's wrong with that?"

"The question is not which ally to choose, but which civilisation," Abu George insisted.

"But we have our own civilisation! Islam is a civilisation, a whole way of life! You want to adopt Western culture? You might as well try to raise penguins on the banks of the Nile!"

Abu George puffed on the narghile and listened to the bubbling of the water in the bowl.

When they parted company, Abu Nabil went to his office, took off his jacket, loosened his tie and let his mind wander. He recalled his student days in Cairo and his work on the daily *Al-Ahram* where he was taught to stick to the truth, to uphold the honour of the written word. What should he do now? He wrestled with himself, and finally made a decision. We are at war, the Palestinian people are sunk in gloom. I cannot stand by. If lies will help restore self-confidence and dedication to the goal, then I'm in favour of lies. Let lies and exaggerations be our fighter-planes and tanks.

He drank some water, crunched an ice-cube between his teeth, took out his favourite Parker 51, filled it with green ink, spread out the newspapers from Jordan and began to write, quoting the reports on the destruction of the Israeli broadcasting house, as if he had not seen with his own eyes that the building remained intact.

The next day when Abu George read the false report and Abu Nabil's lead article he felt sorely disappointed. The culture of exaggeration and lies had triumphed again. Now Abu Ammar and Abu Nabil had formed a common front, one in which he had no place. Perhaps it was time to retire to his house in Jericho and leave everything behind – the newspaper, business concerns and politics.

He went for a walk, his hands clasped behind his back, rolling the *masbahah* beads. He entered the Old City through the Jaffa Gate and walked down the wide steps through the teeming market. He stopped in front of the Church of the Holy Sepulchre in the Christian Quarter. The square was full of tourists and pilgrims sitting on the steps, filling every corner. The entrance to the church looked dilapidated, the front made up of stone patchwork. Four arches, two on either side, rose one above the other. There was the massive stone slab on which, according to tradition, the body of the crucified Christ had been laid out and washed, as shown in the mural. Abu George felt humbled and awed before the great images of saints. A cloud of incense hung in the air of the church, a smell he had loved ever since he had been brought here as a child by his Hilmi grandfather. The place was packed with pilgrims. A long file of Armenian seminarians passed by, chanting softly. Scores of Americans stood in line, singing and lighting candles, their faces beaming. He wanted to climb to the upper floor, but the staircase was crammed with German tourists. Mostly blond and pale-eyed, they too sang and chanted. Abu George gave up and turned towards the crypt, but that too was packed with a noisy Latin American group. Israelis swarmed on the ground floor. Judging by their clothes, he thought they were kibbutz members. A young tour-guide lectured them above the sounds of singing and chanting, and the group listened to him avidly. Abu George watched them mingle among the pilgrims, and felt better momentarily. He found a secluded corner and said a quiet prayer, then suddenly found he was choking and had to hurry outside. The truth is, he said to himself, this land speaks all languages, and this city belongs to no one. It belongs to everyone.

25

"What is there here for us?"

Ghadir and her mother Fathiya were waiting for me at dawn near the southern corner of Damascus Gate. Ahead of us was a long drive to the Galilee – first to Karmiel, where I was due to attend a working meeting with the Mayor, then to their relatives in nearby Ghayna.

I got out of the car to introduce myself to her mother.

"*Sabah al-khair, ya ibni*. My daughter told me about you back then, when you were a soldier on Jebel Sacobos."

The square outside the gate had always been the site of a makeshift market, with stalls selling seasonal fruit and vegetables, choice local produce, but now the area was packed solid with people and no one was selling anything. Cars with Israeli licence plates were parked here and there. People streamed out of the Old City through New Gate and Damascus Gate and joined the hundreds who were already packed in the square. Where were they hurrying to, so early in the morning? The place was unrecognisable.

"What's all this?" I asked Ghadir.

"Don't you know? It's *souk al-abied*, the slave market. Every morning people come here from Silwan and Abu-Dis and Sur Baher, Beit Hanina and Shuafat, looking for work."

When did the fruit and vegetable market turn into a slave

market? And how did I not know? Suddenly I heard a familiar, powerful voice. It was Humi, a Labour Party organiser from my parents' neighbourhood. "*Ta'al hon, itla* – here, get on," he was ordering men in an authoritative voice. In a matter of minutes he filled three pickup trucks with workers and they were driven off. Now I understood why he had recently managed to buy himself a house in wealthy Rehaviah.

We drove through the Jordan Valley, now and then encountering Israeli army checkpoints. The presence of two traditionally-dressed Arab women in an Israeli vehicle aroused suspicion, and this in turn frightened the two women. You can't imagine anything more scary than a bunch of bored reservists, posted to a road in the broiling Jordan Valley and wilting in the heat.

The eight o'clock news reported that eleven infiltrators had been captured on Mount Gilboa, and it was suggested that they had been planning a retaliation for Israel's destruction of the oil refineries in Suez a couple of days before. Fathiya saw my face growing tense and looked at me with alarm. I told her what I'd heard.

"We need the mercy of Allah," she sighed. Then she said, "I thought we would be going through Jaffa."

"On the way back," I promised.

We stopped for a short break and sat under a kiosk awning. I ordered cold drinks, which Fathiya supplemented with pittas and fruit from her basket. We attracted some suspicious looks and for a moment I asked myself what I was doing travelling with two Arab women. I then felt ashamed of myself.

"*Ya salaam, shu halu*, how beautiful this is, I don't remember going this way before '48," said Fathiya, as we drove alongside the Beit Netofah valley, which was broad and lush, checkered with green, brown and black patches, and dotted with woods and olive orchards. The hills surrounding the valley gave it a sheltered look.

"This is a new road," I said.

We climbed up the steep hillside to Maghar. "*Ya binti*," Fathiya turned pale. "What are these houses?" she pointed to the white houses of Carmiel to the left of the road. The town had not existed in her time.

The original purpose of my visit which came at the behest of my Minister, was to see the Mayor of Karmiel to discuss a development project and to persuade him to head it. I was there on time and was taken straight to his office. Ghadir and her mother waited for me on a bench in the lobby.

The Mayor spoke to me at length about the area and showed me on a wall map the clusters of industries and workshops that were being planned for the benefit of the Arab population.

"We shall also open joint schools for Arab and Jewish children, who will get to know each other from nursery age on, like true cousins. We shall open up new vistas for Arab women," he enthused. "Tell the Minister I shall be happy to head any collaborative forum he has in mind."

A few minutes after leaving Karmiel, Fathiya shouted, "Stop, we're here!" Two small road signs pointed to Dir al-Arnab and Ghayna to our right. I drove slowly along the narrow, twisting road up a hill, where on one side there was a field full of recently uprooted boulders and behind them an olive orchard. Dark blue dung smoke rose from the houses, the familiar smell of Arab villages. Two stray dogs barked at us hoarsely, and when I turned towards them they shied away in fear. Alongside ran an overflowing drainage channel, and the streams of sewage flooded the road and filled the many potholes.

The two villages were interwined like a braid, the houses climbing over one another, struggling for a place in the sun. The chilly feel of bare concrete predominated, except in the window frames, which were painted blue to ward off the evil eye. A little boy licking a red ice-lolly ran after us, chanting, "A white car! A white car!" I drove on a little futher and then stopped by the side of the road.

"Everything is the same. I'd know this place even in the dark," said Fathiya excitedly as she got out of the car. She walked quickly, carrying two packages, and stopped in front of a small house: "This is the one," she said confidently.

A big dog lay on the concrete pavement in front, its eyes mournful, wailing like an abandoned child. When we approached he tried to bark, but managed only to whine. I'm afraid of dogs, but I could see he was helpless. A mess of urine and turds was near the wretched smelly creature. I moved away and waited. Fathiya went straight to the open door and a moment later cries of surprise and joy filled the air: "Fathiya!" "Asaliya!" "Haven't seen you for years and years!" The two women fell into each other's arms, hugged and kissed and showered blessings on each other.

Ghadir stood quietly beside me until Asaliya noticed her. "It's Ghadir, isn't it?" she cried, and drew her into the knot of hugs and tears and cries of admiration.

"Are you her husband?" she asked me.

"My husband has been in Amman since the war," Ghadir said. "This is Nur al-Din, of al-Quds." The minor change to my name turned me into one of them. It made me smile, which was taken as part of the introduction.

Fathiya took my arm and said to her sister, "This is a good man who is helping us to apply for family reunification. We have a problem with Ghadir and we've come to ask you some questions. We'll tell you later. First let us hear how you are and what has happened in all the years we haven't met."

"*Ahlan wasahlan*," Asaliya welcomed me into her house which consisted of a single room, narrow and dark like an abandoned railway carriage. There were mattresses on the floor and a scattering of worn cushions. On the wall hung a photograph of a thin, moustachioed man wearing traditional keffiyeh and agal.

"Thanks be to Allah, the smell of home and family," said Fathiya, and another round of hugs and kisses and joyful tears began. Then they started on the family gossip.

"How is your son Karim? Married? With children?" asked Fathiya.

"Not yet. He waited for Ghadir. We showed him the photograph you sent, when she was fiftten, *mashallah*, God save us – a woman! We said she was destined for him. 'She's beautiful,' he said, 'I'll wait for her', and he didn't want anyone else."

A man of about thirty came in. With his narrow dark face and hawk nose, his only resemblance to his father's picture on the wall was in his moustache and mouth.

"Karim *ibni*, come meet Fathiya, your aunt, and your cousin Ghadir," said his mother.

He gave Ghadir a piercing look and from that moment hardly took his eyes off her.

"How are you, *ya* Karim?" asked Fathiya. "It's been almost twenty years since I saw you. I thought we'd find you with a wife and children...We did want you for Ghadir, but it did not work out. After the *Nakba*, we were left in Jordan and you in

Israel. Now, *ya* Karim, get married and we will all rejoice at your wedding."

Ghadir stood in the doorway, looking out, and he went on staring at her back. Then he turned his dark eyes to me, as if sizing me up. To take my mind off him I listened to the women. I noticed that Fathiya spoke Jaffa Arabic with Jordanian intonation, while Asaliya spoke with a Galilean accent.

"How did he go?" Fathiya was asking about the late Abu Karim.

"*Rah*, just went." The two of them began to wail and Asaliya struck her own face, as though he was lying dead before her eyes.

"What happened to him, *ya ukhti*, my sister? He was not old," Fathiya persisted, looking at his picture on the wall.

Asaliya sent one of her daughters to the grocery: "Buy grapefruit juice and orange juice," she said. While the child was out, she made tea and coffee for us. The coffee was, as the Bedouins say, "strong and bitter as life".

After coffee, Asaliya invited us to come with her and asked her youngest daughter to keep an eye on the dog. "He's dying, poor thing," she said. Thin and straight-backed, she led us down the hill to the road linking the two villages, and then to an ancient olive tree that was being strangled by heaps of broken rocks, gravel and sand.

"It happened just here. The Jews expropriated the land, the military government declared that it was an army training area, out of bounds to civilians. Abu Karim and a few others wanted to go on working in the quarries and the olive orchards, and to graze our goats here even though it was forbidden. They were arrested and put on trial in Nazareth – a very quick trial. Abu Karim sat in jail for a month.

"When he came out they said the government wanted the land to build a town for the Jews. There, you see, those tall buildings. I hope they all collapse in one night! They like to live high up in the air. We like to touch our earth. Who could imagine they would really take away our land and dare to uproot our olive orchards? Our fathers and forefathers planted these trees, and thanks to them we worked a little and harvested a great deal. Do you remember, Fathiya, how you used to come and take home olive oil and soap?

"Then the Jews came to our mukhtar and the heads of all the villages here and said they wanted to build a new city, with roads and schools and factories and work places – for us, you know. They said all the villages will benefit and we will be better off. You have seen how our house has become more beautiful," she said ironically.

"We said to them '*Al hamdu lillah*, thank God, we have flocks and pastures and olive trees, we don't need anything.' The Jews offered one hundred and twenty lira per acre. Abu Karim would not hear of it, and made us swear that if anything happened to him we would never agree to sell. A hundred and twenty lira for an acre – thirty lira for a whole dunam? I tell you, sister, that's what the Jews are doing to us, they who are said to be *Ahl al-kitab*, the People of the Book!"

"What is there here for us?" Fathiya asked sadly.

"We did not know what to do. Our strength and our minds were exhausted. Who are we, shepherds and fellahin, how can we take on the military government? Abu Karim did not understand what was going on. He became a different man. His face fell. His legs became heavy.

"One day he gathered the family and said, 'I inherited this land and these olive orchards from my forefathers, and I must leave them to my son. That is the honour my forefathers demand from me, and the honour I owe the land. I will not lend a hand to the Zionists' scheme. Their belly is full but their eyes are hungry. What do they want? The little bit of honour we still have left? What is a man worth when you take away his land? Nothing! He has no foundation and no root. I, Abu Karim ibn Aziz, of the al-Sadek clan, say to them: You came back here after two thousand years – we will come back after forty-thousand years! The land is ours and the country is ours. You cannot take from a man his own self and his own flesh. Life is like a wheel, sometimes up and sometimes down. Now you are up, the day will come when you are down. The day will come when you will fall like a hollow tree. *Kol kalb biji yomo*, every dog has his day.' That is what he said.

"One morning Abu Karim took a mattress and spread it under this olive tree, and he sat here and watched the bulldozers and the tractors crushing the earth. Every road they built he felt as if they were trampling on his body, every tree they uprooted as if they were pulling out his teeth, every rock they moved as if they were pecking at his liver. He did not eat or drink. Mukhtars and dignitaries came from the villages all around, from Dir al-Arnab and Nahf and Majd al-Tin, and they said to him: 'Man brings life to the earth, the earth does not bring a man to life. A day will come when Allah will pay them back.' But he continued to fast, saying: 'The Jews took my land, let Allah take my soul.'

"He stayed like this a few more days. The smell of death came from his mattress…*Hada huwy*, that is it, my sister," Asaliya finished, her eyes red. The tears ran down Fathiya's cheeks.

"We will be back," said Karim through tight lips.

Silence fell. Ghadir broke some olive twigs that lay scattered on the ground. I moved away and sat on a rock, and the same old image from my childhood flashed into my mind – Rashel facing Iraqi soldiers who are kicking her husband Hizkel. Blood trickles from his lips and forehead, and they go on beating and kicking. She cries and pleads, and they slap her face, and she falls down.

We walked back to the house and Asaliya served us food. I had no appetite but did not wish to offend, so I ate a few spoonfuls of rice, then went outside to smoke. Ghadir brought me a plate of freshly picked figs.

After coffee, Fathiya talked about Ghadir who had the misfortune to be married to Issam. "That is fate," she said, "and now Ghadir is obliged to go to him and his family in Amman – unless she can prove she is from here. The official in the Ministry of the Interior says we must prove that we lived in Jaffa and have family in Israel, names of our relatives, their ages, their homes."

Asaliya brought out all the documents she had in the house. I copied the names from the documents, with the dates of birth and identity numbers, and also wrote down all the details she could recall about their family. "In Jaffa there are not many left. Karim visits them sometimes."

Fathiya and Asaliya hugged each other in silence for a long time, two hardworking women who had known much pain, and found a little relief and comfort for a couple of hours. "Come to see us – al-Quds is not far," Fathiya said, and walked to the car with a stooping gait.

We were supposed to return to Jerusalem via Jaffa, which Fathiya and Ghadir had longed for years to see, but it was getting late. I was wondering how to tell them that we had better postpone that visit for another day, but Fathiya beat me to it:

"*Ya* Nuri, may Allah grant you a long life. Let's leave Yaffa for another day." Her expression was desperate, her eyes overflowing. "Forgive me," she apologised. "I am crying for my life. Why was I born in this time?"

"I promise I shall take you to Yaffa."

We returned to Jerusalem in silence, feeling burdened. Evening was falling. When we reached the Rockefeller Museum, Ghadir said, "Drop us here. We'll walk the rest of the way."

"Why? I can take you home. Your mother is tired."

"No, *ya ibni*," said Fathiya. "My husband may be home by now. We don't want any trouble."

26

Thirty Lira and a Special People

"You're looking for justice?" said Mother.

"Mother, thirty lira for a dunam of land? You refused to sell the house in Baghdad, didn't you? Have you forgotten how angry you were at the price the Muslims offered for it?"

"True, I didn't want to sell them the house for pennies, damn their eyes. Better they should steal it than for me to sell it to them!"

"It's the same here. What's the difference?"

"How can you make that comparison, *ibni*? Even if we had sold, what could we have done with the money? Could we take it with us? No chance. They froze our property and bank accounts and drove us out, so why should I care about their feelings? Have you forgotten how they stripped us and searched our bodies at the airport? They even took our shoes apart, to check that we weren't smuggling gold."

"Yes, Mother, but here we're in charge and we can show justice."

"You're looking for justice – when did they ever show justice to us? Our ancestors settled in Iraq during the Babylonian Exile, a thousand years before Mohammed was born. Did it stop them from expelling us? Wasn't that an outrage? Justice, he wants!"

"Why did we have to build a Jewish town on their land, in front of their faces? Do we have to spit in their eyes?"

"Are you defending them?"

"I want to defend us, our morality. We are supposed to be a special people, a light unto the nations, aren't we?"

"I don't know what being a special people means, but I can see that you want the Arabs to dominate the Galilee and Israel and turn us into refugees all over again!"

"Um Kabi," Father intervened, "our son is right."

"What, are you too a defender of Islam now? They threw us out like dogs!" she ranted at Father, furious to hear him siding with me.

"Mother, enough of Baghdad. We're in Israel now, not over there, and we're stronger than all the Arab states put together."

"From your mouth to God's ear! But I'm still afraid, *ibni*. Anybody who's had the experience that Jews had will always be afraid. You want to help them, treat them honourably. Wonderful! What world are you living in? Did they treat us honourably?"

"We are not them," said Father. "And where it is truly necessary to take from them, at least give them decent compensation, without any deviousness."

"It won't do any good, whatever we do they'll hate us. They don't know how to live with others, it's in their religion," Mother told him and turned to me. "*Ibni*, why do you go to their villages, isn't it dangerous? You can't trust them."

"Mother, we have to solve their problems, help them, maybe in the end they'll get used to living with us."

"It's good that he's looking at things with his own eyes," said Father. "And good that he's helping this Arab woman. Isn't she a human being?"

"Whatever I say, he says the opposite. You see?"

When Mother complains to me about Father I can sense a row flaring up. Time to deflect it before it starts. "Where's Hizkel?"

"At Efraim's in the kibbutz. He'll be there all week."

As I was leaving I thought it was a pity Hizkel wasn't there. His presence calmed them, or at least restrained them. The tension between them had been high ever since we left Iraq. They were always arguing, it didn't matter about what.

When we first came to Israel Father dreamed of growing rice. He thought that the Hula Valley was the perfect place for it, and he saw himself as a visionary and entrepreneur of a new agricultural enterprise. He was full of strength and confidence, but bureaucracy gradually wore him down. Disappointment consumed him the way rust corrodes iron. What made it worse was that he had to work as a road builder to support his family. His body shrank, and when he put on one of his smart suits from Iraq he looked like a scarecrow. In the evening, after an exhausting day's work, he would shower and slip out to the café, so we were left without a father. He did not cuddle us or hug us, did not encourage or support us, did not comfort us or fill us with hope, as he once had. He was broken, like the central pole of our tent in the immigrant camp in the winter storms of 1951.

Mother found herself without a shoulder to lean on or an ear to hear her pain. She took charge of the family, traipsed around the immigrant camp market to buy damaged vegetables on the cheap, and made pathetic attempts to grow tomatoes, onions and parsley in the sandy soil. She contrived to produce something out of nothing, and protected her children like a wounded lioness. On rare occasions she tried to cheer Father up, to tell him that the future was still before him, despite the present failure, and would repeat the old Iraqi saying, "When you fall, be a man." She urged him to postpone his dream until his brother Hizkel was released and joined him in Israel, saying that together they could take on the clueless officials. But whatever she said only hurt him more. In Baghdad she submitted to his will and followed him to Israel, but once here she discovered her own strength and stood up for herself. She rebelled against tradition and went out to work. Father, feeling like a lion whose teeth have been drawn, disliked the change in her and did not see it as the fulfilment of her potential but as a symptom of his own decline. Her new activities struck him like a slap in his face, as though she were saying, "You are not a man, you can't support your family." No matter what Mother did to try to patch things up between them, Father wrapped himself in a thick blanket of silence and could not be mollified.

He is so hard on her, I thought on my way out. He doesn't emerge from his shell, takes offence at everything she says, like a little boy. Strange how an intelligent and open-minded man can be so sullen and unmovable around his wife.

27

Their Clocks and Ours

In the morning I arrived early at the Ministry. Levanah was already there, alone in the office. "What good wind has blown you here so early?" she asked.

"Homesickness," I replied with a smile.

"I wish! Can I invite you to coffee? The Minister won't be here until eight, so we have a little time." In the cafeteria she took a seat at a side table and I went to fetch the coffee.

"What's bothering you, Nuri?" she asked point-blank.

"Tell me," I replied with a question, "were you here when the lands of Karmiel were expropriated?"

"No, I was still in the army. You need information?"

"Yes indeed." I told her all about Ghadir and her family's tribulations.

We returned to the Minister's office and I shut myself in the spokesman's room and read classified papers in preparation for the periodic report to the Minister. Barely an hour had passed when Levanah came in with a big and bulky envelope. "Here, I got what you need."

"You're amazing!" To show my gratitude, I slipped out to the Knesset garden and picked a rose, which I laid on her desk.

I opened the envelope as soon as I entered my office in Sheikh

Jarrah and looked through the papers but couldn't get a clear picture; a lot of detailed information phrased in legalese only confused me. I decided to examine them at leisure, and also to consult my old friend Solly Levy at the Lands Office. I put the documents aside and picked up the American newspapers which were regularly delivered to the office.

In the *Washington Post* the face of my neighbour, Senator Antoine, appeared alongside an interview that was seething with hatred and denunciation. Not exactly a kindly old man, I thought. My Minister should see this, take a closer look at the more extreme attitudes among the Palestinians and get a whiff of reality.

Since I was due to see him that evening, I went to the military government headquarters for a current assessment and a chat with casual colleagues, a way of keeping us all better updated. There I ran into Shamluk and told him what I had just read in the *Washington Post*.

"Crazy old man, challenging a major power," he said.

"You have any background on him?"

"I'll send you some," he promised and hurried away.

I didn't have enough time to go out to lunch, so I bought some salami, fruit and bread in a nearby grocery and ate in my office while reading papers and formulating my report.

I'm always rattled when I have to prepare the report. Afraid of the Minister's criticism, I struggle with the wording, write and rewrite, feeling him breathing down my neck. His Hebrew is superb, drawn from geological strata of Bible and Talmud, the Revival writers and poets, innovations made by Bialik, Mendele, Agnon, Shlonsky, Alterman...As for me, I'm an immigrant with limited command of the language.

*

In the car on my way to the Minister's office, Um Kulthoum's voice warbled out of the radio – her daily concert. Just after the war an Egyptian magazine ran a big story on her, calling her "opium for the masses", with the accusation that her singing drugged the soldiers on the eve of battle and dulled the nation's senses. The singer withdrew into silence and did not appear in public for several months, grieving for her people's defeat. Recently she had emerged from her mourning to launch a campaign of recovery in support of the *rais*. She sang about heroism and the battling spirit, the greatness of the *rais* and the victory to come. She, who had never addressed her listeners directly, now made speeches about unity, called on the women of Egypt to donate their gold jewellery to the state, carried the national flag from city to city, appeared in Alexandria and Ismailia, Mansoura and Damanhur, Khartoum, Tripoli, Rabat, Amman and Damascus, even in European capitals. "We are all fedayeen, ready for self-sacrifice," she sang, joining in Arafat's chorus. Now her voice flowed like hot tears in the song *Inta umri*:

> What I saw before my eyes beheld you
> was a lost life – how can it be reckoned my life!

I stopped by at Al-Hurriyeh, but Yasmine wasn't there. Abu George said she was holed up in the Mission library, "writing the concluding chapter of her dissertation." I left her a note which did not disguise my disappointment.

When I reached the Minister's office I was surprised to find Levanah. "You're still here? From seven in the morning till seven in the evening?"

At that point she stood up and began to sing "Happy birthday!"

How could I have forgotten?

"Nuri, you're thirty years old today. It means something!" She handed me a small package. Inside was a gold Sheaffer fountain pen, with a card, "From the Minister's Office."

I stood before her embarrassed and touched. Not since my bar mitzvah, not once in the past seventeen years, had anyone marked my birthday.

"The Minister will be here at any moment," she said in her usual businesslike tone. She looked at my face and picked up her handbag to leave. So you're going to let her leave like this?

"You're one in a million, Levanah," I said, hugging her.

The Minister surprised me too. "Shall we have a drink?" he said, taking a bottle of fine cognac and two glasses out of the cupboard. Interesting. He was usually very Spartan in his habits, even miserly, writing with a cheap pencil on the unused side of papers, filling the whole space, eating ordinary sandwiches from the staff cafeteria, and when he had to spend the night in Jerusalem he stayed at a modest central hotel. Now this cognac!

"To you, Nuri!" he toasted me. "Levanah told me it was your birthday today." He drained his glass at a single gulp. "How was Karmiel?"

"The Mayor was happy to accept your proposal."

"Good. Now we must speed up construction, fill and expand the town, settle in new immigrants. No more delays."

"Minister, I'd like to share with you a disturbing experience I had in the village of Ghayna near Karmiel." I repeated to him Asaliya's story about the land expropriation. "Is it any wonder that the mood there is so hostile?"

"Young man, my advice to you is, leave it alone! What's the point of reviving these memories? Look forward, my friend –

great enterprises lie ahead of us." He refilled our glasses. "The Prime Minister has asked me to chair a committee to consider the future of the territories and their inhabitants and all relevant factors, including how to present the issue to the public in Israel and abroad. It's an exciting challenge!"

"It sounds great! At last we'll have clear directives."

"We must retain the assets we hold and create facts on the ground before the Arabs recover from the shock."

"What about East Jerusalem?"

"It will be our top priority. No need for declarations. We'll work quietly, as in the pioneering days – another dunam of land, another goat, another building…That has always been the strength of Zionism."

"And will the Arabs accept it?" I asked.

"The question is what we want and what we will agree to. The Arabs will adapt and forget, the way they forgot Jaffa and Majdal and Akko."

"They haven't forgotten," I put in.

"Well, all right, I'm not deluding myself," he replied. "But let's not overstate their opposition. So the water will boil and steam, hateful articles will be published by that senator of yours and others, maybe a speech or two in front of an empty Knesset. So what? The dogs bark, and the caravan moves on. Remember, my dear Nuri, the Arabs are the same Arabs and the world is the same world."

"I've made you a translation of some poems by Fadwa Toukan, the Nablus poetess, and a couple of stories by refugees in Lebanon, to show you the trends of thinking…"

"Good, very good. I noticed you have a poetic soul…"

"I translated the poems because it's poetry that shapes their consciousness and their reality," I persevered. "All our leaders should read their poetry, sir, or they won't understand them. After all, our own consciousness was shaped by Bialik, Uri-Zvi Greenberg and Alterman."

"How can you make that comparison?"

"I make the comparison because I believe they should be treated as we would want them to treat us, and this would open the way to a true reconciliation between us."

"It's not as simple as you imagine in your tender heart, young man. Remember that Dayan took their religious sentiments into account, their need to preserve their culture, and gave them the Temple Mount. Did that gesture, which was unimaginably far-reaching, reconcile them to us one little bit?"

"Not everything should be seen in the short term. Perhaps when Dayan took that step he was thinking in the long term, and did it in the hope of reducing the likelihood of future wars?"

The Minister's face showed that he did not see it that way.

"Minister, would you allow me to smoke in your room today, in honour of my birthday? The cognac has left me craving a cigarette."

"Very well, after two thousand years of exile in the corridor, I grant you this birthday gift."

I inhaled the smoke and said, "I'm thinking that among us people have only two or three children, whereas they have a dozen. This demographic diagnosis is keeping me awake at night…"

"I think you mean prognosis. A common mistake. But don't worry, masses of Jews will come from the Soviet Union, and we shall need the land and the strategic space!" he declared, waving away the smoke.

"Will Brezhnev let them leave Russia? Nasser will raise hell."

"Listen, Nuri, Jews are returning to their ancestral land, to the source of their heritage, a vast settlement movement is getting under way. How long shall we wait for the phone call from Hussein? The Arabs reject every attempt at dialogue. Maybe if they see that we are not sitting idle, they'll make a move."

"Their clocks do not run at the same rate as ours," I said. "The question is, what price will we pay for settling in the territories."

"Why are you so pessimistic, young man?"

"I'll tell you, sir. A neighbour of mine, a Labour Party organiser who used to work in the municipality, is now a labour contractor who hires workers from the West Bank, makes a mint of money and has bought himself a fancy villa."

"So because of a few bad weeds we must refrain from planting grass?" he said, and swung his feet onto the desk – his favourite position.

"Something warns me that there is serious trrouble ahead," I said and took from my briefcase a summary of some vituperative polemics published by Abu Nabil. The Minister glanced through it and flung it aside.

"Young man, this is a war between two national movements. It's not a duet in an opera. What we need is a profound belief in the justice of our cause. Fear not, recoil not!" he concluded, took a paper clip, straightened it and began to clean his nails.

"Sir, the question is how we interpret the reality, not the justice of our cause," I said.

"Young man, as you grow older you'll understand," he assured me, ending our meeting.

I went out into the darkened corridor. Everyone had left, only the watchman remained, making himself tea in his cubicle.

28

Father and Senator Antoine

The cold air smelled good, the neighbourhood was waking up. On my brisk morning walk I met the early risers, the dustmen, the driver of the Tnuvah dairy truck and ten men going to the synagogue to form the morning's first minyan. Like theatre ushers, these people opened the gate to the new day.

I returned to my flat and instead of the news listened to a Mendelssohn violin concerto. Having trained myself for years to listen to classical music, I had begun to enjoy it. Gradually I established regular times for listening – classical music in the morning, Arabic music in the evening. Like a pasha who maintains two beloved wives in separate palaces, I kept them strictly apart.

It was time to go to Katamon and my parents' house. This was the day I planned to take Father to my office in Sheikh Jarrah. If Hizkel had been here I'd have taken him too, but he liked Efraim's kibbutz and was staying there another week.

I went into Mother's kitchen to eat breakfast. The corner of the ceiling, just above Mother's Sabbath oil lamp, had a sooty black patch that seemed to be spreading and I thought I ought to repaint the kitchen before Kabi came home on leave. After the war, when he was fully recovered, he told me we had to take our parents out of the housing estate, buy them a new flat. He left out our brother Moshi, "because he's got his own family". It peeved me that he still treated me as he did in Baghdad, where the eldest son is the commander-in-chief. I was even more annoyed at myself for continuing to obey him.

Mother brewed Noumi Basra tea for me and wondered aloud for the millionth time how I could start my day with such a sour drink, and then she spoiled it by sweetening it too much. She gave me two soft-boiled eggs, in which I dunked pieces of brown bread, enjoying every mouthful. I rarely succeeded in making such perfect soft-boiled eggs. To finish, she gave me a chunk of almond halva from Abu Salman. This Abu Salman had a small stall in the "Iraqi" alley in the market, and sold his special halva only on order and only twice a week.

Father was all set to go. His smoothly shaved cheeks smelled of lemony aftershave and he looked both solemn and alert, showing almost no trace of his heart attack. I was as tense as I would be if my Minister was about to visit my office, and hoped Father would like it. On the way we chatted about this and that, and I unburdened myself on the subject of Senator Antoine, who kept attacking us in the foreign press and who turned down all my requests to meet with him.

"Every lock has a key, son," Father said. "I trust you will find it."

When we reached Sheikh Jarrah I parked as usual at the top of the little alley and we walked down towards my office. It was then that we saw my neighbour Senator Antoine opening his garden gate.

"*Sabah al-khair*," I greeted him, and this time added, "My name is Nuri…"

"Yes, I know who you are. *Wamin hadhirato*, and who is his honour?" he asked, looking at Father.

"My father. Will you not pay us the compliment of visiting us in my office? Or perhaps we could come to your place, if you will allow it. We are, after all, next door neighbours…"

He looked at us, surprised and embarrassed. "I'll come to your office…" he said in a low voice, "after I've watered my flowers."

"*Alf marhaba*, a thousand welcomes," I said and walked on with Father, holding him by the arm, smiling that his optimism was so quickly to bear fruit. He knew what I was thinking and warned, "Did you notice his eyes, son? His hands? The Arab is courteous, with very formal manners. If you ask to come into his house it's as if you ask for shelter. Your request honours him. According to their rules of hospitality he should have welcomed you in."

Aliza greeted my father very warmly. I told her I expected the senator in a little while and said she was to show him maximum respect, and to leave the office door open till he arrived.

We went into my room. Father looked around, took in every object, and said with obvious pleasure, "So this was the office of Ahmad Shukeiry, the head of the PLO, may his name be forgotten!" He inspected the house, including the kitchen and the luxurious bedroom, which was now unused and said, smiling, "The man certainly knew how to live and take care of himself." I hadn't seen Father smiling for a long time.

At last, the senator arrived. He stood on the threshold, as if momentarily undecided. I bowed slightly as I invited him inside. We sat down in the conference corner, with its Damascene table and seats, decorated with the fresh flowers Aliza had picked earlier in the garden. The senator sat on the edge of an armchair, holding himself stiffly. His eyes toured the room, suspiciously examining every object. Suddenly he stood up, changed his regular glasses for reading glasses and approached the wall. "I see that except for the pictures you have left everything as it was. I used to come here often. The head of the Palestine Liberation Organisation, Advocate Ahmad Shukeiry, was a friend of mine. He was at my house the night before he left al-Quds."

"I am honoured by your visit," I said.

"Al-Quds al-Sharif is lost, and the world is fast asleep!" the senator lamented, wringing his hands in despair.

"We shall pass away when our time comes, but al-Quds will remain for ever," Father assured him.

Aliza came in, bearing a tray with coffee. "Here you are, your excellency," she said as she served him. The clicking of her heels on the marble floor as she came and went reverberated in the tense silence.

"I have brought you the text of an interview that I gave to the *Washington Post*," Senator Antoine said, putting the paper on a stool. His stomach was distended and now and then he pressed it with his hand and sighed audibly. "The world should be told what you are doing here. I am documenting all the crimes you are committing. Every scrap of information, every newspaper clipping, is kept in my archives. It is my duty to alert the world."

His loud voice sounded shrill in my ears. Father, however, looked at the senator mildly and moistened his lips.

"Your love for al-Quds is very moving, Senator," he said. "No one can understand it better than us. We waited and prayed for it for two thousand years."

"What have you to do with al-Quds?"

"Senator, Jerusalem is mentioned in our Torah 667 times, and the Land of Israel 4,584 times. On the other hand, Jerusalem is not mentioned even once in the Quran."

"Then why did you demolish the Mugrabi quarter?"

"To let our Western Wall out of darkness into light, to enable the thousands of worshippers to approach it."

"Why are you changing the character of the city?"

"It is the nature of war that it alters reality and creates a new balance of power. In 1948 you captured the Jewish Quarter and did whatever you wanted with it – you killed some of the inhabitants and deported others, and destroyed all the houses. Did that policy not change the character of the ancient Jewish Quarter?"

My nerves were wound as tightly as a coiled spring as I listened to their exchange. I was afraid that my father's version of events would make the senator jump up and leave, breaking the fine thread of communication that had only just been formed. What was it about Father's approach that enabled him to enter this sensitive area and emerge safely, I wondered.

"You are behaving like ruthless conquerors towards the people who have lived in this land for untold generations. Was that how you were treated by our brothers in Iraq?"

"We lived in Iraq for thousands of years. Then one day they expelled us."

"Expelled you? You wanted to leave. You are Zionists, you were undermining the regime."

"No, your excellency. They passed a special law forcing us to give up our identity cards, our citizenship. My hands shook when I handed over my card. The roots of seventy generations were severed at one stroke. I became a man without any rights, floating in limbo without anything under my feet."

"That is exactly what is happening to us now."

Father shook his head, as if saying that comparison simply didn't apply. "Our family had land, thousands of dunams, whole villages, tractors and combine harvesters and modern farm machinery. Hundreds of Muslims worked on our land. We were the first Iraqis to export rice and grain to the West. The government of Iraq confiscated all our property, everything! They turned us into refugees." Father was echoing the arguments he had rejected when Mother made them. He took out a cigarette, sniffed it and put it back. "Afterwards came the longings – for the house, the smell of the lemons, for the dates, even for the cemetery where my parents and forefathers are buried...I still have the keys to our house in Baghdad, your excellency. I keep them as a souvenir."

Instead of responding to Father, the senator turned to me. "You people are behaving like *abadhai al-hara*, the neighbourhood bully. Why did you have to take over the office of Chairman Shukeiry? Have you no respect?" I ignored the personal attack and he went on, "People are complaining about the Ministry of the Interior, the Ministry of Commerce, the Lands Registry...You do whatever enters your heads. Who gave you permission? Al-Quds is lost and the world is fast asleep," he lamented again in a hoarse voice.

"Salvation will not come from the outside world, your excellency," said Father. "The question we, the sons of Abraham, must solve is whether to continue the conflict between Isaac and Ishmael, or learn to compromise and live side by side. There is a story in our holy book about a family quarrel between the shepherds of Abraham and the shepherds of his nephew Lot. Abraham said to Lot, 'We are brothers. The whole land lies before us. Separate yourself from me – turn to the left and I will turn to the right, or you take the right and I will take the left.' That was the solution of our mutual forefather, Abraham al-Halil, the friend. Why can't we act like him?"

"You invaded our country."

"Forgive me, your excellency. We have always been here, we went away and returned. Sometimes we were the majority, sometimes the minority."

"You are disrespectful. Your governor summoned our Mayor, Ruhi al-Khatib, and scolded him as if he were a street urchin."

"In this instance you are right, your excellency. Western people are ignorant of the Arab rules of courtesy and respect," Father said, and touched the senator's hand in a friendly gesture. The old man's eyes softened, and he leaned closer to Father.

"We lived together for hundreds of years until the Russian Zionists came and spoiled everything. We and you are their victims – they lit the flames of hatred, they turned us into enemies."

"Your excellency," Father said in a moderate, relaxed tone that aroused my admiration, "surely you remember that there were attacks on the Jews before then? Even in the time of the Prophet Mohammed Jews were slaughtered, and I don't need to tell you about the pogroms that the Christians inflicted on the Jews. The facts are widely known. Is it not time to stop the bloodshed?"

"What was taken by force will only be restored by force," the senator repeated Nasser's slogan. "How can you seek peace and boast about your democracy when you are committing international crimes?"

"Your excellency, in 1941, in Baghdad, on the feast of Shavuot which celebrates the giving of our holy Torah, Muslim gangs attacked us, slaughtering people, cutting off babies' feet to steal their gold anklets, and they raped women, set fire to houses – just because we were Jews. So you see, in this contest over murder and expulsion we can't even begin to compete with you."

Silence fell. Father took a cigarette from the Damascene box and before lighting it offered the box to the guest. "'Does your excellency smoke?"

"Yes. That is, no…" the senator replied vaguely, and again said mournfully, "Al-Quds al-Sharif is lost, and the world is fast asleep."

"Your excellency, it is time to continue the dialogue begun by King Faisal and Chaim Weizmann, Allah have mercy on their souls."

"Weizmann underrated us, Herzl thought we were barbarians with an inferior culture. They were both agents of the West, and Zionist ideas are European, alien to this region, to its culture. That is why you will be defeated in the end."

"We are aliens? This is our home, your excellency. Half the Israelis are children of Arabia, from Asia and the Maghreb, speakers of Arabic and products of its culture. It is time to turn over a new leaf. We offer you good neighbourliness, we court you the way a cousin courts a cousin. Why do you not respond?"

"Because we understand exactly what Zionism wants," said the senator.

"We also understand exactly what your people want," Father responded.

Their exchange, though prickly, fascinated me. No wonder this society respects the old.

"*Ibni*," said Father after the senator left, "for this conversation alone it was all worth it. To face on an equal footing a senator of His Majesty Hussein bin Talal bin Abdullah al-Hashemi, to debate with him on equal terms like a pair of sparring partners – everything was worth it to reach this moment."

29

Fathers and Sons in Hebron

At last Kabi had some time off and came home to celebrate the release of Uncle Hizkel. Now the whole family could rejoice, something we hadn't done for a long time. Moshi, his wife and their children came from their co-operative village and picked up Efraim on their way. Sandra also came, and every time I saw her I felt a twinge that Yasmine was not with us.

Mother, with the energy of ten horses, toiled the whole of that week, shopping and cooking, and preparing all the sabbath dishes we had loved since we were children. It was many years since she'd had all of us around her.

Father became a happy grandfather delighting in his family. There was no trace of the withdrawn, despairing man who had broken down before our eyes after our arrival in Israel eighteen years before. He took a warm interest in everything and everybody, including Sandra – whom Kabi for some reason was ignoring – and even played a little on the oud I had bought him in the Old City. The memory of the notes remained in his fingertips, and his favourite Arabic songs carried him back to his youth. To these he added, in honour of this family sabbath, a special encore, the Hebrew children's song *Agalah im susah* – "A Cart with a Mare" – which he'd picked up somewhere. "To please the little ones," he said, smiling, half-embarrassed. For years I had agonised over the change that befell him when he failed to put roots down in Israel and collapsed with his dreams, broken and helpless by the roadside. Now I understood that he had recovered and found some peace, even though he had never realised his ambition to grow rice in Israel.

What amused the children more than the song, though, was listening to their grandparents' speech. The little sabras, who knew only Hebrew, were entertained by the patois of Iraqi Jewish-Arabic blended with elements of Hebrew, like a new dialect. In one sentence the verbs might be in Arabic and the nouns in Hebrew, sometimes with comical results.

Kabi was more taciturn than ever, withdrawn and intense. He had hugged Hizkel tightly for a long time, but hardly said a word through the entire day. I too had cause for restraint, and with good reason. When my youngest brother Efraim announced his decision to take the plunge and become a fully-fledged kibbutz member, Father and Mother took the news as calmly as if it was the most natural thing imaginable. I was dumbstruck. I couldn't forget or forgive the way they had been so opposed to the kibbutz when I was there. The pressure they put on me to leave was so relentless that eventually I gave in. I left the kibbutz, humiliated and ashamed.

In the evening, when Efraim and Moshi and his family had left, Father suggested visiting Hebron the next day. "In Baghdad I dreamed about two places – Jerusalem the holy and Hebron, the city of the Patriarchs. God be praised, now that Hizkel has been freed from prison and Hebron has been liberated, let's go and see it."

Mother prepared a big basket filled with good food, as she used to do in Baghdad when we made the pilgrimage to the tomb of the prophet Ezekiel. She took out Father's festival clothes – a starched white shirt, a new suit, a tie and a hat.

"A suit?" Father looked at her, appealing for a reprieve, but Mother ignored him. Father had long ago given up thinking about clothes. The elegant tailored suits, worn with striped ties and a flower in the lapel, were long forgotten. He wore the standard "utility" men's outfits, khaki trousers with a white shirt on weekdays, and on holidays gabardine trousers with a pale blue shirt. But Mother, who since the war felt that a new chapter had begun, bought him shirts in East Jerusalem and had an Arab tailor make him a bespoke suit.

At the door she examined him carefully, as if he was a child about to embark on his first day at school, made sure he had his pills, both dark and reading glasses, and when she was finally satisfied that we hadn't forgotten anything she agreed we could set out, kissed the mezuzah, and locked the house.

On the way to Hebron I thought about the change in Father. His behaviour reminded me of a serious argument we'd had a couple of years ago, and made me reconsider what he'd said at the time.

A tall, slender young woman from the Sociology Department at the Hebrew University had come to our housing estate. She said she was researching the question, "To what extent are the new immigrants satisfied with their reception in the country." She asked to interview Father, and I was sure he would refuse – why risk another bout of depression, dwelling again on his shattered dream? But Father invited her in, and while I made her sugarless coffee with milk, as she requested, Father brought her a tray laden with biscuits and oranges. She sat on the bed, took out a long questionnaire and began to fire questions at him. In fact, it boiled down to one question asked in various ways – "Are you content in Israel?" Father said that he did not regret having come here, that he would have done it again, that he was content, his integration in the country was satisfactory, and so on.

When she had finished and I closed the door behind her, I couldn't stop myself asking: "Father, why did you mislead her?"

"What do you mean?"

"You said everything was all right, that you had no regrets," I repeated his words in a mocking tone. "How? You realised your dreams? You started a rice-growing farm in the Hula Valley, as you'd dreamed of in Baghdad? Didn't you live in a tent, then a canvas shed, a tin shed, and a wooden hut? Didn't you wait seven years for this dream palace – a 43 square-metre flat in an immigrant housing estate in the up-market neighbourhood of Katamon Six? When did all this become so perfect all of a sudden?"

Father lit a cigarette and stood up. "Will you have coffee, son?" – his signal that a serious conversation was about to start. He went to the kitchen and prepared the excellent coffee that only he knew how to make, returned to the room and poured it for both of us.

"My son, *behiat iuni wa-iunek*, I swear by my eyes and yours, I did not say to the student one single word I did not think. I thank God that we came to Israel, where we have freedom, independence, and where we're in our own state…"

"But what have you achieved?" I interrupted.

"You think I dreamed of becoming Prime Minister? I immigrated for the sake of your future. Here you and Kabi graduated from university, Moshi has his own farm in a co-operative village, Efraim is being educated on a kibbutz. Thank

God you are all nicely established and have a good future before you."

"But Father, the woman was asking about you, not us."

"It is true that I had a dream, and things happened to me...and now I am out of work. But if we'd stayed there we would have been hostages, and under their boots."

I knew that Father had immigrated to realise his Zionist dream, not because he was thinking of us, his children, and his wife who did not want to leave Baghdad anyway. I had no doubt that before emigrating from Iraq he was not thinking in bourgeois terms, "for the sake of the family", or "for the sake of the children's future." He was an idealist who stuck to his beliefs without considering his immediate family. But now, looking at the stubborn man who had turned into a kindly grandfather, I understood something I hadn't before – Father had changed, and not only in his appearance. At some point that I'd failed to notice he had decided not to remain entrenched in the feeling that his sacrifice was in vain, and he began to appreciate his children's success. Interesting how a man justifies and even believes in his present existence in spite of his old dreams.

The delapidated road leading to Hebron was crammed with cars. Jews were driving from village to village, eager to buy up everything in sight, as if they too, like the Arabs, assumed that Israel would quit the West Bank in a matter of weeks. Burnt-out vehicles stood beside ruined adobe houses, clouds of dust rose from the roadside, out of which appeared herds of cattle driven by fellahin, and here and there someone sat on a low divan with a crate of apples or plums for sale. The land seemed sunk in sleep, neglected, backwards and beaten. This must have been the overall state of the country that greeted Sonia, my kibbutz mentor, and her comrades, revolutionaries of the early twentieth century, full of faith, seeking redemption, hungry for action. That was how I imagined them – sowing and planting and building, drunk with dreams of changing nature and man. And indeed they moved mountains and performed miracles, while here you could see the opposite, the frozen continuity of the age-old past.

We stopped beside a stall selling Hebron glass and Arab pottery jars. Mother admired the blue glassware, and Father bought her a big bowl for fruit, a big open-mouthed jar for pickling and some vases. "For your flowers," he said, smiling.

When we entered Hebron, the city of the Patriarch Abraham, our excitement grew. A small boy rolled an iron hoop on the narrow road, unimpressed by my impatient toots on the horn. He continued to run after his hoop, as if to declare, "This is my place!"

"That's how you boys used to play in Baghdad," said Hizkel.

We left the car and walked through the town. The market was crowded and filthy, with heaps of rubbish and dark, narrow alleys that twisted like the hooks, laden with their hunks of fresh, bleeding meat. Everything was dilapidated and patched, and stinking open drains ran through the centre. Eyes full of suspicion peered at us from the doorways and windows.

We went up to the Machpelah Cave, the Tomb of the Patriarchs. Hundreds were gathered there. Old and young, religious kippah-wearers and secular types who put on head-covering for the occasion, touched the walls lovingly with their fingertips, eyes awash with yearning. The shrine had been forbidden to Jews for centuries.

After a while we entered a little restaurant, where the owner recognised Father's Iraqi accent. "I worked in Baghdad for five years," he said sociably.

"*A'al*, that's good, we've come to the right place then. And how was my city? Tell us, please," Father said.

"*Wallah*, what can I tell you? After they hanged King Faisal and the Regent Abdullah and Nuri es-Sa'id, the city of the Caliphs became the city of hangmen." Father and Hizkel exchanged glances.

A skinny Jew with a long neck and a weird look in his eyes came in and asked the owner about a local furniture dealer. The man, probably suspecting him of being an agent of the *mukhabarat*, evaded the question. Then the Jew explained that he owed that merchant money from a transaction they had made before the '48 war, and he wanted to repay it. Mother looked at him admiringly, and said to him that ten Jews like him would hasten the coming of the Messiah. The owner of the restaurant thought for a while and overcame his suspicion. "That furniture dealer you asked about," he said, "he opened a business in Qatar, but his son lives in Ramallah." Then he thought a moment longer and promised to obtain the son's address.

The restaurateur turned to Father and said, "Allow me to tell you in all frankness, you people are scrambling my brain. We thought you were not human, that you were demons, devils, that you would slaughter us and rape our wives and rob our properties, and here you are…a tiger that does not devour. You behave like noble sheikhs. I am confused and do not know what to think."

Father leaned back in his chair and a smile spread over his face. He was remembering how in Baghdad he used to listen to knowledgeable insiders and search in their conversation for clues to the future behaviour of the Iraqi government. Here, in Hebron, this Arab was searching for answers in what he had to say. And he, Salman Moshi Imari, was *al-wali*, the sovereign. All praise to His Name. He looked straight at the restaurant owner. "*Ya akhi*, brother, we do not want to hurt you, God forbid. On the contrary, we want to live with you in peace, and we are waiting for your leadership to shake our outstretched hand."

After we left the restaurant Mother went to a fruit and vegetable stall and returned smiling. "So cheap you wouldn't believe. These are not like the Muslims in Baghdad – these are innocent and humble as sheep."

"They're in shock," Kabi suddenly broke his silence, "as we were in the immigrant camp. When they recover, that's when the bloodshed will begin."

"Hebron is more run-down and even poorer than the Abu Saifin quarter in Baghdad," Father said. "Tell me, son, what have they been doing here all these years?"

"Dreaming about *al-awda*, the return," Kabi replied.

"But we were refugees like them," Mother said, "and now, thank God, we lack for nothing. All thanks to the Labour Party – it did everything quickly."

"I'll tell you the difference," Father went on. "The Arabs smoked narghiles and waited for a miracle, while the founders of Israel drained the marshes and tilled the soil, changed the face of the country and of the Jewish people."

On the way back to Jerusalem Hizkel suddenly spoke up. "I want to say something that maybe you won't like. I've been thinking and thinking, and I'm not sure that we orientals would have been capable of building this state."

"How can you say such a thing?" I protested.

"After what we saw today, and after twenty years in prison with Muslims, I've come to know them and us. Our culture is not a culture of revolutions. We are also fatalists, like the Arabs. We sat under the palm trees and waited for the Messiah. We lamented 'by the rivers of Babylon' while the Jews of Europe got up and did something. They came from the incandescent world of the Bolsheviks. Such people are irreverent, they have no God, they have decided to become the Messiah themselves. If there is a mountain in their way, they move it. We see a mountain and we stop. That's the difference between East and West."

"I'm not sure you're right, brother," said Father. "We thought of the Land of Israel as the Temple, a spiritual focus, an object of longing. They saw it as a place in which to build a state."

Kabi objected: "It's terrible, what you're saying. In what way are we inferior to those Ashkenazis? Look how we fought in this war, and how many border settlements we have built! The problem was that they never took us into account, and you allowed them to do everything without you, you didn't even demand to be represented in the Zionist congresses!"

"We trusted them," Hizkel replied. "They are Jews, after all."

I decided to enter the discussion: "Before the Second World War there were ten million Jews in Europe, and two to three million would have been enough to establish the state the Zionists were hoping for. In the East, at that time, there were only about a million Jews, scattered among all the Muslim states. They didn't know any Yiddish, and they were rooted in Arabic culture. The Zionist leaders didn't know them and didn't need them."

"Nuri, my son," Father said in an unusually thoughtful tone, "your uncle may be right. Revolution is blood, and these people had the hard heads of world-savers who believe only in their own truth and God himself can't budge them from it. Like in your kibbutz, where the children sleep separately from their parents. Can you imagine such a thing among us? Parents and children getting together for a couple of hours a day, like a committee meeting?"

"Let me tell you something that may astonish you," said Hizkel. "Listen to a 'prisoner of Zion' who had plenty of time to think. Without Israel, the Arab world would have gone on sleeping for another hundred years. All the revolutions – Hosni al-Zaim in Syria and Nasser in Egypt – happened because of the Zionist revolution. They learned from us and envied us for what we achieved here. I keep on rubbing my eyes and can't believe what I see. All that has been done here, the construction, the enterprise, the industry, the creativity – *mashallah*, God help us, is there such a thing in the Arab world, in the entire world?"

"It was a struggle for survival," I insisted. "If we'd been here instead of the old pioneers we would have done the same thing."

"We contributed too," Kabi declared. "The state wouldn't be the same without us. The trouble is, the old guard don't give us a chance."

"Maybe we ought to show more initiative, both in society and towards the Arabs," I suggested.

"It won't do any good," Kabi argued bitterly. "The game has been fixed. The old guard and the Labour Party leadership have sewn up this state. They seized the high ground and left no room for us."

"There is a difference between their soul and ours," Father explained. "To make a revolution the way they did, you must have some ruthlessness in you."

Kabi heard Father only partially and interpreted things his own way. "We're no worse than the old guard!" he said angrily.

"Historical circumstances created this reality, and for now they hold all the power. You also revolutionised the life of the Jews in Iraq – you created a secret Zionist movement, some of your comrades were hanged, others died on the way, you sacrificed everything and here you had to start from scratch."

"The one thing we can say for ourselves, son, is that we wanted with all our hearts to be in the Land of Israel, and we did it without any advance preparation, Now we must move forwards."

"But don't you see, Father," Kabi protested, "we're stuck in jobs that have to do with Arabs and Arabic, and in the minds of Ashkenazi Israelis these are marginal and temporary occupations without any prestige!"

"Kabi my son, don't be angry with me…If you feel this way you shouldn't have gone to Europe on this job, and you shouldn't keep going with Arabic issues. We didn't leave one exile to go into another. How is it that with all your gifts you've been left on the fringes? Maybe you gave up too easily, didn't make enough effort to integrate yourself into Israeli society."

"What choice did I have? If I hadn't gone to work for the Mossad and travelled wherever they sent me, I'd have been unemployed. So I'm also doing something," he concluded, looking at Hizkel.

"You should feel that the State of Israel is yours, that you are in your own house, and it doesn't matter whether you work on Arabic issues or anything else," Father said, looking at the fiery sunset holding back the night on the mountains of Jerusalem.

30

Sealed Lips

"How is it that with all your gifts you've been left on the fringes? Maybe you gave up too easily, didn't make enough effort to integrate into Israeli society." That's what his father had said, and he was so hurt that he almost gave away the secret. But if he had he really would have been a failure.

But this silence was certainly costly. He would never be able to celebrate openly, really rejoice at having fulfilled his wildest ambition. He would never be able to utter cries of joy, as he would have liked to do, to share his profound satisfaction even with the people closest to him. Not one of them would ever know about the months he had spent in Khorramshahr, that remote corner of a hot and humid hell, without a home and without a woman, a monk among crooks and all sorts of dubious types.

He had no one to blame but himself. He had chosen freely to work for the Mossad, nobody forced him. And there, in the outer darkness, he was doing something real, something valuable. Even Amram Teshuvah, the ultra-cautious, tight-lipped head of station, had a good word for him. Had he not searched out and freed Hizkel without authorisation he would have been given a commendation. Never mind, everyone in the Mossad was proud of him, pleased that he was able to liberate a "prisoner of Zion" they had all despaired of.

Amram Teshuvah made things very clear: "Your parents mustn't know that you've been transferred from London to Khorramshahr, it will kill them with worry. Also you must not see Hizkel in the course of this operation. He might recognise you and that will be the end of him and you and our network over there. It could lead to a disagreement between the government of Israel and the Shah of Iran. Whatever happens, your lips must remain sealed!"

And what did Father know now? He knew his younger son Nuri was doing very well, and was disappointed that his eldest seemed to be stuck in a rut and left behind. You could not miss the satisfaction on his face when he saw a newspaper photo of Nuri with some VIP on a visit to East Jerusalem, or when his name appeared in one of the Arab papers. Nuri had replaced him in Father's life; he was the one who helped him with everything, looked after him and Mother, enjoyed their high regard, while he – he was nothing. All they knew about him was that he was working for the Mossad in London. A headline without a story. And even when he achieved the unbelievable and freed Hizkel, no one knew about it and he had to bottle up his feelings.

On the other hand, he did not envy Nuri his work with the Minister, a rigid conservative Ashkenazi who hid behind the backs of prime ministers and behaved as if he was still in the pioneering days, as if the Middle East had frozen in its tracks. How could Nuri get on with such a man?

If he could only reveal the truth to Hizkel! If Hizkel only knew that he, Kabi, had been behind his sudden release, that his favourite nephew was his angel of deliverance. He would tell him all the details of the operation which turned his dream of liberty into reality after all those years.

Maybe he should do this anyway, he thought. What a conversation that would be! Why not? He would invite Hizkel to join him over a glass of good arrack, then drop the information on him like a bomb. Hizkel would laugh, cry, shake his head, pinch him, unbelieving, and demand to know everything.

Then he would describe his wanderings in Iran, tell him about Tehran, about Khorramshahr, where the choking stink of gas is overpowering, tell him about the slick Shahin Pur, the compulsive gambler he had met in the tea-house, about the moment he mentioned his family connection to the governor of the prison in Nograt Salman. Kabi would describe how from his first night in Khorramshahr he felt that this was one of the most important episodes in his life, perhaps *the* most important, and sensed that destiny had sent him there.

He would tell Hizkel about the long weeks of making friends with Shahin Pur, until he agreed to involve him, Kabi, in his smuggling business, then sending Shahin to Baghdad to persuade the embittered head of the prison service to collaborate with the Free Iraqi Forces based in London, a totally imaginary group that he'd invented for the purpose.

He would describe the exhausting process of finding out about Hizkel's condition, the nights when he sat up, calculating and recalculating his resources till he concluded that financing the operation of smuggling his uncle out of prison and Iraq was beyond his means, then his agonising over the decision, whether to tell his superiors in the Mossad about it. The shortage of funds was not the only obstacle; Hizkel's legal status, his passport and all the rest had to be taken care of. In the end he told Amram everything, and was severely reprimanded for acting on his own.

He would tell Hizkel how he, Kabi, left Khorramshahr two days before his uncle's arrival there, and how at the height of the operation he confined himself to a room in a small flea-pit hotel in Tehran, where he sat and bit his nails and calculated the hours: *Now Hizkel is in the smugglers' boat, now he's in the hut in the grove, now he's in Shahin Pur's house, taking off the woman's clothes, now our contact man has come to see him, now he's on the plane to Tehran, now he's in Tehran, now he's on the plane and on his way home…*

If he could also tell Father, expunge the scars of the torments he had endured ever since Hizkel was arrested. How Father suffered when his brother was seized and jailed, when he left Baghdad and immigrated to Israel, leaving Hizkel behind, how he grieved when Rashel had abandoned Hizkel too. The feelings of guilt never left him in all the years in Israel, and even now he could not look his brother in the eye. If he knew that his son, his own flesh and blood, was the one who freed his brother, it would make him feel so much better.

But Kabi was bound by the constraints of the Mossad. Hizkel and Father, Mother and Nuri were all around him, his heart was overflowing, but his lips remained sealed.

31

"You're a minute and a half late"

"Hello, Nuri. Yes, it's me. Yes, thanks, I'm all right. I heard you were looking for me at Al-Hurriyeh. Yes, I'm out of hiding…Of course, I'll be glad to meet you for coffee this evening. No, not at Al-Hurriyeh, it's closed for renovations. How about the Imperial hotel? You know it? Fine, then I'll see you there at seven."

That was Yasmine on the phone, and my heart soared like a bird. I hurried to finish some urgent work, dressed warmly and left for the Imperial. Outside it was dark and the wind was howling, and by a quarter to seven I was in the hotel lobby. I didn't want her to wait for me.

I examined the photographs on the walls, which revealed something of the history of the old hotel and the important people who had stayed there. Ten past seven. Yasmine was usually very punctual. I thought of Abdel Wahab's song, "You were a minute and a half late, not a minute…" I ordered a beer. I kept glancing at the entrance. A pair of young tourists came in, talking noisily in French. Twenty past seven. Where was she? Had the heavy rain delayed her? Maybe she couldn't find a parking space. I finished the beer. I thought back to our short telephone conversation. Did she perhaps say eight, not seven? I asked a waiter to bring me a newspaper, to pass the time.

The wall clock showed seven-thirty-five. I began to worry. Had something happened to her? The French couple kept on laughing loudly, getting on my nerves. What was keeping her? Couldn't she phone the hotel and leave a message? I glanced around the lobby – no desk there, the phone would be in reception. Come on, trade unionist, I told myself, take it easy. They'll call you if anything…Still, I went along to reception and asked them to let me know if there was a call for me. Perhaps she had changed her mind. Meeting in a hotel might seem compromising even to a Jewish woman, let alone an Arab one. Someone might see her. The hotel proprietor was probably a friend of her father's.

Five to eight. Now I was feeling offended. Did I have to hang around for a whole hour, waiting for her? I ordered another beer. I needed to go to the lavatory but stayed put – she might turn up just when I was in there. At ten past eight I got up, went to the lavatory, and when I came out she still wasn't there and there was no message. I'd had enough.

Hail was beating down outside, heaps of tiny beads of ice edged the road. I drove slowly to avoid skidding, back to my little flat, all the while seeing Yasmine's face – her sensuous curved lips, her all-seeing eyes. I had become intensely alert to every flutter of her eyelids and felt the thrill of intimacy, a desire to know her, listen to her, hear her inhaling the smoke of her cigarette. She had entered my bloodstream. Was this the immediate, instinctive love, the kind you can't resist? They say that every person has a halo around his head, a small sun, which dazzles, creates a sweet illusion, an addiction. When two such haloes touch, love happens. Was her halo responding to mine? And where would it lead?

How would Abu George react if this relationship developed? Would he feel that I had taken advantage of his daughter? I was walking through a minefield – one wrong step and it would all blow up. One evening I sat with him in his newspaper office, we drank vodka and he told me about his anguish when they had to flee from their house in 1948. By the time we left we were both drunk and propping each other up. I staggered with him to his Dodge and he said, swaying, his hand on my shoulder, "Nuri, life is short. Who knows when my hour will come. There is no cure for what ails me, and I am teaching myself to look for the good in the bad." He glanced round and chuckled. "There is even some good in your conquest – we got Yasmine back. You will never know how grateful I am to you. You saved my daughter for me." He gave me a kiss on the cheek and climbed into his car. Yes, the situation was complicated, but it was not entirely hopeless.

My phone rang at nine. Yasmine. She apologised. Just when she was going out to meet me her father had felt so unwell that she had taken him to Hadassah. By the time a doctor had attended to him, and she felt she could leave him to phone the hotel I had already left. She apologised again and said they were still at the hospital. I asked if I could visit her father and she promised to let me know when he felt well enough.

In the morning I asked Aliza to get me Shamluk of the Shin Bet.

"Shamluk, you won't believe this – the Messianic Age is at hand! Senator Antoine has finally recognised us. A few days ago he actually came in person to my office and we had a long chat."

"Bastard!" Shamluk hissed, totally oblivious to my hope that the news would cheer him up. "We sent him warnings, told him to tone down his public statements. Nothing doing! We should lock up his mouth."

"He's just a toothless old man, sick and utterly confused," I argued. "Don't turn him into a martyr."

"He can go to hell, he doesn't know what he's got coming to him. If he didn't listen to the words of Moses, he will listen to the whip of Pharaoh."

A few minutes later Aliza came in. "Yasmine Hilmi is here."

"Give me two minutes to get organised." I emptied my pockets of all the things they were stuffed with – bits of paper, a notebook, a handkerchief or two and a wallet – a bad habit left over from my childhood. I went into the bathroom and in front of the mirror tucked in my shirt and tightened the knot in my tie, combed my hair and splashed on aftershave. My face felt hot. What had brought her here, I wondered anxiously. Was her father all right? Hadn't she sworn that she would never enter my office, this symbol of the occupation?

I went out to the waiting room and found her huddled in a chair, her big dark glasses hiding her eyes and a scarf tied round her head. Aliza relieved her of the umbrella and raincoat, and she stood before me in a long black skirt and a long-sleeved brown sweater, as if she was visiting someone in the ultra-Orthodox quarter. I led her into my office and asked after her father.

"He's better," she said and sat down wearily, tucking her legs under the armchair. She took out her slim cigarettes, lit one and inhaled loudly. Slowly she took off her dark glasses and looked around the room. I guessed that she would prefer to leave the important stuff to the end of the visit, following local custom.

"It's good to see you. I think about you a lot, and…" I stopped there. "Have you finished writing your dissertation?"

She shook her head. "Not yet."

"I have news for you, Yasmine. I've located Edna Mazursky. About eight months ago, after the war, she went to join her sister in New Jersey. Apparently for good." I gave her a note with Edna's address and telephone number.

"New Jersey?" her eyes clung to mine.

"Her husband fell in the battle for Jerusalem."

"Oh God!…Where did it happen?"

"In al-Mudawara, the place we call Ammunition Hill. As she is a war widow I was able to locate her through the army."

Her hand slipped down from the arm of the chair.

"Has she any children?"

"No."

"What awful news. Jesus." Her face was very pale. "It's hot in here," she said and took off the scarf and sweater, revealing a short-sleeved beige shirt. She shook out her hair and ran her fingers through it. Seeing her breasts rising and falling made me hot too. I wanted to sit beside her, caress and hug her, sink into her…I took one of her thin cigarettes, lit it and inhaled deeply, but I looked away so she wouldn't see what I was feeling.

"What good angel brought you to me?" I asked in a low voice.

"My father sent me to see you urgently." Looking tense, she replaced the cigarette in the ashtray. "It's about Senator Antoine. Last night he came to the hospital, badly shaken, and told us he heard a rumour that he's about to be deported because of some idiotic interview he gave the *Washington Post*. He says, 'The Israelis took my words out of context.' Father asks if it's not too much trouble, if you could find out if there is any truth in the rumour, and what can be done about it."

"Have you seen the interview, Yasmine? He says some very harsh things. He compares the Israelis to the Nazis. It's not a case of taking words out of context. It's a difficult business. The question is, would he be willing to soften his statements, apologise, explain…"

"We have a saying, *Kif intale lehmar min al-wahle* – How do you get the donkey out of the mud? I've known the senator all my life. He's like a kindly grandfather to me. His head is made of stone, but he's not a bad man. Expelling him from his home and his country would be like a death sentence, especially at his age. He's also unwell." She looked at me and dropped her eyes.

She was obviously tired and worried. She took a small mirror from her handbag, tidied her hair, then smiled. "I dressed up a little, didn't want to be recognised coming here. I look terrible."

"You look beautiful."

"I slept very little last night," she said and rubbed her leg absentmindedly.

I leaned back in my chair, loosened my tie and closed my eyes for a moment, struggling with myself. The office was so quiet I could hear her breathing. She's so near, I thought. I wanted her to stroke my forehead, my face, I wanted to take her hands, smell them as you smell a baby, kiss her fingertips. My heart was beating fast.

"Are you all right?" she asked a little anxiously.

"Yes, a little tired. I've missed you…" I avoided her eyes.

"I'm tired too. Finishing the dissertation is exhausting me, on top of the regular work at the youth village."

"How is it going? Are you getting on all right?"

"I like the work, it's varied, very professional. There is a lot to do and people to work with. There are about two hundred children and it's both a treatment centre and a home for disabled and retarded children, but it also takes children who have simply been neglected. I work as a diagnostician. I see all the new arrivals and assess their condition. I'm very careful about classifying any child as retarded, to avoid damaging those who are not, so that they can be transferred to other institutions where they could develop better. It's important to me," she emphasised, "so from time to time I give repeat tests to all the children in the village, and sometimes we discover children who can be transferred gradually to the normal systems. Of course, there is counselling too. I advise the instructors and nurses and also treat children individually. That's the main satisfaction in the work." She took a deep breath. "That's it, more or less. I'm glad I went to work there. Maybe now is the time to say, Thank you, Nuri." She stood up and quickly put on the sweater and the headscarf.

"You're going already?"

"Have to. Father is waiting for me at the hospital."

"Don't forget to give him my regards and best wishes for a quick recovery."

I always enjoyed the matter-of-fact clarity of her speech. At the same time I wished that she wouldn't insist on speaking to me in English, which she spoke so much better than I did. Sometimes what she said sounded like a complex mathematical equation and I often felt tongue-tied when speaking to her. I could understand why she did not want us to talk in Hebrew, though when working at the village she sounded like any Jewish Israeli woman. But why couldn't we communicate in Arabic, which was our mother-tongue, hers and mine? Why did she set up this language barrier between us, like a throw-back to the days of the British Mandate? I remembered her quoting Franz

Fanon: "Speaking a particular language means, above all, adopting a culture."

I had to move quickly – the conversation with Shamluk was a bad omen. I rang Levanah and asked to speak to the Minister. I told him briefly what it was all about.

"Nuri, the man is an anti-Semite. I read the interview you sent me."

"And what are we, Arab-lovers?"

"Look here, even if I agreed with you, it's not in our hands."

"Sir, the policy of deporting people is causing resentment and giving us a bad name throughout the world. We must enable them to let off steam," I insisted. "We must give them a chance to soften. We can bring them closer, build a bridge for reconciliation. It can't be done by force and under compulsion. Please!"

After a brief silence he drew the conversation to a close. "Thou shalt cast out the evil from thy midst – so says the Bible," he intoned with an air of finality.

I sank back in my chair like a deflated balloon. Perhaps I should have gone to see him, talked to him face to face instead of on the phone. I still did not know what moved him, how to touch his heart. "Appeal to his good side," Levanah always advised me, but deep down inside me I rebelled. This is a national issue, and I'm his advisor, dammit!

"Aliza, please get me Aharon Amitai, it's very urgent!" Amitai was my last hope. I had to speak to him, even though it meant circumnavigating my Minister and acting against his wishes. It took Aliza a whole hour to get hold of him.

"Aharon, does the name Senator Antoine mean anything to you?"

"The die is cast," he replied crisply.

"Please, won't you reconsider? It's a mistake which will harm us. Why use a sledge hammer to swat a fly?"

"Not every fly is simply a fly, Nuri. Some are poisonous flies that can kill you." I heard him puffing on his pipe. "How're things otherwise?"

"Just fine!" I snapped, flinging my pen down on the desk. I put on a raincoat and walked out, seething.

"Where are you going? It's pouring out there. At least take an umbrella!" Aliza urged, running after me to the door.

To hell with it, I fumed, what's the point of my job, if I can't show them that a different approach is possible? The Minister thought I loved Arabs. He paid no attention when I quoted something Charlie Chaplin once said: "I hate the sight of blood, but it's in my veins."

32

"A kosher Christian"

After leaving Nuri's office, Yasmine felt the ground slipping away from under her. Her mind was in a whirl. How did he feel about her? Had he been indifferent and correct or polite and respectful? Where was the relationship with him leading her?

She recalled a remark he made once while walking her home. When they entered Ragheb al-Nashashibi Lane he had told her that it was named after the Arab Mayor of Jerusalem whose wife was Jewish, then in the same breath added that Rashel, his Uncle Hizkel's wife, had abandoned him and remained in Iraq with the Muslim lawyer who had defended him. Was that a hint that he was willing to follow their example, that he would contemplate a cross-cultural marriage?

It was complicated. Though he called himself *ibn Arab* – a son of Arabia – and was indeed steeped in the life, culture and language of the Arabs, he was a Jew, through and through, his mother was a devout Jew, his grandfather had been a rabbi. What would he say to his family: "I've brought you a kosher Christian woman"?

But perhaps she was simply fantasising and there was nothing to it, just a curious male looking to add another trophy to his string of conquests, someone who liked the idea of flirting with a goy female. Oh come on, she said to herself, is that how a flirting man behaves? No, she wasn't mistaken: the sky seemed to be falling in on them when they were together.

What do you know about him, she asked herself, and what can you learn from it? As a boy he had left his family and joined a kibbbutz, then left the kibbutz and rejoined his family in an immigrant camp, left them again and at sixteen moved to Jerusalem, where he lived alone and supported himself, and when he began to do well he moved his family there, lived for a while with them, then left them again and took a flat by himself...All these moves suggested an independent personality, not a soft, malleable type attached to his mother's apron strings. Torn from his roots as a boy, he managed to take root in a new culture, even though the scars of the old uprooting remained deep in his soul. Would he have the strength to break the bonds of nationality and religion? He was rebellious and defied convention, though he did so discreetly, with his casual undemonstrative touches, and his soft voice. He was inquisitive and compassionate. I'd like to meet his parents, she thought, then smiled to herself. And you, Mrs Hilmi, how would you like him for a son-in-law?

He had told her that his older brother had an American girlfriend. Was she Jewish? It's a fact that in America and Europe Jews marry Christian women, so if Nuri had fallen in love with a Christian woman in London or Paris he would not hesitate to marry her. But could he cross the lines for a Palestinian Arab woman? His mother would have a fit, and what would his father say? And he himself might lose his job and his position and his entire world. But maybe he would...After all, he's a different Jew, unlike the image depicted by Fayez and his comrades in their struggle for public opinion. A new kind of Israeli, without machismo, not a battle hero or a hoe-wielding pioneer, as they like to project themselves.

Her head was bursting with questions and thoughts about him and herself. Why not put it to him directly: "What do you want from me?" She longed to start living again, to leave behind the pointless mourning, the bitterness, the loneliness, and the patriotic struggle. Surely life was not all wars and vengeance and restoration of rights and that whole ideology. Perhaps real life was simply loving, finding a partner, raising a family, like her friend Nehad and like people all over the world. Ever since meeting Nuri she had felt that deep down inside she was yearning to conceive, longing for love given and received, for a man's caress, his warmth, his friendship, for life with a twin soul. She dreamed of waking in the morning with her man beside her in bed, of listening to his breathing, caring for him and giving him pleasure, putting her arm through his in the street, dreaming together.

She was gripped by a sudden surge of panic. What was happening to her? Till now she had succeeded in suppressing these thoughts and longings. She'd never considered that he could be brought into her life. Yet now he was constantly in her mind. She was thinking like a woman in love. Why, of all the men in the world, did she have to fall in love with a Jew?

But she was no longer afraid to contemplate every possibility, and it was as if a new flavour had been added to her life. She was sure he would not convert to Christianity for her. Was she willing to convert to Judaism for him? Did he view her as an enemy, the way she saw him as an occupier, teasing him over it endlessly? She treated him with suspicion all the time, as is the way of weak people, and threw unfounded accusations at him. Yet he did not behave masterfully, like a conqueror. Why bring external considerations into the sphere of love? What do they matter? We're just people. Peel a single millimetre of skin from a black or white person, and they will look just the same, sharing the same humanity; how much more so when two people are natives of the same region and speakers of its language.

Why had she insisted on speaking English with him? She didn't want to speak Hebrew – it would have made her feel subordinate to the occupier – but they could have spoken Arabic, as he proposed and as would have been most natural. Why had she refused? Was it to demonstrate her superior knowledge? Or had she subconsciously preferred the international language as a way of neutralising the strident nationalisms of Arabic and Hebrew?

She had appeared with him in public, even made a date to meet in a hotel in East Jerusalem, though you could lose your reputation if you so much as spoke with a man in public. The Arab woman's honour was the highest value in her society. Some honour! Honour my arse, as the Israelis would put it. But no power on earth would help you when minds were scorched by the fire of this honour. Even clever and educated people fell into this trap.

The first time she had set eyes on him he symbolised their life's catastrophe. In fact, she did not see him, but pinned on him all the agonies of the occupation. She did not even speak to him, only threw slogans at him. It never occurred to her that her soul would grow attached to him, that merely thinking about him would wake her body from its long hibernation. Perhaps they really should flee from this insane place, find work and a life somewhere else – in France, America, Australia, New Zealand. For surely they could have no future here.

Suppose she married him and they lived together. Where would she belong? With whom would she identify? With him and his people? How would she feel? Her very existence would be split down the middle, the Arabs would cast her out and the Jews wouldn't accept her.

And her parents? The thought of what this might do to them made her blood run cold. Their only daughter, the apple of their eyes, marry a Zionist? Their hearts would be broken just as if she had died.

And if they married and had a family, what would their children be and what kind of future would they have? To which community would they belong? Would they be Jews, Christians, Arabs, Israelis, Palestinians? In which army would they serve? Or they might grow up with split personalities and escape from this place to seek lives elsewhere.

How she wished she had Edna Mazursky beside her now, she needed her so much. With her alone could she share these thoughts. Or was that an illusion? Perhaps her Edna had become a dream, a mental construct, unrelated to today's real flesh-and-blood Edna. So many years had passed since they last met as eight-year-old girls. She could hardly out of the blue call this woman in New Jersey and talk into a telephone about a man called Nuri who had got into her bloodstream, and about the tenuous filaments holding her world together, a world suspended in the void.

33

"That Yasmina of yours"

At the end of February, soon after infiltrators set off bombs in the Jerusalem neighbourhood of Romema, Yasmine showed up again at my office. She put Naguib Mahfouz's *Bain al-Qasrain*, the first volume of his Cairo Trilogy, on my desk, gave me a friendly smile, said, "Just wanted to give you a little present, a novel I enjoyed reading," and left.

I stroked the book, my heart warmed by the gift from my sharp-tongued "Turquisa". But it also deepened the sadness and loneliness into which I'd been sinking by the day. The longing for her was growing unbearable but still I did not approach her. My relations with her were a little like a tango – one step forward and two steps back. One moment I rose to heaven with her, the next I plunged into the abyss. This rollercoaster was wearing me out. Perhaps I should stick to Michelle? Michelle was cute, clever, full of life, and she wanted me. I did not feel lost with her. Keep knocking on Yasmine's gate, I told myself, and you'll remain a lonely, ageing bachelor.

For some reason I remembered a poem by Leah Goldberg, engraved in my consciousness ever since I heard her reciting it back in my student days:

It is not the sea that lies between us
It is not the gulf that lies between us
It is not the time that lies between us
It is we ourselves – who lie between us

The phone rang – Michelle. At least she remembered me. "Let's go to the cinema this evening," she suggested. We agreed to meet at eight outside Smadar cinema in the German Colony.

At home I found a thoughtful letter from my brother Kabi, who had returned to the mystery country in which he was stationed. "When I finish my service and return to Israel," he wrote, "I think I'll change my home base. Why live in the holy necropolis of Jerusalem? What is there to do in a city of stones and melancholy, in this gathering of the generations? Better to live in a casual, promiscuous, hot city, the city of Bialik, Alterman and Shlonsky. Better still, in Ramat Gan, where the former Baghdadis have settled, a city of *'eyish tanoor'* pittas, hamine eggs, mango pickles and Persian garlic. So don't be surprised, little brother, if when I return from this mission I divorce Jerusalem and turn over a new leaf in the sands of Tel Aviv." What did he mean by turn over a new leaf? Was that a hint that he was thinking of getting married, at long last? The phone rang and interrupted my speculations.

"Nuri? Instead of meeting you at the cinema, I'm coming to your place," Michelle announced.

"Oh no! The place is a mess. Wait for me there, I'm coming!"

"It's no use, Nuri. It's time I saw where you live. Did you say number 13 Elazar Hamodai? I'll be right there."

I hurriedly swept the room, passed a duster over my desk and tidied things up a bit. I took a quick shower and used the aftershave she'd given me. At that moment the doorbell rang.

"This is it?" she looked around critically. "What's this cat doing here? Out, shoo!" she raised her foot to Grushka, who scooted out. "It's awfully tiny. You should have a spacious, elegant flat. A man in your position deserves better."

"This is what I've got."

"Oh look at the wardrobe – where did you get this great heap of junk? You should have modern furniture. And this poster of Marilyn Monroe – are you a teenager?" She dismissed it, ignoring the longing in Marilyn's eyes. "Get an original painting. There are some good and inexpensive Israeli painters. You shouldn't surround yourself with posters and cheap reproductions. We'll go to the galleries in Jaffa, I'll help you to choose."

She came up to me with sinuous feline movements, removed the scarf from around her neck, put her arms around me and sniffed. "Ah, you're using a decent aftershave at last. You're making progress." She offered her lips and I kissed her lightly.

"Would you like a drink?"

"My mother's been taken to hospital," she said in reply. "I've got to return to Paris."

"I'm sorry to hear that. What's wrong with her?"

"What isn't. Why don't you come with me? I'll take you to the Louvre, to St Germain, we'll sit in Café Flor, the café of Sartre, Camus, Greco. We'll have a great time."

"And who will make peace here?" I said, laughing.

"There will never be peace here, *chéri*. I have learned in my profession that there are problems that can't be solved, not even with medication. The trick is to survive them."

"I can offer you a glass of arrack from Ramallah."

"Ah, yes, your famous arrack – that will be interesting. With plenty of ice."

I went into the kitchenette to prepare her drink. "Tell me," she asked, "is it normal that a man of thirty has never been abroad? London, Paris, Rome – aren't you curious to visit them? Why not learn from that Yasmina of yours. She lived in Paris for years, she's a woman of the world. Incidentally, I have news for you. She wants to start a village like ours in East Jerusalem. What do you think? We're bringing them progress, aren't we? I intend to help her. Has she told you?"

"Abu George, her father, told me. He advised her to get Mutran Krachi to help her raise funds and public support."

"Who is that Mutran? She respects him."

"An Israel-hater," I said.

"*Ooh la la*, you're making progress! You're not Hamlet any more. You've finally realised that they're all Israel-haters. I think that your Yasmina is also working against us." She clasped my neck with her arms, pressed her breasts to my chest and started to pull my shirt out and unfasten the buttons.

"You can't do this," I said, blushing. "The neighbours can see us."

"Are you a kid?"

"Come on, let's go! I reserved tickets at the cinema."

"To hell with the cinema, when will you act spontaneously, learn to live a little?" she grumbled, drank up the arrack and exhaled an anise-flavoured breath. "Which film are you taking me to?"

"An Israeli one, *Three Days and a Child*."

"I didn't know there was an Israeli film industry."

"You think this is the Congo? You said yourself Israel is the world's third major power."

When we left the flat Grushka wasn't on the landing . "You see, even the cat is scared of you," I complained.

"You're the only one who isn't," she giggled.

Michelle wanted to walk to the cinema in spite of the rain. "It's romantic, and I've got an umbrella." She slipped her arm through mine contentedly, as if I were walking with her down the Champs Elysées. For a moment I hoped we would run into Yardena, who lived nearby.

She was unimpressed by the film, so I made up for it by taking her to the Peter Café for coffee and apple strudel. Then she suggested going to her place but I suggested mine, knowing she wouldn't want to stay the night there, away from her cosmetics. I returned home alone.

Still no Grushka. Perhaps she was out fighting with a street cat. A few days earlier I saw a tomcat chasing a female, and when he caught up with her he gave a hoarse cry, bit her neck and crouched over her. She moaned and struggled as if terrified of being knifed…Where was Grushka? I worried, but the street was quiet.

I went into my little one-room flat, snuggled down in a winter blanket and listened to the rain hammering at the big window. The phone rang. Probably Michelle, grumbling because she was there and I was here on such a cold night.

"I hereby announce that I'm finishing the dissertation and returning to life!" Yasmine declared gaily, "Next week I'm on cash-register duty at Al-Hurriyeh, your honour is invited."

"My honour is impatient, can't wait to see you. Welcome back!" I replied, and fell asleep with a smile on my face.

Two days later I drove Michelle to the airport. On the way I gave her a record by the Queen of Fado, Amália Rodrigues and a brooch I'd bought in an Armenian shop in the Old City.

"I don't know when I'll be back," she said sadly.

"I'll be here, I've nowhere else to go."

From the airport I drove straight to Al-Hurriyeh. Um George was at the till. "Yasmine asked me to tell you she will be here this evening," she said.

Shamluk was sitting at the table that Yasmine and I usually occupied. He waved to me and I joined him.

"Your nymph is spending too much time with the Mutran," he said. "The man is up to his eyebrows in gambling and he's a womaniser too. He organises demonstrations against us and tells the Arabs in the territories, who are working for us, that they're helping us to establish the third Kingdom of Israel."

"The Mutran is helping her start a youth treatment centre in Abu Dis," I replied.

Shamluk gave me the contemptuous look he usually reserved for Mr Harish of the Ministry of Religious Affairs. "That's a cover story."

I returned to the restaurant in the evening. The canaries greeted me effusively, like an old friend, but Um George seemed a little cool. "Yasmine is not back yet. She's at the Mutran's office. Can I offer you anything?"

I stayed. An hour passed and I began to feel uncomfortable. I was getting up to leave when Yasmine arrived. She was breathing heavily, as if in some distress, and looked like a troubled ghost. She put down a heavy package beside the till and when she spotted me she smiled sadly.

"I'm sorry," she said and sank into a chair. "I'm so tired, completely wrung out." I wanted to touch her, to take away the pain in her eyes. "Please phone tomorrow. Forgive me." She made an effort to smile.

Outside the night was dark and cold. Rain was beating down.

The wind was tugging at the slender palm tree at the end of the street. An old cypress tree had surrendered and collapsed onto the pavement – luckily no-one was hurt. I couldn't get Yasmine out of my mind. I'd never seen her so broken and depressed. What had happened?

34

Hizkel – Integration Blues

I had barely started attending to Hizkel's immigration issues, and already this took up what little free time I had. Michelle's letters remained unanswered, and when I phoned Yasmine she wouldn't agree to meet me and she cut the conversation short. What on earth was going on?

I took Hizkel to the Ministry of Absorption, where we were met by a friendly, roly-poly receptionist. She put him down for a course in Advanced Hebrew at an intensive study centre, and advised him to defer his claims while the status of the "prisoners of Zion" from the USSR was being defined. "Their privileges are being extended," she explained. He stared at her, uncomprehending, but could see she meant well. "In the meantime, get your documents ready," she instructed him.

"What documents?" he asked.

"The verdict from your trial and statements of witnesses that you were a 'prisoner of Zion'…"

"Witnesses? Very well, I have some names for you to write down: Shalom Salah and Yussef Basri, who were both hanged, and Abu-Salah el-Hibaz, my student and subordinate, who kept the weapons for Jewish self-defence in the basement of his bakery and sang Hatikvah on his way to the gallows…"

The woman's eyes widened, and Hizkel stopped, afraid to

slide back into the nightmare from which he had just been freed. "I'm sorry," the woman said drily, "this is the procedure." She frowned and played with the pencil, searching for a solution. "Why don't you go to the Association of Immigrants from Babylon?" she said brightly, as if it was an original idea. "They have people from the Zionist movement who can give you letters of recommendation." She thrust her head forward, eyebrows raised, to see if he would come up with more information. Seeing that there was no getting through to her, he got up and dragged his damaged leg out of the office.

"Come on son, let's get out of here and breathe some fresh air," he said gloomily. From the car park I showed him the government enclave, the offices of Prime Minister Eshkol and Finance Minister Sapir, as well as the new Knesset building.

"Why don't we go to Stad Nawi?" Hizkel cut in. Nawi had led the clandestine Zionist movement in Iraq, and I knew that Hizkel was devoted to him and regarded him as his mentor. "An excellent idea," I said and went to my Minister's office in the adjacent building to tell Levanah I was going to Tel Aviv.

Once there, we went straight to the headquarters of the Labour Federation on Arlozorov Street. The huge building, popularly known as the Kremlin, dwarfed its surroundings. We passed through the gates and crossed the vast front lawn.

"His office is in this building?" Hizkel said in amazement.

At the information desk I asked about the department for the integration of immigrants from Iraq. The clerk stared at me. "Excuse me, comrade" – stressing the last word – "are there any immigrants from Iraq? I thought they all arrived long ago."

"We are looking for Stad Nawi."

"Who? Osnavi? You sure he works here?"

"Stad Nawi – two words. Professor Nawi, sir."

"Here there are no sirs and no professors. We are all comrades, comrade." He leafed through a thick notebook. "Do you mean Comrade Naveh?"

"He changed his name?" asked Hizkel.

"He did not change it, comrade, he Hebraised it. Comrade Ben-Gurion required all public representatives to Hebraise their names," the man explained, clearly enunciating every word. "So, you want Comrade Na-veh," he hummed to himself, then nodded. "He's on the basement floor. Go down the stairs, then turn right and he's at the end of the corridor."

Hizkel straightened his back, tried to overcome his limp, and walked ahead. I had heard a lot about Stad Nawi, a writer who translated the Bible into Arabic, as well as the writings of Mendele and Yosef Brenner, and was the director of the Frank Ini Jewish School. As soon as he arrived in Israel he joined the ruling Labour Party, believing it was his destiny to become the Minister of Education and Culture. Needless to say, this never happened. After a lot of effort his followers found him a position in the Labour Federation as supervisor of the social integration of Iraqi immigrants. About eighteen years yearlier, when he first arrived in Israel, he came to our tent in the immigrant camp to tell us there had been signs of life from Hizkel, but I hadn't seen him since although I heard him mentioned now and then, and I used to see his name on the stencilled newsletters that Father received from time to time, giving details of social and educational activities organised by the Association of Immigrants from Babylon. And now here he was – bent over his papers in a small, damp and gloomy office. He pushed up his reading glasses and looked at us for a long moment.

"Hizkel? Hizkel, my son?" he whispered. He struggled out of his chair, came around and hugged Hizkel, kissed him and wept on his shoulder. "Thanks be to God... Wondrous are His ways..." he murmured. He was an old man, his eyesight and hearing were failing, and he looked tired and distracted. His desk was piled high with papers, pamphlets, stencilled circulars, and on the floor too were stacks of books and yellowing newspapers. "Why was I not told that you were free? Why? A new generation here, they know nothing of the past...But I mustn't complain, what matters is that my pupil who followed in my footsteps has been freed from the clutches of the evil ones, may their name be obliterated...Dear God Almighty, is it a sin to wish to be free in your own country among your own people?"

His speech was disjointed and his loud voice betrayed his deafness. Hizkel looked around the neglected room in a buried corner of the immense building, only half listening to his old mentor, and his eyes showed the depth of his distress.

"May I offer you coffee?" the old man asked, bending down to pick up a thermos flask.

"No, thank you," said Hizkel. "We have just had some."

"Or we can go to the cafeteria. They don't bring refreshments to this office..."

"No, it is not necessary. We've come to see you."

I spotted a big photograph of Stad Nawi in the uniform of an officer in the Iraqi army – a handsome, straight-backed young man with a moustache, a regimental baton tucked under his arm, his eyes staring ahead proudly. I shifted my gaze from the photograph to the man crouched behind the desk, and Hizkel too looked from one to the other. I thought he was seeing himself in that sad transformation.

"Hizkel, my dear," the old man chuckled with amusement. "Who would have imagined it – the whole of Babylon's Jewry upped and abandoned the land of onions and garlic...Who would have thought it? Even Ben-Gurion did not believe it. I met him in his office in Tel Aviv. He paced up and down and showered compliments on our community." His weak eyes glowed.

Suddenly serious, he went on to say: "Only one thing is eating away at my liver. No, not the properties we left behind, not the way that we were driven out of our native land, not that. Such things have been known to happen in the world. What hurts me is that we left behind our spiritual treasures, the rabbinical colleges of Sura and Pumbedita and Salaat Zilkha, the Torah scrolls and the holy books, the books of philosophy, entire libraries, our people's spiritual inheritance...And my own vast library. In my dreams at night I walk through it, clean the dust from the volumes, kiss the wisdom of the ages..." He took a large handkerchief from his pocket, blew his nose and mopped his forehead. "I have spoken here with the people in charge of culture, but their hearts are obtuse. Ignoramuses, simple-minded revolutionaries who want to discard our heritage. Their heads are stuffed with socialism, with vain dreams and nonsense..."

Hizkel was embarrassed. He looked at me and then down at the pamphlets. He almost took one from the stack, but didn't.

"I intend to write the history of the Jewish community of Babylon, the second exodus of the descendants of Abraham our patriarch...The new generation here, they know nothing, they have not even heard of the first exodus..."

"Blessings be upon you, Stad Nawi. You were our column of fire," said Hizkel, and at last he got round to introducing me, mentioning my position in East Jerusalem.

"So you are the brother of Kabi Imari! Why did you not say so? Kabi Imari was my brightest student, the editor of our school magazine. Such talents, the Imaris, always excellent writers. And now, the younger brother, advisor to the Minister on Arab affairs. A very important position, and a great responsibility laid upon you." He sat up straight in his old chair, tightened his old tie and went on.

"Beware, my son, the Arabs here are not the same as the Arabs over there. Here they have the blood of our Matriarch Rebecca in their veins. Cunning and brazen they are. In Jaffa did they not murder Yosef Haim Brenner in cold blood, the man whose books I translated? What harm had that fine, suffering thinker done to them? It breaks my heart…Today everyone is exulting, but who can foretell what the future will bring? An idea is burgeoning in my mind which they will call insane – give it all back to Hussein, and do it now, while the Arabs are beaten and confused and weakened, before the venom of revenge spreads through their veins. Who knows if a second opportunity will arise to purchase peace and recognition. For life is not literature, you cannot write drafts, you write the final version at once. But no one listens to me. Why, they do not even listen to Ben-Gurion!"

Hizkel still said nothing about the reason for our visit.

"Stad Nawi," I intervened. "My Uncle Hizkel needs testimony to prove that he was a 'prisoner of Zion' in Iraq."

"Do you have work?" the old man asked Hizkel. "It is a comrade's right to work," he said, adding bitterly, "So they tell us."

Hizkel said nothing but shrank back in his seat. This fifty-year-old man looked at us like a timid child. My heart ached for him.

"They want testimony that you were a 'prisoner of Zion'? You? Do they not know this without a document?" The anger in old Nawi's voice became more intense, and his face grew more commanding. "Very well, we shall give them a document." He took a sheet of paper and wrote on it in unsteady but curling script all the testimony that was needed, and added a few lines of praise for the man. "I do not have headed stationery," he explained simply, "but they all know who I am." He folded the paper, stuffed it into an envelope and handed it to Hizkel.

Hizkel signalled to me to get up. "May God give you long years," he said to his old mentor.

"Do not fret, my son. I shall talk to the comrades. We may find you a post in the Labour Federation," Nawi said, and wrote down some telephone numbers. "This is my number and this is the number of my niece. She is a nurse in the Federation health service. She lives across the street from me. If you do not find me at home, you can leave a message with her."

Afterwards we sat in silence for a long time on the edge of the lawn. Hizkel kept on pulling up stalks of grass and crushing them. Now and then he rubbed his damaged knee and grimaced in pain. "A great and brave man," he said at last. "His finest hour was in Baghdad."

"Patience, brother," Father advised him when we got back. "Rest a little. Take a week's rest for every year in the prison. What's your hurry? Travel around the country, read…" He offered him books in Arabic and English, newspapers and magazines from the Arab world. Hizkel said neither yes nor no, but took the bundle Father had prepared for him and went into Kabi's room, which was now his.

The prolonged stay at our house was wearing him down.

Mother said he shut himself indoors, woke up often in the night, made himself tea in the kitchen, smoked and stared at nothing, often forgetting to drink the tea he'd made. Noises and voices bothered him. The doorbell or a knock at the door made him jump, and he needed to be told who had come and why. The sound of the power drill on the hill above the neighbourhood alarmed him. He was impatient to get a place of his own and a job and to be independent. Once more we went to see the plump lady at the Ministry of Absorption, and this time he was informed he could have a one-room flat in an immigrant hostel in Kiryat Yovel, on the outskirts of Jerusalem.

"Charcoal on their faces!" Mother protested. "Better a tent in an immigrant camp than such a room." She wouldn't let him leave. "Our house is empty. Kabi is away. You're no trouble! On the contrary, now Abu Kabi has company in the house."

One evening, while we waited for him to return from his regular walk – "a prison habit", he called it – Mother said to Father that it was time to find him a wife.

"What kind of a marriage are you thinking of? What will they live on?"

"Maybe he'll be lucky and have a son to say Kaddish after him."

Father smiled. "A man doesn't beget a son just for the sake of Kaddish...What he should do is go to Hadassah and get his leg treated."

"I am blowing on the dying embers and the soot flies in my face...In Baghdad he was a river, here he's become a desert. I can't bear to see him like this, it breaks my heart. I found him Rashel, damn her, now I'll find him a new wife." It was the first time I heard Mother cursing Rashel.

Hizkel rejected any discussion of Rashel. The very mention of her name caused him grief and embarrassment. Outwardly it seemed as if he had recovered from the torture, the years in prison, the crushed knee, the unfulfilled dreams – but not from his abandonment by the wife of his youth. My Uncle Hizkel never said a bitter word about Rashel or about the Muslim lawyer who saved him from the gallows and later married her. He hated no one, he said, not even her. But he saw her in every woman, and none of them was she.

For some reason he didn't want people to know that he was free, not even his old friends from the movement. He didn't renew old contacts, didn't seek out friends and refused to be interviewed in the papers, even anonymously. He wanted to forget and be forgotten, to merge into the crowds in the streets and be unnoticed.

He spent his mornings in Kabi's room where he went over the papers he'd smuggled from the prison – wrapping paper, the backs of bills, rough toilet paper, all covered with tiny, cramped writing. He read and re-read them, trying to sort them into some kind of order, as if solving a difficult crossword puzzle.

Sometimes in the evening he asked Father to play for him, and Father would take the oud out of its velvet case, play and sing songs from over there, and they would drift back together to a world that would never return. On other evenings he would walk up and down Antigonus Street, back and forth from end to end, as if he were exercising in the prison yard before returning to the cell. The neighbourhood became used to the sight of this thin man who kept his eyes down while he walked lonely as a shadow, deep in thought, dragging one leg.

*

He didn't find work. He was offered a job as a substitute teacher in the Arab suburb of Beit Safafa, and decided to give it a try, saying he wanted to get to know the Palestinians. But it never materialised. "Charcoal on their faces," Mother protested, "is that how they treat a 'prisoner of Zion'?"

Salvation came from far away, from my brother Kabi who was "somewhere" overseas. Kabi consulted his superior in the Mossad, who spoke with the director of the Arabic service of Voice of Israel, and he invited Hizkel to an interview. Mother made sure he was looking his best – she ironed his shirt and trousers meticulously, with a wet cloth to make a sharp crease. She used to do the same with my clothes, and when I started sending them to a laundry she was offended – "My work is not good enough for you any more?"

Hizkel returned from the interview somewhat depressed. "They proposed a temporary job as night editor," he said.

"Go for it, brother! Just start to work and *Allah karim*, God is generous," Father urged him, despite the disappointment on Hizkel's face.

The work did him good. It obliged him to read the papers, listen to broadcasts from the Arab countries, open up to the world. His journalistic curiosity was aroused and with it the pleasure of reading and writing. Mother bought him a second-hand radio, so he wouldn't depend on Father's set, and the two of them exchanged information and analysed speeches and political moves like a pair of old viziers. Gradually he emerged from his shell, finished the advanced Hebrew course, joined the Labour Federation and the Medical Insurance Fund, and took out membership at the main library. Doggedly, if without enthusiasm, he began to patch up his daily life.

"What did I tell you?" Mother said to Father. "Get him to start working and the colour will return to his cheeks. And now he must take a wife. I have found someone for him – a widow from a good family, good-looking, healthy. It's true that she has a small son, but that is not a serious flaw. What do you think?"

"Why a widow with a child?"

"You'd prefer a sixteen-year-old virgin? Hizkel is fifty, and he is not Baron Rothschild. Can't you see?" she said in a softer tone. "A new wife will flush Rashel out of his heart."

The Ministry of Absorption sent Hizkel an invitation to a gathering of "prisoners of Zion" at the Beit Elisheva culture hall, in which all participants would speak. As usual, he asked me to go with him. Most of the people there were immigrants from the Soviet Union. One by one they came up on the stage, spoke about their expectations, made demands, some even threatened violent protest. They looked dynamic, ready to start a new life, spoke freely in a mixture of Russian, Yiddish, Hebrew…

"You should speak too," I urged Hizkel.

"Here?"

"Where else? Even your radio job will be coming to an end soon, isn't that what they told you yesterday? Stand up, speak!" I insisted.

He shrank back in his chair, looking defeated. Now and then he turned his head to glance at me with despair in his eyes.

The meeting ended but many remained behind in the hall, continuing the discussion in small noisy groups. Hizkel and I made our way out, when suddenly the roly-poly woman from the Ministry came up and said to Hizkel, "The Deputy Minister wants to see you. He would like to hear from an Iraqi 'prisoner of Zion.'"

Confronted with the Deputy Minister, Hizkel concealed his anxieties and chose to appear as a journalist specialising in Arab affairs. I urged him to speak about his own problems, but he ignored me. Inspired by the Deputy Minister's close attention, he held forth at length about the Arab world. "Honour and shame are the two axes around which Arab life revolve," he explained.

Afterwards I asked to speak privately to the Deputy Minister. I introduced myself and told him about Hizkel's suffering, his shattered knee, Rashel's abandonment, the uncertainties over accommodation and employment.

"Why didn't he tell me about all this?" the Deputy Minister asked in surprise.

"The honour! The shame!" I said, and he smiled.

A few days later the Deputy Minister phoned my office and invited Hizkel and me to come and speak about the Israeli-Arab conflict at a conference of the Labour Party's youth wing that he was organising.

Hizkel was alarmed. "How can I speak at such a gathering?"

"You must not miss this opportunity," Father urged him.

"*Ibni*, son, save me from this, my Hebrew isn't up to it!"

"I promise to help you with the material and the Hebrew."

It was hard to believe that he had once been the leader of an underground movement, a lion of a man who captivated everyone with his charm and whom women adored. Now he was insecure and withdrawn, and whenever he opened a small window, he locked seven doors.

35

The High Windows

A brazen wind lashed the trees, stripped their branches and tossed their leaves on the ground. The rain beat down without mercy and streamed in rivulets along the verges of the streets, flooding courtyards and fields. The days, bitterly cold, wet and grey, grew shorter. In my office the lights stayed on till late.

I knew I should phone Yasmine but put it off, from morning to evening, from evening to the next morning. My office was always full of people seeking help, and the situation was difficult – a sure prescription for delay. Finally I just picked up the receiver to call her when two families came in. I could hardly let them wait outside in the rain and the cold so I replaced it but after they left I rang her. "Yasmine, I'm terribly sorry. I failed. The senator will be deported. I talked to the Minister, to the 'Colonel', everyone…They rejected my arguments."

She remained silent, but I could hear her breathing. Finally, in a low voice she said, "Thank you," and hung up.

A veiled young woman knocked on my half-opened door. I recognised her immediately – Ghadir. "May I come in?" she whispered, and closed the door behind her as if finding refuge. She took off the veil and the soaked abaya, rubbed her hands to warm them and sat down facing me. But before saying a word, she put a box on my desk and opened it, and the room filled with the strong scent of cloves. I could never get her to abandon the habit of bringing me presents. Then she handed me some sheets of paper covered with a schoolgirl's large, neat handwriting. "These are our relatives from Yaffa and Ayn Mahel that Mother remembers. It is possible we forgot someone…"

"These will be enough. Don't worry."

"When will my problem be solved?" she asked, obviously distressed. "I cannot sleep at night, I do not know what to do. My husband Issam sent me a message that if I do not come to Amman immediately, he will cross the lines and take me back by force. Now I have a new worry. My cousin Karim from Ghayna – you remember, we saw him when we went there – he says he wants me, that I was promised to him before Issam. He follows me wherever I go, he says nothing but his look is evil, it frightens me. If they let Issam come back here Karim will leave me alone, he will have no other choice…Help me, Nuri!" Tears ran down her cheeks.

"It will be all right, Ghadir. I'll speak to Haramati."

The rain had eased up a little and I advised her to take advantage of the respite and leave. I considered taking her in my car, but didn't want to get her into trouble with the jealous cousin, who might have followed her to my office.

I asked Aliza to get me an appointment with Haramati as soon as possible. I had to persuade that pain-in-the-arse to finish the business – he had all the necessary information.

Aliza tried for three days but was unable to fix an appointment with him – he was either busy or out of his office. She became more and more determined to get hold of him, and discovered that he liked to spend his evenings at the American

Colony café. "Go and surprise him there," she advised, so I did that very evening, waited and waited and he didn't show up, but I wasn't going to let the sonofabitch get away with it.

The next morning I went to the Ministry of the Interior very early, determined to catch him when he arrived. Though it was before opening hours, there was already a long queue in front of the door. A clutch of people were gathered around an elderly bespectacled woman sitting at a folding table typing on a little Hermes portable. It turned out she was an Egyptian-born Jewish woman who came each day to help the applicants by typing their applications and translating their documents, entirely voluntarily. The people around her showered her with affection. Someone brought her a glass of tamarind juice, but she refused politely, pointing to a little basket which contained a thermos flask, a bottle of water, a carefully-wrapped sandwich and some fruit. Quietly, without wasting words, she listened to another person, translated another document, typed another letter…Inside, I thought, Haramati ruled in lordly style, while his work was being done on a folding table outside by a saint in spectacles.

"Oh Mister Imari, good morning, this is a great honour, do come in!" Haramati's grating voice proclaimed his arrival, and he led me inside.

I laid out before him the list of Ghadir's relations and those of her husband Issam, whose father had moved to Palestine from Amman and settled in Ayn Mahel in the north. I added my own detailed and reasoned recommendation to approve her application. Haramati glanced at the papers and addressed me.

"I wanted to save you the trouble and come to you, believe me. At the same time I intended to see the villa of that senator, damn him, which he calls the garden of Eden and from which he will soon be deported. I don't know if you've had a chance to see what a fuss the Jordanian television and newspapers have made about the deportation of this Israel-hater. Outrageous! And I say, good riddance. One less! What can we do, the Gentiles hate us. It doesn't matter how kindly we treat the wretched population of East Jerusalem and the West Bank. After all, what are we here for if not to help them? I don't recall if I told you that my family was saved by a miracle in 1936, when the Arabs were slaughtering Jews here. I ask you, where was the world when that slaughter was going on? But I needn't tell you – you immigrants from Babylon also experienced a massacre in '41. And where was the world during the Holocaust? Good God Almighty, is it only Jewish blood that may be spilt with impunity...So I ask you, do we have to swell the number of our enemies here?" He stopped for a moment and lit a cigarette. "I'm not supposed to smoke," he explained, "but no one could withstand the pressures of this thankless work of mine."

His mouth spouted pearls, but his heart was as murky as the smoke he exhaled. I wished he would choke on it, but forced myself to urge him to conclude the business at hand.

"Mr Haramati," I said firmly, "I believe that now that you have all the necessary information, as well as my own written and reasoned recommendation, and in view of the fact that these are relatives in the first degree, it should be possible to approve the application."

"I'm not denying," he said, "that there is some justice in the case but tell me, if you'll be so kind, why do they covet our meagre little patch? After all, we are receiving immigrants from the United States, and we pray that before long the gates of the Soviet Union will also open. Your Minister, incidentally, is a shrewd and far-sighted man. He's talking about that dearly-expected immigration day and night...They have twenty-one Arab countries and fifty-five Muslim countries. I ask you, why can't their precious family reunification take place over there and not here?"

"They don't want it, and it is their right to object."

"Patience, my dear Mister Imari, patience! My experience has shown that the longer it takes to get a response, the better the chances that the reunification will take place on the other side – and so much the better for us!" He laughed aloud and drummed on his desk with obvious pleasure.

A strong smell of sweat greeted me in the crowded corridor. Anxious, quiet, resigned faces looked at me. Some pressed close to me and showered me with questions, and their pain almost suffocated me. "*Inte al-mustashar,* you are the advisor," an old woman seized my hand, weeping. "I saw your picture in the newspaper. Allah's blessing on your father. Help me, please. My son is abroad, and I am alone." I was ashamed to have no answer for her. Enlightened occupation! A special people! A light unto the nations indeed! Mr Haramati, you broker of people's destinies, vicious bastard, you should live under occupation, I wanted to yell, I hope your ulcer bleeds! I cursed him and Shamluk too, these "New Jews". Shit! Why didn't I throw it all away and get out? Better to sell kebabs in the market than be roasted here.

But then I told myself, Come on, you can't give up that easily! I got in the car and drove to the government sector in West Jerusalem.

"I want to see him immediately," I said to Levanah, pointing at the Minister's door.

She gave me a long look and a faint smile. "Would you like a cup of coffee, Nuri?"

"Levanah, It's urgent. I must see him right away!" I insisted.

"He'll be free in a little while, he's with someone," she said in a soothing voice. "In the meantime, let's go to the cafeteria and have a pastry."

"What's troubling you?" she asked when we sat down.

I told her.

"It's unbelievable. What is happening to us?"

"You've no idea what these poor people are going through. Why?"

"May I give you a piece of advice, Nuri?" Her light brown eyes looked straight into mine. "Speak to the Minister very calmly and moderately. You know he dislikes emotional scenes. He interprets them as personal attacks on himself."

"Minister, you know I'm always looking for ways to strengthen our position in East Jerusalem, to restore normal life, calm the population and thereby avoid unnecessary suffering and complications which will be difficult to get out of later on."

He nodded and placed his feet on the table, his favourite posture.

"I realise that problems to do with land and property are difficult and painful, but the greatest suffering is in their personal lives – identity cards, family reunification. I suggest that you ask the Minister of the Interior to include me as your representative on the committee that deals with personal issues."

"You want to get me into trouble?"

"No, sir, I want to help in an area in which there is great bitterness and many complaints directed at you and at the

Prime Minister, cases where the husband is stuck in Amman and the wife in Jerusalem, or a daughter who went abroad to study and is not allowed to return."

"What I see is that you want to liberalise the system. What are we, a charitable organisation? We are faced with a demographic problem of immense national importance! You yourself have pointed it out to me more than once."

"Minister, I'm speaking about humanitarian cases, families torn apart…"

"So you suggest that we go behind the backs of the security forces and the Ministry of the Interior, who are entrusted with this task."

"There is an Arabic saying, 'The baby is not ours, but his excrement is soiling our clothes'…"

"Oh you and your Arabic sayings! What's wrong with thinning out the population density over there?" He stood up to indicate that the meeting was over.

I left his office on leaden legs.

What did I expect? That he would be an Albert Schweitzer?

36

Ghadir

Ghadir was murdered, her body shattered against the rock on which she used to sit with her sheep around her. A local Arab woman, probably a neighbour, was waiting for me at the office to give me the terrible news. I informed the police and then made my way to the foot of Mount Scopus. Ghadir's broken body was still lying on the boulder, helpless under the wide blue skies and the hot sun, covered with her darkening, drying blood. Who killed her? Her husband? Her cousin Karim? Her father? Or all three?

I couldn't work. I said I was taking a few days off, went home, disconnected the phone and closed the shutters. I lay in bed, tormented by the thought that I had failed to save her.

After two days my doorbell rang and there was an impatient knocking on the door. It was the postman with a registered letter from the Income Tax Department. The next afternoon again there was a knock, much softer but persistent. Finally I opened the door and there was Levanah. I was unshaved, dishevelled, in a sweaty pyjama top and shorts, the room stank of smoke, the kitchen was a mess, but without a word she put down on the table a newspaper with a photo of a bloodstained rock. I recalled that not long before, when I stormed in demanding to see the Minister after my exchange with Haramati, I had told her about Ghadir. She connected the dots.

Levanah opened all the windows and the door to the balcony, rolled up her sleeves, washed the coffee dregs from the cups, and tidied up the flat as if she knew it well. Then she sat with me in silence for a long time, without asking why I'd shut myself away. I didn't say anything either. What could I say? Suddenly she got up, said, "I'll be right back," and returned with her arms full of groceries.

"Will you eat supper with me?" she asked and set the table. I nodded.

"Nuri, come back to work. You're needed."

"You look pale," Aliza said when I returned to my office. My desk was heaped with letters and a stack of newspapers. *Al-Quds* did not report the murder, and *Al-Wattan* had only a brief notice: "The body of a young woman was found at the foot of Mount Sacobos." No name or address, no possible motive for the murder or the killer's identity. Nothing.

Aliza buzzed me. "Haramati wants you."

"Later. I'm busy."

"He called yesterday and again this morning. Talk to him or he'll keep on phoning." She tranferred his call.

"Good morning, my dear friend. How are you? It's been a while since I heard from you, and I didn't see you at the meeting of the consultative team yesterday. I have some good news. I can tell you it was a tough debate, but I told them, I'd bend over backwards for him, believe me, I said we can't turn down a request from a respected member of our team. I put it as a personal favour to me, you see? The poor woman was so desperate, she even approached the director general. Well, never mind, how could she know about our procedures? In the end I managed to persuade the committee to approve the application. We'll inform her officially, of course, but I wanted you to be the first to hear."

"She's been murdered."

"What? When? Who murdered her?"

"Probably her husband. She didn't want to follow him to Amman," I said and slammed down the receiver. Damn you to hell, I cursed him silently, may your shrivelled soul be stained with her spilt blood.

In the evening I went to Mount Scopus – and there was Ghadir sitting on the boulder, in a black dress that was turning gold in the light of the setting sun. I was stunned. Then I remembered a passage from the *Book of Legends*: "Said the prophet Jeremiah: On my way to Jerusalem, I looked up and I saw a woman sitting on top of the mountain, dressed in black and her hair loosed, crying and pleading, who would console her? And I too am crying and pleading, who will console me?"

When I approached I saw that the woman was not a spirit, nor was she Ghadir – it was her mother Fathiya. "Come, son, sit with me," she said. She told me that after our visit to Ghayna, Karim, Ghadir's cousin, began to visit their hut in Wadi al-Joz. He said he loved her, that she had been promised to him when she was eight, and he would not give her up. "He was full of lust, like a wandering Bedou. He followed her, shouted at her, threw a tantrum once when she visited your office. I did not keep silent. I told him you were kinder to her than ten brothers.

"Then one day, one evil day, Issam her husband also showed

up, may God break his neck. He said he had slipped across the border to take her back to Amman. He found Karim at my place and they went out to the mountain. After many hours passed and they did not come back I went to look for her, and found her here on the rock...I begged our neighbour to go to your office and tell you...That is all, she is gone. Since then there has been no sign of Issam, may his name be erased, and Karim has also disappeared, may Allah cut off his head, and my husband too, may his days be short." She fell silent, evening came down and soon all was dark. "I had only her, one ray of light, and they went and extinguished her too." She sighed and stood up to leave.

Ghadir's death elevated her in my mind, drew all the light to her, forced me to clarify to myself what I had taken for granted while she lived, to understand what I had unconsciously sensed in her.

I had always seen Ghadir as a sweet, appealing creature, an innocent girl-woman walking down a quiet marginal path, far from the centres of power and influence, simply living and letting others live, like a little bird under the sky, a flower of the field. In a way she was the opposite of Yasmine, the educated, analytical, political Yasmine, who lived at the heart of things and rallied to the flag.

I had always thought that the politicians, the aristos, ran the world. I didn't think of the masses of ordinary people, those who led their own lives far from politics and untainted by its poisons, as factors in the unfolding of events, capable of leaving their mark on history.

When Ghadir died, this one little bird under the sky, a stream of pure water, brought back to my mind some lines from

Bialik's poem, "Let me be a part of you", which I had learned at the evening school for working boys:

Let me be a part of you, the humble of the world, the mute souls,
  Spinning their lives unseen, modest of thought and destiny…

37

Kiddush Wine

Michelle's mother died. When I phoned Michelle in Paris to say how sorry I was, she told me she planned to come back to Israel after the seven days of mourning, together with her fiancé Jean-Claude. But she kept on postponing her return, sending colourful postcards in which she complained she was lonely, bored and homesick for Jerusalem.

Reading between the lines I guessed that her relations with her fiancé were at a critical stage. To be honest, I missed her. I missed her energy and the racket she created around her, her nosy curiosity about my private life and her efforts to manage it, the gossip, the gourmet meals and pampering she gave me, and the sex that was always available. She asked, in her direct way, about my plans, but I evaded the issue. I never thought of her as my future wife.

In her absence Yasmine took her place in the youth village and worked full-time, though still as a volunteer. Caring for the children, and the responsibility laid upon her, brought her closer to the place and its staff. The director even phoned to thank me for "the excellent match". But it was always very difficult to get hold of her. When I did, she would say, "I'll phone you," which I interpreted as "Don't call us, we'll call you," American-style. My stomach tightened at the thought that she might not.

I was wrong. In the weeks leading up to Passover she phoned often, almost every day, if only for a quick chat during working hours. Our talks, especially the long ones at night, when we would exchange ideas and views, warmed my heart and I lived in anticipation of them. We talked about everyday matters, the women's magazine she wanted to launch, work, the family, even the weather. We didn't clash on political issues and our exchanges were relaxed, intimate, caressing.

One day I was out for a walk in the quiet lanes of Sheikh Jarrah, taking a break from the pressures of work, when I ran into Yasmine, smiling and surprised to see me. I was so delighted that I had to stop myself rushing to take her in my arms. She said she'd heard about an explosion in the Mahaneh Yehudah market, and decided to come to my office, instead of telephoning, to see if all was well.

"The market again!" I said. "Today is Thursday…I hope my mother didn't go there." Despite all the string-pulling, our parents still did not have a phone. Yasmine ran with me to the office and I turned on the radio – still no details – so I phoned the sector commander and was told that the bomb had gone off on Agrippas Street. A falafel seller and a postman, who just happened to replace his colleague that day, were killed, and several people were injured. I tried to reassure myself: Mother did not shop in that street, she usually made her purchases in the Iraqi market on the Jaffa Road-side, some distance from the site of the explosion. This was a re-run of what had happened the time I had driven to Katamon like a madman.

"Why don't you go home and make sure?" Yasmine suggested. "I'll come with you if you like." I agreed but only in part. First I took her home and then rushed to Katamon. Thank God, Mother hadn't gone to the market that day.

And so Yasmine's boycott of my office was broken. She would walk in sometimes, usually in the evening after a long day's work, and we'd make a light supper. Standing side by side in the kitchen I longed to touch her shoulder, stroke her hair, take her arm, pass my finger over her crescent lips, but did not dare. Once her hand touched mine and they held together. A warm thrill passed through our fingers. We looked at each other, then lowered our eyes and returned to the task of washing and drying the glasses.

I was impressed by her dedication to the project of a youth village in Abu Dis. Without telling her, I asked Solly Levy of the Lands Registry to help find a plot of land for the purpose. He opened maps, checked this and that, and marked two possible locations. Then he suggested that Yasmine visit the plots with us and select the one that suited her. He promised to obtain the necessary permits. I couldn't help myself, I ran to tell Yasmine but instead of rejoicing she said, "Thanks. I don't want help from your side. It could damage the project."

It felt like a stab in my flesh.

"Don't be offended," she said. "It's not personal. I really appreciate what you've done, but…life is complicated."

She's crazy, I told myself. But, on the other hand, she had eased her boycott of West Jerusalem, and didn't confine herself to the youth village, making her way there like a blinkered horse. Now she could be tempted to visit places. She asked to go to the Israel Museum to see an exhibition of Chinese painting, and once to visit the house of Anna Ticho, the artist. She wanted to sit in the Atarah café on Ben Yehudah Street, another time in Café Savyon near the Terra Sancta building. Besides the pleasure of accompanying her, I enjoyed the admiring looks she attracted.

She suggested dining at Chez Simon. Needless to say, I couldn't make head or tail of the menu, but she guided me confidently through the foreign dishes. The women in my life were turning me, a product of the immigrant camp, kibbutz and Katamon housing estate, into a connoisseur of fancy restaurants, and what Michelle left out Yasmine filled in. After the meal she insisted on paying. I felt like the proverbial plucked chicken, but when Yasmine made up her mind there was no moving her.

Another evening I suggested coffee at the YMCA. We walked slowly across the city park in the twilight and afterwards went up to the roof. There we stood all alone, and took in the surrounding view. The flood-lit Old City walls, the minarets and steeples, and the tops of the recently planted palm trees on the skyline, were mysterious and magical.

"It's so beautiful," she said. "My father brought me here when I was a child."

"As for me, I couldn't afford to be a member so I never went up on the roof. But I did sneak in to do my homework in winter, because the place was heated. I was always afraid they'd ask me for a membership card and throw me out."

A pleasant Jerusalem evening breeze was blowing. I moved close to her and she put her head on my shoulder. Her breasts rose and her nostrils widened, as if she was smelling the orange blossom in the orchards. We stood like this for a long time, listening to the silence.

After I drove her home, she stepped out of the car without a word and we waved goodnight to each other, like a pair of undercover agents, acting with discretion.

*

I didn't see Yasmine for the next two days, nor did she phone. When I asked for her at Al-Hurriyeh I was told she'd gone to Jericho. I longed for her and desired her like a boy in love for the first time. Yasmine awakened in me a virginal excitement, as if I'd never known a woman before.

After her return from Jericho a new chapter began in our relationship – without spelling it out, we began to act as a couple. We went together to concerts and films. She, like her father, was especially fond of the Edison cinema. "There's something majestic about the spacious entrance hall, the lights, the big mirrors, the red upholstered seats. It has a special atmosphere, like an epic novel," she said.

The first time we went to the Edison I was afraid that she would be disappointed, as the place had declined somewhat over the years, but she enjoyed it and liked to see and be seen in the foyer. "Suppose I hug you here," she whispered, her face flushed, "in front of all these famous people, then everyone will know you have an Arab girlfriend."

"You're mistaken, they won't know. With your Oxford English and your turquoise-blue eyes, they'll be sure you're a new immigrant. Some will envy me because of your beauty, and others because of your new immigrant privileges." And then I let slip the words, "If you convert to Judaism and marry me…"

"Is it worth it? And what would your *mukhabarat* say?" she challenged me.

Studying her reflection in the big mirrors in the foyer, I reckoned she looked like a foreign tourist from a far away country. From time to time I had thought that my colleagues on the committee might be under the impression that Yasmine was tapping me for secret information, like the legendary Mata Hari, although if anyone had said such a thing I'd have dismissed it out of hand. Everyone knew Abu George favoured co-existence, and was in touch with the "Colonel" and other figures in the Israeli establishment. My real worry was that Mother would be devastated if she found out about Yasmine. Then I'd say to myself, take it easy, nothing has happened between us yet.

When Yasmine brought me the book *The Dove's Necklace – On Love and Lovers*, a masterpiece written in 11th-century Cordoba by the Arab author Ibn Hazm, I imagined that we would leaf through it together and enjoy its subtle treasures. I did not expect it to fall by the wayside while our love was swept into the vortex of a cataclysmic storm, overwhelming and devastating in its effects.

The evening began with a pleasant walk in the neighbourhood of my office and then we drove to the Intercontinental Hotel for a drink.

"I admire your courage in being seen with me in public," I said to her.

"I have an obligation to be myself, and never mind what people say about me. And don't forget I'm a widow. Anyway, I really don't care."

"What does your mother think about our meetings?"

"I haven't told her. Don't forget I lived on my own in Paris."

"This isn't Paris."

"I'm a lost cause, anyway. A girl who is not married by the time she's eighteen is already a cause for worry. If she's divorced or widowed and approaching thirty, she's had it. Remaining single is considered shameful, but to me marrying an unsuitable man without love is out of the question, and my mother and father know this."

"Where do young people in your community meet?"

"At the universities. They're the chief match-making institutions. There contact between the sexes is open. We're not such a backward society as your people like to think."

I went to the bathroom, and when I returned she crossed her ankles and said to me with a provocative grin, "My lackadaisical conqueror, you're not at all the same man I first met at the American Colony. Then you had a mischievous, greedy look in your eyes." Her full lips laughed.

"I've learned to hide my intentions," I replied and pressed my leg against hers under the table. I could feel her warmth.

"You know, after we visited the youth village together I went for my father – how could he let you exploit him, why was he seeking your help? Then I avoided all contact with you."

"I remember. Thank God those days are behind us."

"Then, when I began to work there, your name would come up in talks with Michelle. I could tell there was something between you two. I also had an idea that the pair of you were conspiring against me."

I couldn't understand why she was telling me these things now, and signalled to the waiter to bring another bottle of beer.

"That was how I felt until that day in Al-Hurriyeh when you amazed me with your knowledge of Nasser's speeches. You probably don't remember, but you were eating watermelon and I noticed your hands, your fingers – you have long fingers, like a musician – and I wanted to touch them, to stroke them," she laughed. "The next time you talked about Um Kulthoum like a poet in love. Then I said to myself, this is a different sort of Israeli, not like the others. But just then you stayed away, you kept your distance. I couldn't understand why." She fell silent and lit a cigarette.

There it is, I thought, she's getting at me for that time when I learned to hide my feelings even from myself, though my soul felt tied to hers and my body burned for her, and every meeting with her was a celebration.

"I thought it was because of Michelle," she said, putting out her cigarette.

"By the way, Michelle is getting married."

"I know, she wrote to me." She gulped down her beer. The omelette she had ordered was untouched.

"I'm sorry," I said and wiped the puddle of condensation left by the beer bottle on the table. "My uncle, who was a prisoner in Iraq, arrived in Israel and I had to take care of him. I also tried to help in a case of family reunification for a shepherdess I knew on Mount Scopus. When she was murdered I blamed myself for failing to push her case through. I was miserable and shut myself at home. I wanted to quit everything."

"Don't take on the sorrows of all the world, you're doing your best," she said gently, and before I could explain that this wasn't the way I felt, she cut me off: "Let's go somewhere quiet. I can hardly hear what you're saying."

I suggested going to my place. I knew it was a serious matter for a woman like her, but I took a chance and she agreed.

Grushka was on the stairs, blocking our way.

"*Tali ya hilwe*, come, my beauty," Yasmine said to her in Arabic and stroked her back. Grushka accepted the stranger's gentle touch and revelled in the caresses.

I turned the light on inside and with a deep bow invited her to enter. "Please come in, your highness!" The place was immaculate – luckily I'd recently found a cleaning woman who took real pride in her work.

"What a nice, intimate studio," she said and made a beeline for the Arabic shelf of my bookcase. She examined the spines, then took out *Al-Ayyam*, and leafed through it. "You like Taha Hussein?"

"Very much. I feel he has something in common with Agnon. You remember I lent you *The Doctor's Divorce*, that my brother's girlfriend Sandra translated into English?"

"Yes, a sad and complicated love story. I felt close to Dinah, the heroine. It's beautifully written."

We stepped out onto the balcony. My Orthodox neighbour was sitting opposite, on her own brightly-lit balcony, peeling potatoes. Her bearded husband was there too, bent over a big volume and rocking back and forth.

"He looks like a member of a Sufi order," Yasmine commented.

"We're cousins, after all…What will you have – arrack from Bethlehem, French liqueur or Scotch whisky?"

"*Yayin lekiddush*," she said, and laughed.

I thought she was poking fun at me, using Hebrew to ask for a drink, but nonetheless I poured us both some kiddush wine and we toasted each other, then moved on to arrack.

"With water and a lot of ice, please!"

Half a bottle was soon gone. I brought out olives and salty cheese and anchovies from a tin, peeled some cucumbers and sprinkled them with salt, and cut brown bread into triangles.

"Forgive me, princess, this was unexpected. I did not prepare refreshments for your visit. But I do have nice music." I put on a tape that Kabi had recorded for me before he went to Europe, Arabic songs broadcast on the Israeli Arabic service.

"Fairuz?" she said, delighted, settled down in the big green armchair that before the war I'd sworn to throw out, tucked up her legs and sipped her arrack.

I could hardly breathe. All my life I'd longed for a tremendous passionate love, a love with an eagle's wingspan, and here it was...

"Where are you drifting off to?" Yasmine startled me. "Hey, do we have to start arguing about politics for you to wake up?"

"We can do other things, talk about music, literature, architecture, cookery..."

"Silly!" She threw a cushion at me.

"No, really – I can cook. For example, an Iraqi thumia. You fry chopped onion in sesame oil, add two spoons of tomato paste, add little meat balls, salt and pepper, and cook till the meat is done."

"Motor-mouth!" She threw another cushion.

"Here's the main part – peel three cloves of garlic, add a handful of mint leaves and cook on a low flame..."

"Would you like to be the chef at Al-Hurriyeh?"

"I dreamed of you for a hundred generations..." I sang to her.

"I'm not Jerusalem..."

"Oh no, please not Jerusalem! Let's go back to the thumia, before it gets overdone...Frozen vodka is terrific with thumia!"

"You learned that from Michelle."

"My beauty, it's you I've been longing to eat, ever since the American Colony."

"What happened since then?"

"My hands are tied, you're a protected person, a pledge entrusted to me by your father. It's a matter of honour."

"Hell, you're not an *ibn-Arab*, as you claim – you're an Arab through and through, squared!" She threw her arrack glass on the floor, smashing it.

Instead of asking if she'd gone mad, I went mad myself. I took all the glasses from the cupboard and pleaded, "Yasmine, *mon amour*, smash the glasses, all of them, but don't be angry with me and please don't speak to me in English. Speak Arabic, Hebrew, only not English!"

"*Habibi, widadi, hiami, fuadi, dalili, ruhi, albi…*" she trilled a string of Arabic endearments, poured herself another glass of arrack, climbed on to the coffee table and, when she finished the drink, she again flung the glass on the floor. Pieces of glass flew everywhere. "My dove, my lovely, my sister, do not mock me, I beg of thee," I sang, fetching a broom and a dustpan. "We must eliminate the effects of aggression, as Nasser said, the hero of our youth. O Yasmine of my soul, who are you? A spy, a fedayeen? And how will you eliminate me – with a bullet in my heart? A knife in my back? Poison in my coffee? With fatal love?"

"That's enough, you're drunk."

She looked at the floor, which was covered with shards of glass, and suddenly clutched her head and burst into tears. I brought her a glass of water and hugged her. She was trembling all over, desperate for comfort.

I set a coffee pot on the stove, but the coffee boiled over and blackened the range. I served what was left of it in glasses instead of tiny cups, and apologised for giving her Arabic coffee as if it was the usual Israeli-style milky brew.

"You keep changing, Nuri. Who are you, what are you doing with me?"

With the glass in my hand and a lot of arrack inside me I

launched into a full-scale speech. "I'm an *ibn-Arab* Jew who admires the wonders of the West. I listen to classical music in the morning and Arabic music in the evening. I'm a bird of passage wandering between two worlds, a foot here and a foot there, and sometimes my feet get mixed up.

"I'm in conflict with myself and with those who are supposed to be my brothers. Sometimes I feel close to them and sometimes they horrify me. I long for the Tigris and the palm trees and my home in Baghdad, but I'll never go back there, never again live as a second-class citizen.

"I'm furious with you Arabs. You don't know how to agree, how to accept the other and to compromise. Compromise is not a weakness, it is knowing how to give up in order to get more. Yasmine, you know that the Arabic language doesn't even have a word that means compromise. There is *musawameh* and there is *hal wasat*, bargaining and interim solution, but there is no compromise.

"I love the East, the family feeling, the good manners, the human warmth, the colours, smells, crowding, sweat, but I also detest the East for its stench, its falsehood and betrayal, blind fanaticism and cruelty, and I prefer the openness, alienation and airy distance of the West.

"I'm a Hebrew-speaking Israeli who dreams in Judeo-Arabic, my mother-tongue, my warm home." I poured myself another glass. "In my mother-tongue and with this arrack I'm closer to you than to many of my own people. And I must tell you, my lovely, that your foolish caprice of speaking with me in English is driving me crazy. Language, Yasmine, is the key to the heart."

I'd wanted to say all this from our first meeting, but it was only tonight, when I was drunk, that it all came pouring out. Why had I bottled it up? What was I afraid of? Yasmine did not get angry, did not turn away from me. I think she even smiled. My eyelids became heavy. The ice-cube I sucked in the hope that it would wake me up slowly dissolved, and I drifted away on distant clouds.

When I opened my eyes she was bending over me, her small ears translucent like a baby's, her neck smooth as silk, and her breath smelled provocatively of arrack and cigarettes. I gathered her in my arms, feeling her heart beating against mine. My hand slipped under her clothes, attracted to the destination that stopped my breath.

But how could I when she was drunk with arrack, had broken my wine glasses, wept, and didn't know what she was doing? I wanted her when the arrack faded away, when she was sober and aware, sure of herself.

Yasmine didn't say anything. She lay beside me in silence and I felt her looking at me. Suddenly she got up, buttoned her blouse and straightened her clothes. "Take me home," she said.

Idiot, I said to myself. You've hurt her feelings. But I couldn't help it. I drove to Sheikh Jarrah slowly, drunkenly, but by a miracle also very carefully. When we reached her house she forbade me to drive back, so I spent the night in my office.

As I lay down on Ahmad Shukeiry's sofa, the ache in my balls forced me to confront the question, why did I not make love to her? Was it really because she was drunk? Michelle was also drunk when she dragged me to her bed. You can't make that comparison, I told myself. Come on, don't take the easy way out. How is it that after growing up in the kibbutz and twenty years in a Western society you're still a primitive Easterner? Or perhaps, for all your crowing, you're still afraid of commitment? You'd better make up your mind, or you'll lose her the way you lost Yardena, and then you'll spend the rest of your life mourning for what you missed.

*

The ringing of the telephone woke me up.

"A sweet morning to you, my love. I miss you. I want to see you opening your eyes and hear the first word you say," Yasmine whispered.

"A bright morning to you, my sunshine," I replied, and started a new day.

38

An Ordinary Weekday

We agreed to meet in the evening, but Yasmine couldn't wait and she showed up at my office at three o'clock. Smiling mysteriously, she said, "Come with me, those papers won't run away."

The mystery was solved at the entrance to the Smadar cinema in the German Colony. A matinee performance of *Jules et Jim*! I'd forgotten such things still existed.

Leaving the spring brightness outside we entered the darkened hall. Jeanne Moreau, my boyhood goddess, smiled at us from the screen, superb as ever with her wide forehead, penetrating eyes and sensuous lips. How wonderful to watch her with Yasmine beside me, her soft warm hand in mine.

"Did you know that Jeanne Moreau had a passionate affair with the homosexual Pierre Cardin?" Yasmine said when we came out into the quiet green street. "She was his first woman, and they were in Venice, at the Danielli hotel, in the room of George Sand and Alfred de Musset."

"No one could resist her," I said, as if to account for Cardin's deviation from his normal habits, and pointed with a smile at Yasmine herself, implying "or you".

"Don't exaggerate," she replied, smiling back.

In the twilight a pleasant breeze was blowing, soft and caressing. How this gentle mood took us after the weird night in my room, that had left us both stunned, I could not imagine, but I didn't try to understand it. Everything was flowing sweetly, and how good it felt to flow with it. My soul was singing. Yasmine wanted to go for a drive. In the car she took off her shoes, folded her legs under her in her favourite posture, tossed her head back and sang Jeanne Moreau's song from the film:

> Once more together heart to heart
> Together we shall go round again
> Hand in hand you and I.

We drove around the narrow streets of the German Colony, admiring the old Templar houses, then on to the still older Yemin Moshe neighbourhood, where we stopped to look at the floodlit walls of the Old City as the evening fell, munching on sandwiches we'd bought earlier. I buried my face in Yasmine's hair, breathing in the sweet warmth of her body, the leeches of anxiety disappearing. I wanted to stop time, to make the moment last and last for ever.

We decided to go together to the Writers' House, for a literary evening with a gifted young Israeli author who had recently caught the public imagination with his first novel. The week before I'd bought two copies of his book, one for me and one for Yasmine, which I inscribed with some lines from Bialik:

> Take me under your wing,
> And be my mother and sister,
> And let your bosom be my haven,
> Abode of my forlorn prayers.

*

We both read the book but decided not to discuss it till we heard what the author himself had to say. He was a young man of about my age, very handsome, with fine expressive features, his eyes burning and intense. His hands were square, strong, not large, the fingers short and sturdy as a farmer's. I knew he'd spent time on a kibbutz – perhaps milking cows had given him his powerful hands.

He spoke very eloquently in perfect sabra Hebrew, with emphatic gestures. Complete sentences, idioms and original metaphors tumbled from his mouth like a cataract. His thought was structured, crystallised, highly persuasive. By the time I had digested one polished sentence it was followed by a second, a third and a fourth, a string of colourful, glowing pearls. Where did all this abundance come from? It flowed, it ran in a mighty current, like the Tigris in winter.

We were sitting near the podium and I was leaning forwards, listening attentively, afraid to miss a word, when suddenly I felt dizzy. I leaned back and shut my eyes, covering them with my hand. Yasmine took my other hand and stroked it, not knowing what was happening to me.

When the young author finished speaking there was enthusiastic applause, and people crowded around him with copies of his novel to sign but we didn't join the queue: Yasmine put her arm through mine and drew me outside.

"You felt unwell," she said. "What happened?"

"His Hebrew, ya Allah! Another wonder of the world."

"Nuri my dear," she announced an unexpected discovery, "you can't get away from it, you're going to be a writer!"

"I'll be a writer and you'll be a fortune-teller."

"It's not a joke," she said authoritatively. "It's a simple

linguistic fact. Perhaps you're not aware of it. Such a sensitivity to words, the way you reacted this evening, it's a natural disease of writers, perhaps it's part of their creative force. I know it well – my father is a poet too."

We went into Fink's, the old bar on King George Street, and Yasmine gave me her impressions. "The whole of that lecture I was trying to reconcile the contrast between this gifted and impressive writer and the characters in his book. He is brilliant, confident, solid. Even his complexity is solid and tangible, but his characters are airy, anguished, conflicted. They're imaginary protagonists, without bumps or bulges, clean and smooth, without body wastes, without smells of flesh or pus. I asked myself if a Jew could write about Arabs and depict their substance, their actions and motivations, their customs and their ability to break out of them, without flattening them into stereotypes, and without exaggerating their good or bad qualities."

"Doctor Yasmine, you're fascinating," I said, trying to sound playful while expressing my appreciation of her analysis. Why couldn't I tell her she was a shrewd judge of literature, I wondered? Would I have said to a man who impressed me with his ideas and insights that he was "fascinating"?

We were sitting at the bar and two couples crowded us wanting us to move away. Normally I would have left, but not this time. I ordered two more beers, we drank them at leisure, and only then slid down from the high stools and walked to Ben Yehuda Street.

"You remember you promised to take me for a trip around the country?" she asked. "Is the promise still good?"

"*Avec plaisir, madame.* How would you like to visit my old kibbutz? I've been asked to give a talk there, and we can combine it with a trip."

"A talk about what?"

"About the Israeli–Arab conflict. A few days ago an Arabist from my kibbutz, a guy called Haggai, came to my office. I took him on a tour of East Jerusalem and we had a long chat. Before he left he asked if I'd be willing to speak to the members. 'There is a lot of interest in the Arab issue,' as he put it. I said all right, but it's not definite yet. He has to get approval from the kibbutz culture committee. So we have to wait for a positive reply from Haggai. There is also another problem, Yasmine," I added. "The talk will be in the evening and the kibbutz is in the Jezreel Valley, a four-hour drive from Jerusalem. We'll have to stay overnight."

"That's fine."

"We may have to share a room."

Did she smile, or did I imagine it?

39

"Either I'm crazy, or they are"

I began preparing material for the lecture at the kibbutz. I didn't want to read out something structured and prepared in advance, but to speak naturally to the audience. I read somewhere that Toscanini said it is better for the score to be in the head than for the head to be in the score, and I didn't want to have my head immersed in written notes. This meant a lot more preparation – storing the material in my head so I could deliver it naturally.

Now and then I was gripped by a paralysing fear. How would I stand before them and hold forth? Added to this was my self-consciousness due to Yasmine's presence. I was afraid that it would affect me too much, that I'd want to please her and not speak freely. I was also afraid that she would see me fail, unable to reach the audience, get stuck or confused. At the same time, I wanted her to be there and to like what I would say and the way I said it.

The phone rang. It was Pe'era Shadmi. She said the Professor was unwell, but added hesitantly, "He would be happy to see you."

The following morning I went to their home in Rehaviah. The living room was a mess – books, magazines, all kinds of things from the study were scattered all over the place. In the midst of the chaos Professor Shadmi, in a dressing-gown and tie, lay sprawled in a big leather armchair. He who was usually so pedantic about his appearance. When he saw me he closed the book he had been reading – *the Muqaddimah*, Ibn Khaldun's introduction to the science of history that had influenced both East and West. Pe'era apologised for the disorder and brought us tea on a hammered copper tray.

"We decided to enlarge the study by enclosing the adjoining balcony," the professor told me, "but the work seems to go on forever. For the past five weeks we've been living with the dust and the mess and the end is not in sight. I'm afraid that's what is making me unwell."

"The builder says he can't get workmen," said Pe'era. "He says nowadays every Jewish worker has become a boss…I suggested hiring Arab workers, but Shadmi objects."

"We wanted our society to be built with Hebrew labour, to provide for our needs with our own hands," Shadmi said. "If we start relying on Arab labourers we will become dependent on them to our own detriment." He put on his horn-rimmed glasses, picked up the Ibn Khaldun and turned the pages. "He has a passage here that describes how a military victory and its fruits affect the victors. Though it was written centuries ago, when I read it I feel that he was describing us and what we are facing: 'The tribesmen will lose their ability to live the desert life and to be satisfied with little, their communal sense will decline and their bravery slacken, and they will indulge in a life of ease and plenty…Their sons will exist in an atmosphere of superiority and think it beneath them to serve themselves and to provide for their own necessities…Their bravery will weaken in succeeding generations, until it disappears altogether.'"

"My dear, you are feeling unwell, which is why you overstate everything," Pe'era told him. To change the subject she asked, "Have you shown Nuri the latest research publications?"

Shadmi picked up two handsomely produced Arabic periodicals, one from Saudi Arabia and one from Iraq, leafed through them and showed me the articles bearing his name. "They published the papers exactly as I sent them, only omitting the fact that I'm an Israeli Jew," he said with a chuckle. Then he began to question me, as he always did, about the situation in the territories.

"I'm finding it hard," I told him. "The attitude of our side towards the Arab population often causes unnecessary problems. I'm uneasy, and as time goes on my mind is more divided." Shadmi gave me a sharp look, sat up and said, "Remember, my dear Nuri, that we are dealing with two cultures, two different psychological systems. Theirs is a culture of shame and honour, and among us Israelis, to put it simply, chutzpah and rough practicality are gaining ground. Their way of doing things is to follow the well-trodden path. With us the tendency is to improvise. So quite often we don't understand them and they don't understand us, which is another tragedy in this conflict. It is a dialogue of the deaf. We will get nowhere if we judge them by our criteria, and that is why I don't foresee a solution in the near future. The euphoria and the overconfidence that followed the victory are a bubble, and it will burst.

"There is another matter, which seems trivial but is not – the way people behave towards one another. We are a nation without manners, we encouraged our children to show off their cheeky precociousness, to use a direct, loud and brusque attitude. The Arabs, by contrast, are polite, have exquisite manners, charm and a flattering tongue. This gives rise to misunderstandings that can be dangerous.

"You know that I've liked you since we first met on Mount Scopus when you were doing your national service, so I'll tell you something else. You, the immigrants from the Arab countries, you have known the Arabs since infancy, and could have served as a bridge between us. But that didn't happen. You failed to pass on to the rest of us what your intuition and knowledge told you about our Arab neighbours. You became assimilated, whether of your own will or not I can't say, in our local low-grade culture. It's a great and serious loss on the national scale.

"The people here are sitting on top of a volcano, but are quite unaware of it. It would take the combined wisdom of Weizmann, the foresight of Moshe Sharett, the decisive courage of Ben-Gurion, and the down-to-earth sober mind of Eshkol to get us out of this predicament. But here I'd better stop, because I'm entering the unstable sphere of politics."

"Professor, why don't you come and address the Labour Party's youth wing on the subject of the conflict? My Uncle Hizkel, who I told you about, is going to speak at their conference. The views you've spelled out are important and could be very useful precisely because they will provoke controversy."

"Let me get better first. When this nuisance" – he pointed to the broken wall – "is behind us, I'll come with pleasure." Before I left he patted my back and said, "I'm glad you came. Don't forget – *al-bait baitak*, my house is your house."

From the professor's house I called in on a solicitor to sign the contract for my parents' new flat. I'd found them a pleasant three-room flat in the German Colony, with a balcony overlooking the street. I could see Mother sitting on it, smoking a reflective cigarette as she watched the passers-by. My brother Kabi had sent a substantial sum for the down payment, I obtained a mortgage from the Civil Service bank and another one, at a higher rate of interest, from the national mortgage bank, and there it was – a new flat! After the signing I drove to my parents' house, to give them the news.

Mother hugged me and kissed me, then burst into tears: "Why did the two of you have to get into debt for us?"

"I knew you'd say that, which is why I didn't tell you about it, or take you to see the flat. Otherwise you wouldn't have let us buy it."

Father was grateful but embarrassed. He hugged me, clearly distressed at needing his sons' help. "You must have borrowed a lot of money. But as soon as we sell this place you'll be able to repay most of the loan."

"Soon Kabi will come from London," Mother said. "Then we shall hold a proper housewarming with the whole family."

Hizkel had a lecture of his own to prepare, and he worked on it with renewed enthusiasm. He no longer looked like a shadow of his former self, and his self-confidence was improving. He went on his own to Nablus and Hebron, to Tulkarem and remote villages, made notes of his impressions and conversations with people he met. He read articles and books and consulted Jewish and Arab commentators. He wrote and crossed out, and finally gave me his lecture to translate into Hebrew. The work called for a lot of discussion and rewriting, and took up a lot of time. Once I even had to cancel a meeting with Yasmine.

"You've forgotten me," she said, only half in jest.

"If I forget thee, may my tongue cleave to my palate! Are you free tomorrow?"

"No."

"The day after?"

"No."

"Yasmine, please! You know about Hizkel, what he's been through. This lecture is so important to him. I had to help him. Come, my flower, don't hide your face from me! I miss you so much. If this was a video-phone you would see an unhappy man on his knees, begging for his life."

"Flatterer. You always win with your smooth talk."

The invitations to the conference arrived. Hizkel went to East Jerusalem to buy a ready-made suit, but because he was abnormally thin, the salesman persuaded him to have one made to measure. In the end, of all the styles and colours they showed him, he chose to have a black pinstripe suit, in the fashion of Baghdad in the 1940s.

Two days before the conference Kabi arrived and brought Hizkel striped ties and Aero shirts, the kind he used to favour in Baghdad. "Will it be all right if I invite Sandra to Hizkel's lecture?" he asked.

"Of course!" I said, and felt a twinge of envy because I couldn't bring Yasmine.

Back at my place I was met by Grushka, who scowled at me. She stood at the door, holding her tail upright like a sword. I left the door open in case she wanted to come in, but she didn't. Perhaps she was annoyed with me because I hadn't seen her for several days.

The cold empty room depressed me and I went out onto the

balcony. The sky was clear, the moon was shining brightly and there was a kind of tense calm, the kind that grabs you by the throat. It reminded me of the beautiful but nervous nights of waiting outside Gaza before the war. I recalled how, deeply moved and anxious, I stared at the pure heavens, wondering if I would live to see them the next night. I understood then the blessing implied in the biblical verse, to "dwell safely, every man under his vine and under his fig tree". The fear had eased now, but was not quite gone, and peace seemed as far away as ever.

Some nights I couldn't sleep, kept waking again and again, sticky with sweat, staring into the darkness, afraid that the concrete ceiling would crash down and bury me alive. My friend Trabulsi wouldn't let me rest, rising from the flames with a silent scream and nobody responding. The son who was born to him when we were called up was now a one year-old orphan. I felt a powerful urge to tell Yasmine I loved her, and repeat it in seventy different ways. But I could hardly telephone her at such an hour.

The evening of the lecture Kabi and I went to pick up Hizkel.

"This is how you dress, in a short-sleeved shirt?" he rebuked me.

"These people are socialists, they have no use for suits and ties," I explained.

"Then I'm not dressed correctly?" he asked, worried.

"The suit is fine. The beret I'm not so sure about."

"Leave him alone," Kabi told me. "Let him wear whatever he wants."

The square in front of the Labour Federation building was packed with members of the Labour Youth movement in blue shirts, waving both the national and the red flags. The hall and the podium were also decorated with these flags, as well as slogans and flowers. The place slowly filled up with members of the youth wing, the Working Women's Council, Labour Federation activists, party leaders and functionaries. We were seated in the front row, beside the VIPs. Hizkel looked very much the new immigrant, in his beret, his Clark Gable moustache, the pinstriped black suit and tie.

He was also very pale. "I didn't know there would be so many people," he said to me in a low voice. The tension was visible in his face. I tried to joke him out of it but failed. When I gave him a mint to suck he put it in his pocket and when I handed him a cigarette, he didn't light it.

First the choir sang, then came a long series of speeches and encomiums, but at last the Secretary General introduced Hizkel and invited him to address the gathering. Going up to the podium Hizkel almost stumbled on his damaged leg. He stood before the large audience, cleared his throat and began, despite the advice I gave him when we worked on the lecture, with the story of the Jewish underground in Baghdad. The microphone magnified his heavy Iraqi accent.

The story of the underground read from the written page failed to hold anyone's attention. The young people giggled, others exchanged whispers and some began to chat openly. In the end the Secretary General stood up and called for silence.

Hizkel stopped speaking and looked at the audience.

Suddenly he took off his beret and jacket, loosened his tie and took off his reading glasses. He pushed aside the lecture notes and held up his head. The underground hero and freedom fighter emerged from the pinstriped suit.

"I am a new immigrant, I don't yet speak good Hebrew," he began slowly, making every word count. "But I do understand a movement of national liberation. For twenty years the hangman's rope hung over my head because I fought for freedom. My best friends, who were with me in the underground, were executed. We gave our lives to the struggle for independence, for a state of our own. Now, in the Land of Israel, what do the Arabs and the refugees want? They want independence, a state, like ours. Exactly. Now we must pay attention to the *Nakba*, the catastrophe, their catastrophe. We must listen to their pain, we must remember that they also have dignity. We must also remember that a weak man hates the strong, and that life is a wheel – it turns up and it turns down. And I am afraid of the time when we shall be down. We have our Jewish morality, and we must make justice for these Arabs too. Churchill, who defeated the Nazis, said, When you are victorious, be generous!"

There was total silence thoughout the hall. Hizkel made a little bow and turned to leave the podium, but changed his mind and returned to the microphone. "Recently I travelled among the Arabs, I wanted to see how they were faring. One day on the road from Jericho to Jerusalem the bus stopped. On the road lay a dead Arab – they said he was killed by mistake. His blood was on the road. Then what did I see? A Bedou took his son, showed him the dead man, and said, *Ibni*, do not forget this blood!"

Again he stopped, gazed at the audience, then read out the final passage in the speech he'd prepared: "We were a persecuted people, humiliated and rejected, we were hunted down and massacred. I am afraid that the the evil demon in our souls will raise his head and demand revenge for the humiliation of our fathers, and that we will fall into the sin of pride and treat the Arabs the way the Gentiles treated us. I have been to Jericho and Nablus, to Tulkarem and the West Bank. I saw beautiful lands, a sweet and spacious country. It is true that it was the land of our ancestors, but another nation has been living there for generations. How can we drive them out if they and their fathers were born and lived there? We have to decide what we want and what we must do. We have no other place, but we must also think of them, we are not alone in the world. We must not be a ship of fools. We have to make the peace we always prayed for."

There was uproar, shouts of "Shame! Coward!...The Arabs understand only the language of force. Give them a finger and they'll demand the whole hand! You're talking like the Arabs!"

The conference descended into pandemonium, a deafening chorus of denunciation. The Secretary General tried to reimpose order, and Hizkel climbed carefully down from the podium. Facing the outraged audience he signalled to Kabi and me and we left together.

"Either I'm crazy, or they are," he said outside, trembling all over.

40

A Dowry without the Bride

To my amazement, the very next morning the Deputy Minister phoned me to say that Levi Eshkol wanted see Hizkel. He added that the attacks on my uncle not only did not deter him, but in fact reinforced his view that such statements needed to be heard at the highest level. I have to admit that I too had been surprised and impressed by Hizkel's courage.

When I told him the news I could see that our underground hero was deeply moved, though he tried to hide it.

"The Prime Minister? The Prime Minister!" he repeated. Then he said with a smile, "Tell me, Nuri, is this their way of making it up to me after the reception I received yesterday?"

Before entering the Prime Minister's office, Hizkel smoothed down the striped tie Kabi had given him, winked at me and grinned. Levi Eshkol, big and broad-shouldered, rose from his chair as we walked in. He was not the man I'd seen three years before in Nazareth, when he seemed full of vitality. Now he put me in mind of Samson after his haircut. His small moustache had turned grey and he looked old and weary, though still warm and sociable.

"Welcome! Blessed be He who frees the captives!" he said in

his thick voice as he shook Hizkel's hand. "And welcome to you too," he said to me with a smile. I wondered if he remembered me from the Nazareth visit of three years before and last year's tour of East Jerusalem.

His office was spacious, with a big desk, a bookcase packed with books on law with blue bindings, the works of Berl Katznelson, one of the fathers of the Labour movement, and others, and on a small table beside him four telephones, two black, one red and one green. He invited us to sit on a divan, and he sat facing us with a leg over the armrest. "*Vos hert zich?* How are you?" he asked, flavouring his speech with his trademark Yiddish phrases.

"So where shall we start?" asked the Deputy Minister, also in attendance.

"Start from the end," said Eshkol, as a woman came in with a tea tray. "Here comes Dinah with the chai."

He put a sugar cube in his mouth, Russian-style, and began to sip the tea with noisy relish. Next he took a pretzel and ate it, then another sugar-cube, and by the time we were all served, he had already finished a glassful.

"*Krasabitza*, eh? She's pretty, isn't she, our Dinah," he said with a smile that obviously pleased the woman. Then he turned to Hizkel. "Well, and this Zion that you dreamed about – how does it strike you?" He might have been asking a groom how he liked his bride.

"It is more beautiful even than my dream," Hizkel replied, and went straight to the subject that troubled him. "Also very big and complicated. I am asking myself, what should be done with all this?"

Eshkol's brow creased and his glasses slid down his nose. "*Reb Yid*, my good man, you've touched the heart of the matter.

What do we do now with the territories and the Arabs? It's mashing my brain…"

"Prime Minister, you defeated Goliath. The cards are all in your hands!"

"This Goliath is making a lot of trouble even when he's lying on the ground," Eshkol said thoughtfully. "He's stuck there like a stone, not moving or trying to get up. You must have heard about the three "Noes" of the Khartoum conference – No peace, No recognition, No negotiations. What are we to do with them? How can they expect to change their situation unless they are willing to change? The heads of the churches and the Christian communities in East Jerusalem came here, showed respect and asked for this and that…And I, who came like you from the diaspora, dreaming about the Zion of our forefathers, I didn't put them off. I said to myself, God in Heaven, how great are your deeds, how wise. Perhaps in victory the wisest thing is to be generous."

"That is precisely why I thought you should meet Mr Imari," put in the Deputy Minister.

The Prime Minister's secretary came in and pointed at one of the telephones. "Excuse me, Mr Eshkol. Pinhas Sapir on four."

"I should hope so too," he growled, picking up the green phone, and the grin re-appeared on his face. "Pinya, what's going on?" He listened to the Treasury Minister for a moment, then said, "Pinya, get me the money, we'll build the state, then go and eat dinner." He hung up.

"Tell me, Mr Imari," he returned to Hizkel. "Was your life in danger in prison during the war?"

"It was hard. Especially in the days of waiting before the fighting."

"The days of waiting…" Eshkol sighed, then said, "The time

will come when people will understand that our decision to wait till the goy finished all his shenanigans at the UN was the right one."

"It was a wise decision, sir," Hizkel said.

"We're living in a madhouse. The end of one war can easily become the beginning of another. We've got to finish all this," the Prime Minister declared. "But our cousins, they should be so healthy, have an inflated sense of honour, a great sensibility…Ay-ay-ay, it's impossible to conclude the business and move on," he said and looked at us, seeking confirmation.

"Sir, they have time. We do not."

"Tell me, please, what the Iraqi intelligentsia are saying, the officers? This time they didn't risk getting involved, not like the Egyptians and Jordanians, who fought very well. What's it like in Iraq now?"

"Well, sir, in my prison there were communists and nationalists and dissident officers, and we talked a lot. Every new intake is a great improvement on the previous one. Since the Jews left, they have taken over all our professions in the economy, in art, law, even music."

"So the gap between us is getting smaller," Eshkol sounded worried. "And you, what are you thinking of doing?"

"I don't know yet. I'm still looking for a place to live."

"Have you arranged it?" Eshkol asked the Deputy Minister.

"We're taking care of it."

"Mr Imari, you've come from over there, you know the Arabs. Do you have a suggestion?" Eshkol asked, gesturing with his hand with the amputated finger.

Hizkel was silent for a while, considering the question. Then he spoke. "Sir, first of all the Jews must agree among themselves and decide what they want."

The Prime Minister laughed. "What the Jews want is the dowry without the bride."

"The Palestinian refugees, sir. This problem must be solved quickly, otherwise it will generate a lot of trouble."

"*Das iz eine a ganze mayseh*, now that's a whole story, and a long one too. It takes money, a lot of money, and co-operation."

"We must give them a state, sir."

"But there is nobody to do business with! I've met their leaders from Hebron and Nablus and Bethlehem – ten men with a dozen views, just like us, and nobody willing to take responsibility."

"Then we must return the territories to King Hussein. He himself says, 'Jordan is Palestine and Palestine is Jordan'. What could be better? Leave the problem to him," said Hizkel.

"The point is, there must be some give and take. Something given in return for these territories – peace, security…" the Prime Minister arqued.

"Sir, they are confused. And how could it be otherwise? Every Israeli minister says something different. It's driving them mad. Could you not address them directly, on our Arabic radio service and in their newspapers in East Jerusalem?"

"That's an idea." Eshkol summoned his secretary and told her to bring in the text of an interview he had given to an American journalist. He leaned back and read out the crucial passage: "The territories we conquered in the war that was forced upon us are almost in their entirety a pledge that we are holding until we make a permanent peace. Until then, it is a hammer without an anvil, and we're playing chess with ourselves." He sighed and handed the paper to Hizkel.

"Sir, we were brought up to be a light unto the nations. How can that be when we are ruling over them?"

"*Oy vay*," Eshkol laughed. "You don't have any easier questions? Before we become a light unto the nations, we should try not to be a darkness unto the Jews…We could learn from the nations a little modesty and a sense of proportion." He got up and went to the bookcase, humming a Hassidic song, "The Rebbe says rejoice, for hard times are coming…"

He drew out a copy of his book and inscribed it for Hizkel in large, curly handwriting, ending with a signature right across the page.

"I'm glad to have met you," he said. "I'm sure you will contribute much to us with your knowledge and experience, and I promise you we shall not rest till we achieve peace."

41

Ramleh and the Immigrant Camp

One morning in early summer, the kind of morning when heaven and earth compete in singing paeans of praise to the Creator of all things, I picked up Yasmine at her house. Her cheeks were as rosy as the flowers, and when she climbed into the car I sang Abdel Wahab's song.

"When the wind told the butterfly about your lips, it abandoned the roses for you…"

"How come you know so many Arabic songs?"

"From my fathers and forefathers, from the dawn of my life."

"I've never heard you singing in Hebrew."

"That's because I rarely sing in Hebrew. Do you know which Hebrew song I learned first? *Shibbolet basadeh* – 'An ear of corn bowed in the wind, burdened by its grains'. I heard it when we arrived at the immigrant camp. It smelled of the country, of the earth, of roots. I thought if I sang it I would become a true Israeli, a sabra. I don't know what I've become, exactly, but the songs that come up spontaneously in my mind are the same as before."

"I didn't sleep much last night," she said and opened the window. Her hair fluttered in the breeze, and she gazed at the passing views with wide-open, curious eyes.

*

We descended from the mountains to the plain, passed stables for horses and donkeys, and reached a narrow, potholed road where stray dogs and cats wandered freely. Ramleh. I liked that neglected old cowboy town, which greeted visitors with cheap eateries and a colourful market. A mixed town, with Arabs, Bedouins and Jews living together, each community in its own corner.

Yasmine asked if we could stop, and she got out of the car to take pictures. Soon these photos would join the vistas of al-Quds and Paris hanging on the walls of her house.

"Come on, let's have coffee," she suggested, and added with a sly smile that reminded me of our first meeting: "Perhaps this time you really will tell my fortune."

We went into one of the cheap roadside restaurants – a perfect contrast to the American Colony where we'd first met as two distrustful strangers. This time my lovely flower smiled at me, and I was as happy as a king in his court. When the coffee arrived Yasmine opened her handbag, but instead of her foreign cigarettes she brought out a small package tied with a ribbon. "A present for you," she said, her eyes radiating affection. "Open it and see." Inside was a wristwatch in a simple modern design. "It's self-charging," she told me.

I put it on, imagining that it throbbed to her heartbeat. Then she took the watch I'd taken off, an old one with a worn face and a sweaty leather strap, and put it on her wrist. "I want this one. May I?"

"That old thing, why? I'd rather buy you a new one, an elegant feminine one. This one is almost twenty years old, Father bought it for me before we left Baghdad."

"I want your watch."

I looked into her eyes and my heart missed a beat. I took her emptied coffee cup and tilted it this way and that. "'Shall I tell you your fortune?"

From Ramleh we drove through orchards and orange groves that stretched for miles along the road, like the carriages of an endless green train. Here and there rose tall palm trees, their feathery tops whipped by the wind. The intoxicating fragrance of citrus blossom permeated the car. We proceeded to Beit Dagan and from there to Jaffa's ancient port which seemed unchanged, eternal – high-masted trawlers and small fishermen's boats floated on the blue water, overlooked by the ancient stone fortress. An idyll from another world. Yasmine rested her head on my shoulder and I nuzzled her hair, enjoying its scent mingled with that of the sea. But the beauty of the scene reminded me of Ghadir, who was born in Jaffa, and my mood darkened.

"What's the matter?"

"I was rememberimg Ghadir."

Yasmine held my hand and led me towards the sea. We took off our shoes and walked along the sandy beach. Two elderly men, bent over fishing nets they were mending, smiled at us. The air smelled of fish. A flock of gulls circled above us and then took off over the sea.

Driving along the sea front we were soon in Tel Aviv, the topless city, as frivolous as the waves. The beach was crowded with small children and wrinkled old people, sexy girls and muscular beach boys, men and women, sprawling in the shade or tanning themselves, exercising, running or eating.

"It's a modern city, secular, and materialistic," I said. "Here you can live. In Jerusalem you can pray."

"What a wonderful name you chose for it – Tel Aviv, Tel alrabia, Spring Hill, Colline de Printemps..." she tried it in various languages.

"It's the cradle of modern Israeliness. Still, things wouldn't work without Jerusalem which has most of the beauty as well as the sorrow. It's like the two arms of the scales, the ancient and the new, the root and the branch."

As we drove northwards I asked, "How is your youth village project coming along?"

"It's stuck," she replied and looked away. "I approached the wrong partner. Instead of helping me establish a youth village, our saintly Mutran just wanted to get me into his bed. Once he almost raped me. That was the evening I was supposed to meet you at Al-Hurriyeh."

His cynical laugh echoed in my ears. Even back then, in his church, he had the look of a hungry hyena.

"It took me a while to realise that all he cares about is women and money. He's a compulsive gambler. Would you believe it, he gambled away all the money we'd raised to build the village?"

Before long we reached the site of the immigrant camp near Pardes Hanna which had once been my home. There it was across the road – empty, abandoned, like a scruffy scarecrow. Desolate white dunes extended in all directions. Here and there a torn canvas tent, a rusty tin shed, but chiefly the latrines – tall rounded concrete structures with gaping dark holes in them – had refused to surrender to the drifting sands. They had been built for the troops of the British Mandate, and remained as memorials to a departed empire. I remembered the narrow road that crossed the camp, muddy and windswept...

"Here I met my Tower of Babel," I told Yasmine, "of languages and cultures, people uprooted from their homelands and gathered in this place in the hope of liberation. But being stuck on this bare ground we felt like beggars. Perhaps this is where my dreams were born; to break through, to live, to make a difference in the world."

What had come over me? I never imagined I'd talk like this. I'd never even said these things to myself. But Yasmine's attentive eyes made me open up.

"You see this wilderness? Here there were hundreds upon hundreds of huts. Thousands lived here, refugees, displaced people. And now – nothing, just drifting sands.

"Not far from here is the venerable village of Pardes Hanna, a much more substantial place. Solid houses, green lawns, red roses, prosperous farms and orchards. There were noticeboards and clubs, a cinema and a school, a clinic and shops and groceries, all the normal amenities of permanent inhabitants. We used to invade it like locusts, steal vegetables and oranges, out of hunger but also out of envy. Refugees' envy. The need to steal, to hide the loot inside your shirt, to elude the householder for the sake of a tangerine or a cucumber, was so demeaning. I don't know whom we hated more, them or ourselves.

"It was a miserable, lawless, wretched camp. All the same, I learned something here and that was that a stray dog who rummages in garbage to keep alive is better than a fat lion lying contentedly in his kingdom."

We drove on. Yasmine was silent. In Wadi Ara, with its surrounding Arab villages, she said to me, "I never believed that our conquerors also had wounded hearts, as we have." Then she suggested, "Shall I drive, to give you a rest?"

"Thanks, no need. We're almost there."

I could see Kiryat Oranim, my old kibbutz, from afar, clinging to the hillside, hugging the boulders and the woods, firm and prosperous.

42

The Flight of the Gulls

Reaching the kibbutz I slowed down and stopped before the avenue of palms that lined the access road like a palace guard. Not all the palms were still upright. Eighteen years had passed since I had first come here, as a thirteen-year-old boy who spoke Hebrew haltingly with a heavy Arabic accent, a little refugee from Iraq taken from his parents' home in the immigrant camp and sent to join the youth group in the legendary kibbutz.

I restarted the engine and drove down the avenue. The smells of the silo and the cowshed, the flower beds and the laurel hedges, the quiet and the intimidating cleanliness trickled into my soul as they always did. Yasmine said nothing but stroked the back of my neck.

Noa, the wife of Haggai who had invited me to give the lecture, was waiting for me in front of the dining hall. She was surprised to see Yasmine, because I hadn't said I was bringing a girl friend, but immediately recovered and gave us a meaningful smile.

"Noa, this is Yasmine. She's an orientalist researching the Israeli-Arab conflict at the Sorbonne," I said.

"It's a pleasure. My husband Haggai is an orientalist too."

You'll soon meet him," she said to Yasmine and shook her hand. Noa had filled out a little and become very attractive. Her hair was neatly gathered on her nape, her back was very straight and her eyes were full of warmth. The years had been kind to her. Even in the old days she was always a good-looking girl who had a style of her own in clothes. She favoured colourful shirts with a bandana at her throat and the white shorts of a tennis player. Now she took us to the guest apartment, stopping on the way at the linen storeroom to pick up sheets and towels, and then leading us up the cypress walk. Pinkish-purple redbud bushes were blooming everywhere.

Yasmine looked around at the rich greenery and said to Noa, in Hebrew, that it was her first visit to a kibbutz.

"But you speak such good Hebrew, without an accent!" Noa said admiringly.

"I was born in this country," Yasmine replied.

"What happened to the orange grove and the vegetable garden and the olive orchard?" I asked.

"Times have changed," Noa said. "We did away with the orange grove and the vegetable garden, and uprooted the olive trees to grow fodder for the cattle and the poultry. Nowadays the fruit and vegetables from the West Bank are so cheap that it doesn't make sense, simply for the sake of Zionism, to keep on growing them."

The guest apartment, consisting of a room and a half, was furnished with monastic simplicity but was clean and pleasant. There was a basket of fruit on the table, and in the kitchen there were tea bags, coffee, biscuits and bottles of juice and soda water. Noa went into the bathroom and turned on the tap. "Good, the water's hot. Dinner is at seven. We'll meet you at the entrance to the dining hall."

"That's some title you gave me," Yasmine laughed. "An orientalist researching the Arab-Israeli conflict at the Sorbonne, no less!"

A profound peace, and the pleasant and familiar cooing of the wood pigeons, enveloped me like an old lullaby. "Try to get some sleep, we've got a long evening ahead of us," Yasmine advised and went to take a shower.

I tried to breathe quietly, listening to every rustle. The squeak of the door when she came out of the shower, her barefoot padding on the way to the tiny bedroom. There was no door or curtain between us, and I imagined her removing the towel from her head, shaking out her wet hair. I love wet hair. Now she was taking off her dressing-gown, revealing her naked body, which I'd never seen…My heart began to pound madly and my whole body grew hot. I wanted to get up and love her crazily, make her mine, my desired, my adored…but I held myself back. I took deep breaths and forced myself to calm down, to repress the storm inside me. I needed to sleep – tonight I had to face a double test.

Crazy, restless dreams filled my sleep, and one image shook me: the ruddy Tigris overflowed and flooded the loamy soil, bursting furiously on to the white dunes of Pardes Hanna, washing over the immigrant camp, submerging the tents and swallowing everything in its path.

I woke up in alarm. Where was I? It was dark. My head felt heavy. The lecture! Oh no, I'm late! I turned on the light and looked at my watch. Five past six. Where was Yasmine? She was not in the apartment. I opened the blinds, and found it was still light outside. I looked around till I saw her on the path, her camera case slung over her shoulder and a bunch of wildflowers in her hand.

"This place is like a village from another world," she said.

"Pastoral, peaceful. The people are relaxed, sitting on their balconies and on the grass with the children. Nobody stopped me or asked who I was and what I was doing here. Everything is wide open, like one family…It's perfect, just like the descriptions in your propaganda booklets."

I gave her coffee and stroked her arm. "I also thought so when I was a youngster. It looks idyllic, everything is left open, there are no locks and no divisions, everyone is equal. But behind it there are tensions and disappointments. You won't believe it, but an old kibbutz member wrote in his diary, which was found after his death, that all his life he felt like a second-class citizen because he came to the kibbutz three months after the founding group."

"All the same," she said, "what they've done and built here is really enviable." Then she looked at me severely. "You're not going to put on a jacket and tie?"

"In the kibbutz? You know what they call a tie round here – a kipper!" I laughed.

"But you're not a kibbutz member, you're a lecturer, this evening's guest."

Outside, red hibiscus and long-stemmed poppies glowed in the twilight. Yasmine took my arm, giving me a feeling of confidence and belonging.

"When shall we visit your old instructor?" she asked.

"After dinner."

I stopped outside the dining hall, which had been enlarged since my last visit, uneasy about entering without someone from the kibbutz. People nodded to me, a few came over and shook my hand, and they all stared at Yasmine, who stood beside me, slender, elegant and unassuming.

The practice in the dining hall had changed from table service, as it had been in my time, to self-service. This evening the supper was lavish – boiled chicken, potato puree, red cabbage and a green salad. Yasmine took a tray and helped herself readily. No one could have guessed who she was, not even Haggai, who bombarded her with questions about her research and asked her to send him a copy of her dissertation, talked to her at length about his own research, and said he was willing to lecture at the Sorbonne.

Yasmine turned out to be a good actress. She said her doctoral thesis focused on Nasser's influence on the Israeli-Arab conflict and the national identity of the Arabs in Israel. She showed great interest in the kibbutz, asked about the way of life, communal property, the upbringing of children, education, the status of women. Then she surprised me by saying, "I'd like to spend a week or two here. Perhaps work in the fields or the kitchen. Could I?"

"You're very welcome. Just let me know and I'll get a room ready for you," said Nili, an old friend from the youth group who had stayed on and married a kibbutz member.

A group of blond youngsters came into the dining hall. I raised my eyebrows.

"Volunteers from Europe," Noa explained. "Better than hired labour."

"And that's not hired labour?" Nili commented.

"No, the volunteers are something else altogether," Noa replied. "The young people enjoy their company, party with them and have fun. There are already some mixed couples. One kibbutz-born guy married a girl volunteer and went to Holland with her."

"How did the kibbutz react?" I asked.

"It's not such a big deal these days," Nili said. "You know, of our youth group only I stayed on. All the others left sooner or later."

We spent the hour before the lecture visiting Sonia, my immortal former instructor. When she opened the door and saw Yasmine beside me her eyes lit up. "Your girl friend?"

Yasmine and I smiled. For a moment the world was ours.

Sonia, now sixty, had changed. Deep lines framed her mouth, etched by the hard years in the valley. Her thin frame exposed the signs of passing time, which in the fuller-bodied are cushioned by fat. Her room remained as small and simple as ever, and the refreshments she offered were also the same – plain chocolate, a homemade cake, and coffee.

Yasmine took a piece of chocolate. I watched it cling to her lips and wished myself in its place, but Sonia's presence inhibited me from showing my feelings, like an adolescent feeling bashful before his mother. Instead, I took an apple from the fruit basket. "The kibbutz has changed," I said. "It's developed."

"Every bit of this land is soaked with our blood, sweat and tears," Sonia responded with her familiar phrases. "We started from nothing. There was nothing here, only fallow soil, marshes and malaria…"

"And Arabs who had lived here for generations, surely?" Yasmine put in with an innocent expression.

"Yes, of course," Sonia agreed, slightly taken aback, but went on to explain, like a patient teacher: "You see, they were very backward, and we brought them Western values and culture."

Yasmine's face changed colour. I was afraid that a war of words would break out, which would have been inappropriate. Sonia's heroic narrative was a perfect example of what Yasmine called "obtuse Zionist condescension", but she kept her temper and only added ironically, "That's right, we came here to benefit the Arabs."

Sonia ignored the irony and went on: "From our first day in the wilderness of the valley we made every effort to cultivate friendly relations with the nearby Arab villages, because to us they were part of the world underclass that was suffering under capitalism. We hoped they would understand that their real enemies were the landowners who exploited them. Our tractors ploughed their lands and prepared them for sowing, in times of drought we filled their water-cisterns, and they were free to use our clinic. We wanted to be good neighbours and we believed we could live with them in peace."

"Then we started another war and conquered more territories..." Yasmine could not resist saying.

Sonia stared at her, amazed, as Yasmine went on in the patronising first-person-plural style, borrowed from her: "We wanted to help, but we thought we were better than them. Who gave the Arabs stereotypes if not us? – poor quality Arab labour, monotonous music, social and technological backwardness...And what we attributed to the Arabs we also attributed to the Jews from Arab countries."

I wanted to cry out, Yasmine, who needs this now?

"You can't bracket the Jews from the Muslim countries with the local Arabs," Sonia said, visibly upset. "As for the Arabs, did you know that we always supported a bi-national state? It was they who didn't accept us and didn't want to live with us in peace. They rejected the Biltmore Programme and the Partition Plan of 1947, and went to war, and then another war, to wipe us out..."

"And now you...sorry, we, are subjugating and oppressing another people," Yasmine responded. Sweat appeared on her forehead. She lit a cigarette, poured herself a glass of water and drank it down.

"You don't understand. We settled here as idealists. We believed, we still believe, that we are tested by our treatment of minorities. Here, let me read you what Ahad Ha'am wrote, and remember we were brought up on his thought." Sonia got up, took a volume from the shelf and read aloud: "We must be careful in our conduct with the strange nation amongst whom we have come to live anew, treat it with love and respect, and needless to say, with fairness and justice."

"You mean, we're enlightened conquerors," Yasmine smiled sarcastically. "Is that possible? Why should we succeed where others failed? The French tried it in Algeria, and that ended in a bloodbath."

Sonia protested, half apologetically. "Look, we're doing everything we can to avoid bloodshed, to protect human rights, to preserve justice, and not to hurt or humiliate."

"I am sorry to have to disagree with you," Yasmine said, "especially since I'm your guest." She became openly critical. "You live inside the kibbutz and you don't know what is going on outside. I move around and collect information and I've found cases of harsh treatment, sometimes very harsh. We don't seem to care what we are doing to them – our military government, land expropriations, everything depending on permits, area closures, cultural and national repression…A lot of injustice, even if unintentional."

Her inner conviction and passion overwhelmed me. If only she were Jewish and I could marry her according to our law! I looked at my watch and became impatient. The bitter exchange was lighting a fuse that I wanted to steer away from, especially since I was about to face an audience.

"You're saying very hard things. I…" Sonia struggled with herself, then her voice softened. "There may be a grain of truth in what you say, and some bad things are happening…Perhaps it's difficult for us to admit to errors and see ourselves in the mirror…About the lands – you're making it sound worse than it is. You're young and there are things you haven't found out. The landowners and the heads of the Arab clans from whom we bought the lands made a lot of money from the sales. The Arab labourers who worked for us also earned well, and Arabs from neighbouring countries came here to look for work, so their numbers grew. Without the renewed Jewish presence in this country the Arabs wouldn't have come here." She fell silent, then added in a weary but confident tone, "Injustice is done when you want to do it. Our intentions were pure."

"Ladies," I broke into the silence, "it's time to go to the dining hall. The lecture is about to start."

On the way there Sonia whispered to me, "I'm afraid your girlfriend has been too much influenced by Arab propaganda." Then she asked sadly, "Are you moving in the same direction, away from us?"

43

"What could you have done?"

The dining hall was full. An accordion player was on the podium, his fingers flying over the keys, and the entire audience burst enthusiastically into song, including myself (off-key as always):

> Sing, O Youth, of our future,
> Revival, building, aliyah!
> In will come our brethren
> homeland from Diaspora.

Yasmine pinched me. "It's the first time I've heard you singing in Hebrew."

I whispered, "The religious start their meetings with Bible commentary, and the pioneers with a singsong. It's a new culture!"

A man with a violin and a young woman at the piano, both kibbutz members, played the first movement of Beethoven's Spring Sonata. "Are you sure those two are agricultural workers?" Yasmine murmured.

Finally Haggai stood up to introduce me. My mouth was dry and my head felt empty. The old guard of the kibbutz, with their hard sunburnt faces, scared me stiff.

"Comrades," I began, "I feel like a bar mitzvah boy standing up to read the weekly portion. Only yesterday I was a pupil here and sat on the back benches of this dining hall, now I'm on this podium. So forgive me if I am a little nervous.

"Today we need a new beginning, a revolution that will take into account both the Arabs of Israel and us, the immigrants from the Muslim countries, who fought in this war shoulder to shoulder with you.

"The question is, what will be our place in the leadership? Will our knowledge, our intuition, our cultural connection to the Arabs, be put to good use, will we be a formative element in the culture and the new political reality, or will we continue to be second-class?

"And another question – Will the Arabs of Israel continue to be the third-class? I believe that what we do today will determine whether the Arabs of Israel will be our neighbours or our enemies. Are we capable of sensitivity to the Other and consideration for his difficulties? Will we have the wisdom to carry out the necessary revolution and usher in a future of peace and co-existence?"

I then talked briefly about the population of East Jerusalem and the West Bank, illustrating the distress and the hardships these people were suffering with examples drawn from my personal experience. I talked about things that weighed on my mind, and when I finished speaking my back was wet with sweat.

Many disagreed with me, and some of the same arguments were repeated in different forms. Dolek was the first to speak. "Nuri, you were educated here and you know what this place means to us. We are tied to this soil with an umbilical cord. We fertilised it with our blood, we watered it with our dreams. As for peace, perhaps it is your youthful impetuosity that makes you lay the whole burden of it on us alone, and makes you forget the harsh facts of reality. Hasn't our hand always been extended to make peace? But what can we do, if they always push it away? The responsibility for achieving friendship and peace can't be only up to us, even if we want it with all our heart."

Guerman, a history teacher at the secondary school, said: "This is the land of our forefathers. The Arabs came here after us. The people who call themselves Palestinians came from Jordan, Egypt, Iraq, Saudi Arabia, Lebanon and Sudan to settle here. If we recognise them, they must recognise us. Young man, your open attitude towards the Arabs is impressive. When I was young I also wanted to view the world from such a beautiful standpoint, but it can't be done. Life is not so simple. The fine vision which you presented refers to a very narrow section of reality, it ignores both the terrible fanatical violence of the Muslim world and the hideous suffering of the Jews. You speak as if what we have here is a hard-hearted Jewish conqueror confronting a wretched Arab, and nothing else. This is so narrow and so superficial! That is not how it is. We keep questioning ourselves, examining our own actions, wondering what to do in order to survive, as simple as that, and what is the right thing to do? Are we responsible for the problem of the refugees? There was a war, and they started it! Do they ask themselves how come Holocaust survivors like myself and refugees from the Arab world like you have built up a successful state, while they remain bogged down in their refugee camps?"

"And what about Jerusalem?" asked Shaike.

I had to answer them, and tried to work out a comprehensive

response that would cover the various questions and arguments.

"In my opinion this country has two histories, two languages, two cultures, two visions, two dreams. Anyone who tries to claim the whole thing will end up with nothing..."

"You haven't mentioned Jerusalem," Shaike interrupted.

I felt Yasmine growing tense. Her eyes were on me.

"Shaike, Jerusalem the holy is a difficult place. Its entire history is paved with conflicts and wars, and precisely because it's holy, it attracts messianic weirdoes and religious nuts. The Christians have left the battlefield to the Jews and Muslims. We'll slaughter each other and they will be the observers. In my opinion, Jerusalem should be open to all, and if you ask me, the Temple Mount should fly not just the flag of Israel, but the flags of the Vatican and of all the Arab states."

There was a deathly silence. I was afraid I'd gone too far, though in my heart I believed it was the right answer. I was standing before them as an equal, not a boy under their protection. This time my background and my knowledge of Arabic were a source of strength and respect.

When I stepped down I was surrounded by friends, both close and distant. Dolek, who had opened new vistas to me as a boy, was especially moved, and he pressed me to his chest with his huge paws.

The severe-looking Tirtzah, one of the oldest members, spoke solemnly as always, but with a little stammer. "That was...I should say...well, anyone can prepare a written lecture, look things up, summarise and read it out. But to speak like this and answer questions, off the cuff? Spontaneously? That is..." She couldn't find the right words, or perhaps she wanted to compliment the boy from the youth group who had grown into a man, but was unable to praise him wholeheartedly.

Yasmine, who was noting everything in her balance-sheet of justice, swallowed a smile. "What's this, you're being tested?"

"Absolutely! And it's a strain on the nerves, but it also drives you forwards."

"You know," Haggai said, summing up, "you've broken three records this evening: people stayed till after eleven, asked a lot of questions and applauded, which is not customary among us."

"Come to us," Nili urged, "and we'll celebrate. You've earned it."

"I'm bushed. Let's have breakfast together instead."

Hand in hand, Yasmine and I walked up the dark cypress path, just the two of us, closer than we'd ever been before. Here, in Kiryat Oranim, my first home in Israel, the barriers between us finally fell.

As soon as we entered the guest apartment we turned into each other's arms. Yasmine clasped my head with her hands and I pressed her to me with all the tenderness in me. Her hands ran down my back and her nails dug into me. I had dreamed of this moment and feared it ever since the day I met her, and always knew it would be a point of no return. I undressed her and kissed every cell in her body which was revealed in all its beauty and freshness. I laid her on the bed and stretched out my hand to turn off the light, but stopped. No, let there be light tonight!

"I want to see you, to love you with my eyes as well."

"You are my gentle conqueror," she murmured, her eyes moist.

I'm no conqueror. I don't want to conquer. I want to live you, love you, come to you with silky caresses, envelope you with my heartbeat and my soul and the yearning of my body.

She was bleeding and I was smeared with her blood. "Sorry, it's my period," she said, but I entered her with a sense of compassion I'd never known before. She cried and pressed me to her warm spring, and I was sucked into her with infinite sweetness, surrendering to her my essence, my seed and my being, body and soul, blending with her. We were intertwined, coiled in and around each other. We were one flesh. I wanted to say to her, in Hebrew and Arabic and all the languages of the world, all the words of love I'd stored up for a year, but the release and relief made me swoon and forget everything. I fell asleep inside her, sinking into the sweetest sleep I'd ever known.

We woke early, before it was fully light, and with my eyes still half closed I covered her face with kisses.

"I love you, Yasmine."

"I love you, Nuri. I love your thoughts and your feelings, your speech and your passion. I love your skin and your smell and your sweat."

"Will you live with me?"

"Are you asking me to marry you, my love?"

"Is it possible?"

She buried her face in my chest and wept. My eyes were not dry either.

On our way to breakfast with Nili we stepped into the dining hall. I wanted to smell again the old familiar odours of omelettes, semolina porridge and cocoa. Nor could I skip the two youth group houses. The lawn in front was overgrown and weedy, the sand plot in between, which served us for athletics, was covered with planks and timber, and our beloved plum tree was gone, like all the rest of our world.

An abundant breakfast was waiting for us at Nili's. As we ate I told her that the municipality of nearby Netanya had decided to name part of a public park after our "Mister Universe", Amram Iwa, who was killed in the war. They had invited Amram's old classmates from the youth group to the naming ceremony. In parting, Nili gave me a bottle of her home-made cherry liqueur, and we left.

We drove up Mount Tabor and visited the shadowy church on its summit, our arms around each other, locked in love. It was a breezy, pleasant spring day. I stopped beside a tangle of bougainvillea bushes that bore pink, purple and white blossoms, picked handfuls of their flowers and scattered them on Yasmine's face and neck and on the car, as they do for brides on their wedding day. In my heart I sang to her the verses of King Solomon: "Thou art fair, my beloved, thou art fair…Come with me from Lebanon, my spouse, with me from Lebanon…"

We drove on to the Sea of Galilee and visited the cemetery on its bank. We walked in silence among the tombstones: here was Berl Katznelson, a towering Zionist intellectual with his wife to his right and his mistress to his left, here Ben-Zion Israeli, the founder of Kibbutz Kinneret, and here Rahel, whose book of poems lay on her tomb. Yasmine picked it up and leafed through it:

> Facing each other – the twin banks
> of a single stream.
> Fate's verdict:
> Forever apart.

*

Yasmine looked around at the greying stones and then at the blue lake and the distant gulls. "Tell me about the founders of the kibbutzim," she requested, "but without the slogans that Sonia spouted. Talk without thinking, without straining to get things exactly right, just the way they come to mind."

"What can I tell you? To me, the founders were the people of what we call the Second Aliyah, the first organised Zionist settlement. In fact, it all began right here, the great drama opened here in the hellish summer heat. There were not more than two thousand stubborn pioneers – solemn revolutionaries, with powerful motivation and strange moods, highly romantic.

"They arrived in the early years of the century, most of them from Russia, after the dreadful pogroms and the failure of the 1905 revolution, and had extravagant and colourful visions of the life they would lead here. They were like seagulls, they spread their wings and flew to a different country that was both old and new, dreaming about the revival of the Hebrew nation. Again and again they failed, but every failure led to another creation, another social institution.

"They saw themselves as secularists who rebelled against religion, but they lived like devout believers in an ascetic order. Many of them were poets and writers. Yosef Brenner, one of the most outstanding among them, once took a pioneer of the next wave of immigration, showed him a worker's room and said, 'No woman has entered this room for months.' Then he took him to the cemetery and said, 'Of the eleven buried here, only one died a natural death. The others were either murdered or committed suicide.'"

"And the Jews who were here before, the old community, how did they receive them?" Yasmine asked.

"They didn't want them! The Jewish farmers wouldn't employ them, they preferred Arab labourers, who were more skilful and cheaper.

"What else can I tell you? Perhaps about the achievement which moves me most – the revival of the Hebrew language. There's a story about a pioneer who took two vows when he came – one, never to return to the diaspora, two, to speak only Hebrew. He was sent to work in the winery of Rishon Lezion. There he was asked if he had any knowledge of French and of bookkeeping, and though he knew both, he said he knew only Hebrew and wanted to work as a common labourer. They thought he was an idiot and made him wash barrels and vats. The foreman kept nagging at him, talking to him in Yiddish, but he ignored him unless he spoke Hebrew. One day he was told to fill the barrels, and at a certain point the foreman ordered him, in Yiddish of course, to shut the spigot. He paid no attention and the wine was spilt. The foreman yelled, again in Yiddish, 'Shut the spigot, idiot!', but he stood over the flowing wine, asking, 'What did you say?' 'I said turn off the spigot, you fool, then get out of here!' the foreman yelled in Hebrew. 'Now I understand,' the man said, shut the spigot and was left without a job."

"Charming story," she smiled. "Amusing but worthy of respect."

We decided to return to Jerusalem via Beit She'an and the Jordan Valley. On the way we stopped at a small Arab village. A woman was drawing water from a well, slices of tomatoes hung on strings between two adobe houses, an old man sat on a wooden crate, rolled a cigarette and smoked it in a leisurely way. A bored cat looked at us without stirring from the soft ground. Apart from barefoot children who took us for tourists and ran up to us, there was a great stillness about the village, as if it was outside time. Everything was done *shwai-shwai*, without haste, moved by an ancient tradition in which a son followed his father and the father his grandfather, and the world remained unchanged. The Western frenzy had not reached this place.

When we reached Jericho we ran into a roadblock. A young Israeli soldier demanded our identity cards. Yasmine handed him her papers and French passport which immediately aroused his suspicion, and he told her to get out of the car. I got out with her and gave him my identity card. He looked at the photograph and the personal details, looked at me closely and handed it back to me.

"It's all right, you can leave," he said.

"She's with me, friend," I said in an informal tone.

"I'm not your friend and I don't know you."

"I know her, her father is — "

"Sir, I'm doing my duty and you are obstructing me."

"I tell you she's my friend. What's the problem?"

"How many times do I have to tell you you're obstructing my work?"

"Listen, soldier, you don't know who I am…" I produced a document issued by my Minister and another one authorising me to enter any military compound in the territories.

"Sir, to me you're a citizen like any other, I'll have to take steps against you," he threatened.

"What do you mean?" I raised my voice.

Yasmine shushed me. "You want to light a fire or to put it out?" she whispered.

The soldier searched the car thoroughly. The camera and the

rolls of film fanned his suspicions, and he asked a girl soldier to take Yasmine into a hut and check her out. "There's a gang of terrorists in the area," the girl soldier explained.

"Does she look like a terrorist?"

Yasmine signalled to me to move away. I'd promised to do everything for her, and here I was paralysed. I wanted to scream, but stood by helplessly as my love was led away to be questioned and physically examined. She was detained in the hut for a long time, and when she came out she walked slowly, her head bowed.

We got back into the car without a word. I stopped near the little square in the centre of Jericho. "I need coffee, my love."

"Please just take me home."

"I'm so sorry for what happened."

"What could you have done?"

44

"There's no comparison! She's a woman!"

Invariably, when debating with Abu Nabil, Abu George maintained that it was necessary to do some real soul-searching after the recent cataclysm. Why was Israel flourishing while the Arab world was languishing? He thought about it constantly, trying to decipher the secret of the Jews' success. Was it democracy, which respected the individual, rather than repressing and exploiting him? In our society, he argued, and throughout the Arab world, there was neither place nor hope for the individual – all were subsumed in the clan, in the mass, in the painful history.

Perhaps the secret of the Jews' strength was in their women, playing an active role in society. A woman felt equal to a man. Among us the woman is silenced, veiled, bundled in a robe of shame and honour and chained with religious and traditional prohibitions.

Yasmine had once accused him of being a collaborator. Of late, so it seemed to him, her attitude towards the enemy had changed and grown more clear-headed. She appeared calmer, and perhaps she too was beginning to understand that life mattered above all else, and it made its own demands. Perhaps it was young Nuri's influence. They exchanged views, sometimes dined together at Al-Hurriyeh and met to discuss their work. Just yesterday they travelled together to the north of the country. This was unexpected, but he had not intervened, afraid to spoil his relations with his daughter and encourage her to return to the Fatah crowd in Paris…Perhaps when she was occupied with her own youth village and the magazine her world would be complete.

The telephone rang. It was Abu Nabil. Unexpectedly, he suggested a trip to the Israel Museum in West Jerusalem. To see an exhibition of Islamic art.

During the drive to the museum that afternoon he felt that Abu Nabil wanted to say something but was holding back. After the exhibition they went to the King David Hotel, and there, on the terrace with the view of the walls of the Old City and the church steeples, he suggested to Abu Nabil that he join him and another partner, a Jew, in opening a fish restaurant in East Jerusalem.

Abu Nabil smiled his cynical smile and twirled his moustache. "Half my money belongs to Um Nabil, who is after all my life's partner. Of the remaining half, a quarter belongs to Nabil, my only child. Of the remainder, I save a half and invest the other half, and since we haven't done any business since the war, I'm holding on to what's left of my assets against a rainy day."

"Come on, Abu Nabil! Who knows how long this damned occupation will last? You rejected my suggestion to build a hotel on Mount Sacobos, refused to start a tourist transportation company. How long are we going to sit here doing nothing?"

"*Ya akhi*, brother, their government is behind it all! They want to pull our teeth, take over the business and the newspaper and use them in their propaganda. Can't you see that?"

Abu George was simmering with frustration.

"Patience, brother," Abu Nabil went on. "Soon it will all be ours, without any effort on our part. Israel has swallowed more than it can digest, its stomach is about to burst and its heart will stop."

"Forget Israel for now. Let's talk about our business."

"My son Nabil, Allah preserve him, is fighting against them – how can I do business with them? You know," he said in a low voice, leaning closer to Abu George, "it was Nabil's group that placed the landmine under the school bus near Be'er Orah."

"How can you let him risk his life like that?"

"Will he listen to me?" Abu Nabil sighed. He lit a cigarette and blew out a cloud of smoke. "You've no idea of the pressures I'm under…" He stopped, not wanting to tell his friend, in his delicate state of health, what Abu Ammar's people were saying about him and his daughter. But when could he speak? Every time they met he intended to get it off his chest, but held back. Then he heard himself saying, "Listen, brother, they are saying Yasmine is collaborating with the Zionists." He paused, to give his friend time to rally, and added: "I gave them my word of honour that if Yasmine knew how to use a gun, she would be fighting the Jews just like Nabil."

Abu George was horrified. "They're crazy!" he snapped.

"I said to them, 'By Nabil's life, kill me, but don't touch a hair of Yasmine's head.' But I must ask you, why does she work for them in that youth village?"

"My friend, she is only doing her practical work there, for her doctorate. There is no suitable institution on our side," Abu George explained, but sensed that his friend was not convinced.

431

"What else are you keeping from me?" he asked, and began to cough.

Abu Nabil felt his heart melting with compassion. "How come the doctors can't find a cure for you? By Allah, I wish I could raise our genius Abu Bakr Mohammed al-Razi from his grave to take care of you." He sipped his coffee, then went on, "*Ya akhi*, brother, you're as dear to me as my flesh and blood, and Yasmine is as precious to me as my son Nabil. Did I not want her to be his wife? I do have something more to say to you." He lit a cigarette.

Abu George clenched his jaw.

"Brother, people in this town gossip, they drip poison. What has Yasmine to do with that Jew Nuri, curses upon him?" Abu Nabil asked, puffing smoke.

"Can I tell her what to do?"

"Who else but you? You're her father!"

"And you cannot tell Nabil what to do, is that not so? Yasmine is not a child, she's a grown woman, an independent person," Abu George argued. "That's the problem. We treat women as we did in the Middle Ages. If we allowed them to be independent, as the Jews do, our lives would be transformed."

"There's no comparison, brother! She's a woman! I'm talking to you about her honour, your honour, everything that is precious to you and to us, and you babble about women's liberation...That would destroy the foundations of our society!"

"Or give rise to a new, advanced, enlightened society, without vendettas and the enslavement of women," said Abu George.

"Forget society, I want to talk about Yasmine. You should know that people are talking about her, saying bad things. Something must be done to stop it."

"The devil take them, what business is it of theirs? Abu

George's heart sank and he was filled with helpless rage. "They are smearing her because they are not real men. An educated independent woman like Yasmine scares our little cockerels. And the fact that she's a widow makes their jibes all the more vicious."

"Did you know that she has been meeting that Jew at night?" Abu Nabil did not let up.

"I know. They eat at my restaurant, meet for coffee at the American Colony. She makes no secret about it. It is nothing but a friendship. So what?"

"Make it stop now!" said Abu Nabil firmly. "You must cut off the snake's head before it grows too large. Don't let things get out of control!"

Abu George remained silent.

To lighten the mood and ease the tension, Abu Nabil reverted to the suggestion of starting a fish restaurant with a Jewish investor. "Understand me, brother, how can I do business with them? I'm a Muslim. The Muslim is superior, the Muslim rode on a horse and carried a sword, while the Jew walked on foot. A Jew may not carry arms, he may not walk in the rain lest he splash a Muslim. How can he be my partner?"

But Abu George's mind had drifted away. On his way home he felt people's eyes on him, as if he had sprouted a hump. If his friend and partner talked to him about Yasmine and Nuri, and went on and on about it, that meant the whole town was talking. *Ya rab al-alamein*, O Lord Almighty, she is due back this evening! What's to be done? Anxiety was corroding his veins. He had known suffering, had been deeply hurt when his friends denounced him and almost ostracised him as a collaborator, but the attack on Yasmine's reputation was a knife thrust into his heart.

But perhaps all the rumours had been started by the gang of that scoundrel Arafat, and were meant to drive him out of the newspaper business? The Fatah people wanted a newspaper of their own, full of lies and propaganda, like the Russian papers. How can you build a national identity on foundations of falsehood and fantasy? His anxiety turned into anger. These fanatics, he fumed, they would destroy everything and prevent others from building anything. Things were falling apart and nothing would satisfy them. Perhaps he really should retire from the newspaper, avoid public activity, spare himself further anguish and damage to his health...But how was he to tell Um George about the malicious gossip, and what would happen to Yasmine?

45

A Refugee, Son of Refugees

I couldn't get over Yasmine's humiliation at the Jericho roadblock. I was torn between hope and anxiety, belief in the power of our love and despair in the face of the inevitable complications. I couldn't wait for the morning, hoping she would telephone before leaving for the youth village. At six, after my brisk walk, having picked up my favourite, slightly scorched, rolls at the grocery, I went out on to the balcony.

It was a fine morning. I stood and watched the red kestrels. They came to Jerusalem from thousands of miles away and built their nest under the tiled roof opposite. The male had his work cut out, coupling with his mate many times. The eggs had recently hatched and the parents were feeding the fledglings with such care and devotion that I was touched. Before long they would all spread their wings and fly away, to return the next winter.

And here was my Orthodox neighbour, back at home. She came up to the window and showed me her new baby, turning its face for me to see. "Mazal tov! Congratulations!" I said aloud, and she smiled.

I put the kettle on, made Noumi Basra tea and took the halva out of the fridge. The phone rang – Yasmine? No, it was Levanah, kind-hearted as ever. She had just returned from abroad and brought me some chocolate. "Come in here before you start your day. The chocolate will sweeten it."

Levanah greeted me with her lovely smile. "I'm glad you came in. The Minister wants to see you." She took a packet from her drawer and put it on the desk. "The chocolate is waiting for you." I smiled at her and went into the Minister's office.

"Good morning, sir."

He did not return my salutation and looked worried and annoyed.

"Is it true," he asked grimly, "that you appeared at a political forum in Jerusalem at a conference of the Labour Party's youth wing, alongside your uncle, the 'prisoner of Zion'?"

I felt as if I'd been hit in the stomach. "It's true."

"It's against civil service rules."

"I asked the civil service regulator, and was told I could appear as an expert. Anyway, I didn't get to speak because the audience became unruly," I said, breaking into a sweat.

The Minister took a piece of paper from his jacket pocket and read out some quotes from my lecture at the kibbutz. "Are these quotes accurate?" he asked, piercing me with his big eyes.

"They are."

"Is it true that in that lecture at the kibbutz you said we should give up the liberated territories and give the Arabs a state, and that Jerusalem, our people's eternal capital, should be an open city and fly the flags of the Arab countries and the Vatican?"

"True."

He threw his pencil down on his desk, laced his fingers together and looked at me as if I were a stupid child. "I promoted you, I appointed you to an important post, I opened doors for you, trusted you. Tell me, how can we go on working together? How did you dare speak like a defeatist in public? You, my advisor and the head of my office in East Jerusalem! Do you know how much political damage you have done to me, and to my status as a public figure?" He was deeply agitated.

"I am very sorry if I caused you any distress. I never intended to do so. I have no earthly reason to want to harm you," I said. He closed his eyes as if to say, That's irrelevant. He took a paperclip and started cleaning his fingernails.

"Have I not followed your instructions? Have I acted in defiance of your policy?"

"We're not talking about your loyalty or your actions, but about your views! Why can't I get through to you?"

"Because I think otherwise, Minister," I said quietly. "We are orphans and they are orphans, we suffer from the victim complex and so do they, we have the refugee complex and they do too. The difference is that now our belly is full and theirs is empty. We have a home and they don't. They are consumed with envy and hatred and frustration. We have a saying that you should open your umbrella before the rain begins. If we do not give up the territories and help them establish their state, and do not help to solve the problem of the refugees, even God will be unable to sort out the mess."

The room was silent. The Minister threw down the paperclip and began to tear at his eyebrows. "We can't continue like this," he said at last.

"With your permission, Minister, I'd like to go out for a smoke," I said and went out into the front office. I stood by the window, immobile, my thoughts racing in the effort to reassess the situation in view of his attack. This was not a discussion, it was a confrontation between world-views. He refused to legitimise my position, and I'd have to sell my soul, become a chameleon. Once again I was a refugee, the son of refugees, one who for a little while seemed to belong, seemed to be one of the bosses, but only conditionally. He wanted me so long as I followed in his footsteps, since I was little more than his factotum, to be periodically reminded whose hand fed me.

I took a sheet of paper from Levanah's desk and wrote a short letter of resignation. In the afternoon I collected my belongings from the office in Sheikh Jarrah. I never went back there.

46

A Broken Branch

Nuri my love,

By the time you receive this letter I'll be in Paris. I'm disappointed with myself and ashamed that I didn't have the strength to tell you face to face that I'd decided to go away. It turns out our dream journey was in fact a farewell trip.

I didn't intend it to be like this. On the contrary, I tried to remove the obstacles in my heart. I'm trying, in the middle of this mental turmoil, to reconstruct things, to figure them out. One thing is clear to me – you stole my soul. Steal is not a nice word, but I haven't got another. With the persistence of an ant you succeeded in blunting my fears, awakening my curiosity, melting my resistance, seducing me – a plot for a true romance.

You took me back to the scenes of my childhood, to the YMCA, where my parents met and where I got to know Edna Mazursky, my dear friend and perhaps my only friend, a place which still holds familiar smells and even has good coffee… You took me back to the Edison cinema, a site of nostalgia for me, and the Smadar cinema which stands near our old home among the picturesque Templar houses. You fed me falafel in

Mahaneh Yehuda. I stood there with you in the crush, tehina dripping on my dress, wondering what it is that binds together distant people, uniting in a shared pleasure.

My dear conqueror! With your shy, sly courting, with silky caresses, you got me to peer surreptitiously at the gate of Al-Hurriyeh, waiting endlessly for you to turn up. In a certain sense you won me with your weakness – like Azme, who was the only man in my life until then. I've told you almost nothing about him. When he died I shut myself in my room, scratched the walls and licked the whitewash. I was sure I'd never again get close to another man. Until you appeared – a twin soul rising from the chaos of our defeat.

I looked forward to our journey. I wanted to be with you, just the two of us in a small room, in one bed, to breathe your smell and feel your warmth and search for a little opening of hope. I wanted you for a long time, once I even came to your room, but you were afraid and didn't want to take me, pretended to be stupid, as if you didn't understand what a woman wants when she comes to a man's room.

My beloved, the trip to the kibbutz was also a journey of farewell to my old dream of tearing you, the Jews, out of this place. In the cemetery in the Galilee I saw the tombstones that tell your stories. I saw that you too are buried in this soil, alongside those who "drowned in the lake while hauling sea-sand" and the one who "died of yellow fever", and I understood that you also belong in this place and I knew how complicated it would be to uproot you. I realised that the past can never be undone. I envied the shrewdness with which the pioneers planted themselves in this place, thrusting their roots deep into the ground.

A year ago I returned to this land and almost as soon as I got off the plane I had to go through one of your army checkpoints. The day before yesterday I had to go through it again. Everything is closed off to me. What kind of a future awaits me, even with you, if I give up my identity?

I couldn't escape from myself even if I wanted to. To you I'm Yasmine, but beyond that I'm an Arab woman in the Jews' country. How naive I was to think that I could fit in with this country which was once my home. I never told you about the blow that opened my eyes as to who I am in this place. A while back, after I'd worked as a volunteer in the youth village for almost ten months, I went to the director and asked to become a regular employee. "Ah Mademoiselle Yasmine, so you would like to work for us?" he said, as if till then I'd been working in Somalia. "You're a good and dedicated worker and I'll be happy to have you stay with us..." He kept me coming and going for a couple of weeks, then announced, "Mademoiselle Yasmine, I'm sorry, it can't be done. I mean, what will the parents of our pupils say if they find out that you're..." He was careful not to say "Arab", as if it was an obscenity, or a crime that must be concealed. He also omitted to mention that the problem didn't exist so long as I was a volunteer.

I know that not everyone is like him, but even the best of you, unconsciously, unintentionally, look down on us, as if you're doing us a kindness. It's a permanent insult to live in a country where you don't belong, as a second-class citizen, if not lower than that.

Your father and my father are two parts of a broken branch. My father tried to walk on hot coals, to preserve himself without hurting you and without being injured and robbed, but he failed, defeated on all sides. It breaks my heart to see that he's become bowed and ailing with a mysterious illness. I can see how hard he's trying all the time to hold on to life, to behave as if it's "business as usual", while everything slips through his fingers and he increasingly loses the will to keep going. He even wants to break up his newspaper partnership with Abu Nabil. The occupation has damaged a wonderful man of goodwill and made him sick and pain-ridden, a stranger in his own country. Now Abu Nabil will inherit everything.

For me, our trip to the kibbutz was an exploration of your other side, of the source from which you are drawn. I saw the blend between the "son of Arabia" who adores Um Kulthoum and knows our culture, and the new Israeli, advisor to the minister-in-charge, our *wali*. I wanted to discover the roots of my anxiety, our anxiety, why we fear you and what is so special about the kibbutz, the holy of holies of Zionism, and what kind of people built this cathedral. Listening to Sonia's accounts of their origins I felt as if something was invading my body and tearing chunks out of it. But who the hell wants to hear my story?

Sweetheart, I meant to talk about you but ended up with generalities, jumping from subject to subject. There is much I don't understand. I started to write this letter when I got home, draft after draft, and everything became confused in my mind. I feel as if there is a lump in my throat, blocking the words, fighting my consciousness.

Our first and only night together I cried from pain and joy that I couldn't contain, and now I'm deserting…If there is one thing that distresses me about going away – besides leaving you and the house and al-Quds – it's the return to what awaits me in Paris: Fayez and his macho cronies. I've got used to your way of speaking, the gentleness with which you treated me, this hesitancy that does not head straight for the finish. It pains me to admit that Fayez has won, but no other path is open to me.

I wanted you to be my man, my complementary other half. Two days before our trip to the kibbutz I was scared and feared the worst. I felt I was about to enter the jaws of a dragon. Perhaps the fear brought on my period ahead of time, I haemorrhaged and had piercing cramps, like the time I miscarried Azme's baby. The morning of the trip the pains stopped and my heart filled with joy. Like a starry-eyed girl ignorant of the world, I thought only that I was going on a trip with you and that you'd take me away, for ever, to another place that would contain the two of us. I sang with your Um Kulthoum, '*Ya aghla min ayyami*':

> O my dearer-than-life,
> O my loveliest dream,
> Have pity and carry me
> Far from here,
> Take me far far away –
> You and me all alone…

As soon as we left al-Quds I saw the thriving settlements, your passionate activity. Among us life is lived at the pace of the narghile – one leisurely lungful after another, getting stoned. What a lost opportunity! I was confident that Nasser would change the Arab world. Another youthful dream bites the dust. Now it's all up to my generation. We're condemned to fight till we regain what is ours.

During our few days of happiness I loved every moment of being with you, and for the first time sensed also your "as-sumood" your love for this soil, the sweat and blood with which you watered it. Your story and ours are more difficult than the judgement of Solomon. Here neither side will give in and no one will be spared. You must understand, my love, I also have no other place to go.

What am I taking away with me? All of you! You cleverly instilled your ethos and myth into the Bible, into your prayers. You made them your homeland, carried them everywhere with you, like a gypsy with his violin. The Bible became your mobile homeland and your prayer-books a temple in a rucksack. Simple and brilliant. Your laden cart was emptied when you realised your dream of *al-awda*. Now everything is reversed, and we're the wronged ones! You are Goliath and we are David, you are Pharaoh and we are in bondage. Now we shall carry our dream with us, perhaps for two thousand years, until we take back our land and our honour. How could you be so bold? Was it really the power of "no other choice", as your Sonia said? Well, then, we also have no other choice.

Oh my Son of Arabia! When Azme died I withered like a desiccated tree, and you watered it and made it flower. I even enjoyed arguing with you about politics – in other matters there was practically nothing to squabble about…When I outgrew the suspicions that blackened my soul, I saw that we had everything in common, love and friendship and the language of body and soul, deep worries and shared anxieties and tastes.

I think about your confession that time when I went mad and smashed all your glasses, and about how you stood on the stage in the kibbutz with a shining face – how good you looked in the white shirt and black trousers – and your voice was soft and pleasant and your words wise. I wanted you, I loved you, you were my heart's sun and tears. I feel the love that we made real, and I'll never forget its flavour. I dreamt of leaving everything behind to follow this love, but when you stood there on the kibbutz stage and supposedly spoke up for me and represented me, I realised that you were not mine and never would be, that you belong to your people and your country.

What do I have left? Your song, the song of Um Kulthoum:

> I forced myself
> and abandoned you,
> hoping to forget
> your love.
> Since then I have fretted:
> How shall I forget you
> and your love.

Yasmine